THE HARROWS OF SPRING

JAMES
HOWARD
KUNSTLER

THE HARROWS OF SPRING

A WORLD MADE BY HAND NOVEL

Atlantic Monthly Press
New York

Published simultaneously in Canada
Printed in the United States of America

FIRST EDITION

ISBN 978-0-8021-2492-0
eISBN 978-0-8021-9037-6

Atlantic Monthly Press
an imprint of Grove Atlantic
154 West 14th Street
New York, NY 10011

Distributed by Publishers Group West

groveatlantic.com

16 17 18 19   10 9 8 7 6 5 4 3 2 1

This book is for Anne Poole
Annie on the Mountain in Bear Creek, PA
My ideal reader

In a dark time, the eye begins to see

—Roethke

THE HARROWS OF SPRING

ONE

In late April of the year that concerns us, a year that has not yet come in the history of the future, in the strange new times that followed the collapse of the American economy and the country's political breakup into several new, quarreling nations, mild spring weather finally arrived in the village of Union Grove, Washington County, New York. Spring came to this region of tender hills and hollows in the morning shadow of the Green Mountains, a two-day ride north of Albany, after a drawn-out winter of brutal storms and freakish cold that seemed to defy two decades of rising temperatures. At Easter, a crust of icy snow still lingered on the ground, coated with a dingy film of woodstove fly ash. Then it rained on and off for two weeks. Now, the last patches of snow had melted away and buds were close to bursting in trees along the village streets where automobiles had not been seen for many springtimes.

Twenty-three men labored in their shirtsleeves this day in and around the new Union Grove Hotel, under construction on the site of the former Union Tavern, which had been burned down New Year's night by a disgruntled farm laborer named Travis Berkey. The new hotel was one of several pet projects of Brother Jobe, pastor, patriarch, attorney, and head honcho of the New Faith Covenant Brotherhood Church of Jesus, an evangelical outfit of eighty-two souls that had fled the disorders of the southern states and pilgrimaged north seeking peace and the chance to be fruitful in these difficult new times. They had arrived in Union Grove the previous spring, bought the abandoned high school, and made countless improvements to their "New Jerusalem," as Brother Jobe liked to call the group's new headquarters. They had laid out gardens and fenced in paddocks on the athletic fields, planted fruit trees, nut trees, grapes, and berries, converted the bus garage into a barn with forty stalls, dug earthen root cellars, built several greenhouses, de-paved the parking lots and used the tar extracted to fix the school's vast flat roof, created dormitories and workshops in the classrooms, and rigged a wood-burning furnace to run the heat system. They had also entered into beneficial relations with the populace of Union Grove, a secular people much beaten down by their broken economy and the failed promises of technological rescue, as well as repeated visits of so-called Mexican flu and other epidemic diseases that winnowed the town's population down to 712 from the 3,245 who had greeted the millennium before the times turned.

Lately, Brother Jobe walked over to the new hotel each after-noon to check on its progress and visit with his counterpart among the townspeople, Robert Earle, mayor of Union Grove and journey-man carpenter, who was straw boss on the construction site. Robert worked side by side with Brother Shiloh, a bona fide engineer, who had put up buildings all over North Carolina for the Days Inn hotel chain back in the old times. Construction methods weren't what they used to be, though. The men had no power equipment. All the work was done with hand tools. Brother Mordecai did nothing but sharpen saws all day. Brother Shiloh had designed an ingenious oaken crane run with gears and counterweights to hoist materials to the upper stories. The materials were largely salvaged from existing vacant buildings in and around town. Some new custom stock for trim and moldings was milled by Lloyd Hokely at his sawmill on the Battenkill River, which ran through town and then down to the mighty Hudson four miles west of town. The roof was slate, a regional favorite, originally from the quarries of nearby Granville up by the Vermont border. The slate, too, was salvage, along with the copper nails needed to hold the slates on.

Brother Jobe was anxious to complete the new hotel as he was working hard to reestablish trade in the region whose economy now centered on farming and the activities that supported it or depended on it. Among other things, the New Faith group was breeding mules and trying to popularize them in a part of the country that, before the old modern times, had been partial to oxen and draft horses.

Brother Jobe held that mules were superior in brains, temperament, and handling for any kind of work. They even rode better than saddle horses, he insisted. His own personal mount, Atlas, was a handsome bay mule of great conformation and personality, fully sixteen and a half hands tall.

This mild spring afternoon Brother Jobe was inspecting progress on the masonry heater at the heart of the new hotel. It consisted of a massive column of salvaged brick with an interior of baffle chambers designed to maximize the retention of warmth in the masonry mass. On a winter's day, you could fire it once in the morning and again in the evening, they said, and steady heat would radiate into the building all day long and into the night. The masonry heater occupied the center of the new building. One side incorporated separate fireboxes, steel cooking surfaces, and ovens for what would be the hotel kitchen in the new tavern portion of the first floor. The old tavern, meant to be a place of fellowship and community in troubled times, had been a labor of love for Brother Jobe. When it burned down a mere week after its grand opening, he had to weigh the mysterious intent of Providence in the matter, but determined after much reflection and prayer that he was commanded to rebuild something bigger and better, hence the added hotel. He had decided to name the new tavern the Cider Barrel, after the most popular beverage of the region.

Brother Jobe, forty-six, plain made and burly like a barrel of cider himself, paused to admire the colored-glass transom window above the door to the new barroom. Made in a New Faith workshop, it depicted a federal eagle with wings spread, meant to convey the idea that the sympathies of Washington County and the village of Union Grove in particular lay with the remnant of the national government that called itself the Federal Union. Since the bombing of Washington, DC, that political entity was now centered at its capital of New Columbia in Michigan on Lake Huron. It had little practical influence on affairs in and around New England these days, but the people of Union Grove had political allegiances that went back beyond the battlefields of Ball's Bluff, Gettysburg, and Malvern Hill. Even the New Faith bunch had let go of their southern political leanings and come over to the federal fold after the indignities they suffered when leaving Virginia three years earlier. Now hostilities had broken out between the two new nations east of the Mississippi: the Foxfire Republic centered in Tennessee— still reeling from the assassination of its leader, the evangelist and country singer Loving Morrow—and the deep south states of New Africa, led by the former check-cashing mogul Milton Steptoe, better known by his military moniker, Commander Sage. With the paucity of news and the absence of radio, television, and Internet these days, it was hard for people as far away as Union Grove to get a grasp of these doings.

Brother Jobe wended through the ground floor. Carpenters were fitting beaded wainscoting into what would be the hotel's reception room. It already looked cheerful and welcoming. The masonry team, New Faith brethren Gideon and Ithiel, were pointing up a few final joints on the big heater. Brother Jobe peered inside the firebox and was surprised to see ashes in it.

"You test her already?"

"We fired her up today, sir," Ithiel said. "It was thirty degrees when we come down to work this morning."

"How'd she run?"

"Perfect, sir," Gideon said, grinning broadly. "She burned like a charm and kept us toasty till the afternoon when the temperature come on all springlike. Here, feel."

Brother Jobe placed his palm on the bricks, which still radiated warmth. A smile briefly lighted his face.

"You done a fine job, boys."

He left them and climbed the main stairway. The paint crew was already finishing some of the guest rooms in the second and third floors. They used a milk paint colored with iron hydroxide ochre mined off an outcrop on nearby Colfax Mountain (really just a big hill at 1,200 feet elevation). They sealed the chalky paint with a finish coat of linseed oil and turpentine. The result was a lustrous patina over a warm, sunny hue. Brother Jobe then went up a steep, narrow set of stairs into the attic, where a two-hundred-gallon salvaged water tank stood on a masonry ledge of the thermal brick mass before the chimney's final ascent through the roof. A hundred feet of salvaged copper coil pipe ran from the tank and was mortared within the thermal heater to deliver warm water to washrooms on the second and third floors and the tavern kitchen, another contrivance of the engineer Brother Shiloh. Union Grove was fortunate to have a gravity-fed water system that did not depend on electricity. The old village reservoir on a shoulder of Pumpkin Hill still worked reliably, though every once in a while a dead animal had to be removed from the grate over the intake pipe.

Satisfied that work was proceeding nicely, Brother Jobe returned downstairs and found Robert Earle in the new barroom of the tavern, where Robert was at work installing the new cherrywood bar-back cabinetry he had built based on the design of the handsome woodwork that had gone up in flames months earlier.

"You got a moment there, old son?" Brother Jobe said.

His features generally crowded toward the center of his broad face, as though he were in a constant state of perturbation, but this mild afternoon Robert detected more than the usual tension in a man who bore many burdens and responsibilities.

"Sure," Robert said, and put down the rubber mallet he had been using to coax a beaded fillet into a tight spot.

"Let's go set outdoors and enjoy the vapors of spring."

"All right."

They settled down on the top of the four broad steps that connected the deep hotel veranda to the sidewalk. Brother Jobe produced a flask from the inside pocket of his black frock coat.

"Taste?" he said. "This here's the Tiplady rye from up Hebron way. I like it fine. You folks is definitely learning the finer points of the distillery craft. My own people were the leading moonshiners in Scott County, Virginia, back in the day. They turned out a corn beverage that would take the varnish off a fiddle."

"Why would anybody drink that?"

"Our competition put out a product that could flat-out kill you. Poor quality control batch to batch. We was more careful. And our price was right. You couldn't get a half pint of aftershave for what we charged on a half-gallon jug of Tway Hollow Three-Hog Stand-Pat corn."

"Where did the hogs come in?"

"That'd be my grandfather Royce and my great-uncles Fen and Cool-Ray, partners in the operation. They was all in the First Cav in the Kim Son Valley of Vietnam. Survived a night ambush, scaring the devil out of the VC with their hog calling. All received the Silver Star for valor."

"Cool-Ray? How'd he come by that?"

"He had a kind of voodoo love magic that made him catnip to women. Wore sunglasses day and night. Played the Fender Telecaster and sang in a honky-tonk band. The other two, one being my daddy, was no slouches for high times, though they was married, obviously, else you wouldn't be talking to me now. Go on, take a pull on this here. The workday's most done." He proffered the flask again.

Robert knocked back a dram. Then Brother Jobe took his turn, a long pull that made him shake his jowls and suck in the spring air across his teeth. The sound of hammers and handsaws filled the air.

"The squire's at it again," he said, referring to Stephen Bullock, owner of the sprawling plantation four miles west of town—Bullock, the leading citizen, wealthiest freeholder, elected magistrate, and employer (some said feudal lord) of three score laborers and craftspeople, plus children, who lived in a village constructed by them on his property. Bullock, it was said, wanted to take America back to a society like thirteenth-century England's.

"It happens that I received a letter yesterday from him," Robert said. "He's resigning as magistrate."

"Oh . . . ?" Brother Jobe perked up.

There had been considerable trouble just after Christmas concerning the disappearance of a murder suspect, a woman named Mandy Stokes, alleged to have slain her husband and infant son while her brain was addled by the aftereffects of meningitis. She had been in custody at the New Faith compound—the jail in the old town hall was unheated in January—and apparently escaped a few days before Bullock could convene the grand jury. It was further suspected that Brother Jobe and his men had contrived to help her get away. In any case, Mandy Stokes had not been seen nor heard from since New Year's Eve. Stephen Bullock had threatened to bring charges against Brother Jobe for facilitating the woman's escape but he had not acted.

"He wasn't no good in that position anyhow," Brother Jobe said. "Bad law or arbitrary and malicious law is worse than no law at all. Do you get to appoint a replacement now?"

"I'll have to call a special election."

"There ain't but one other competent attorney in town: Mr. Hutto."

Sam Hutto, respected as he was, ran a turpentine still on the backside of Pumpkin Hill for a livelihood these days. The absence of functioning courts, deeds registries, jails, and all the other accessories of the law had obviated any paid work for lawyers.

"There's you," Robert said. Indeed, Brother Jobe held a law degree from Duke University, as well as the bachelor of divinity from Roanoke College.

"Your town folks wouldn't stand for that," Brother Jobe said.

"Well, who's Sam going to run against?"

"He can run uncontested."

"You could run just to give the appearance of a contest," Robert said. "Sam's well liked, but you might get more votes than you imagine."

"I ain't got time for the job, anyways. It's all I can do to run my own outfit. I s'pose I know why it annoyed Mr. Bullock to get elected, busy as he is."

"Well, does the magistrate absolutely have to be a lawyer?"

"It'd sure help," Brother Jobe said. "The fact is, what we got going in the way of law don't bear much resemblance to the system that used to be. Mr. Bullock's right about one thing: we making it all up as we go along now. The situation kind of compels us to.

Remember, this country used to have vast networks of judges, justices, jurists, arbitrators, mediators, social services, juvenile services, and so forth, and now there ain't none of that left. All we really got is tradition and precedent. The tradition is pretty strong—innocent until proven guilty, habeas corpus, and so on—but the precedent in case law is withering away cuz you need institutional support for it: functioning courts, law schools with legal scholars, access to records, up-to-date publications. It's all gone."

"I'll meet with town trustees and set a date for an election," Robert said. "Think about what I said."

"Oh, all right. Anyways, Bullock's up to some new mischief we got to talk about. He's withholding trade goods from my folks."

Bullock owned a boat that made regular trips down the Hudson to Albany to get goods that could not be made or grown in Union Grove, everything from cloth and tools to wholesale groceries such as cane sugar, wheat flour, and, once in a while, exotic commodities like coffee and lemons. It was Union Grove's chief connection with the wider outside world of commerce, or what remained of it.

"Why don't you just buy what you need at Einhorn's store?" Robert asked.

"Einhorn seems to be cut off too.

"What?"

"Yessir, as of yesterday. I confabbed with him at lunchtime. He sends his boy to Bullock's landing Tuesdays, and they blew him off. Told him they didn't have nothing."

Terry Einhorn ran the town's only general merchandise and grocery. He received trade goods from Bullock's boat runs, too, while he also purveyed local produce, meat, and handicrafts from around the county. But it was the time of year when local supplies of last year's crops were running low—potatoes, onions, turnips, cornmeal—and no new crops were far enough along to eat. The farmers were just now planting corn and potatoes. Peas and lettuce, already in the ground, wouldn't be ready for weeks. Apart from the New Faith operation very few farms had greenhouses, since agricultural-grade plastic was no longer available for hoop tunnels, nor were manufactured metal sashes to hold glass panes, nor silicone for gaskets, nor so many of the materials that made things so magical in the old times.

"Did you talk to Bullock?" Robert asked.

"Naw. He don't talk to me anymore," Brother Jobe said. "But I send a wagon over to his landing once a week, same as Mr. Einhorn, and he told my boys he didn't have nothing for us neither."

"Is he still running the boat at all?" Robert asked. "You know last year we had all that trouble on the Albany docks. Maybe they're back at it again?"

Dan Curry, the boss of Albany, had gotten into the hostage and ransom business and made the mistake of taking Bullock's four-man boat crew into custody on trumped-up charges. He threatened to hang them. It was clear that any bail collected would never be returned. For his trouble, Dan Curry was shot in the head by one of Brother Jobe's rangers, who were enlisted by Bullock to go down and find the boatmen.

"We didn't hear nothing of the kind," Brother Jobe said. "And I expect we would, since we helped him out of a jam last time. My boys said that the boat was setting right there at the landing, all rigged and ready to run, far as they could tell. I'd say it's up to you to go confab with Bullock. Maybe take Mr. Einhorn over with you. Find out what the heck he's up to."

"All right," Robert said. "I'll do it first thing tomorrow."

"I suspect he just wants to punish everybody over here. My bunch, your bunch, all of Union Grove. Is he really like that? You know him better than I do."

"He's headstrong, all right."

"Ruthless, I'd say. Vengeful sumbitch."

"He can't not trade with us out of spite," Robert said. "People will go hungry around here if we don't get goods from outside."

"Looks like that's exactly what he wants," Brother Jobe said and handed his flask over to Robert again. "I don't know. Maybe we got to get our own dang boat."

Two

Late that same afternoon, Britney Blieveldt, twenty-seven, Robert's girlfriend and housemate, had gone a mile out of the village "gathering wilds," in the parlance of the new times; that is, she was searching for things to eat that grew naturally in the woods, meadows, and along the banks of the Battenkill River. Lithe and athletic, yellow hair tied in a ponytail, wearing a plain skirt sewn together from pieces of old leisure wear and a sweater she had knitted herself out of wool from the Deaver farm on Pumpkin Hill, she approached the railroad bridge warily. The old steel bridge across the Battenkill, built in 1917, would have been condemned by now if there were any bureaucrats left to decide such things. An actual train had not clanked over it since 1981—and that was just two excursion cars with tourists admiring fall foliage. The bridge was lately a favorite place for a considerable number of townspeople to come and end their lives—people impoverished, discouraged, beaten down, sick, disappointed, and driven mad by the rigors of the new times. It was generally avoided by those not interested in suicide, and in the new dark air of superstition that rushed in to fill the vacuum left by the collapse of modernity, many considered the bridge haunted. Because of all this, not many people foraged on the far side of the river and Britney favored it for that very reason. This day she was out for ramps, fiddleheads, and trout. In one hand, she carried Robert's treasured fly rod and, in the other, a long ash-splint basket made by herself. She carried a jackknife and a dandelion weeder in a canvas shoulder sack.

Britney looked forward to making a supper of fresh food for Robert and her eight-year-old daughter, Sarah, for the menu items of early spring had grown tiresome. At this time of year, the evening meal was usually corn bread and soup, an ongoing mélange of whatever had been put into the pot night after night, sometimes for a week or more, and called simply "soup" because no particular ingredient stood out. Of course, some people were better soup-makers than others, and Britney was a good one. The other staple of the new times cookery was the dish called "pudding," a casserole of stale corn bread, eggs, cheese, sometimes a bit of meat, potatoes, turnips, onions, kale (which, when protected by mounds of straw, wintered over in the garden row), or really anything on hand or leftover. Robert had built two cold frames, in which he grew lettuce and spinach beginning in February when the days grew longer, but this spring they had attracted an infestation of leaf miners. In the older times that had preceded the machine age, this phase of the year had been called "the six weeks want" for lack of fresh food. The phrase had come back into use.

Britney stood before the bridge taking in the beauty of the river below. The snowmelt runoff was over for the year and the current ran clear now. A hatch of late day mayflies fluttered out of the water and made the air above appear to vibrate in the lowering light. She eyeballed the bridge to determine how far gone it looked. The process of dilapidation was accelerating lately. Every time she came out this way, there were alarming new signs of structural failure. In places, she could see clean through the rusted girders and plates attached to the crumbling concrete abutments down to the water rushing below. Above, an osprey had built a huge nest at the point where the top chord met the front strut. The railroad tracks themselves had been torn up during the years of the Great Collection, when steel was desperately needed for the war in the Holy Land. The wooden cross ties had been disturbed in the process and were rotting too. There were holes here and there that a person could easily fall through. Some rude planks had been laid down on them over the years to make crossing the decrepit bridge on foot a little less scary. Britney had been on the middle school gymnastics team years before, specializing in the balance beam. She crossed the bridge in a firm, economical stride, marveling as she did that something built only a bit more than a century before was already a ruin. Someday, she mused, it would crash into the river and then the forest behind the far bank would become a tract of untrodden wilderness. The next town to the east, Bennington, was fourteen miles away, and people didn't range very far from their towns in the new times.

A quarter mile beyond the bridge she came to the sunny, south-facing embankment where the ostrich ferns liked to grow along a curve in the railroad bed. Hundreds of the curled green sprouts poked through the leaf litter there. They looked like the scroll at the top of a violin peg box. She set about methodically collecting the fiddleheads with her jackknife, dropping them into a cotton sack that had once been a pillowcase. In a little while she had enough for the evening meal and some additional to pickle, and she moved on to a lower place nearer the river where the ramps grew. These wild leeks, with their strong garlic overtones, spread profusely along this half-acre patch, their broad double leaves like flags against the umber forest floor. The dandelion weeder was the perfect tool for extracting them without bruising the tender pink and white bulbs. She would pickle some of these, too, and made a bundle of them in a damp dishrag to keep them fresh. She stuffed the bundle into the sack with the fiddleheads.

Next, she proceeded back down the railroad bed along the river to a place she knew well. Many trout lurked in the riffled feeding lanes between a quartet of large boulders anglers had always called the Four Brothers. She laid her basket in the shade of a blown-down sycamore tree and the rod with it, kicked off her leather, wood-soled clogs, and waded up to her shins in the stream with an old plastic jar that, years before, had contained factory-made mayonnaise. She hitched up her skirt and tucked the hem into the waistband to keep it out of the water, which was so cold her feet quickly went numb. After a quarter of an hour of foraging under rocks in the gravel streambed, she'd captured half a dozen crayfish in the jar, little ones, two inchers, the kind the trout adored. She held one in her left hand and placed the jar with the rest of them on the exposed gravel bed beside the blown-down tree and her basket. Robert was an adept fly fisherman but Britney had not learned the difficult particulars of the art. Instead, she had tied a bare number 12 hook to the end of the leader with a small lead split shot eight inches above it. She ran the hook between the carapace and the first tail plate of the squirming crayfish, then pulled out several yards of the flourescent green fly line, manufactured out of miracle polymers in the old times, and used the line's weight to roll out a cast so that the crayfish landed with a delicate plop in a riffled run behind the nearest of the four toolshed-sized boulders in the stream. The crayfish sank and not a second later something seemed to snap in the frothy riffle where it landed as if a rat trap had sprung underwater.

Britney clamped the loose fly line to the cork butt of the rod to get it taut, then jerked it. The rod tip bent parabolically down and quivered. A speckled trout exploded out of the water and danced on its tail trying to throw the hook. The crayfish had broken off, but the hook held fast in the fish's lip plate. It remained up in the air for such a long still moment that she could make out all its vivid colors. The native speckled brookies had made a strong comeback in the new times, with the human population down by two-thirds and many of these surviving people working long days on the farms, with little leisure for sport fishing, and dwindling supplies of the old manufactured fishing tackle. The imported European brown trout, stocked assiduously every year by the state in the old times, were almost all gone now, but the native brookies were better fish. They had gorgeous red fins and bellies and red spots in a blue aureole on their flanks, and their meat was pink, like salmon.

Britney let the fish tire itself out and landed it carefully on the gravel beach. It was a good fourteen inches. She placed her thumb in the trout's gasping mouth and bent its head back until its spine snapped so it would have a quick death instead of suffocating slowly. Then she took her jackknife out and made a slit from its anal vent to its gills. She removed the guts and flung them onto the bank for the raccoons or the fisher cats or the minks, and then ran her thumb along the inside of the cavity to remove the dark blood sac along the spine. Finally, she cut out the gills, which would give the meat an off flavor if they remained attached. When the trout was laid in her basket under the damp bundle of ramps and the fiddleheads, she rigged up another crayfish, moved about ten yards upstream toward another of the Four Brothers, and roll-cast her line into the riff behind it, with similar results.

Britney fished that stretch until six o'clock, when the sun fell below the ridge of Schoolhouse Hill and the first intimations of nighttime dimmed the corridor of the little river valley. She had five nice trout, three for the table and two for Robert's smoker. The basket was heavy enough that she had a bit of a struggle climbing the steep bank to the old railroad bed for the walk back to the bridge and then town. She had gone perhaps two-tenths of a mile up the track when she stopped to pick a trout lily from a little patch of them growing behind a bent and rusted bridge signal stanchion. She was just fitting the stem behind her ear when an unusual odor came to her attention. She turned slowly and looked down the track where she had come from. A black bear lumbered toward her some fifty yards away. As she stood up and straightened the bear stopped.

She took out her jackknife, opened the blade, and gripped it tightly against the butt end of Robert's fly rod. The bear's head swayed back and forth. In a person, that body language might be interpreted as something like sheepishness, but Britney was not at all sure that was the case for the bear. She took her eye off it a moment and glanced down the tracks at the bridge. It was about a hundred yards away. When she looked back at the bear, it was on the move again, slowly stalking forward.

"You stay the hell away from me!" she shrieked at the bear. It stopped and sat on its haunches like a dog. "I'll cut your heart out!" she shrieked again. She turned and began walking briskly toward the bridge, thinking that if she ran she would surely prompt the bear's instinct to chase her. The bear continued to follow her anyway and was closing the distance between them. She remembered with a shudder that it was her time of the month. She was wearing a simple napkin of cotton batting, made by herself, in her underwear. She wondered if the bear could scent her the way she scented the bear.

This time of the year, a female bear would almost certainly have a cub or two with her, and this being a solitary animal she supposed it must be a male. She quickened her step and broke into a trot. Glancing over her shoulder, she saw the bear break into a lope.

Britney was twenty-five yards from the bridge. She dropped the basket full of trout and the sack of wild gatherings, hoping the bear would be satisfied with that, but he loped right past them. She now broke into a sprint thinking if she could just get onto the rickety structure made by clever and fearsome humanity, the bear would not dare to follow. She could hear his paws hit the ground as he loped up to her heels, and then she reached the bridge. She had taken perhaps three strides onto the planks laid across the disintegrating cross ties when she felt the weight of the bear on her back, inhaled its vicious stink, felt its forepaws encircle her torso, and sensed both of them go suddenly weightless. And then everything—bridge, treetops, pale sky, black fur—spun wildly as Britney and the bear fell clean through the bridge and made a full rotation until their sickening and wondrous descent through the air came to a violent stop as the bear, with Britney in its arms, landed on his back on another glacial erratic boulder in the streambed under the bridge, this one known as the Priest.

The fall knocked the wind out of Britney but the bear took the brunt of the impact—his spine snapped and the force of the collision drove a piece of shattered clavicle bone into his heart, killing him instantly. Both Britney and the bear then slid down the sloping boulder into the water, whereupon Britney came free of the bear's embrace as the cold current sucked her into a deep eddy and she submerged completely for a moment. Her spasming diaphragm saved her life, for her temporary inability to breathe prevented her from inhaling any water and thus drowning. The swirling water propelled her out of the eddy into the main current, which deposited her gasping on a gravel bank some thirty yards downstream of the bridge. Soon, she stopped gasping and resumed breathing—hungrily but regularly, though her solar plexus ached. Eventually, she began to shiver and her teeth chattered. She slowly groped onto all fours as the water poured out of her clothes. The gravel hurt her knees. But what impelled her upright was the recognition that she had let go of Robert's precious fly rod, and after establishing that nothing else was wrong with her, nothing broken, she set about searching for it along the gravel banks in the fading twilight. Her skirt was so heavy now that she took it off, wrung it out, and slung it over her shoulder as she moved down the river.

She did not have to search long or far. She found the graphite fly rod in a tangle of willow stems where a sharp bend in the river formed a little island. The fluorescent green fly line was easy to spot in the low light. She waded a chest-deep backwater pool to get it. Many yards of line had come off and gotten tangled in the willow branches but the rod was completely intact. She freed the line, reeled it in, and secured the hook in the little wire loop at the top of the cork butt. There was no sign of the bear, which had floated farther downstream in the main current. She wondered whether what had just happened was real and not imagined as she slogged back upstream in the gathering darkness. The iron bridge came into view against the green and orange twilight, a weird, looming reminder of times past and gone. She was able to climb up the steep bank there on the old path worn by generations of fishermen. She walked back down the track a little way on the wild side of the bridge and retrieved her basket with its trout and wild edibles. The cold of a spring night was coming on. She hurried back across the bridge barefoot, careful where she stepped in the dim light, fly rod in one hand and basket in the other. It wasn't until she got to the road another quarter mile down the track that she realized she had lost her jackknife, probably forever.

THREE

Robert Earle's son, Daniel, twenty-one years old, who had recently returned from two years of wandering in the interior of America, was the chief suspect named in the assassination of Loving Morrow, president and "Leading Light" of the theocratic Foxfire Republic, a breakaway nation comprised of both Virginias, the Carolinas, Kentucky, Missouri, Arkansas, and Tennessee, with its capital in the town of Franklin just south of Nashville. The name of Daniel Earle spread slowly across the broken United States in the scant broadsheet newspapers published here and there, and the news eventually reached the town of Union Grove in a paper published in Kingston, New York, and distributed in the port of Albany on the Hudson River, where Stephen Bullock's trade boat made weekly trips.

The story, which was a compilation of official reports out of Franklin adumbrated by retelling and rewriting and republishing as it moved through the states, accumulating rumor and myth as it churned along the way like a political hairball in the continental gut, was accurate in some respects. It characterized Daniel Earle as a federal spy, which was partially correct in the sense that he was an agent of the Federal Service, as the severely pared down agglomeration of intelligence bureaucracies from the old times was now called. But in fact he was not so much a spy as a trained assassin sent on a singular mission, one he had accomplished. He was not sent to the Foxfire capital merely to collect information. The original story out of Franklin, released by the Foxfire government news office, left out the fact that Daniel Earle had been enlisted as the Leading Light's sexual plaything in the weeks before her death, the last in a long string of young men who had occupied this role over the years since her ascendance from being a star of country music and a television evangelist to chief executive of the breakaway nation.

In the aftermath of the death of its Leading Light, the Foxfire Republic formally declared war on the remnant Federal government. The Foxfire army, underequipped and ragtag as it was, had been visibly preparing a siege of Cincinnati on the Kentucky side of the Ohio River for weeks before the assassination of its leader. So a de facto state of war already existed between the two countries. But the Foxfire Republic also had been openly at war for months with the breakaway nation of New Africa (formerly Georgia, Alabama, Mississippi, and Louisiana) led by the wily and elusive Milton Steptoe, aka Commander Sage. Steptoe's army not only had chased the Foxfires out of Atlanta, which they had only briefly controlled, but had pushed them back beyond Chattanooga in their home state of Tennessee. Steptoe then put Chattanooga to the torch. In the event, additional Foxfire troops had been rushed from the vicinity of Cincinnati to the outskirts of Chattanooga where 2,900 were taken prisoner and then massacred by Steptoe's army after the battle of Soddy Daisy in retaliation for the detention camp deaths of thousands of black civilians who had resisted being run off their property in the Foxfire secession.

One other detail in the broadsheet report about these faraway events did not escape the attention of those who read or heard it: a reward of one hundred ounces of gold had been offered for the life of the suspect Daniel Earle, said to be a businessman of Covington, Kentucky, but more likely an agent of the federal government now at large somewhere in North America, probably in Federal territory. It said he was more than six feet tall with light brown hair. Nothing else was known about him. The small printed picture of Daniel's supposed face under the headline was a crude woodblock engraving of a conjectural likeness drawn from a recollection of witnesses in Tennessee. It looked no more like Daniel Earle than an old times comic book drawing of Daniel Boone.

By the time Daniel Earle straggled home on Christmas Eve from his long and arduous journey that started in May back in Ohio, he was a scarecrow of a young man, near death from exhaustion, starvation, disease, and parasites. It became known around town that he'd ventured west along the Erie Canal to the Great Lakes and had endured hardships, including shipwreck in a storm on Lake Erie. But of his doings in Tennessee on behalf of the Federal Service, the only one he had told was his father, Robert, and then just the barest outlines.

In February, Daniel moved out of his father's house. In the weeks of his recovery, he had discovered the abandoned office and equipment of the defunct *Union News Leader*, a "pennysaver" type newspaper in its final incarnation, whose owner and publisher, one Paul Easterling, had frozen to death in his car years earlier trying to make it back from a Christmas visit to his daughter's home in Medford, Massachusetts, during one of the serial gasoline crises that had paralyzed the nation before the DC bombing put an end to the old times for good. Daniel staked a claim on the *Union News Leader*. There were many abandoned properties in Union Grove and in the absence of a functioning court system people could and did take casual possession of property in title limbo, as it came to be called. Daniel had seen a number of broadsheet newspapers as he made his way through Pennsylvania, Ohio, Michigan, and the Foxfire states and he imagined that this was a business he would like to try his hand at, a good alternative to manual labor on some rich farmer's land or at a trade such as carpentry, like his father. He had to find a livelihood somehow. In the new times there was no other way.

Rummaging through decades of accumulated junk in the *Union News Leader* office on Elbow Street—originally a temperance hall, built in 1883—Daniel found an 1891 Albion nonelectric hand-operated flatbed proof press, along with drawers of movable type and related equipment for typesetting. The discovery helped reanimate him and he became determined to produce a regular broadside for a county starved for news, information, commercial advertising, and public notices. He set about cleaning up and reorganizing the old newspaper office, a massive job in itself. He arranged for Frank Ramsdell, the "salvage wizard" of Battenville, to fabricate a sheet metal woodstove for him. His father gave him three ounces of silver to pay for it and Robbie Furnival gave him three cords of stove wood on a note. He rounded up a few pieces of furniture, a bed, a long plank table, and some chairs and cast-off sofas. A fine oak rolltop desk was hidden behind the junk he cleaned out. His father's girl, Britney, gave him a well-seasoned cast-iron skillet. It was the first home of his very own.

Once the place was warm, tidy, and coherently organized, it took Daniel weeks to figure out how all the printing equipment worked. He sought help from the polymath Andrew Pendergast, who had some formal training in letterpress from his college days at the Rhode Island School of Design. Andrew suggested some recipes for a suitable printer's ink that could be cooked up with materials at hand (linseed oil boiled and then burnt, lampblack, pine tar, and turpentine), and found the book *The Practice of Printing*, by Ralph W. Polk, for Daniel in the town library, which Andrew ran. Daniel read it backward and forward. He practiced setting type with the composing stick, and mounting the composed lines of type in the form case, and designed a four-column layout that would allow him to cram as much information on a single page as possible in 8-point type. He'd considered attaching a new name to the publication, but he'd found an elegant old engraved end-grain print block of the *Union News Leader* logo made decades before Paul Easterling's time as publisher and so he decided to stick with the established name. Besides, he liked the idea of continuity. On fair days near the approach of spring, he went out of the office to collect items of news and gossip, notify local tradesmen of advertising opportunities, and went door-to-door soliciting subscriptions at one silver dime a month. By the vernal equinox, Daniel felt ready to produce a first edition, though he lacked a supply of newsprint paper.

It was about that time that he was visited in the office one rainy night by a delegation consisting of his father, Robert Earle, Loren Holder, the Congregational Church minister (and his father's best friend), and Brother Jobe of the New Faith brotherhood. In one corner of the office, Daniel had set up the old sofas and a battered club chair around his woodstove. When the three visitors stepped in, Daniel had been engaged in the never-ending task of sorting boxes of old odd-lot pied type into their proper upper and lower case drawers.

"We saw the light burning," Robert explained. The light was a single beeswax candle.

"Dang," Brother Jobe said, taking in the big old room with its fourteen-foot-high ceiling, tall arched windows, and small prosce-nium stage at the far end where temperance crusaders had inveighed against whiskey in another, different America. "Ain't this a grand place."

Robert found the first proofs of specimen layouts that Daniel had run off on various odd scraps of paper with the Albion press.

"Looks like you're getting the hang of this," he said.

"Thanks. I've had some help," Daniel said. "But before I can really get started, I need to get a supply of proper newsprint paper."

"You might have to go to Albany to find that," Loren said.

The small talk ceased.

"Come on over and set down, son," Brother Jobe said.

Daniel could not fail to notice the grave demeanor of the three men. He ran a little turpentine on a rag over his fingertips to get the ink off and joined them over by the stove with the candle. Brother Jobe drew his flask out of his coat and put it on the wooden crate that served as a table in front of the sofa.

"Try some," he said.

Daniel hesitated, then went for it. Loren took a turn. Robert pulled a packet of paper out of his inside coat pocket, unfolded it to a single sheet, and passed it to his son. It was an edition of the *Kingston Pilot*, dated March 28. An item in the lower right column was circled and some words underlined. The headline read, REWARD FOR FOXFIRE ASSASSIN. The story named Daniel Earle in the second paragraph.

Daniel took it all in and then looked up at the men without speaking. His face seemed red in the candlelight.

"Interesting," he said at length.

"Inneresting?" Brother Jobe said. "That all? It don't concern you?"

Daniel shrugged his shoulders and tried to look away but Brother Jobe captured him in his gaze. Brother Jobe was not just an adept hypnotist. He had an aptitude for preternatural empathy that allowed him to enter the interior lives of others, like an explorer crossing the frontier into an uncharted territory. It was not an ability he could account for, or even explain to himself. But he had learned to be comfortable with his gift. Daniel's mind was as transparent to him now as a glass of spring water.

"I'm advising you to take more'n a passing interest in this," Brother Jobe said.

"Maybe it's some kind of coincidence," Daniel said. "Or a mistake."

Brother Jobe noticed how Daniel's leg was jiggling.

"Young man, I'm amongst your thoughts even as we speak," he said.

"What's that mean?" Daniel glanced at his father and then at Loren.

Robert, too, had some prior acquaintence with Brother Jobe's strange talents.

"You can trust him," Robert said.

Loren just raised his eyebrows.

"Do you read minds, sir?" Daniel asked.

"I have a sympathetic susceptibility," Brother Jobe said. "It don't really matter what you call it."

"What did you tell them?" Daniel asked his father.

"That you were in Tennessee," Robert said. "That something happened down there."

"Son, your name's in the papers now," Brother Jobe said. "Probably in papers all around the states."

Daniel left his seat, stalked across the room, and stood by his composing table in a pool of darkness with his arms crossed.

"A hundred ounces. That's a hell of a lot of gold these days," Loren said. "Why the hell did you use your real name down there?"

Daniel sighed. It pained him almost physically to talk about what he had done, but he found that he could not resist.

"They figured I'd be less likely to slip up if anyone asked who I was, my name, my background," he said. "But I had a cover story too, a *legend*, they called it in the service."

"Did it occur to you that something like this might happen?" Loren said.

"I wasn't thinking so clearly at the time."

"Maybe they didn't expect you to get out of there alive," Robert said.

"Getting out was a big part of the training."

"Anyway, for all these Foxfire people knew, Daniel Earle might have been an alias," Loren said.

Nobody spoke for a long moment. Robert reached for the flask.

"The thing is," Brother Jobe spoke across the room to Daniel, "now that you're about to start this here publication, it would be prudent to keep your name out of it."

"Everybody in town knows that it's my paper," Daniel said.

"Maybe so," Robert said. "But people outside of town don't know that. They don't even know you live here or who you are. You see how these news sheets get carried far and wide. You can't advertise yourself as editor and publisher of this thing right there in the paper the way it's usually done."

"The masthead, it's called," Daniel said.

"Just leave it out. Use the space for an ad or something."

"I have to put the office address somewhere on it so people can come in if they want to advertise or want me to do a print job."

"Okay, put the office address on it somewhere, but leave your name out of it."

"They have to ask for somebody."

"Make up some other name," Robert said.

Daniel rolled his eyes and snorted.

"Pen names are an old tradition in journalism," Loren said. "James Madison wrote the Federalist Papers under the name *Publius*."

"Mark Twain done it too, didn't he?" Brother Jobe said. "Who was a bigger draw in letters than Mark Twain? See, I don't even remember his real name."

"Samuel Langhorne Clemens," Daniel said.

"That's right," Brother Jobe said. "A fine appellation. It's got music in it, don't it? And he give it up? Was the law after him or something?"

"No, he was just crafting a persona for himself," Loren said.

"How's that?" Brother Jobe said.

"Inventing a comic character for himself to play," Loren said.

"There you go," Brother Jobe said to Daniel. "You could do the same."

"I'm not funny," Daniel said. "And I'm not trying to be some made-up character."

"Look, if you run a newspaper, you're going to be a public figure," Robert said. "You must understand that."

Daniel heaved a sigh. He'd been in the shop since just after daybreak. He returned to the woodstove and the others.

"All right. I'll do what you say. How does I. P. Daley sound?"

"Kind of made up," Loren said.

"Put a little more thought into it," Robert said. "You can do better."

"Can I have some more of this?" Daniel asked, reaching for the flask.

"Have at her," Brother Jobe said. "Maybe it'll get some funny going for you."

"Where I've been and what I've done wasn't funny," Daniel said, and everyone retreated into themselves again for a while.

"The thing is, anybody who tried to collect that reward would have to go all the way down to Tennessee to get it, wouldn't they?" Loren said, eventually.

"That's true," Brother Jobe said. "Any jackass could turn up there and claim he done you in."

Brother Jobe looked up and discovered Robert and Loren scowling at him.

"Just saying," Brother Jobe explained. "I don't see how anyone might prove it, though. Anyways, the news, such as it is, travels slow and there ain't no regular mails in most places, so my advice to you, young man, is to keep well to the background in this here endeavor of yours. Maybe after a year or two it'll blow over."

Robert lingered in the office after Loren and Brother Jobe departed.

"Hey, apart from all that," Robert said, "I'm proud of you for pulling this together. You did a great job in here. It's a fine place to work."

"Thanks," Daniel said. "Do you happen to know if there are any more copies of that Kingston paper around?"

"That's the only one I've seen around here," Robert said.

Daniel picked up the sheet lying on the sofa and studied it for a moment. "It's a good print job, I'll say that. Nice paper. Hope I can do as well." He crushed it into a wad, opened the door to the woodstove, and laid it on the glowing embers within where it flared for a few moments and lit up that part of the big room dramatically. They both watched for a little while and then Daniel turned to his father. "I'm not proud of what I did," he said. "It makes me sick to even think about it."

"I know," Robert said.

Four

That was some weeks before the evening that Britney was assaulted on the railroad tracks by the bear. There was nothing else she could do but walk home, cold, wet, and barefoot, with her recovered basket of wild gatherings.

Darkness had just overcome the last glimmers of daylight when she arrived home. Robert had been teaching her daughter Sarah how to play the tune "Hollow Poplar" on the fiddle. She was learning quickly and had developed a nice shuffle rhythm with her bow. Britney walked glassy-eyed through the front door to the kitchen in the back of the house, put her basket on the counter there and the fly rod in the corner by the back door, and stripped off all her damp clothes, which she placed on a warming rack near the woodstove. Robert and Sarah watched, and then followed her progress as Britney came back into the front room, all without a saying a word, and went up the stairs.

"Mama's naked," Sarah whispered.

"I know. It's okay," Robert said, though he suspected something was very wrong. He was torn between staying with Sarah and following Britney upstairs. But before he could resolve that quandary Britney came back down in a bathrobe. She went directly into the kitchen and stuffed more billets in the cookstove.

"I made corn bread, Mama," Sarah called in from the front. It was the child's duty to make corn bread every other day. Britney did not reply.

Robert watched Britney begin to go about her tasks in the kitchen as if nobody else was in the house. There was something oddly mechanical about her movements, he thought. He put his violin on the table among the candlesticks and sheet music and rose out of his seat to go to her. She had just set a big iron pan on the stove when he came behind her and put his arms around her. As he did, she began to shriek and then she slipped through Robert's arms onto the floor in a heap.

He picked her up, bundled her in his arms, and carried her over to the sofa in front, where she came back to herself sobbing and racking. After he brought her some whiskey, she was able to tell what had happened to her. The tale rendered him speechless.

"Does that mean we can't go back to the river, Mama?" Sarah asked.

"It's our river too," Britney said. "We'll go back there."

Robert wondered if he might convince her to carry a pistol next time.

FIVE

The following morning, Robert and storekeeper Terry Einhorn, a brawny man of forty-two with red hair and whiskers and a usually cheerful demeanor, set out from Union Grove for Bullock's plantation, which lay four miles west of town, near where the Battenkill River entered the larger Hudson. They rode on Einhorn's spring-mounted store wagon behind a big Belgian gelding named Lancelot. The weather had turned cooler again and clotting clouds threatened showers. Robert wore a long waxed canvas raincoat over layers of shirts and a sweater.

"Where'd you come by that coat?" Terry asked as they went by the abandoned Ford dealership on the edge of town.

"My girl made it."

"I could sell those. You tell her that."

The freezing and thawing of the seasons had added another cycle of damage to the pavement of Route 29, the old state highway. It had been years since the government gave up on road maintenance and there were no prospects whatsoever of it resuming. In places where the potholes and fissures were especially bad, horse-drawn vehicles had departed from it and made a parallel carriageway off the shoulder in the soft dirt alongside the highway.

"You're tight with Mr. Bullock, aren't you?" Terry said.

"Yeah, we're friends, I guess."

"How'd you get to know the squire?" Terry asked.

"Carpentry jobs," Robert said. "I built a Japanese teahouse on his pond years ago. He lived in Japan for a while after college. He's crazy for it."

"We'll never travel that far again," Terry said. "The young ones, they'll be lucky if they get to see the Atlantic Ocean."

"My boy sailed on the Great Lakes," Robert said.

"I heard. Maybe he should get a boat and take over the Albany trade from Bullock."

"He's set on starting up that newspaper."

"Yeah. Well, it's a good thing, I suppose," Terry said and added, as if talking to himself, "I thought me and Bullock had a nice arrangement. I always paid him hard money for his goods. I don't get why he's turned on us."

"I think he's a little bipolar," Robert said.

Terry cut him a nervous glance.

"You mean, like, crazy?" he said.

"Just real moody. You know, up and down."

At that moment, as they rounded a curve on the River Road about a quarter mile from Bullock's Old Manse, as the main house on his vast property was called, they came upon a man nailed through the forehead to the trunk of a black locust tree with a twelve-inch spiral-shank landscape spike. He hung there with his feet suspended at least three feet off the ground, and his arms tied behind his back, and great gouts of dried blood crusted down his face and his clothing as far down as his ragged pant legs. He was barefoot, suggesting that someone had taken his boots. He had a full head of brown hair and was slight of frame, but with all the gore it was hard to tell whether he was twenty-five or forty-five years of age. Both men let out more than a few oaths of astonishment at the sight of him. Terry reined in Lancelot. Robert leaped down from the driver's box before the wagon came to a stop.

"Is he one of our people?" Terry said.

Robert stood on his tiptoes to examine the dead man's face.

"Nobody I recognize," he said.

They regarded him silently for a minute. Crows could be heard quarreling in the distance somewhere.

"I hope they killed him before they did this," Terry said eventually.

Robert did not voice his own thought: that the man must have been alive considering how much he bled out on himself.

"Yeah, you'd hope," was all he said.

"Do you think this was Bullock's work?"

"I dunno. His men, anyway."

"Moody, you say?"

"Well . . ."

"There's got to be something really wrong with him."

The previous October, nine marauders had invaded Bullock's property, as deep as the sanctity of his very bedroom. Bullock killed three of them himself with a Japaense sword. His men captured the other "pickers," as such roving bandits were called. Bullock ordered them hanged along the same River Road and left them to rot until his wife Sophie complained about the odor.

"Are we just going to leave him here like this?" Terry asked.

"We'd need a hacksaw to get him down."

"You want to just go back to town then?"

"No," Robert said.

"A man who would do this," Terry said. "Sheesh."

"We still have to talk to him about the trade boat," Robert said. "People are running out of things in town."

He climbed back up onto the driver's box and sat down beside Terry.

"Are you going to tell Bullock that we came upon this?" Terry asked.

"How can we not mention it?"

"Your call," Terry said and geed up Lancelot. "This is beyond moody, if you ask me."

They passed Bullock's river landing on the way. His sloop, the *Sophie*, sat quietly in its crib dock with its rigging bare and sails stowed. There was no sign of any activity around the warehouse. Since Bullock began his trade runs to Albany three years prior, there was usually a man posted on the premises to keep an eye on things.

"Looks like he's closed for business, all right," Terry said.

Shortly, they turned up the drive to Bullock's house. Eddie Flake, a young man with a lopsided head and a touch of palsy, hitched Lancelot to a post beside the soapstone water trough and ran awkwardly up the gravel lane and across a field of new pale

THE HARROWS OF SPRING   31

green timothy grass to fetch his master at some unknown remove.
They watched him lope toward the horizon till he was out of sight.
Lancelot drank from the trough.

"This is a hell of an outfit he's got going here," Terry said, taking
in the big old house, the several barns, the workshops, the distillery,
and the fields sloping up from the river valley. "He lives like some
kind of royalty, doesn't he?"

"He saw what was coming from a long ways away," Robert said,
"and he was well prepared when it hit."

"How many people, you figure, has he got living on this place
now?"

"Twenty families, maybe. New ones turn up all the time. Some
single people too. It's not a bad life here, considering how things are."

"But basically he rules the place," Terry said. "Like a lord of old."

"Pretty much," Robert said.

"Do you suppose they like being told what to do?"

"I think they knew what they signed up for," Robert said. "They
can always leave and strike out on their own, or move to town if
they prefer a different life. He doesn't hold them against their will.
The thing is, most of them came here without any skill for the new
times, how to farm, manage animals, the useful crafts. They had
office jobs in the old times, like you and me. They learned these
things after they came here."

"What keeps them here then, after they learn a few things?"
Terry asked. "There are plenty of abandoned farms around."

"An ordered existence. Community. Security. A sense of belonging to a successful enterprise in a time when everything else is shaky
and there's nothing to hang your life on to. Whatever else you think
of Bullock, he's a good organizer and a commanding personality."

"I'd take liberty over security any day," Terry said.

"Liberty's great, but first you've got to feed yourself and your
family."

"It smells like serfdom, if you ask me."

They heard hoofbeats. Bullock and his right-hand man, the
versatile Dick Lee, crested the hill cantering down through the

field of timothy grass on big bay Hanoverian mounts, Bullock's preferred saddle breed. When they got to the soapstone trough under
its canopy of budding old maple limbs, Bullock dismounted with
surprising agility for a large man of sixty-one. Dick Lee remained
in the saddle. Bullock's long silver hair, aquiline nose, fine riding
clothes, high brown boots, and erect posture gave him the air of
someone born to a high position. But his face was inflamed with
dudgeon and his eyes burned as he stood before Robert and Terry.

"The electric's out," Bullock announced.

"Oh?" Robert said. "Back in town the electric's been down for
more than a year."

As it happened, one of Bullock's far-seeing preparations for life
in the new times was to rig up a hydroelectric system for his property.

"I mean out for good here," Bullock said. "As in over and out.
That's all she wrote. Good night, Missus Calabash, wherever you
are."

"Uh, gee. Sorry about that, sir," Terry said.

"I laid in three goddamn replacement Pelton wheels for that
turbine, and now the last one's shot to hell. I can't believe it."

"What are you going to do?" Robert said.

"I'm going to scour the countryside to see if anyone can fix the
goddamn things. You can't weld them without special equipment
and materials. And, of course, you'd need electricity to do the weld-
ing. I should have bought twenty or thirty of the goddamn things
instead of just three. Goddamn shortsighted of me."

Robert and Terry shared a glance.

"Uh, Stephen," Robert said. "We just saw something kind of
horrifying down on the River Road—"

"So that's it for the goddamn stereo, among other things," Bullock continued undeterred. "I suppose I could get hold of some more
musical instruments for my people and have them put on live music,
like you folks do over in the village. But, hell. I couldn't summon
them every time I wanted to, like at the dinner table. And there
are things they'd never be able to perform correctly: Erik Satie,
Mahler, the Doors—"

"Uh, Stephen, there's a guy nailed to a tree down there," Robert said.

"Oh?" Bullock said, coming out of himself. "Is that so?" He craned around and looked up at Dick Lee, still mounted. "Is that so, Dick?"

"Yessir," Dick Lee said.

The men swapped glances all around.

"What did he do?" Robert asked Bullock.

"Remind me: what was it, Dick?"

"Stealing a horse," Dick said. "Attempted, anyhow."

"There you go, horse thief," Bullock said. "I'd forgotten in all the excitement today, I guess."

"Isn't the punishment a little harsh?" Robert said.

"Hell no," Bullock said. "Historically it's punishable by death in many jurisdictions. Horse theft is serious stuff."

"Was it necessary to nail him to the tree through the head like that?"

Bullock appeared to flinch slightly.

"Was that your idea, Dick?" he asked.

"Yessir."

"He was alive when they drove that spike through his head, you know," Robert said.

Bullock again glanced up at Dick Lee, who rolled his eyes.

"How's that?" Bullock said.

Robert explained about all the blood.

"Well, it's a bit over the top, I guess," Bullock said. "But what's a fellow to do in these times, with savage riffraff everywhere creepy-crawling around the property, filching things, threatening life and limb? You remember those jokers who broke into my bedroom last October? We can't have that sort of thing. Now this fellow down on the River Road was a solitary picker, skulking about the property. Imagine how many more like him are out there. You have to send a message. By the way, I'm done serving as magistrate for a town that just can't even keep a homicide suspect in lockup. You got my letter of resignation, I presume."

"Yes, I did," Robert said. "And under the circumstances it's a little shocking to see you take the law into your own hands out here."

"Well, Robert, there is no law anymore, is there, really?"

"Sure there is," Robert said. "But the system for running it is broken."

"Well, exactly," Bullock said. "Which is why we do what we can over here in our domain to protect our people and our property. I also presume you'll hold an election and get yourself a new magistrate."

"Yes, we will. I think Sam Hutto will make a fine one."

"Last time I heard, he was operating a turpentine still on the back side of Pumpkin Hill."

"That's right. We all have to make a living somehow."

"I wouldn't trust him to draw up a prenuptial," Bullock said. "Did you handpick him already? I thought you said you were going to hold an election."

"Yes, we will. And he'll win, don't worry."

"I'm not worried," Bullock said. "About that anyway. I'm worried that I'll never get to hear a recording of Satie's *Reveries and Nocturnes* ever again. That would be goddamn tragic. But I think we can keep the vagabonds and riffraff in line."

Dick Lee's horse pawed at the ground restlessly.

"Uh, that's actually not why we've come out here to see you, sir," Terry Einhorn said.

"What else do you want?"

"I thought we had a good system worked out with you for getting wholesale trade goods from Albany on your boat, and all."

"You always settled your accounts straight up, Terry," Bullock agreed. "I appreciated that."

"Well, I'm a little confused, sir. My boy has come down to the landing for pickup twice lately on the regular schedule only to be told that you have no goods for us."

"I've discontinued the service for now."

"Like, temporarily or what?" Terry said.

"At least through planting season. Turns out I need all the men I've got around here."

"When exactly do you expect to resume?" Terry asked.

"I dunno," Bullock said. "Midsummer maybe. And then there's the harvest to contend with."

"The town has come to depend on you, Stephen," Robert said.

"That's not my fault. I'm not the Union Grove's sugar daddy. Maybe you should make other arrangements, be more self-reliant."

"There is nobody else sending a regular trade boat downriver."

"Then get your own goddamn boat and build a landing for it like I did. There's plenty of vacant riverfront property."

Terry and Robert shared a long fraught look.

"Now, let's talk softball, shall we?" Bullock said, rubbing his hands together.

"What?" Terry said rather loudly.

"Robert and I were talking last fall about reviving the old soft-ball league," Bullock said. "Remember? We had regular play for a couple of years before that Mexican flu epidemic."

Robert nodded reluctantly.

"Wait a minute," Terry said. "You don't want to bother getting trade goods that everybody around here needs, and is willing to pay hard cash for, but you want us to play softball?" Then to Robert: "Is he serious?"

"Are you serious, Stephen?" Robert said.

"Of course I'm serious," Bullock said.

"What kind of silly-ass idea is that?" Terry said.

"What's silly about it?" Bullock said, his voice rising. "Sports builds character, confidence, morale, community spirit. It's whole-some recreation. The national pastime. It's just the thing for those long hot summer evenings soon to come."

"Come on, let's go back to town," Terry said and climbed back up to the driver's box of his wagon.

"My girls have already sewn up some nice softballs," Bullock said. "Real horsehide with cork centers and everything. Close to factory-made."

"Good luck with your electric outfit, Stephen," Robert said. He unhitched Lancelot and joined Terry up above in the driver's box.

"Don't be soreheads," Bullock said as Terry reined the big horse around the circular drive. "Or losers."

When they were back on the River Road, Robert said to Terry, "You're right. Moody doesn't quite cover it."

Six

Dr. Jerry Copeland, forty-three, stood atop a steep slope above the Battenkill River beside a magnificent sycamore tree with a lit pipe in one hand and a silver flask of Mount Tom whiskey in the other. The pipe contained a mixture of tobacco and marijuana, both grown locally. Eighty feet below, white billows of river water dashed over the spillways of the dam built to power factories in the old times, beginning with a cambric mill that turned out officers' dress uniforms for the Union Army followed by manufacturing ventures that made cotton shirts, cardboard boxes, wallpaper, and lastly toilet tissue. The early factories ran on direct water power; after 1899, they switched to hydroelectric. Nothing remained of these industrial works except some ragged fieldstone and concrete foundations and the dam itself.

The damp air rising off the river felt soothingly cool on the doctor's face. He had walked over to the river from the makeshift surgery in the carriage house where he maintained his medical office. He had spent much of the morning there removing an eleven-inch black locust splinter from a sawmill worker named Edward Tenant. The splinter had penetrated clear through the transverse abdominis muscle and perforated the ascending colon. Assisted by his wife, Jeanette, the doctor had scrupulously cleaned and sewn up the various layers of the wound and the patient was resting comfortably in the small infirmary on the second floor under the influence of the opium suppositories that the doctor manufactured himself from a supply of poppy gum that several local farmers produced for him.

The catch was the doctor had no way of knowing whether Edward would develop fatal peritonitis and he had no antibiotics, nor did he have access to X-rays, CAT scans, ultrasound, or any of the diagnostic equipment he had been trained on years ago at

Johns Hopkins. He just had to wait and see how God Almighty was disposed to the fate of Edward Tenant, and the doctor was not convinced that the deity existed, or was especially fair or generous if He/She/It did exist. It was bad enough to preside over the epidemics that swept the county like a drag rake over a field of dandelions, but he saw cases every week of common accidents and illnesses that would have been easily fixed or cured in the old times and now sent their unfortunate victims straight to the graveyard. The phrase *not what I signed up for* reverberated in his mind as he let out a plume of smoke and followed it with a gulp of the whiskey. The responsibility, he thought, was literally killing him. The smoke and the drink temporarily eased the pressure crushing his soul.

Upstream of the dam hundreds of black, brown, and white Canada geese were marshaling on an eddy and making a conspicuous racket doing it. Flights of several dozen would land and others would take off as though the geese were practicing some sort of war game maneuvers. Airborne, they assumed the familiar flying-V formation. The population of these geese had surged even before the old times ended as weather patterns changed. More of them wintered over than migrated now. The people of Union Grove killed and ate them as they could, but there were far fewer people than there had been a decade earlier and fewer of them had working firearms or factory-made ammunition. One townsman named Tommy Pernelle had affected to work occasionally as a market hunter with a gun he made himself that fired any kind of scrap metal and even pebbles, and occasionally he sold a brace of geese to Terry Einhorn. But then his dog died and he couldn't find another retriever—the dog population being depleted even more than the human—and Tommy did not like going into the water to fetch the geese himself. Eventually Tommy preferred working in the comfort of Holyrood's cider works to the life of a market hunter.

Standing high above the river on Salem Street, the doctor watched the sqwonking geese below, realizing what a perfect disease vector they were for the next epidemic, and the arresting thought entered his mind that he would rather die than go through another epidemic as the town's only doctor. It startled him because he had two children, Jasper, twelve, and Dinah, six, whom he loved desperately, and a wife, Jeanette, he was very content with, plus a beautiful home, a position of high regard in town, a good living by the stringent standards of the new times—he was often paid in hams, chickens, candles, crafted goods, liquor, and whatnot when he was paid at all—and days filled with purposeful activities, many of them life-and-death matters. In fact, the brief retreat from the office on this damp spring day was one of the rare tranquil intervals he had had in a long time. But anytime he managed to free himself of the hubbub that was his life, despair came over him and hung over his shoulders like a cold, wet mantle.

On nights when he had seen a last patient, or finished checking on one confined in his infirmary, or returned from some house call, he more and more sought refuge in a bottle of pear brandy or rye whiskey, and his pipe, stuffed with some of the Afghani weed that grew wild everywhere along the roadsides these days. Lately, sometimes he had even taken to ingesting some of the laudanum, a tincture of opium, that he had learned to make, telling himself that he was merely doing *quality control.* In the past several days, he had gotten to feeling twitchy, anxious, nauseated, and horribly sore in all his muscles and joints if he didn't help himself to a few drops of the stuff at regular intervals. In the cold clarity of the outdoors, watching the geese on the river, he could see where that path might lead.

He could also see where society was going and it spooked him to the jellies at his core. It was going to a dark age. All of the old certainties of the Enlightenment had come to seem like a bad joke with the electricity out for good and circumstances making a mockery of his medical training—and, by extension, the entirety of science. Antibiotics were only the beginning of the supplies and equipment that were no longer available to him. About the only thing that couldn't be taken away, that couldn't plunge him all the way back to the eighteenth century, was his knowledge. For instance, of basic sanitary procedures such as scrubbing before examinations and surgery and sterilizing his instruments in the nonelectric auto-clave he'd found in a barn among the effects of one Dr. Raymond Triffen (1878–1939), offered for sale up in the town of Argyle by Triffen's descendants. Nobody could take the germ theory of disease away from him. He knew, unlike the physicians even of the great Benjamin Rush's day, that disease was caused not by miasmas, humours, spells, impure thoughts, or supernatural agency but by microorganisms, toxins, and genetic programming. He was well trained in the minutiae of anatomy and physiology. When things didn't work—limbs, eyes, organs—he was able to deduce what might be happening with them, even if he was not able to treat them successfully anymore.

But how long would such specialized knowledge persist in this darkening age? Without the solid institutional support of the medical schools and the professional associations and the journals, what would people know three generations ahead? Would they remember genetics? Germs? Basic hygiene? After the Romans left Britannia, the doctor ruminated, the Britons stopped bathing and even forgot how to make pottery. The archaeological record showed it conclusively. He took a last hit on his pipe and a sip of whiskey, and his thoughts turned again to his son Jasper, who by now would have finished his chore of cleaning up the surgery. Jasper had been training with him for more than a year and the doctor was quite sure that he would become a competent physician before he was out of his teens, without the ridiculous hazing ceremonies of internship and residency that the doctor's generation had been subjected to. Perhaps Jasper would become a better doctor than his father, given what he had to work with. At least he would not be tortured by the same regrets about what he had lost.

Seven

Daniel Earle had finished drawing a proof of his latest trial newspaper layout at about 5:30 that evening down in the old temperance hall that was his living and work space. Daylight waned in the big windows and he was tired after working twelve hours with only a break for lunch, which would be the same as his supper: a days-old soup of this and that he kept simmering atop the woodstove. He hadn't spoken to another human being all day, he realized, when somebody knocked on his door. He wiped the ink off his fingertips and navigated around all the stuff in the big room in long graceful strides to find his father's girlfriend, Britney, waiting outside the door. She bustled right in and went over to the long oval table near the woodstove. It served as his kitchen prep area and dining station and he often read and studied there when he was not working.

"I brought you some things," Britney said. She put a basket down on his table and began taking items out of it. "Here's some corn bread. Turnip and onions for your soup. Some preserved pork. It's salty. I'd soak it for a day and change the water a few times before you put it in your pot. Oh, and here's a little honey."

"Thanks," Daniel said. "But maybe it's time you stopped bringing me things."

"We have extra," she said.

They stood in place, regarding each other without words for an elongated moment.

"Are we playing 'stare down'?" Britney asked.

"I'm not."

"Do you want some company?"

Daniel had to think about it. Britney excited his senses in a way that set off alarm bells in several parts of his brain.

"Sure," he said. He sat down at the long table and began skinning the onions before chopping them.

"Mind if I sit too?" Britney asked.

"Go ahead," Daniel said. He lit a candle on the table.

"Maybe I'm bothering you."

"Does my father know you're here?"

"He hadn't come home when I left."

"Does he know you bring me stuff?"

"Of course. He wants you to . . . to thrive."

Daniel dumped the onion skins into a battered plastic garbage pail.

"You should start a second soup pot and put your vegetable peels in it so you always have some fresh stock to add to the regular pot," Britney said. "That's how I do it."

"I don't have another pot."

"I can bring you one."

They sat in silence again while Daniel peeled and trimmed the turnip.

"I'm surprised you don't have a woman yet," Britney said.

"What's surprising about it?"

"You could have your pick. All those girls doing farm labor."

"I can barely take care of myself."

"You could take care of each other."

"Maybe I'm not ready for that."

"A full-grown man like you? Do you like women?"

Daniel swept the chunks of turnip into his hand and dumped them in his soup pot.

"Did my father tell you what happened in Tennessee?"

"He said you went there."

"Is that all?"

"Pretty much. Why?"

"Did he tell you I killed a woman there?"

Britney recoiled.

"You?" she said. "You killed someone?"

"I did," Daniel said. He looked straight at her for an awkward interval, but then his eyes clouded and moistened and he averted them back down at the empty chopping board on the table.

"What did she do to you?" Britney asked.

"Nothing."

"I don't understand."

"She was evil."

"Evil? How?"

Daniel shook his head. Britney saw his shoulders hump and shudder as he began to weep. She watched for a while, then got up from her seat, hurried around the table, stooped down beside Daniel's chair, and attempted to put her arms around him, but he stood up abruptly and turned away.

"Excuse me," he said, trying to get hold of his emotions.

"It's all right."

"It'll never be all right," Daniel said. "But that's not your fault."

He turned in place. Britney stepped toward him.

"Maybe I better go," she said.

Daniel did not reply but merely stood his ground studying her as if the two of them were chess pieces on a board come to life, able to decide for themselves which way to move. He could not fail to notice her chest heave under her lumpy brown sweater.

"Yes, you should go," he said.

EIGHT

Robert Earle called the village trustees to a meeting in the upstairs of the old town hall on Main Street the following Monday evening. The big room, with its hand-painted ceiling, was the scene of many a seasonal ball and holiday levee. Here, too, Andrew Pendergast's community theater company put on their plays and musicals, beloved by a people who had lost their access to recorded entertainments. The scenery flats of the New England seaside village left over from last fall's production of Rodgers and Hammerstein's *Carousel* stood onstage at the far end of the room. Auditions for the spring production of *The Boys from Syracuse* would get under way in a week. Most of the seats were stacked up against the wall. Eleven chairs were deployed around a long table at the center of the room. At seven p.m., a salmon-colored sun could be seen through the tall, arched windows, hanging just above the crest of Schoolhouse Hill behind a band of wine-dark clouds and a scrim of budding pink treetops. Robert threw open a lower sash to let in some spring evening air.

Shortly, the trustees could be heard climbing the wooden stairs: Ben Deaver, Todd Zucker, Ned Larmon, all wealthy farmers, Loren Holder, minister of the Congregational Church, Jason LaBountie, the veterinarian, Robbie Furnival, the cordwood cutter, lawyer Sam Hutto, storekeeper Terry Einhorn, and Brother Jobe. Robert chaired the meeting from one end of the long table. Leslie Einhorn, recording secretary, sat at the other end taking notes. She'd brought to the meeting a tin of the popular oat and nut cookies sold in the store. They resembled the granola bars of yore. Her husband, Terry, lit three candles along the table as the daylight dwindled.

Young Daniel Earle arrived minutes later amid the brief pleasantries and took a seat outside the charmed circle of the trustees' conference table. He brandished a clipboard holding some loose sheets of paper and a pencil stub.

"What do you think you're doing here, son?" Jason LaBountie said. He'd been up since one in the morning the previous night with a colicky horse and his brain ached. "We've already got a recording secretary."

"Haven't you heard? He's the press," Ben Deaver said.

"You starting a newspaper, sonny?"

"I'm bringing back the old *News Leader*."

"I used to line the cat box with it."

"You'll find it much changed, sir. Would you like to advertise?"

"I've got all the work I can handle," LaBountie said. "It was the news media that brought down this country, you know."

"Quit talking out of your ass, Jason," said Robbie Furnival, who was a very large man, physically powerful from wrangling logs every day, and unafraid of expressing himself.

Robert tapped the butt end of his Swiss Army knife on the tabletop to get everyone's attention. The trustees dutifully took their seats.

"Some of you might have heard we have a situation with our supply line for trade goods," Robert began, and explained what he and Terry had learned at Bullock's the other day concerning the trade boat. He omitted mentioning the picker pinned through his skull to the tree, in order to avoid a distracting ruckus over it. "Bullock's right, of course," Robert continued. "We ought to get our own boat instead of being at the mercy of his moods and whims. To that end, I suggest we take up some kind of collection around town—"

"Sounds like a tax," LaBountie said. "A coming-at-you-sideways tax."

"No, it isn't. Nobody will be forced to pay anything," Robert said. "And frankly I'm going to ask the farmers to dig a little deeper than the rest."

Ben Deaver made a face and appealed to his fellow farmers Todd Zucker and Ned Larmon, but they would not venture to argue about it. In the new times, in the absence of big corporations and a so-called consumer economy, wealth came from land used productively, putting farmers on the higher rungs of the economic ladder.

"We'd be looking altogether for about a hundred ounces of silver," Robert said. "Is that right, Daniel?"

"Maybe a little more depending on the boat," Daniel said. "Or four, five ounces of gold."

Ned Larmon whistled through his teeth.

"Wait a minute," Jason LaBountie said. "He's not a member of this board. He can't participate in the discussion at the same time he reports on it."

"Relax, will you, Jason—" Loren said.

"Anyway, we didn't vote to admit any news media to village board meetings."

"Move to vote to admit journalists to the meeting," Sam Hutto said.

"Second," Robbie Furnival said.

"Call to vote," Terry Einhorn said.

"All in favor?" Robert said.

Nine hands went up, plus Leslie Einhorn's.

"She's not a voting member of this board," LaBountie said.

"Motion is carried in any case," Robert said. "Press is welcome to observe the meeting,"

"Move for public discussion," Loren said. "So he can speak too."

"Second," Terry Einhorn said.

"Oh for chrissake. What does the kid know about boats anyway?" LaBountie asked.

"I bought a cargo scow at Buffalo summer before last, sir," Daniel said, "and sailed on Lake Erie."

"Did you run freight?" Todd Zucker asked.

"Never got to," Daniel said. "I lost her in a storm on the shoals off Sandusky."

"Not much of a sailor, then, were you?"

"It was a wicked gale, sir, as they are on the lakes, and it came up fast without warning."

"Sorry to hear it. But how'd you get the money for the boat in the first place?" LaBountie asked. "A hundred ounces of silver, or so you say."

"I had it," Daniel said.

"Oh, you just had it? A veritable fortune?" LaBountie said. "Got any more where you had it from? Maybe you can buy the town a boat. And, by the way, what did you pay for this newspaper? And who to?"

"You're out of line, Jason," Robert said.

"It was an abandoned property," Daniel said.

"Well, shouldn't unclaimed, abandoned property become an asset of the town, of the common weal, so to speak?" LaBountie said. "An editor, for one, ought to have some sense of the public interest, don't you think? Oh, and I assume this newspaper is intended to be a moneymaking operation."

"Of course I intend to make a living at it."

"Maybe you should kick back some of your profits into the village kitty and then we don't have to levy a coming-at-you-sideways tax at folks that barely have a pot to piss in, pardon my French."

"Other commercial operations are being run in abandoned properties," Daniel said. "Schroeder's creamery was a garage in the old times owned by one Butch Casper."

"Butch was a friend," Todd Zucker said. "Influenza got the whole family."

"McWhinnie's Boots and Harness used to be a restaurant," Daniel said, "and before that a butcher shop and the building was owned by a George Hazen."

"He was a village trustee back in the day," Sam Hutto said. "Coached Little League too. I was his attorney. Died without issue just before that bomb destroyed our nation's capital."

"Allison's Livery used to be the video rental store owned by Paul Michaelides—"

"Encephalitis," Sam said. "Strange to relate, the building was originally built as a livery stable, way before Paul had it. What goes around comes around, I guess."

"And of course we've started up the town laundry in the old Union-Wayland mill without any formal legal arrangements," Robert said. "The property was last owned by National Grid as a potential hydro site. I don't know if they have a beef with us about it, but the electric service has been off for more than a year and there's a good chance the company no longer exists. We haven't heard from them."

"That's all very well, but you know this can't go on indefinitely," LaBountie said. "People just appropriating land and buildings like some communist revolution happened. This is America! With no property law there's no property rights. Titles and deeds were invented for a reason. You can bet we're going to have a mighty mess sorting all this out when things get back to normal—who really owns what and so forth."

The room fell stark still. A horse could be heard distantly clip-clopping down Main Street. A chair creaked. Someone's stomach growled. A breeze from an open window made the candles flicker. LaBountie looked from one board member to another, but all evaded his gaze except Brother Jobe.

"I got news for you, friend," Brother Jobe said. "Things ain't never getting back to normal ever again."

"Sure they will," LaBountie said. "Just wait and watch, you'll see. The Bilderbergers and their banker amigos are just trying to put the squeeze on us. We're on to them. Once we get the electric back up they won't be able to hide so easily."

More than one board member rolled his eyes.

"Tell you what, Jason, we'll just stand by on all that," Robbie Furnival said.

Todd Zucker chuckled.

Leslie Einhorn passed the tin of cookies around the table. To avoid saying anything, the village trustees kept their mouths busy savoring the oats and hickory nuts in a matrix of honey and butter.

Finally, Ben Deaver cleared his throat and spoke up. "A hundred ounces of silver is a lot of money to come up with, Robert. I can't speak for the others but I'm cash poor. I'm feeding the twenty-five families of my employees on what we produce and living on the little that's left."

"How little is it?" LaBountie asked.

"Are you hectoring me, Jason?" Deaver asked.

"Just asking."

"Well excuse me but it's none of your goddamn business."

"I know these other gentlemen have plenty of surplus for trade."

"Well maybe I'm not such a good farmer as they are. I was busy running an airline till you and your Tea-bagger pals ran the country into a ditch, you deluded son of a bitch."

"You can't talk to me that way."

"Of course I can. I just did. Bilderbergers! It's too bad there's no mental ward anymore. You belong in one."

"You'll pay me in hard silver before I ever come back to you again about a sick animal, and you'll have to beg me too."

"You can go to hell. I'll send over to Bennington for the vet there before I let you work on mine ever again."

"I'll tell him your sheep have got the scrapie."

"Well that'd just be a goddamn lie, Jason—"

Robert rapped on the table with his knife.

"Gentlemen, can we get back to the matter at hand, please," he said.

"Spending public money we don't have on a business venture we're not competent to run is the matter at hand," Jason said.

"You can shut the fuck up now, Jason—" Loren said.

"Oh, nice mouth there, Reverend."

"—before I kick your ass down the stairs."

"Big man!"

"That's right. I'm a lot bigger than you are, so mind what I say."

"Okay. That's it," LaBountie said. "I quit this board. Goddamn thugs and socialists!"

The others watched the portly veterinarian withdraw from the pool of candlelight and waddle across the big, dim room to the stairwell. They waited until his footfalls on the stairs ended and the oaken door of the main entrance slammed shut.

"As we were saying," Robert resumed, and the others around the table burst into tension-relieving laughter.

"Bilderbergers?" Sam Hutto said. "I haven't heard that one for a while."

Brother Jobe passed his whiskey flask around.

"Lookit, everybody," Terry Einhorn said. "I'm about out of sugar, salt, walnuts, peanuts, phosphate, saltpeter, alum, candle wicks, sisal rope, canvas, grommets, and a hundred other things our people need. Do you really want to go without for the rest of the year?"

"He's right," Todd Zucker said. "We can't shut ourselves off from trade with the outside world. And we don't have to."

"Who is going to crew this boat, exactly?" Ned Larmon asked.

"It doesn't take navigational skills to run the river to Albany and back," Robert said. "Bullock ran with a crew of four."

"Well, my bunch is good for fifty ounces toward purchase," Brother Jobe declared. "I can't spare any hands to sail it, but surely y'all can locate some town men looking for gainful employment off field and farm, and maybe a little adventure to boot."

"Motion to vote on proposal to raise enough silver to purchase a cargo boat," Loren said.

"And volunteers to build a crib dock on the river," Terry said.

"In favor?" Robert asked. "Against."

The vote in favor was unanimous.

NINE

Sarah Watling, daughter of Britney Blieveldt and Shawn Watling (deceased), had skills and responsibilities that would have seemed impossible for an eight-year-old back in the old times. She knew, for instance, all the steps to making a splint basket from a black ash log. She could slaughter, pluck, and butcher a chicken, and then roast it perfectly. One night a week she was required to cook the family dinner and it was her job to make corn bread every other day. She could sew well enough to make her own skirts and trousers. She could knit a pair of socks. And it was also her task to milk Cinnamon, the family cow.

Cinnamon lived in the barn on Salem Street that once had belonged to Sarah's grandparents Denny and Marge Watling, Britney's in-laws (also deceased). The accompanying house burned down the previous spring. Only the foundation remained, with blackberries now beginning to creep over the dry-laid fieldstones. The barn behind it, built in 1889, had replaced an even earlier, cruder structure erected by a veteran of the Revolutionary War, one Dyer Goodsell, partner in the town's first flax mill. It was Sarah's favorite place because she felt it truly belonged to her. It came down through her father's family and she was the one who spent the most time there, mostly alone. Sarah loved the forecourt with its old mossy marble pavement, and the Dutch door with its diamond-shaped windowpanes, and the old dark wood of the interior. The floor was made of chestnut planks four inches thick when they were new. She loved the animal fragrance that seemed to carry the memory of every horse and cow that ever lived there.

The back of the barn opened up to a third-of-an-acre fenced paddock that had once been a shady lawn in Denny and Marge's day, scene of barbecues and children playing ringolevio in the summer twilight. Most of the big maples had since been cut down for fire-wood and to allow the grass to grow better in the paddock for Cinnamon to graze on. Evenings, Cinnamon also got some hay, which was stored in the loft.

Robert had made considerable improvements to the building in the year that Sarah and Britney came to dwell with him. He replaced the sill atop the stone foundation on the north side of the structure. He rebuilt the milking stall, replaced the stall gate and the rolling door to the paddock, and removed decades of miscella-neous clutter from the unused stalls and the loft. He put a salvaged three-sash diamond-paned window (to match the one in the door) in the milking stall now that the electricity appeared to be out for good. It admitted more daylight and made milking and caretaking much easier.

Robert had tricked out one of the other three stalls as a chicken coop, with a small hatch door to an exterior pen covered in salvaged chicken wire to keep the skunks and opossums out. They generally kept four laying hens there along with as many as twenty meat birds, which Britney and Sarah raised for trade as well as for their own table. The barn was on the village water system, gravity fed from a reservoir on the shoulder of Pumpkin Hill. It was the gift that kept on giving, though the purification system no longer operated and had to be bypassed.

Cinnamon was a 950-pound, fawn-brown, five-year-old Jersey cow. On her diet, she gave about two gallons of milk a day. She had been "freshened"—bred to produce offspring—sixteen months ago and was still milking reliably. Her calf had been weaned and sold. Sarah was told not to name the calf because Robert and Britney did not want her to become too attached to it. But she named it Cleo after a friend who died in the encephalitis epidemic, and it was hard on Sarah when they sold her. They didn't have the means or the need to keep two cows, and good livestock was in short supply these years directly after the collapse of the old economy.

This evening, Sarah entered the barn on the Salem Street side and passed through the churchlike interior to the sliding door and the paddock. Cinnamon looked up, seemed to be glad to see her, and began walking toward the barn. Cinnamon knew that it was time to be milked and was eager to feel more comfortable. Sarah gave the chickens some cracked corn while she waited.

Cinnamon came directly to her stall and turned around facing a manger where Sarah had placed a flake of hay. She put a halter on Cinnamon's head and clipped the end of the lead line to an iron ring on a nearby post. Then she filled a plastic pail at the standing faucet in the aisle outside the stall and wiped down Cinnamon's udder with a wet rag, which got specks of manure off and massaged the teats to let the milk down. Next, she squirted each teat twice onto the floor to get any old liquid out of the way. Her three-legged stool was made by Robert, with a heart-shaped seat. Her milking bucket was stainless steel, with a lid, the sort of thing that might never be manufactured again. Cinnamon was an exceptionally calm and gentle cow and cooperated with every step of the procedure. While Sarah milked, squeezing the teats alternately with both hands, she sang a song that Robert had been teaching her called "The Blackest Crow," a traditional Appalachian ballad in a minor key that was sad and beautiful and grown-up sounding. She sang her harmony part as a shaft of low evening sunlight beamed through the window into the stall.

The blackest crow that ever flew would surely turn to white
If ever I prove false to you bright day will turn to night
Bright day will turn to night my love, the elements will mourn
If ever I prove false to you the seas will rage and burn

Sarah could tell when Cinnamon was empty from the hash mark inside the pail and the shape and heft of the udder. She clipped the cover on the pail, took off Cinnamon's halter, and that was that. With new spring grass up, Sarah knew that Cinnamon would want to go back out to her paddock for a while in the remaining light and wander back inside when it was full dark. They went their separate ways. As she stepped toward the door on the Salem

Street side, Sarah misstepped and her left foot jammed up against the doorsill, sending a jag of pain up through her leg. She knew at once it was more than a stubbed toe. She was able to set the pail down without the lid popping off, and that was more immediately important to her than the injury. She limped outside, sat down in the early weeds, and tried to take her moccasin off but it would not come off. Lifting her lower leg close to her face, she saw a round metallic button at the tip of her shoe. She touched it and it seemed rigidly fixed to the meaty part of her foot between her big and second toe. Understanding instinctively what it meant, and without thinking the matter through any further, she pulled on the metallic button and drew out a brown five-penny, 1¾-inch box nail, manufactured in Elyria, Ohio, in 1957. The slightly bent nail had lain loose in the space between two floorboards for decades. Though she hyperventilated and shed some tears drawing it out the wound did not really hurt much afterward. She angrily tossed the nail into the street and removed her moccasin and sock. The tiny hole barely bled at all. Mostly, Sarah was afraid of getting in trouble, specifically of not being allowed back in the barn by herself. So she dried her eyes, put her shoe back on, got up off the ground, picked up her pail, and hurried home so her mama could make some fresh cheese out of the milk, as planned.

TEN

Robert Earle, Loren Holder, and Brother Jobe met for breakfast in the town laundry in which they were all business partners. The venture was a great success in its second month of operation. They employed four townspeople in the old repurposed Union-Wayland mill building on the river, charging ten cents (in pre-1965 silver coin) for ten pounds of laundry, the problem being that nickels and pennies did not circulate, not being silver. Customers who brought in less than ten pounds could carry over their credit in cents to the next load. Accounts were recorded in a ledger. The three partners were surprised that the number of customers did not level off in the first month, but continued growing as farm people out in the county heard about it and began to bring their wash in on trading days.

It was also evident just walking about town these fresh spring days that the people of Union Grove were looking better, taking more of an interest in their appearance. As their off-the-rack, mail-order casual clothing from the old times wore out, they began to sport some of the apparel sold in Brother Jobe's "haberdash" on Main Street, where garments sewn in the New Faith workshops were sold, simple cotton shirts, canvas and wool trousers and coats, skirts and jumpers for women. Likewise, in the New Faith barbershop, where the gloomy but skillful Brother Judah presided, some townsmen said good-bye to their beards, so that altogether the denizens of Union Grove, both New Faith and regular, were looking more like one unified people in manner and costume. The Reverend Loren Holder now went in for a shave twice a week, while Robert Earle still wore a full beard but trimmed it in the manner of General U. S. Grant. Brother Jobe, of course, was shaved daily at headquarters by his factotum Brother Boaz.

Brother Jobe had been waiting for the other two in the office down at the laundry for a little while. He came early, enjoying the look, smell, and feel of a successful new enterprise. At eight o'clock the operation with its wood-fired furnace, copper wash kettles, and water-powered machinery was just getting under way for the day. The office was already so warm Brother Jobe took off his black frock coat. Sister Miriam had packed a basket for him with a thermos of "coffee"—brewed from roasted barley and chickory root, with plenty of cream and honey—and generous squares of breakfast pudding for three—cornmeal mush baked with cheese, onions, and flecks of New Faith ham. Robert and Loren arrived a little after eight. After pleasantries, the men settled into the comfortable seating with their mugs and rations.

"How come you didn't tell me the squire done pinned some poor sumbitch to a tree down on the River Road like a ding-danged luna moth in the natural history museum?" Brother Jobe commenced the meeting.

Loren looked up from his steaming beverage with his eyebrows hoisted. "Say, what?" he said.

"Some poor, lone picker," Robert explained to Loren, who hadn't heard. "Bullock says they caught him trying to steal a horse. He nailed him to a tree clear through his forehead."

"Oh, that's lovely," Loren said. "Why didn't you tell the trustees?"

"Things are complicated enough right now," Robert said.

"That ole boy is off the reservation," Brother Jobe said. "Of course, you can't feel sorry for a fellow that'd steal a horse, but these public displays of barbarism and cruelty gonna demoralize folks for miles around."

"I can't talk to him anymore," Robert said. "I tried the other day when Terry and I went over there."

"Why don't you go see Mr. Bullock, Reverend Holder, in your clerical capacity?" Brother Jobe said. "Appeal to the better angels of his nature."

"He's an atheist," Loren said.

"He don't have to believe for you to read him the riot act. Some-one's got to get through to his moral sense, if he's still got any left."

"I wouldn't know what to say to the bastard."

"Seems to me you're the man for that job," Robert said to Brother Jobe.

"I'm liable to hurt him if he sasses me like the last time we were alone together in a room," Brother Jobe said and puffed out his cheeks in frustration. The others studied their breakfast, letting the subject pass. "Anyways, Mr. Einhorn proposes to send his boy to Albany along with your boy, and I can lend two of my rangers to accompany them there, with horses, and some small arms in case of any monkey business, and with some luck they'll bring a boat back. They better leave soon, though. Mr. Einhorn says things are getting a little desperate amongst the town folk, so many being common laborers and of small means. Speaking for my own outfit, we put aside plenty of cornmeal, potatoes, smoked meats, and a few other things, but we're nearly out of sugar, salt, cotton duck, and like that, and I hope to fetch me some ding-dang real coffee up from Albany, if there's any to be got. My men can leave on Sunday with our fifty ounces of silver and whatever you-all can scare up."

"I'm up to thirty-two ounces soliciting my people," Robert said. "If you lend me a mount, I'll ride out to Holyrood's cider mill and over to Temple Merton's farm at Coot Hill tomorrow. They're men of means."

"They must be anxious to get some of their poteen to market, too, if that'll inspire them," Brother Jobe said. "By the way, I'm fixing to officially reopen my tavern on Saturday night. We'll be putting on the dog. You tell folks that. Mebbe it'll take their minds off their empty larders for a little while."

"I'll hit up my congregation for last-minute contributions," Loren said. "Hey, did we decide what to do about Bullock?"

"Tell you what, don't do nothing," Brother Jobe said. "I'll send Brother Joseph over. He don't brook no aspersions from the hoity-toity."

Eleven

Brother Jobe gave Robert a brindle mare named Belle to ride out into the county on Friday afternoon. The mare had been rescued the previous Christmastime from the possession of the indigent homesteader and would-be murderer Donald Acker (deceased), who had lacked the means to keep her in feed and was too stupidly proud to ask for help. She was in sorry condition then, but four months in the New Faith stables and paddocks had restored her to health. Robert was not an experienced rider, but Belle was smart and tractable, and being at large in the landscape burgeoning with new life in fine spring weather exhilarated both of them.

He rode out to the north toward Hebron first, to Temple Merton's orchard and distillery, past men and women laboring in the fields, plowing behind horses and oxen, clearing drainage ditches, coppicing in the hedgerows, burning heaps of bark and woodland trash to spread ashes on the crop rows, and attending to new lambs and calves in the pastures. Some of the smaller holdings were slovenly subsistence farms, where people seemed to be barely hanging on, overworked, scarecrow-thin, ill-clothed, like figures out of a medieval woodcut of the plague years, grubbing around in the soil with hand tools. In the new times, it was hard to go it alone on the land. Places organized for production with many hands were more successful, though there were many ways of organizing the hands.

Robert got to Temple Merton's house near Summit Lake just before noon. He'd been there more than a few times over the years and he was always thrilled by the beautiful orderliness of the establishment. The proprietor was a formalist, like his father before him, who had built walled gardens, planted an allée of blight-resistant American chestnuts from the road to the front of the house and its dependent barns and workshops, and kept his animals clean. The farm gave the impression that at least one corner of the universe was safe and secure. The housekeeper directed Robert out to the orchards where he found Temple and two other men mulching a stand of pears. They had a load of velvety black compost in a cart pulled by a goat. Without even inquiring about his reason for dropping in, Temple invited Robert to lunch. He chucked his shovel onto the cart and told the others he was taking off for an hour and that they could, too, once they fetched the goat some water.

Temple Merton's people had fought in the Revolution and then farmed the same four hundred acres afterward going down the generations to Temple's father, who shifted from dairy to fruit in the 1970s. Temple himself had fled the farm right after high school, gone off to NYU in the theater arts program, and emerged as a highly employable character actor, best known for his role as the carefree Victorian-era poisoner Lamont Circe in the cable TV series *Boomtown*, which ran for six seasons. Before that, he'd been a regular in the Coen Brothers ensemble, beginning with *The Big Lebowski*.

The week of the Washington bombing, he managed to drive all the way back to the family homestead from a James Cameron film location in the Sonoran desert outside Tucson in one of the on-set Escalade limousines, which he'd simply commandeered in the confusion. He was already separated from his actress wife, Fannie Dana (the fortune hunter Maggie O'Toole in *Boomtown*), and left behind all his chattels in Santa Monica, which were blown up nine months later anyway in the Los Angeles bombing. His alcoholic older brother, Jess, occupied the farmhouse back home and had been letting the orchards go to hell for a decade, but the economic collapse finished him psychologically and he lasted less than a year after Temple arrived back home to take charge. He shaped up the place in short order, relearning everything his father had taught him as a boy.

Temple Merton was renowned now in Washington County, New York (and southern Vermont), for his Coot Hill apple brandy that was too fine to be called "jack." He also raised beef cattle and mixed poultry: turkeys, ducks, chickens. His house was red brick, with a curious Dutch stepped roof, and he'd added several new buildings: quarters for workers, stables, a wagon barn, and a bottling works, forming a handsome courtyard arrangement that reminded Robert of establishments he had seen in Europe years ago. At sixty-seven, Temple was hale and athletic. He employed twenty laborers and a household staff of four. His divorce had never been finalized back in California, so he felt unable to marry again, but he found a girlfriend half his age named Lorraine Moncalvo, esteemed as the finest cook in the county. She'd run a Boston catering company in the old times and published two cookbooks, and literally walked out of that city during the post-crash troubles with little besides a change of clothing and three of her best kitchen knives in a back-pack. Temple met her three Septembers ago along the road driving home from Bennington, where he'd traveled with five cases of his brandy to sell. He gave her a ride, of course, on the deadhead trip home. It took mere minutes of conversation for him to discern that she was an extraordinary person, and she wasn't bad looking either, though she wore many layers of clothing that concealed her figure. She was looking for a situation, she said, as opposed to a job. Temple liked the way she put that. Once she got talking about food up there on the bench seat beside him in cool autumn weather, he told her that she may have found her situation. And so she had. And Temple Merton was a happier man in the new times by far than he had ever been back in Hollywood.

Robert was quite hungry that day, having forgotten to pack so much as a square of corn bread in his excitement to saddle up. Temple sat him down in the sun-filled dining room. Lorraine, full bodied with loose curly auburn hair and a winning lopsided smile, brought out duck legs preserved in their own fat with beans and cabbage and pickled beets, onion and pepper relishes, and delicate cornmeal pancakes with sour cream. By-and-by, Robert turned to the matter at hand: the need to resume the Albany trade. The couple were interested and receptive, being short of many necessities from grape-stake wire to veterinary supplies. Temple averred that he had always respected Stephen Bullock without particularly liking him, and he gave Robert twenty ounces of silver toward the purchase of a proper boat.

Robert made it to Felix Holyrood's cider mill eight miles south by four o'clock. Holyrood was desperate for priming sugar, clean copper tubing, tin solder, and other things he was used to sending to Albany for when Bullock was making regular runs there. He gave Robert fourteen ounces of silver coin on a promissory note and sent him home with a bottle of his Normandise bouche brut blush, a particularly fine, dry sparkling cider, which Robert could not help sampling on his return trip to Union Grove in the glow of his successful venture raising additional funds. In fact he was a little high coming down the ridge behind Holyrood's place when something caught his attention in the distance in the low-slanting late afternoon light.

He saw the smoke of many fires curling up out of a pasture on the east side of Lewis Hill, a mile and a half away. Squinting and shielding his eyes with his left hand, he made out colored patches behind the curls of smoke. His eyesight was not what it used to be. Tents, he supposed. He spied movement among them. People. He'd heard nothing of any encampment on Lewis Hill, which was five miles east of Union Grove. Whoever it was had not been there very long. Possibly they had just arrived that afternoon and made camp. He could only guess at the number of people there, figuring perhaps twenty tents were pitched on the hillside. If there were more than one person per tent, the encampment might have amounted to, say, fifty people, maybe more. He wondered if they were displaced persons, or pilgrims of some sort like the New Faithers had been, or perhaps an organized horde of pickers. Certainly they were not out there for the fun of it with nighttime temperatures still dipping into the thirties. In the years since the collapse, the county had not seen a gang larger than the nine who invaded Bullock's place back in October. But such a thing wouldn't be out of the question in these times. If men like Temple Merton and Stephen Bullock could organize many hands to work on their farms, surely some talented criminal could organize a brigade of marauders. He decided not to ride over there by himself to make inquiries, thinking that if they were not friendly he might be detained. Instead, he corked the bottle of cider, tucked it in his coat, and rode Belle at a brisk trot the rest of the way back to town.

TWELVE

After Robert returned Belle to the stable, he sought out Brother Jobe in his personal quarters in the converted high school, formerly the principal's office suite. The New Faith honcho sat behind a fine old oak desk composing his sermon for the coming Sunday. He looked up and slid his reading glasses down his button-like nose as Robert was shown in by Brother Boaz.

"Why, good evening, Mr. Mayor," Brother Jobe began. "I've been studying up on Pentecost. You know, the followers of Jesus were frightened in the days after he took leave of his bodily raiment there on the cross. We take it for granted nowadays that we know how that story developed—the resurrection and the start of a church and so forth—but the disciples, they didn't know nothing at the time, and they were scared. Jesus had wanted to provide for the spiritual fortification of his followers, you see. Now, according to the Nicene Creed, the Holy Ghost was present at the creation of the world and the birth of Jesus and the crucifixion and the resurrection and was lodged also in the hearts of the disciples of Jesus, and he had prayed to the father that this Holy Ghost spirit would be the protection that his disciples needed and would be the very expression of their faith, too, in those parlous days—you following all this, old son?"

"Sort of," Robert said.

"Well, it don't matter, I guess. But there you have it. You get some cash money out of them apple knockers?"

"Yes, enough to go ahead and look for a boat in Albany," Robert said. "But on the way back I noticed there's some people camping out on Lewis Hill. A pretty sizable bunch. I don't like how it looks."

"Campers?" Brother Jobe said. He removed his eyeglasses altogether and rubbed his whole face with both hands. Then he blinked vigorously. "These ain't campin' times. People don't sleep out in the weather 'less they ain't got nowhere to go, or are out ranging for some purpose."

"What I thought too."

"Did you go mingle amongst them?"

"No, I did not. It seemed to me that they might be trouble."

"Yes, I see what you mean." He swiveled in his oak chair to gaze out the window. A three-quarter moon was rising over Schoolhouse Hill to the southwest in a lustrous blue green sky the color of a tropical sea. "You better show me on the map where these birds are. I'll send my rangers over for a look-see."

THIRTEEN

Mary Beth Ivanhoe, known as the Queen Bee or Precious Mother among the brothers and sisters of the New Faith, lay in bed in her quarters, which was a jewel box–like windowless room at the center and apex of three levels of chambers up in the old high school gymnasium, where she and the young women devoted to her care resided. A cupola at the top of the ceiling let in the first rays of evening moonlight in a room otherwise lighted with a few candles. Mary Beth was the group's epileptic clairvoyant spirit guide. She'd been grievously injured by a speeding Jeep Cherokee in the parking lot of the Hunter's Ridge Mall, outside Raleigh, North Carolina, in 2006, when a boy of sixteen with the laces of his Kobe Bryant Nikes untied managed to jam his loose right shoe between the gas pedal and the floor panel in such a way that the throttle opened to the maximum and stuck. The Jeep accelerated rapidly down the loading lane and was going sixty-three miles an hour when Mary Beth happened to back out of her space in its path to get perfectly T-boned on the driver's side of her Toyota Celica. She was in a coma for weeks and was altogether a different person when she came out of it.

Though she was afflicted with horrific seizures and many other chronic disorders, Mary Beth's massive injuries had also endowed her with extraordinary mental abilities to view events at both a geographical and temporal remove, which allowed her to guide the New Faith people out of the tumult of Dixieland ultimately to the group's "New Jerusalem" in Union Grove, New York. Her health had declined markedly over the preceding year, especially after she gave birth to quadruplets the previous fall. The pregnancy itself had been a matter of intense and mysterious wonder, regarded by the sisters and brothers as a miracle.

Following the brief visit of Robert Earle and his report of strangers encamped on Lewis Hill, Brother Jobe laid aside his unfinished sermon on the Pentecost and hurried to Mary Beth's chamber. At the door, intricately figured with a hexagonal honeycomb pattern executed in marquetry of stained hardwoods, he heard the sound of shape note singing, a musical form derived from the group's place of origin in the southern mountains. This so-called sacred harp music had a shrill and somber beauty to it. Behind the door, eight female voices sang the traditional hymn "Idumea" in a minor key. Brother Jobe knew the song full well and hearing its lyrics in a four-part harmony chilled him.

And am I born to die
To lay this body down
And must my trembling spirit fly
Into a world unknown

A land of deepest shade
Unpierced by human thought
The dreary regions of the dead
Where all things are forgot

The door was heavy but so exquisitely balanced that it opened soundlessly and it took more than a moment for the women to discover Brother Jobe standing there. Their voices stopped in sequence until the contralto Sister Zuruiah finished the verse alone. All faces turned to him expectantly.

"You done that real nicely, sisters," he said. "Could you give us a moment?"

The women picked up plates, a tray of uneaten food, a wash basin, towels, and other sundries and exited the chamber in a swirl of coordinated activity. When the door clicked shut, Brother Jobe dragged a chair closer to the bed. The room was extraordinarily warm—Mary Beth demanded it that way—and mingled odors of cloying sweetness and decay hung thickly in the air.

"What all is going on?" Mary Beth asked in a phlegmy, reedy voice. "I was enjoying that."

"They'll come back, dear. Relax."

"Don't tell me to relax. They was easing my pain. Who all are you, anyways? I can't hardly see no more."

"It's me, Precious Mother. Lyle," Brother Jobe said, going by the old times given name she knew him by, Lyle Beecham Wilsey. "You all right?"

"Of course not. I'm done for. What do you think they's singing about?"

"Why, you look a durn sight better than I seen you in years, slimmed right down and all like you done."

It was true. Mary Beth had weighed in at well over three hundred pounds around Christmastime and had shed a hundred fourteen pounds since. She was no longer virtually entombed in the folds and wattles of her own flesh and was beginning to somewhat resemble the ordinary Carolina girl she had once been, the girl who had worked in an Old Navy store at a Raleigh shopping mall, dated athletic young men, and vacationed at Rodanthe on the Outer Banks in her stepmother's time-share. But now she could hardly eat a thing, and her cells were starved, and the synergies of progressive organ malfunction as a result of her injuries were hastening her toward a definite mortal completion. She remained sentient enough to know it. For a while, Brother Jobe didn't speak but dabbed at his eyes with handkerchief and sniffled.

"I could send down for some pie," he said, "if that would make you feel better."

"I'm done eatin'."

"Don't say that."

"I'm awful weary of this life is all," she said.

"Want me to git the doc in here?"

"I don't never want to see no doctor again. Sumbitches treated me like a goldurned science project, and look what I come to." Her breathing sounded labored. Brother Jobe felt the veil of denial fall away in his own mind as he watched her battered body heave and shudder under the bedsheet. The yellow turban she wore to conceal her hairlessness glowed like a lamp in the meager candlelight.

"I don't know what we gonna do if you leave us, dear," he said.

"Don't worry. I'll be up yonder with you-know-who and my kin," she gasped as a rogue pain shot up the back of her neck like the jab of a pithing needle. Brother Jobe cringed in sympathy. "I expect you-all gonna run around like chickens with no heads for a while," she added. "By-and-by you'll be all right. I known for some time there's a gal out there fixing to replace me."

"Who?"

"It ain't clear. Some new blood, I think. Say, what all'd you barge in on me for anyways? Surely not just to pass the time of day in idle chitchat. I was at peace with that there sing-along."

Well, Mary Beth, I was wondering if you got any of that far-seein' mojo left."

"I ain't hardly tried in a while, I been so weary."

"I'd be obliged if you give it a go."

"What's up?"

"That man Mr. Earle, the mayor here, saw some strange doings out east of town. Folks camping on a hillside, he said. Put your mind to what that might be about."

Mary Beth squeezed her eyes and emitted a set of grunts and groans expressing tremendous interior effort. Beads of sweat appeared on her forehead.

"Ain't no use," she said with a final rasp. "I'm drawing blanks. I don't see nothin' but bare planting fields and livestock. Wait!"

"I'm here, dear."

"Green grass," she muttered.

"Well, it *is* springtime—"

"Naw, this green grass ain't about that. It's green but it's dead."

"Huh? Pardon me, but that sounds like a riddle—"

"Aw, I ain't tuned in right. It's all a muddle. Something about green grass is all. Oh, dear Jesus!"

With that utterance Mary Beth jerked back so hard the headboard of her bed hit the wall. Her body spasmed, her eyes rolled up under the lids, her mouth clenched, and her lips retracted displaying only a partial array of teeth. Whitish foam began to run out of her nose and mouth. Brother Jobe stolidly waited it out, knowing that there was nothing he could do to arrest her seizure. She emerged from the fugue state panting. Brother Jobe found a rag on a washstand and wiped the spittle from her face as her chest heaved.

"Oooowee, that was a . . . a humdinger," she croaked, her breathing like chords on a broken harmonium. "I seen something . . . out there."

"What's that? What'd you see, Mary Beth?"

"That green grass. It's a person."

"How can grass be a person?"

"I don't have no idear. I'm so tired. Got to sleep. Send them gals back in and leave me be."

FOURTEEN

Brothers Seth and Elam, veterans of the war in the Holy Land, the first a wiry half-Cherokee and the other a former NFL prospect in the last days of the old times when pro sports still ruled the land, rode out east of town in the light of the waxing three-quarter moon. They were glad to be at large in the landscape, on horseback, out in the springtime night air, after being shut in much of the elongated northeastern winter. As army rangers specializing in reconnaissance night was their natural element. They had studied a topo map before leaving and committed the rather simple route to memory. Eventually, riding east, they made out the campfires on the side of Lewis Hill. In a little while, they turned off old state highway 372 onto a wagon track in a field. The wagon track followed a hedgerow past other fields not yet plowed and up to the edge of a high pasture where twenty-seven tents were pitched in no discernible arrangement.

"These ain't military types," Elam observed.

"I don't believe they's even Boy Scouts," Seth whispered back.

They hitched their mounts in a locust grove at elevation and crept up to a three-hundred-year-old stone wall washed with sprays of bramble canes and wild rose, just barely budding at this time of year. Most of the individual campfires before the tents were merely smoldering now. But, deeper within the encampment, they saw one larger brighter fire, around which dozens of figures sat. The rangers could hear voices ringing in song.

"I know that tune," Seth whispered to Elam. "What all's it called?"

"'This Land Is Your Land.'"

"I be dog. They's socialists for sure."

"Shush."

They watched at a remove for a time. People came and went. Sparks flew as tree limbs were tossed on the fire. The rangers smelled something sweet roasting. The singers ran through a considerable repertory: "Where Have All the Flowers Gone," "Joe Hill," "Michael, Row the Boat Ashore," "Goodnight Irene," "Wimoweh."

Seth studied the gathering through a pair of compact binoculars.

"Hey, quite a number of them is women," he whispered. "Young'ns at that."

"Lemme see." Elam took the optics. "Hmm. They're wearing men's clothes."

"Want to introduce ourself?"

"What's our cover?"

"Men of Jesus and like that?" Seth said.

"I dunno," Elam said. "Nighttime and all. That won't wash. Let's say coon hunters for start."

"Copy that. Fall back to Jesus."

"All right, let's go."

They clambered over the stone wall, entered the pasture, and made their way past the tents to the big fire where the strangers were disposed in various postures: sitting, reclining, couples cuddling, some women with women and men with men, several with guitars and one banjo. They had been singing "Swing Low, Sweet Chariot," swaying in time with the music, when the rangers emerged into the orange halo of firelight.

"How you-all doin'?" Seth said.

"Evening ladies," Elam said. "And gents. We was out and about and heard you-all."

The people around the fire greeted them with silence and stared emptily back at them, many with their mouths open, as if amazed or perplexed. Then, a figure on the far side of the fire stood up.

"Are you regulators?" the person asked, rather sternly. Seth and Elam could not tell whether they were being addressed by a man or by a woman. The voice was of middling register, and the standing figure, dressed in high boots, trousers, and layers of flannel and expeditionary polarfleece from the old times and a wool Sherpa hat with dangling earflap ties, presented an ambiguous picture in the firelight. Then the person moved sinuously through the throng of seated campers until a handsome, big-boned woman stood before the rangers. She was just under six feet tall, with wisps of sandy-blond hair curling out of her Sherpa hat and raptor eyes that suggested steely determination. "This is a no-gun zone," she said, straight deadpan, her delicate mouth downturned into a self-consciously dramatic frown that worked against her natural appeal.

"We just out for coon," Seth said, adding "ma'am" and making sure to point the muzzle of his rifle toward the ground.

"Please don't use the 'c' word in our company."

"Huh . . . ?"

"It's offensive."

"Uh . . . coon?"

"That's right."

"Oh, it's the animal, not a person," Elam tried to explain. "You know, raccoon, ma'am."

"First of all, we don't call it that anymore," she retorted. "Too much room for misunderstanding and offense. To us it is the ring-tailed handwasher."

"You kidding, ma'am?" Elam said.

"No, I'm not kidding," she said. "Anyway, we're vegetarians. We don't approve of killing animals. And don't call me 'ma'am.' That term is an instrument of systematic patriarchal oppression. It smacks of binary opposition and invites unwanted penetration."

"Say what?" Seth said.

"That's our analysis of the associated cultural production," she continued. "Nobody's privileged here. Now is there something you wanted—besides the meat of little animals that are just out minding their own business, not bothering you in any way, shape, or form?"

"We just saw your campfire from a ways away," Elam said. "Thought we'd see who was out and about. So what do you want to be called by if 'ma'am' won't do?"

"By my name," she said. "Flame."

"Pardon me," Elam said. "Like that fire there?"

"Yes . . . ?" she said, the interrogatory uptick meant to display her impatience with yokels.

"She do burn bright," Seth said.

"And hot," Elam said.

Flame bristled visibly again. "Did I ask what you two wanted? I thought I did."

"Well, uh, Flame," Elam said, "it's part of our duties to keep an eye on things, who's coming and going in the area and like that."

"Then you are regulators."

"Uh, no. More like lookouts?"

"Who for?"

"Our people back in town."

"You sound like you're not even from around here," Flame said.

"Well, we're not, ma'am—"

"Flame."

"Darn it you're hard to get on with."

"Lookit," she said. "You barge into our camp with guns—"

"I'm sorry about that," Elam said. "We don't mean any harm and we'll be on our way shortly. To answer your question, we are from down South, mostly Virginia and North Carolina . . ."

"'Cept for me," Seth said. "Oklahoma born."

"And with all the troubles back home, violence and fighting and all, we come north, first to Pennsylvania, which didn't work out so well cuz of its proximity to Washington, DC, and then we lit out again further north to find some security. We are the New Faith Covenant Brotherhood Church of Jesus. There are eighty-two of us in all, counting the young ones. We have settled in Union Grove, some five miles to the west of here, and we are getting on pretty good there, considering these times. Now, who all are you, if I may ask?"

"We're free citizens of the Berkshire People's Republic," she said.

"Berkshire—where's that at?"

"Those are the mountains of western Massachusetts. Our capital is the town of Great Barrington."

"You got your own country?" Seth asked.

"Nature hates a vacuum."

"What's there to hate about a vacuum?" Seth said. "Anyways, the electric's out and all."

"A political vacuum," Flame said. "What's wrong with you?"

"Nothin'—"

"You never heard the phrase? *Nature hates a vacuum*?"

"I guess I have," Seth said. "Do the federals know you gone and seceded from the USA?"

"They're irrelevant now," Flame said. "After Washington was destroyed, we formed our own government. We had to. The Commonwealth of Massachusetts has no presence anymore in the Berkshires either, no resources, no law enforcement, no social services, no outreach, no funding. Of course, you can't have no government."

"Why not?"

"There would be no justice. Rights would be trampled. Oppression and rape would rule. The poor and disabled would be cut loose to die. Discrimination, economic inequality, unfairness in the workplace, gender coercion, environmental degradation, bad schools, and creeping theocracy would be the order of the day."

"We got some problems here," Seth said, "but nothin' that bad."

"How do you monitor excessive privilege?"

"Privilege of what?"

"Race, gender, income."

"I dunno. We have some rich and some poor. Like always, everywhere."

"Is it right, though?"

"It's normal, far as I know."

"Surely you know these aren't normal times, mister."

"Even the rich ain't that rich—not like in the old times," Seth said. "They don't have no airplanes and like that. Around here they's just farmers, mainly."

"And they employ a lot of people," Elam said. "There's work for anybody that wants it."

"Is your community diverse?" Flame asked.

"Well, it takes all kinds," Elam replied, flustered, as though teacher had singled him out for humiliation.

"You know what I mean."

"Not really."

"Then you must be politically unconscious, living in happy anarchy as you do, with no government."

"We're not living in anarchy," Elam said.

"Who monitors diversity?"

"It takes care of itself."

"What about your homeless?"

"Homes are a dime a dozen around here. The population's way down. Abandoned properties everywhere you look, and folks just move in where they please. Nobody has to go homeless."

"It sounds like paradise," Flame said with a sardonic snort and the others in the big circle around the fire giggled. "Utopia! Satori! Nirvana!"

"We're looking out for our own affairs well enough, considering," Elam said. "You still haven't said what y'all are doing over here in New York state."

"Every year we go on an outreach," Flame said. "We call it the Spring Fling, but it's a serious political organizing mission. The People's Republic wants to invite the neighboring regions into our federation for the greater good. Eventually, perhaps it will become a replacement for the broken United States government, and our poor country will be reborn."

"Who you got besides yourself so far?" Seth asked.

"The towns of southern Vermont will be coming along, I believe. Brattleboro, Wilmington. We met with the Bennington council the other day."

"Have you heard of the Foxfire Republic in Tennessee and the New Africa bunch down in Georgia, Alabama, and like that?" Elam asked.

"Of course. We've seen reports."

"Are you worried that they coming up to git y'all over in Berkshire?" Seth asked.

"Foxfire is fascist and racist," Flame said. "We're not comfortable seeing that in what used to be America. Maybe that's okay with you."

"Not really," Elam said. "We're live and let live."

"Except for harmless little animals."

"Well," Elam said. "We like a little meat with our vegetables. Anyway, Tennessee is a far piece from here. And it appears the leader of that outfit been assassinated. Mebbe they'll change their ways now. Like if someone had nipped that Hitler in the bud before he went and started the second world war."

"They're still committing atrocities against people of color down south," Flame said.

"We've heard where it's plenty of wickedness on both sides," Elam said. "I guess me and my partner'll shuffle along now."

"Is he your partner?" Flame said, a smile suddenly lighting her face.

"We hunt and patrol together and like that," Elam said.

"Oh," Flame said, affecting to look abashed. "But you're not . . ." She made a little twiddling gesture with her index finger. Elam and Seth swapped a glance, both genuinely perplexed.

"We go back to army days," Seth said. "The Holy Land war."

"Oh? Did you kill people?" Flame asked.

"Yes, we did," Elam said. "That's what you do in war, ma'am . . . er, Flame."

The crowd around the fire groaned and grumbled.

"Have you ever encountered the teachings of Glen Ethan Greengrass?" Flame asked, the tone of her voice rising again.

"Who's that?"

"The founder of the Berkshire People's Republic. Our leader and teacher. You two can read, can't you?"

"Of course we can," Seth said.

"Someone, give me a green book," Flame cried over her shoulder. A young man with a sunken chest about twenty stepped up and presented a slender volume with a green cloth cover to Flame's outstretched hand. "This is our bible," she said, handing it, in turn, to Elam. The title on the cover read: *Birthing the New Knowledge Economy: Teachers as Midwives for the Skills Agenda of the Future.* Elam opened the book and turned to examine its pages in the firelight. He read a paragraph.

"*The path to victory in this great war for the minds of youth demands that we achieve radical inclusion,*" he read. "*It's not enough to know that we are created equally. We have to act on it every day or surrender to ignorance and failure. In the absence of diversity, stereotype rules. It fills the voids of truth that should be occupied by morality and justice.* Is the whole book like that?"

"It's genius," Flame said. "He'll be coming soon. Do you understand? Glen Ethan Greengrass is coming to your town!"

"We're honored, I guess," Elam said. "Pardon me for asking but does he have Jesus, your Glen Ethan? Does he carry the word of Jesus? Just wondering. You-all have that missionary tone."

"Jesus?" Flame recoiled, almost spitting the name out. "We don't have any use for Jesus. This is political. We're not in the twelfth century."

"Oh. I see," Seth said. "Jesus ain't part of the inclusion deal? He's *ex*clusioned out?"

"Everybody's free to believe what they like," she said. "The People's Republic is a secular enterprise. We don't persecute anybody based on creed or color."

"Speaking of color," Seth said, "I don't see that your bunch here is anything but white folks."

"New Africa has had a polarizing effect," Flame said. "No question about it. Milton Steptoe is a very effective demagogue."

"He ain't no demigod," Seth said. "They say he ran a chain of payday loan shops is all."

Flame just glared back disdainfully.

Meanwhile, a girl of eight came forward from the dozens huddled around the fire. She carried two sticks with smoldering coals at the end and proffered them to Seth and Elam.

"For you," she said.

"What all you got there, little missy?" Elam said.

"Toasted marshmallows," she said. "Glen Ethan Greengrass said to always be generous of spirit."

"Is that so," Seth said. He helped himself to the blackened confection at the end of the stick and made a show of savoring it. Elam took the other one. "Mmmmm," Seth said. "That's tasty for sure. It's been a while since I had one. Is he here amongst you, Mister Greengrass?"

"He's asleep," the child said and went back to the others.

"Tell him thanks, when he wakes up," Seth called after her.

"You-all have a nice campout," Elam called out to the crowd over Flame's shoulder. "Don't forget to bury your fires and your latrines." Then to Flame, he said, "Maybe I'll see you again if you come to our town."

Her mouth clenched and her nostrils flared.

"Maybe you will," she said.

The rangers turned and walked back out into the moonswept landscape.

FIFTEEN

Robert Earle came to the bedroom late, having worked after supper to begin setting up the summer kitchen under a shed roof off the back of the house. Mice had built nests over the winter in the oven of the wood-fired cookstove out there. Cleaning it had been a messy business. Then he'd had to heat up enough water to bathe the soot off.

When he came to her, Britney lay on her side of the bed with her back turned to the door, as though meaning to signal discontent. Also, a candle burned on her night table. Britney was generally fastidious about snuffing the candle out when she was not reading in bed, so he surmised she was awake and fretting. Robert had carried a candle of his own in from the bathroom. He set it down and knelt on the bed. Britney seemed inert. Weeks earlier, she might have rolled over to face him expectantly when she sensed his entry into the bed. He bent close to her ear.

"Are you still awake?"

"Yeah."

"Is something the matter?"

She didn't answer.

"What's troubling you?"

"Nothing," she said. Her voice sounded high, a little cracked, muffled.

He thought he could scent tears.

"I'm here if you want to talk about it."

"Okay," she said, though she remained frozen in place.

Robert reached over her and pinched out the candle on her night table, then found the side of her face under the blankets and kissed her on the cheek. Since her encounter with the bear she had been acting sullen, withdrawn, unreachable. He'd tried to talk to her about it since, but he could not penetrate the emotional shield she had erected. Their sex life, formerly avid and regular, had fallen away. Robert wondered if the incident had exhumed some painful memories of things she never told him about, some dark family incident, some buried childhood violation or secret shame. He knew she'd had trouble with her husband, Shawn, deceased now. Shawn had had a romance with a dairy girl at the Schmidt farm, Britney said, and maybe others too. Toward the end, they weren't sleeping in the same room. Shawn was angry at a world that had left him a farm laborer. Robert wondered if he ever hit Britney. After nearly a year of living together, a large part of her persona remained mysterious and inaccessible. He even wondered whether her encounter with the bear had involved more than she had let on, maybe even some kind of frightening sexual injury. It was a stretch but he couldn't help returning to it. He'd never heard of a bear raping a woman, but he knew that he knew very little about the behavior of wild animals.

With a sigh he reached for and opened the weighty tome that was McCullough's biography of John Adams, taking comfort that he was only at the beginning of its seven hundred–odd pages and that he could lose himself, and many hours of his own dubious life, in somebody else's exciting and momentous history. It did occur to him that the new times of his present life had more in common with John Adams's time of the late eighteenth century than the period of his childhood and of his parents in the late twentieth century. Modernity, he mused, was no longer up to date. Content with the warm presence of Britney's body next to him, he entered the world of the book and let go of himself.

Twenty minutes later, he was reaching to snuff his own candle when he heard three timid raps on the door. The knob turned and then Sarah opened the creaky door.

"I'm sick," she said.

Britney fairly spun around as though she had been lying awake all that time. She propped herself up firmly on one arm.

"Come here."

Sarah padded over in her long cotton nightdress.

"What is it? Your tummy?"

"No. Hot and achy. Head hurts."

Britney felt the child's forehead. It was hot and damp indeed.

"I'll get the thermometer," Robert said, already on his way to the bathroom. There was no need to communicate that sickness had to be taken seriously. Robert handed the old reliable oral thermometer to Britney, who reminded Sarah how to place it under her tongue. In the meantime, Sarah crawled into bed with Britney. After a few minutes, Robert took the thermometer out of Sarah's mouth and brought it over to his side of the bed to read it in the candlelight.

"A hundred-point-five degrees," he said.

"She's got a little something," Britney said.

"We can take her to see Jerry in the morning," Robert said, meaning Dr. Copeland.

"Okay," Britney said.

"Will I go to heaven?" Sarah asked.

"You're not going anywhere," Britney said.

"What if it's Mexican flu?"

"Then a lot of other people in town would have it," Britney said. "There's no sickness going around. It's probably just a spring cold."

Britney spooned up behind the child and petted her damp hairline tenderly.

Robert was grateful to have Sarah in the bed with them to give Britney something to focus on beyond whatever was roiling her spirit. And he liked the physicality of feeling he was part of a family. Robert resumed reading *John Adams*. By-and-by he was satisfied that Britney and Sarah were asleep and he snuffed out his candle.

Sixteen

When they returned from their scouting excursion, Seth and Elam went directly to Brother Jobe's suite, the old school principal's headquarters off the lobby. At eleven o'clock, the building was quiet. Brother Jobe had been occupied with one Sister Miriam of the New Faith kitchen crew, an excellent baker given what they had to work with, and incidentally a long-legged beauty with chestnut hair, laughing eyes, and a figure as soft and creamy as the sweet potato buns that were her particular specialty. She had expressed an interest in biblical hermeneutics, and so Brother Jobe began with her by elucidating his thoughts on the Pentecost, but they had moved on to other things. Now, mantled in an old tartan bathrobe, his thick black hair disheveled and his face pinker than usual, he padded into the outer office, his study, so palpably anointed with pheromones that the two rangers found their heads swimming slightly in a way not accountable to just the lateness of the hour.

"Well then," Brother Jobe began, "did you learn who those birds are out there on the hillside?"

"Quite the flock of odd ducks," Elam said. "They claim to be missionaries from over in Massychusetts. Say they come here on a spring fling."

"Spring fling?"

"Their very words."

"Sounds like some old-timey college nonsense."

"They look the part, believe me," Elam said.

"They got their own country," Seth said.

"Huh?"

"Berkshire Republic, they call it."

"They gone Foxfire?" Brother Jobe asked.

"Something like that. They can't stand not having gov'ment. They crazy for it. Can't get enough. It's all they talk about."

"Sound like socialists."

"I believe that's so," Elam said.

"They got Jesus?" Brother Jobe asked.

"Scoffed at Jesus' name, when we brung it up."

"That so? What kind of missionary is that?"

"Political missionaries, they say. Got their own bible. Showed it to us. Some kind of handbook for schoolteachers, near as I could make out. They was thumping for diversity, homeless, share-the-wealth, and all like that. Some of 'em is same-sexers, I'm sure."

"That's your socialist right there," Brother Jobe said. "What all they want with us?"

"Want us to join up in some kind of federation they putting together. They say southern Vermont's fixing to join. They had a meeting with the honchos in Bennington on the way here. They want to be the new U.S. gov'ment."

"Well, what's in it for us, according to them?"

"I don't have a clue," Elam said.

"They wasn't real clear on that," Seth added.

"Hmph . . ." Brother Jobe said and waddled over to his desk, took a seat, and slumped in it. He opened a bottom drawer and lifted out a square glass bottle of Rupert Road Tawny double malt whiskey and an old jelly jar glass, poured out five fingers of the sunlight-colored liquor, swallowed a dram, and passed it to the rangers, who sampled it in turn. "What's their strength out there?"

"'Bout the same as ours in numbers," Elam said. "Sixty-five, seventy. But they's pretty much kids out on a lark. Young softies. Even a few outright children. I counted eight horses, some simple box wagons."

"No soldier types amongst them."

"Not as we could tell."

"Who's in charge of the outfit?"

"Big strapping gal dressed up in man clothes," Seth said. "Twenty-something. A looker if she put a little effort in, but I don't think she goes that way. Calls herself Flame."

"Flame?" Brother Jobe said, the corners of his mouth lifting in mirth. "Sounds like a pole dancer."

"Don't tell her that," Elam said. "She's a fire-breather. Got all huffy when I called her ma'am. Thought she might try to paddle me."

"She don't have nothing on her mind but socialism," Seth said. "She's hell-bent."

"How'd the country get so full of crazy people?" Brother Jobe said, shaking his head and smiling. "Well, this bunch seems harmless enough. We can resist the heady vapors of socialism, I'm sure. Life is improving enough for folks around here without it. Now, you got my leave to ride down to Albany with these two young fellows Mr. Einhorn's son and the mayor's son. His papa has rousted out enough silver from the home folks to procure a boat, which they will sail on back up here. I got a long list of supplies I want you to get while you're down there and put on that boat. Meantime, we gonna construct a landing just south of Mr. Bullock's, show him a thing or two about taking care of our own bidness."

"What do you want to do about them campers?" Elam asked.

"Don't do nothing. If they want to come into town and confab with me or the town trustees, we ain't goin' nowheres. Sounds like it'd be amusing to meet 'em."

SEVENTEEN

In the morning, little Sarah Watling was still unwell. Robert went and fetched Dr. Copeland at one of the rare intervals, as it turned out, when no one was waiting in his outer office with an illness or an injury. He walked over the two blocks with Robert and his son Jasper, who came on house calls as part of his training. It was a glorious spring morning with the air full of lilac and the foliage of the street trees forming a soft, cathedral-like ceiling overhead. Crabapples, dogwoods, and loquats were in bloom in dooryard gardens that had once been lawns. Robert and the doctor talked about trout fishing. The doctor had come by a fine old-times graphite fly rod in trade for an emergency caesarean delivery he'd performed at Cossayuna. The Hendrickson mayflies (brown bodies, gray wings) were pouring off the Battenkill that week, he said, and he was hoping to get out on the water around four in the afternoon when the nymphs rose from the gravel bottom, shucked their exoskeletons, and flew off to mate during their one ecstatic evening of adult life. Their mass emergence generally drove the trout wild, and there were many more large trout in the river now than in the old times, when great numbers of anglers from elsewhere drove up to the county and mercilessly pounded the good beats. Robert said, alas, he could not go out because he was needed to finish the work at the new hotel, due to open that night. Their bright mood darkened when they entered Robert's house on Linden Street, where Britney was waiting with her brow knitted, her arms crossed, and a baleful aura around her. Robert felt strangely intimidated in her presence in his own house. She took the doctor and his son upstairs to Sarah's room. Robert followed them.

"How are you feeling, dear?" the doctor asked the child.

"Things hurt," she said.

Sarah's temperature had risen half a degree to 101. She had a headache and complained of a stiff neck. Jasper took her pulse. It was rapid at ninety beats per minute.

"Is he a doctor too?" Sarah asked.

"I will be," Jasper said.

"Do you think I'm going to die?"

Jasper put his hand on her forehead, feeling the warmth tenderly. She blinked at him in awe.

"You're going to be all right," he said.

"Sarah," the doctor said. "Did you cut yourself or step on anything sharp recently?"

"No," Sarah said. She remembered pulling the wire nail out of her foot in the barn, but she was afraid *to tell on herself*, as she put it in her own thoughts, afraid that she would get in trouble and would not be allowed back in the barn to spend time with her animal friends whom she loved dearly.

The doctor merely nodded. Then he rummaged in his black doctor's bag and took out a six-ounce glass bottle.

"Give her a teaspoon of this every four hours," he told Britney. "It's a tincture of willow bark with some ginseng and honey. The active ingredient is salicin, which is sort of related to aspirin: an anti-inflammatory. It will help with the fever and the aches." Then, to Sarah: "This stuff tastes a little funny, but it'll make you feel better, so be a good girl and take it."

"Okay," Sarah said.

Robert, the doctor, and Jasper left the room and went back downstairs.

"What do you think?" Robert asked.

"Was she vaccinated before the shit show started?"

"I don't know."

"Could be the start of chicken pox or something. All that crap is coming back. I hate to see it. But they usually get over it. I did when I was a child."

"Me too," Robert said.

"There's nothing going around town for the moment, at least," the doctor said. "Keep an eye on her. If anything changes, we can get her over to my infirmary."

"All right," Robert said.

EIGHTEEN

Later that day Robert worked on hooking up the bar sinks of the Cider Barrel, the new hotel tavern, until a few minutes before the doors opened and the townspeople began swarming in to inaugurate the place. Its predecessor had been open little more than a week between Christmas and New Year's before it burned down, and in that brief time it was already becoming a beloved institution in town. There had been fellowship, a warm, comfortable place to pass time, live music, and a game attempt at pub fare, but mainly it had gotten the people in town out of their houses during the darkest time of the year after many years of having almost nowhere to go at night. So they were very eager to see its replacement and the first wave was not disappointed.

For one thing, the new tavern was considerably larger than the original, both the spacious front bar and the dining room. It featured not only the big central masonry heater that was shared with the hotel next door but a traditional Rumford fireplace on the outside wall of the dining room. Some old sofas and soft chairs were arrayed before it. With the temperature in the low fifties this spring evening, a fire was burning there. Vases of lilacs stood at each side of the broad mantelpiece, drawing attention to a large oil painting by Andrew Pendergast hanging there, a view of the Hudson River from Stark's Knob, an ancient volcanic plug across the river from Bullock's plantation. The vista, captured the previous October with the fall foliage in full blaze, showed the mighty river wending north toward Glens Falls and the Adirondack mountain wilderness beyond. Candles burned in mirrored wall sconces between the tall windows, outside of which purple twilight gathered over Union Grove's old business district.

Brother Jobe bustled all around the place from the front porch to the bar to the kitchen to the basement to the loading dock in the back alley—where a late delivery of Juniper Swamp pale ale came in just after he opened the tavern's doors. (The deliveryman and brewer, one Dutch Dahlgren of Shushan, arrived drunk on his own product; his team of two horses was unhitched and taken to Allison's livery and Dutch was left to sleep it off in the empty box of his utility wagon.) Waddling to and fro in his best frock coat, wearing a green satin cravat to mark the season, Brother Jobe paused to chat with the townspeople, who uniformly expressed their gratitude for the miraculous and heroic resurrection of the establishment. He had advertised free food and libations opening night—the handbills were Daniel Earle's first paid print job—and that was no small part of the attraction for the crowd pouring in. For many, stores of food at home were running low. New Faith waitresses in their long skirts circulated through the rooms with pitchers of cider and ale and platters of tidbits—ham biscuits, sausage bites, cheese grit squares, deep-fried pickles, and the establishment's own trademark tater tots. There had not been a public social gathering since the levee at the Easton Station grange hall to mark the spring equinox in March. Many of the arrivals, young men and women who worked on different farms all week long and saw little of other people off their own workplaces, flirted eagerly with each other.

One of these farmworkers was a dark-haired nineteen-year-old named Karen Grolsch, who worked on Carl Weibel's farm over on Schoolhouse Hill. She was in charge of his considerable side operation in raising ducks, and it was a busy time of the year now with more than two hundred ducklings hatched the past week. Karen lived on Grove Street with her mother, Kaycee, who had been a local ski champion in her own youth and radiated good health at forty-six. In the last years of the old times, Kaycee did physical therapy at an assisted living establishment in Manchester, Vermont, a long commute then. Now she worked in the new Union Grove community laundry, which was warm indoor labor and paid wages in hard money. The rest of Karen's family—father, Emmet, and brothers Hunter and Logan—died in the Mexican flu epidemic. Karen came to the tavern opening with Kaycee. On the way in, Karen had noticed Daniel bundled up in a rocking chair on the porch with a pint of cider in one hand and a crudely wrapped cigar made with local tobacco in the other. She knew who he was. After she'd downed a pint of Temple Merton's Catamount Creek dry amber cider, and filled up on ham biscuits and sausage bites, she left her mother chatting with Bob Bouchard, woodcutter and widower, and ventured back outside. Daniel was still there. He'd draped his wool scarf over his head like a bonnet to ward off the chill. She slid into a rocking chair beside him and pulled up the hood of her thick wool sweater, dyed mauve from a decoction of black hollyhocks.

"They say you're starting up a newspaper," Karen said. It was only then that Daniel turned his head and made eye contact.

"They're right about that," Daniel said.

Both rocked awhile.

"When people say 'they,' don't you want to know who 'they' are?" Karen said.

"I thought you might know," Daniel said. "You brought them up."

"I could find out," she said. Both attempted to smile, each looked uncomfortable trying.

Daniel turned his gaze back outward and puffed his cigar. He dimly remembered the girl's face from long ago, from the last years before the school shut down. She would have been several grades behind him, still a child, more or less. He noticed that she no longer was one. She had big bright eyes, a wolfish nose, and a full lower lip that gave her an appealing pouty look, as though she was never quite satisfied. She slouched elegantly in the rocker with her legs crossed under a long patchwork skirt.

"I'd like to work for a newspaper," she said.

"Where are you working now?"

"I'm the duck boss at Weibel's."

"You like it?"

THE HARROWS OF SPRING 91

"It's okay. It's hard sometimes. Winter and all."

"Well, yes," he said. "Do you like duck?"

"They're friendly and funny."

"I mean to eat."

"Oh, sure. Slow cooked in its own fat. You put it up in jars and it keeps forever. It's how they do it in France. I like to read cookbooks."

"Do you ever make it like that?"

"We put up quite a bit at the farm for trade. Probably five hundred quarts last season. Mr. Weibel's preserved duck is known far and wide."

"I'd like to see France," Daniel said. "I doubt we will, though. No more airplanes."

"They still have boats."

"They?" Daniel said.

"That's right," she said, narrowing her eyes. "They. Them."

"We'd better find out who they are," he said.

They took each other in again. This time it wasn't so hard for him to smile. He realized that he couldn't remember the last time he felt like smiling. When she smiled, crinkles formed at the corners of her mouth. He liked that. It made her look sage beyond her years. He liked several things about her.

"Are you . . . on your own?" he asked.

"I live with my mom," she said. "She's inside. Are you on your own?"

"I'm living over in the newspaper office for now," he said. "It's a big old place. I finally got it cleaned up. Took a couple of months."

"It sounds nice."

"It's an easy trip to work."

"I walk out to Mr. Weibel's farm every day. I love to get out and walk."

"So you read cookbooks?" he said.

"And lots of other books. I write stories too."

"What about?"

"Animals. I have a cast of characters. They stand in for people. Ambrose the porcupine, Tallulah the fox, Boris the 'possum."

"No ducks?"

"I can't give a name to something that ends up as food."

"Of course."

"Maybe sometime you'd consider printing one in your news-paper. I could bring you a sample."

Just then, one of the New Faith waitresses swung by with a pitcher and refilled their glasses.

"I hadn't thought about running any made-up stories in the paper," Daniel said. "The idea is to cram as much news and advertis-ing as possible on two sides of an eleven-by-seventeen-inch sheet of paper. It's called a broadside."

"How often would you print it?"

"Weekly, for the present time. It's called an edition each time it comes out. There's a whole vocabulary for the printing business. I'm learning it."

They rocked again and sipped their ciders.

"I'd like to see your animal tales," he said. "They sound like fun."

"Oh, they're very serious. Full of lessons and morals," she said. "I could write other things too."

"Such as what?"

"I could find out news and events of the day. I could go about collecting gossip and rumors."

"I can only publish what's true."

"Then I would collect only what's true."

"Well, you see it's called being a reporter," Daniel said. He squinted, trying to take her in at such close range. "Maybe you'd make a good reporter."

"I'm very fond of my ducks, but I don't want to be the duck boss all of my life, and there are plenty of others who could do it just as well. Who else is going to work for your newspaper?"

"Well, nobody yet," Daniel said. "I can't even start until I get some decent paper to print on. I'm leaving for Albany tomorrow to find some. Teddy Einhorn and I are going to buy a boat there and sail it back. Then the town will have its own boat so we won't have to depend on Mr. Bullock."

"Yes, I heard that he's stopped trading with the town."

"Where did you hear that?"

"Mr. Weibel was talking about it with a gentleman from Bennington who sells grain drills. Mr. Bullock is angry at the town, he said. Nobody seems to know why. But I could find out."

Daniel pictured her sitting down with Bullock, furiously scribbling notes.

"The truth is, I'm a shy person myself," Daniel said.

"I can tell."

"I'll have all I can do in the office. You seem . . . comfortable with strangers."

"I'm interested in people."

"I don't know what I could pay you," Daniel said. "How does Mr. Weibel pay his people?"

"Shares and bonuses," she said. "We get plenty to eat and a little money at planting, harvest, holidays. Things are a little sparse just now, of course, this time of year. It's getting chilly out here. Would you like to go inside. There's more food and a nice fire."

"Okay," he said and rose from his chair. "I'm ashamed of myself. I haven't asked your name."

She told him.

"Karen," he said. "I like it. It's gentle and dignified."

"I know you're Daniel," she said.

"How did you know?"

"It's around. You've been noticed."

NINETEEN

Brother Jobe happened to be at the bar, in surcease of motion, enjoying a brief rest and a pint of Bald Mountain farmhouse cider, when Brother Jonah, who had been laboring over on the hotel side, came along with a message.

"We have got some check-ins, sir," he said.

"Huh? Who all is that?"

"Out-of-towners."

"Son, hotel customers generally come from somewheres else," Brother Jobe said. "If they was from here, they'd sleep at home."

"Oh, uh, of course . . ." Jonah said. Barely twenty-one years old, he did not have much experience with the business. "Well, anyway, there's three of 'em," he said, "one grown man, one not quite a grown man, and one woman of a sort."

"Of a sort? What sort would that be?"

"Mannish type."

"Hmm. They look like socialists to you?"

"I can't say for sure what one looks like," Jonah said.

"You got rooms ready over there?"

"The sisters are making up beds now. Thing is, they asked to meet with you."

"Is that so?" Brother Jobe said. He stood a little taller, pulled up his pants, adjusted his cravat, and smoothed the collar of his frock coat. "Tell them to come to the office behind the front desk in ten minutes. Oh, and get a bottle of whiskey and five glasses in there."

Brother Jobe worked his way through the crowd to find Robert Earle, who had brought his fiddle and, having finished the plumbing job, was about to start playing tunes across the barroom with several other members of the Congregational Church music circle.

"It's them birds from Massachusetts," Brother Jobe explained. "I think they want to parley. Can you come with me for a bit?"

"Okay," Robert said. "I shall return," he told Andrew Pendergast who was warming up on accordion along with Leslie Einhorn on cello and Eric Laudermilk on guitar. Robert, fiddle and bow in hand, followed the bustling Brother Jobe back into the crowd and then through the door connecting to the hotel.

The office was sparsely furnished because the hotel had not quite officially opened for business. It contained an old schoolteacher's desk with an oak swivel chair, a salvaged fainting couch against wall, and two padded armchairs before the desk so that people conducting business would be comfortable. The mounted head of an eight-point buck, somewhat motheaten, was the sole wall decoration. A window, swagged with simple muslin drapery, looked out on the back alley, but night had fallen and the vista was dim. Robert parked his fiddle on the desk and set about lighting candles in four wall fixtures and one on the desk. Brother Jobe opened a ledger book, found a pen among many others in the desk's top drawer, and made as if to appear busy with figures. Just then, there was a knock on the door and he said, musically, "Come on in."

The three sojourners entered. The first was a man about forty, sturdy and athletic with an open, freckled face that suggested he spent a lot of time outdoors doing rugged things. He wore old time expeditionary casuals of the kind that were sold in catalogs years before, in exceptionally vivid colors: a plaid shirt in motifs of turquoise and rose that did not denote any highland clan but rather had been made in China, a plum-colored polypropylene vest under a teal mountaineering jacket with many zippered pockets, and a pink baseball cap with an NPR logo on the crown. All his clothing was in strikingly fresh condition, as though the UPS driver had only just dropped off the order that week. The second figure was the Amazon who called herself Flame wearing spandex leggings, riding boots, several layers of shirts, two lint-colored sweaters that did not altogether conceal the contours of her body, and a turquoise silk scarf at her throat. She'd removed her woolly hat with the dangling earflaps, but her blond hair was askew and somewhat matted from wearing it. The third figure was the physical opposite of the others: a little less than average height, skinny, frail-looking, dressed in new-times woolens and a high-buttoned vest with round collar flaps peeking out the top that gave him the look of a schoolboy. He carried a kind of canvas bag on one shoulder. His dark hair hung in ringlets. He held a butternut-colored slouch hat with an odd conical crown and a stingy brim and rotated it in his hands as from nervous habit.

The hearty man in sporting togs strode to the desk and extended his hand forthrightly across it to Brother Jobe, with a smile that seemed calculated to appear self-possessed and modest. "Goodfriend," he said earnestly.

"I hope and expect that will be the case," Brother Jobe said, shaking hands.

"Call me Buddy," the man said.

"All right, then," Brother Jobe said with an amused tilt of his head. "You can be our buddy and we'll be your friend."

"No, that's my name. Buddy Goodfriend."

Brother Jobe just stared back a moment, then pointed at him and cackled.

"You're a double threat there, son," he said.

"I'm no threat at all."

"Well, we can't pick our parents, can we. And they're the ones that name us."

"You are so right," Buddy Goodfriend said, and looked at the others, who nodded in agreement. "You see, my given name was Sylvester."

"That's a mouthful."

"Exactly," Buddy said.

"My given was Lyle, which I was never too fond of and gave up on, actually," Brother Jobe said. He formally introduced himself and Robert and explained in a little more detail their relative responsibilities in town. "You must be the famous Flame," he said to the strapping young woman. "I've heard about you."

She nodded, saying nothing.

"Don't worry, I won't call you 'ma'am.'"

The remark didn't elicit a smile. If anything, the corners of her mouth turned down slightly.

"This youngster is my nephew," Buddy said. "Big sister's son. His name is Ainsley Perlew but I call him Sonny Boy. He assists me in this and that and, of course, he's learning. For him, being at my side is what college used to be for some."

"I see what you mean," Brother Jobe said. "Nothing beats hands-on training. Go ahead, set down, you-all."

Buddy and Flame took the stuffed chairs and Sonny Boy settled primly on the settee against the wall, cloaked in a pool of dimness. He put his hat on so his eyes especially lay in shadow. Brother Jobe remained behind the desk and Robert leaned against the window sash. More pleasantries were exchanged about the fineness of the new hotel, the gaiety of the tavern opening, the welcome spring weather. Whiskey was offered. Buddy and Flame partook. Brother Jobe cleared his throat.

"My rangers tell me you-all formed your own country over in Massachusetts."

"You are correct, sir," Buddy said, theatrically. "The Berkshire People's Republic. We're doing what we must in the absence of greater authority. The Commonwealth of Massachusetts has ceased to operate, and of course the Federals have lost all influence in our region. Did your boys say what we are up to over here in New York?"

"Some kind of springtime jamboree, I think it was. But frankly I gather you are trying to enlarge your territory. To what purpose, I don't know."

Buddy smiled as though to allay any distrust.

"We're trying to form regional governance that will mutually advantage all parties in this neighborhood of the late, lamented USA," he explained.

"Yes, I heard that you parleyed with the Bennington folks."

"All of southern Vermont will be joining our federation, it appears."

"And what kind of mutual advantage are we talking about?" Robert asked.

"Security. Enhancements to trade. Fiscal benefits. Rule of law."

"Well, that last one there is a selling point," Brother Jobe said. "If I may say so, we are rather desperate to get the courts up and running again."

"We can help with that."

"And what are we obliged to do at our end?" Robert asked.

"We'd expect you would contribute to the general fund."

"You mean, like, taxes?"

"I wouldn't call it that," Buddy said, wrinkling his nose. "Subscription or endowment is more like it."

"So how's that work?" Brother Jobe asked. "We collect money from folks here and send it to you over yonder in Massachusetts?"

"We could collect some while we're here?" Buddy said.

"Are you serious?" Robert said, sharing a skeptical glance with Brother Jobe.

"Let me give you an idea of how serious we are," Buddy said. He withdrew a wad of colored papers from one of the pockets inside his coat and proceeded to deal them out like playing cards in two stacks on the desk."

"Is that money?" Brother Jobe asked. He leaned forward and peered at the bills as Buddy continued to stack them.

"Go ahead. Look close and hard," Buddy said.

Both Brother Jobe and Robert took bills off the top and held them up to the nearest candle in its wall fixture. They were scribed with red ink on paper that was not currency grade. The engraving quality was less than middling. A scrolled banner at the top said *Berkshire Peoples Republic*. At the center in an oval cartouche was a landscape depicting Mount Greylock, the highest peak in Massachusetts. The denomination was 50.

"You forgot the apostrophe in *People's*," Robert said.

Buddy snatched a bill off the desk and looked.

"Darn, we'll have to correct that," he said; then to Flame: "Didn't anyone proofread this?"

She shrugged.

"And what does the fifty stand for, exactly?" Robert said.

"Yeah, what do you call this paper?" Brother Jobe inquired.

"Dollars, of course," Buddy said. "The people nicknamed them Berkie bucks, but they're our dollar?"

"What can you buy with them?" Robert asked.

"Why, anything?"

"What's the equivalent in silver?"

"We don't use silver."

"How can you not?" Brother Jobe said. "Everybody else does now. Everything's priced in it."

"We discourage traffic in barbaric metal relics," Buddy said. "We refuse to go back to the Middle Ages."

"Silver ain't of any age," Brother Jobe said. "It's timeless."

"It's very inconvenient," Buddy said. "So heavy in the pocket."

"All right then. If you don't trade in silver how are we supposed to pay taxes—excuse me, subscription, did you say?—in these pink coupons? We don't have any. I've never seen 'em around here."

"That's the thing, exactly!" Buddy said, becoming highly animated, as if suddenly thrilled by a great challenge, say conquering an unclimbed mountain peak. "We're willing to exchange these dollars for your silver!"

"We don't even use the old federal greenbacks anymore," Robert said. "And this stuff is like Monopoly money compared to that."

Buddy smiled again, this time ruefully, and shook his head, as if he were dealing with simpletons.

"Is it possible that you folks here don't know how much times have changed?"

"We've got a pretty fair idea," Robert said.

"We're up to speed," Brother Jobe agreed.

"The USA is toast," Buddy said, rather vehemently. "My country tis of thee . . . *phhhht* . . . It's done. Stick a fork in it. Sorry to be the bearer of bad news. We're on our own now. We have to reorganize a viable regional government or you can forget about the Middle Ages—we'll slide straight back into a dark age. And we have to do it now. Are you aware that other regions have reorganized into new political jurisdictions? The Foxfire Republic and New Africa?"

"Yes, we've heard—"

"And the remaining federal piece is just a little rump operation in some backwater on Lake Huron," Buddy continued.

"Yes, we know about all this—"

"And they're at war with each other," Buddy went on. "I've heard terrible things. Crucifixions of prisoners. Cannibalism. Imagine that! All kinds of atrocities. They may be coming up here next. Yes here, gentlemen. New England is still a valuable chunk of real estate. And there's talk that they covet it. They love making war, these peckerwoods. It's in their blood—no offense sir." Buddy nodded to Brother Jobe, who indicated with a wave of his hand that none was taken. "Anyway, we've got to start organizing to defend ourselves. We're asking for your help and, in a way, we're telling you to help yourselves, unite with us for the sake of all. You can't just wait until the last minute, for instance, to raise an army. There are public works to consider. I'm sure you'd agree that the roads are in deplorable condition. We are going to fix the major routes between the regional centers. We have a program for founding local health clinics. Do you folks have a clinic here?"

"Dr. Copeland has an infirmary—"

"And what does that mean? A couple-few beds and one physician? We intend to do better than that. Now, I can see how you folks have pulled yourselves together. You've got good-looking, well-cared-for farms in this county. Your towns are coming back. Why just look at this grand new building we're in. I admire the heck out of it. I'm just asking you to look at the bigger picture here. And by the way, you could cover your subscription without exchanging for the Berkshire dollar."

"That's big of you," Brother Jobe said. "You mean just hand over our silver?"

"Well, for now," Buddy said. "Give us a month to set up offices here and by summertime you'll be in the currency union with us and the Vermonters. By then your status will be settled as to full admission to the BPR following the formal application procedure, of course, and the nod from our legislative council."

Brother Jobe poured himself three fingers of whiskey in his pony glass. He sipped meditatively, shifting his gaze between all three of the strangers. For an elongated moment nobody said a word.

"Well," Flame finally spoke up. "What do you say?"

"We have to consult with our town trustees," Robert said.

Of course," Buddy said. "Think you can make it happen this week?"

"Not sure," Robert said.

"Our head guy is arriving tomorrow," Buddy said.

"You're not the head guy?"

Buddy made comical face. "No-o-o-o-o."

"Glen Ethan Greengrass," Flame said. "Our mentor, teacher, and leader."

Brother Jobe, who had been slumping deep in thought, perked up in his seat.

"Greengrass?"

"Then you've heard of him?" Flame said.

"I believe I've heard the name."

"He's only the leading political thinker of our time," Flame said. "Then you haven't read *Birthing the New Knowledge Economy*?"

"Well, no—"

"Sonny Boy," Buddy said, snapping his fingers. "Green books."

The young man took two books with green covers out of his shoulder sack and handed them to Flame, who in turn gave them to Robert and Brother Jobe. The two pretended to inspect them.

"He's a great man," Flame said. "A genius, a bridge builder, a caring, tireless fighter for social justice, diversity, dignity, tolerance, income equality, gender fairness, and hopeful humanism."

"Sounds like Superman," Brother Jobe remarked.

"He's my father," Flame said.

"Oh?" Brother Jobe digested the information. "I guess every man's a hero to his little girl."

"Do I look like a little girl to you?"

"Anyways, I can't wait to shake his hand," Brother Jobe said, opting to forgo further disputation.

"To be honest, he's not well," Buddy said. "He's old and pretty frail. But he wanted to come on this outreach and see with his own eyes how the federation is taking shape. It might be his last journey away from home. And, well, we just love having him with us."

"Is he here now?" Robert asked.

"Soon," Flame said.

"Any day," Buddy said. "But I'm so glad we were able to reach an understanding,"

"Uh-huh," Brother Jobe said, looking to Robert, who nodded once.

"In the meantime, you know where to find us." Buddy pointed overhead.

"That we do," Brother Jobe averred. "Night, gentlemen . . . and, uh . . . Ms. Greengrass, is it?"

Flame scowled and walked out first.

As the other two were making to leave, Ainsley Perlew tugged on Buddy's sleeve and whispered something in his ear. Buddy turned back to Robert and Brother Jobe.

"Do you happen to have any factory-made ammunition in town?" Buddy asked.

"Old-times ammo is hard to come by," Brother Jobe said. "You might talk to Mr. Einhorn at his store. My people prepare some reloads—you know, recycled cartridges. What size?"

The young man whispered again in Buddy's ear.

"He can talk to me directly," Brother Jobe said.

"Forgive him. He's extremely shy. Probably just a phase. Thirty-ought-six, he said."

"I'll look into it. What's he want them for, by-the-by?"

"He's mad for hunting," Buddy said with another of his incandescent smiles.

"Well, the deer population's way down. No wildlife enforcement nowadays and open season all year round and folks being hungry and all. I expect the situation ain't much different over in Massachusetts."

"It doesn't matter," Buddy said. "For him it's just about being out on the trail after something, whether it's really there or not. Well, thanks and good evening."

"I think you forgot your money," Robert said, pointing to the twin stacks of red bills on the desk.

"No, that's for the two of you. In consideration of your time and attention."

"We don't do things that way."

"Then redistribute it among the needy. Bye now."

Twenty

Britney Blieveldt rushed into the tavern at the very height of the opening night festivities in desperate search of the doctor, Jerry Copeland. She'd gone first to his house and infirmary, but he wasn't there and his wife, Jeanette, attending to one of Robbie Furnival's log skidders who had been kicked in the knee by a horse, said her husband was at the opening festivities of the Cider Barrel. Britney hurried downtown to the new establishment, fought her way inside past smokers on the porch, and shoved through the crowd within, shouting for the doctor. She soon found him at the far end of the bar, drinking with Tom Allison, the former college VP who now ran a successful livery, boarding horses and renting out wagons, carts, gigs, and buggies, of which he was acquiring quite a collection. Britney ascertained almost at once that the doctor was very drunk.

"It's Sarah," she implored him. "You have to come. She's having spasms. Please! I'm afraid it's serious."

The doctor appeared to stare dumbly back at her, breathing through his mouth, weaving slightly on his bar stool. "All right . . ." he said. He got off his seat, took a few steps, and crumpled. Then he struggled to get back on his feet. Britney watched him, horrified. When others stooped to assist him, she felt a hand on her elbow and turned to see the massive figure of Loren, looming beside her.

"Where's Robert?" she asked.

"I don't know. He was here a while ago."

"Something's terribly wrong with Sarah," she told him, struggling to be heard above the din. "I don't know what to do."

Loren saw the doctor fight off those assisting him only to end up sprawled on the floor.

"Oh Christ," he said. "Maybe Jason LaBountie can help."

Britney's face screwed into a mask of contempt. "He's a god-damn vet!" she said.

"I know," Loren said. "But he's what we've got."

The doctor struggled onto all fours just in time to vomit on his friend's shoes.

Britney watched in disgust as the doctor slipped in his own vomit attempting to stand up.

"Oh God!" she shrieked. "Where *is* Robert?"

Bonnie Sweetland, standing close at hand, too, said, "They're looking for him now. He's not in the tavern."

"Go home," Loren told Britney. "I'll fetch Jason and bring him over."

"Please hurry!" Britney said, her face torqued in anxious exasperation. She pulled the wool shawl back over the top of her head and sidestepped the spectacle the doctor was creating to make for the exit.

Loren hurried to Jason LaBountie's substantial Queen Anne–style house on River Street, a storybook heap of bays, turrets, and oriels with an American flag hung conspicuously on the wide porch and the first paragraph of the Declaration of Independence on a sign board beneath it. The paint job was chipped and fading like most houses in town, even those of the better-off citizens. Candles burned deep within the first floor. The town's sole veterinarian had been playing a game of eight-ball pool in the library with his fifteen-year-old son when he answered Loren's knock on the door. Loren rapidly explained about Britney's sick child and the doctor's unfortunate condition.

"He's a goddamn disgrace," LaBountie said.

"His responsibilities get him down," Loren said.

"We're all carrying a heavy load these days, Reverend. In the old times, they'd take away his license."

"Will you go over there or not?"

"Yes. But there may be little to nothing I can do."

"I guess we'll just have to see about that," Loren said. "I'll meet you over there."

Before Loren could step away LaBountie caught his sleeve.

"We take a vow, too, you know," he said.

"I know," Loren said. "Do what you can. But don't delay." He snatched his arm away and hurried off down the dark street.

Britney had left the door open. Loren knew the house well and hurried directly upstairs. He entered the small, stuffy room to find the eight-year-old girl's head cranked way back, her face thrust upward with her mouth stretched into a tortured grimace, teeth clenched and hands desperately clutching at the bedsheets. She made sounds that were not quite language but just desperate squeals and grunts. The room smelled of eliminations.

Britney knelt at the side of the bed with one hand on Sarah's shoulder and the other beneath her head. The child's hair was sopping wet with perspiration. Sarah's midsection suddenly bowed upward, straining unnaturally, like a yoga position carried too far.

"This is what's been happening," Britney told Loren.

"Oh, dear," he said, not a little frightened by it. Just then, LaBountie entered the house and called up the stairway. Loren and Britney replied and he clattered up with his own veterinary doctor's kit in a canvas mason bag.

Britney looked up pleadingly at the two big men. "Do something! Please!"

LaBountie asked Britney to give way and told Loren to hold two candles over the bed. He examined Sarah, palpated her face, neck, and shoulders, took her pulse, and pressed his ear to the center of her chest. He examined both of her hands closely.

"What are you looking for?" Britney asked impatiently.

"Signs," LaBountie said. Then he turned down the bedclothes, drew up the hem of her nightgown, and examined her feet. Her legs were thrashing so violently that he had to clamp them under his arm one at a time to have a look. He eventually found the small infected puncture wound between the big and second toe on her left foot.

"There it is," he said.

"What?" Britney cried. "There's what?"

LaBountie didn't reply directly. He quickly drew down Sarah's nightgown again and covered her legs.

"What is it?" Britney pleaded. "Tell me."

"Tetanus, I believe," he said.

Britney appeared both stricken and confounded. LaBountie stood upright and chewed on his lower lip.

"There must be something you can do," Loren said.

"Did she ever have a tetanus shot?" LaBountie asked Britney.

"Of course not," she said. "There are no more shots. Don't you know that?"

"Yes, I know that," LaBountie said. "I thought maybe when she . . ." He trailed away. He knew Britney was going to implore him again to do something and he knew of only one possible treatment. He turned to Loren. "Hurry over to Jerry's," LaBountie said, "and ask his wife if he has any TIG, tetanus immune globulin. She's a nurse, she'll know what it is. TIG."

Loren left right away. As he did, Sarah's whole body strained and arched upward again, more strenuously than before, her agonized grunts becoming awful animal shrieks. LaBountie knew there was nothing he could do in the meantime besides clean the small wound on her foot, which would do little to alter the course of the disease. He gave Britney his pocketknife, opened to the small blade, honed razor sharp, and told her to boil it and bring whiskey and clean rags back with it.

TWENTY-ONE

The scene over at Dr. Jerry Copeland's home had turned chaotic as the doctor was trundled a few blocks from the tavern in a wheelbarrow pushed by his friends. And then when Tom Allison, Danny Russo, and Walter McWhinnie tried to get him inside, the doctor let loose cursing and striking at them with his fists, doing everything he could to resist being manhandled, while his wife, Jeanette, and their two children stood by weeping and humiliated. When Loren arrived on the scene he watched in amazed fury for a moment before he shoved Walter and Danny out of the way and seized the doctor by the shoulders and hollered an inch away from his face to get a hold of himself. Loren being a large man the doctor shrank from him and gave up struggling. They were good friends through the years of hardship, but Loren had put a lot of time and effort in trying to help the doctor with his drinking problem and his anger now was sharp. Meanwhile, the doctor slumped back in the wheelbarrow. Loren was not sure if he had passed out.

"Can you hear me, Jerry?"

"Didn' you tell me to shuddup?" the doctor mumbled.

"The little girl at Robert's house is very sick with tetanus, we think. She's convulsing. Jason is with her. He sent me over for TIG. Do you have any TIG in your office? Do you hear me?"

The doctor nodded his head but then commenced blubbering.

"I hear you," he said.

"Tell us where to look."

Now the doctor just shook his head. "I can't help you," he moaned.

Loren looked to Jeanette. "Do you know where he keeps this TIG medicine?"

"We don't have any more," she said, and she put her hand over her mouth as if shocked that her words had escaped from there.

"Are you sure?"

"I'm absolutely certain," she said in a voice still inflected with the tones of her native Normandy. "I remember when we used the last of it. A young man on the Schmidt farm. More than a year ago."

"Wake the fuck up, Jerry!" Loren hollered. He smacked him smartly on the face, but the doctor appeared to be truly unconscious.

"Stop it!" twelve-year-old Jasper screamed. "Leave him alone!"

Loren left the doctor and reached for Jeanette's hand. "You have to come help," he said. "Right now."

"Okay," she agreed and hurried away with Loren in the direction of Robert's house. The boy followed them down the street a little way but Jeanette admonished him to go back and stay with his little sister, Dinah, while the other three men resumed their struggle to get the doctor inside the house to his bed.

Twenty-two

Just a little earlier, Robert and Brother Jobe lingered over whiskeys in the office behind the hotel desk after the Berkshire delegation had left.

"They puttin' the grift on us," Brother Jobe said. "Subscription! I never heard such bushwah. We gonna have to let them know we won't be pushed around."

"We can just say the trustees met and decided to take a pass on joining their so-called federation."

"They going to put the strong-arm on us somehow. You know, my rangers Seth and Elam, they went and parleyed with these jokers at their bivouac. Said they was just a bunch of Kumbaya kids, and many of 'em was girls. But I think that's some kind of diversion. I think they got some other backup out there we don't know about."

"Maybe we should think about raising our own people into some kind of defense force," Robert said. "We could get fifty men from town if we had to. Don't know where we'd find firearms, though."

"Don't worry about that, ole son."

"You've got weapons?"

"'Course we do. Plenty of iron and ammunition. Something I been working on all year on my travels, whenever I could work it into some bidness."

"We should bring Bullock's people in on this," Robert said. "He's got some very capable men over there."

"I wouldn't depend on that sumbitch to show up for a Sunday school fund-raiser," Brother Jobe said. "Anyways, I can't tell Bullock on the one hand don't display no dead bodies of pickers and robbers and such along the River Road, and by the way now we got to put the fear of judgment on this pack of grifters that come to steal the town's money—"

Just then, young Brother Jonah knocked on the door and they told him to come in.

"Your wife was looking for you in the tavern, Mr. Robert, sir," he said.

For a startled moment, Robert flashed on his wife, Sandy, who had died three years earlier in the encephalitis epidemic. Then his head jerked back as he realized that was not who Jonah meant. He was a little horrified to realize that he had not thought about Britney and Sarah all evening.

"Tell her I'll be right out," he said.

"Oh, she already left," Jonah said. "With your minister. Something about a sick girl at home."

Twenty-three

Robert got to his house before Loren returned from the doctor's with Jeanette. He heard desperate voices and a commotion upstairs and hurried up to Sarah's room, where he found Jason LaBountie seated on the bed with Sarah's left leg jammed under his arm, as attempted to clean and dress the small infected puncture wound between her toes as her upper body thrashed and convulsed. Candlelight made the scene appear the more frightful, all glare and shadows, like a German expressionist horror movie of the last century. Britney knelt by the head of the bed, cradling Sarah's head, desperately trying to comfort her as the child bucked unnaturally, shrieking and squealing. Jason glanced up at Robert standing in the doorway. Robert's mouth had fallen open. Jason nodded at a candlestick on the seat of a chair.

"Pick that up and hold the light closer, will you?" LaBountie said.

"Where were you?" Britney snarled at him, firmly gripping Sarah's head and shoulder as the girl bucked violently again. "I came looking for you."

"The hotel office," Robert said, reaching for the candlestick. "What are you doing here, Jason?"

LaBountie ignored the question. "Hold this," he said, passing the bloodied pocketknife to Robert.

"What's wrong with her?" Robert asked.

"Tetanus, I have to say. Hold this too," he said, handing Robert the whiskey-soaked rag he used to disinfect Sarah's wound. "I sent Reverend Holder over to Jerry's a little while—"

"He's dead drunk!" Britney screamed.

"Loren?" Robert asked, confused.

"The doctor!"

"He's a disgrace," LaBountie said. "I sent the rev to get a particular medicine over there. I'm hoping he'll bring some back."

"He's so drunk," Britney moaned. "He can't even stand up."

"His wife's not drunk," LaBountie said, struggling to finish dressing the wound. "She knows where everything is."

Sarah bucked upward again with exceptional force and a choking shriek. They all heard something snap, like a bone breaking.

"Oh gosh . . ." LaBountie said. He let go of Sarah's leg and corkscrewed around to face the child, who continued in a series of subsiding, ratchet-like jerks, shuddering violently as though an engine inside of her had disastrously malfunctioned, until she was ominously still. Her eyes rolled up into her head and a stream of pink foam flowed out of her mouth. Britney goggled at her daughter as she felt all the tension come out of the girl's small body. She pressed Sarah's head against her breast, wailing, "No, no, no, no!" Robert stood frozen with terror behind LaBountie. Another commotion, this time on the stairs, signaled the arrival of Loren and Jeanette Copeland.

"Something just happened," LaBountie told the doctor's wife, who was a nurse of long experience in both the old and the new times.

"Get out of the way!" she commanded them. "Let go of her head!" she barked at Britney, who backed away from the bed cringing and bawling. Sarah had stopped moving completely. The pink foam flowing from her mouth had turned darker and redder. Jeanette searched for a carotid pulse but failed to find any. She reached into Sarah's mouth attempting to clear the airway but the red foam was too profuse. She puzzled for a moment.

"Do something!" Britney shrieked.

"What are you waiting for?" Robert said.

Jeanette suspected that cardiopulmonary resuscitation would only add to the damage as she assessed it. But she could not even begin explaining, because it was too complicated, and because she was panicking she was suddenly stumbling over her English, thinking only in her native French. But importuned by the others she attempted a set of chest compressions. The first two had only the shocking effect of pumping gouts of blood from the little girl's mouth, and Jeanette stopped abruptly, breaking down in tears herself. The vet shoved her out of the way and tried a few compressions himself with the same horrific result. Jeanette batted at him and screamed "*Arrêtez!*" repeatedly, though he, too, quickly comprehended the problem.

Then, all that could be heard in the room was the sound of the two women weeping and the men breathing. Sarah lay still on the bed, blood pooling in the little depression between her turned head and the pillow. No one had to state that the child was dead, but the awful apprehension of it filled the air in the small room like a noxious gas. Jason LaBountie sidestepped toward the door, muttering, "We tried . . . I'm very sorry," and exited the room. His heavy footsteps resounded on the stairway and the others heard the front door close.

Britney crept onto the bed, sitting in the pool of warm blood as she hoisted her daughter's body up into her embrace. More blood dripped from Sarah's lifeless lips onto Britney's clothing. The child's eyes remained open and empty as windows in an abandoned house. Robert took a step toward her but Britney snarled, "You stay away from me!" He didn't know what to say or do. Loren touched Robert's arm. "Come," he whispered gently to him. Loren took Robert by the elbow and steered him gently out of the room.

It would have been determined by an autopsy that Sarah Watling had died from a one-centimeter tear of the superior vena cava, the large vein supplying the right atrium of the heart, caused by a broken second right vertebrosternal rib due to the violent spastic hyperextensions (opisthotonos) resulting from the potent toxin produced by the tetanus bacterium, *Clostridium tetani.* But no autopsy would be performed because Britney would not allow Sarah's remains anywhere near the doctor, whether he had sobered up or not.

TWENTY-FOUR

Elam woke up in strange surroundings. It took him five seconds to comprehend that he was in a second-floor room of the new Union Grove Hotel in the bed of the young woman named Flame Aurora Greengrass. He had run into her at the bar of the Cider Barrel with the raucous crowd all around and the music playing and she had allowed him to buy her several whiskeys. The drinks didn't seem to soften her up much, and it was so loud in there they could barely converse, but around ten o'clock Flame leaned forward on her bar stool and said, directly into Elam's ear, "Follow me upstairs, okay?"

"What for?" Elam replied, close to her ear, too, although as soon as the words came out of his mouth he knew he sounded like an oaf. He did, however, get to inhale the subtle natural perfume of her hair and skin, suffused as it was with alluring enzymes. Flame replied by making a face that communicated her awareness of exactly what Elam was thinking himself. She knocked back the last of her whiskey—it was a Dutchtown sour mash—jerked her head to indicate the the barroom exit, and climbed off her stool. She was only a few inches shorter than Elam, who was a very big man.

He followed her out of the tavern and into the hotel part of the building, then up a dim stairway lighted by a single candle at the landing and onto the second-floor hallway, also dimly lit, and into room number 22, which was lighted only by the glow of a waxing gibbous moon. The room was spare but comfortable: a double bed, two nightstands, a desklike table, a wooden chair, a chest of drawers, a mirror, a row of four hooks on the wall for coats, and one plain double-hung window. The curtains were simple muslin. Flame drew them closed, which diffused the moonlight.

"Let's get down to business," she said, unwinding her turquoise silk scarf.

Elam said, "All right," though he did nothing more than stand in place as if awaiting further instructions.

Flame began very methodically removing her layers of sweaters and shirts, pausing between each to watch Elam register the changes as she revealed the extraordinary fullness of her figure. Finally, she got down to a plain cotton camisole. The exact contours of her breasts, visible under that filmy garment, Elam thought, were like two small children sleeping in hammocks. She paused again, enjoying his look of rapt, frozen discomposure. Then she sat on the edge of the bed, removed her spandex leggings, and reclined on the bed in the briefest bikini underpants. In the process, her camisole hitched up enough for Elam to see the rippled muscles of her abdomen.

"You must work out," he said.

"No," she said and emitted a little yelp of amusement. "Do you know what we're here for?"

"You mean on earth?"

"No, just in this room."

"Well, uh, yes, I think so, ma'am."

"What'd I tell you about that—?"

"Sorry. I'm nervous."

"I can tell."

"I can't figure you at all," he admitted.

"What's to figure?"

"Everything."

"Don't try so hard."

They examined each other in the dim light for a long moment.

"How come you picked me?" Elam asked.

"How come you followed me up?" she said.

"Human instinct?"

"Exactly!" she said. "Like being hungry. You don't have to puzzle it out. You just find something to eat. Don't you ever get hungry?"

"Yes I do," he said. He took off his sack coat, pulled off his boots awkwardly standing by turns on each leg, stepped out of his pants, and began unbuttoning his shirt, but he fumbled so badly with trembling hands that he lost patience and pulled it over his head.

"All the way," Flame said as he stood there in his drawers.

"You first," Elam said, deciding at last that he'd had enough of being ordered around. "Go on."

She hesitated a moment and then pulled the camisole over her head with arms crossed and wiggled out of her briefs.

"You're magnificent," he said.

"Shut up," she said.

And then they were upon each other with the moonlight lambent through the thin curtains. They feasted until well after the moon moved out of the window frame. When they'd concluded their exertions, Flame fell asleep with her back to Elam, who remained awake awhile longer marveling at the feel of the deep curve where her waist met her majestic hip. He fell asleep trying to construct some concrete notion of what her life was like back home in the place called Berkshire, some kind of mansion on a hill, he imagined, like a college hall, surrounded by the Kumbaya kids, a swimming pool out back, much bigger than the one behind General Stannart's house off base at Fort Jackson, South Carolina, where Elam had trained in the reconnaissance leadership program at the outbreak of the war in the Holy Land. He pictured a wing of her mansion stuffed with professors wearing Coke bottle eyeglasses, all figuring out how to improve and perfect society. It seemed like something out of a long-ago sci-fi movie he'd seen in a mall cinema when he was a little boy. Somewhere down the slippery slope of that elusive fantasy he fell off into a few hours of oblivion. But his irrepressible internal alarm clock, a residue of the military life, brought him back to room 22 at exactly a quarter to six in the morning.

He could see pink daylight just beginning to glow through the curtains and remembered that he was obliged to report to the New Faith stables to commence a journey to Albany with the mayor's boy and Mr. Einhorn's son. Flame still slumbered with her back to him. She was snoring just enough to charm him with the deep animal commitment to sleep that seemed equal to her carnal devotions. She radiated a delicious warmth and a complicated female sweetness with a slight note of rot, and he repressed, with some difficulty, the impulse to press his body against hers one last time before departing. He suspected that he would never be this way with her again. Then, with his ranger's discipline and catlike stealth, he left her bed, retrieved his clothing, and soundlessly slipped away into his duties.

Twenty-five

Daniel Earle, Teddy Einhorn, and Brother Seth were waiting in the New Faith stable when Elam came from his quarters, where he had stopped to fetch his traveling necessaries, his firearm, his saber, his dagger, his toothbrush, and his waxed jacket. Brothers Eben and Zuriel had prepared four mounts for their journey. Seth was already aboard his blue roan, Ollie.

"You taking your time this morning," he observed as Elam shambled in.

"I wish I could have took more," Elam said.

"You wasn't in your room."

"That's true."

"I went looking. Where were you?"

"I was elsewheres."

"Since when are you steppin' out?"

"Since when you become my daddy?"

"I'm your guardian angel, brother. Don't never forget that." In fact, Seth had rescued Elam from the carnage at Dimona, in the Holy Land, when his mechanized unit was wiped out in an ambush and Elam spent two nights in the latrine of an abandoned kibbutz hiding from the enemy, stung by scorpions while watching his shrapnel-shredded leg swell to nearly twice its diameter. Seth's unit had chanced along after the Hezbollah regulars pulled out and they found the sole survivor of one of the last battles of the war in that god-awful hole. Seth's own outfit was reduced to one remaining MRAP vehicle. With Elam half out of his head, they managed to evacuate back to Ashkelon on the coast and the doctors on the U.S. naval hospital ship *Forbearance* saved Elam's leg.

"You know I won't forget that," Elam said with absolute sincerity and then turned to the others. "Good morning, gentlemen. Ready for a little sightseeing?"

Teddy Einhorn, the youngest, giggled nervously.

Daniel nodded respectfully. "I'm good to go," he stated and straightened his beehive crown flat-brimmed straw hat, a product of the New Faith workshops. In anticipation of the journey, he found himself reimmersed psychologically in the training he received at Channel Island, Michigan, two years earlier with the federal division that called itself, simply, the Service. They had gone into the core of him and inserted things there that made him effective in situations that ordinary people rarely entered. However, Daniel was unaware of the dreadful events that had passed the night before at his father's house. He had not stopped in to say good-bye just as dawn was breaking when he walked across town from his lodgings in the newspaper office. His father had already provisioned him with a heavy purse of silver coin.

Eben brought out a black American standardbred gelding named Raven, sixteen and a half hands high, for Daniel, who was nearly as tall as Elam. Daniel used the mounting block to climb aboard. He was comfortable in the saddle, having ridden his Kentucky hunter Ike from Cincinnati to Tennessee and then back all the way to northeastern Ohio in his flight from the Foxfire Republic.

Zuriel, the New Faith farrier, inspected the hooves on Elam's Percheron-Appaloosa mix, Lad, with its massive brown and white spotted rump. Teddy Einhorn was much more used to driving the double spring-mounted box wagon for the family business than riding saddle horses. A compact, calm, and reliable bay mare quarter horse named Rosie was all tacked up waiting for him. Teddy had brought more clothing and equipment than could fit in the panniers provided to him and was now sorting things into two piles (take and leave behind) on a poncho laid down in the center aisle.

"You don't need that fry pan," Daniel told him from high in the saddle. "Pick one of those books, but don't bring both."

Teddy, who was smallest of the four men at five feet and eight inches, red-haired and stout like his father, had not been more than twenty-five miles from Union Grove since he was a small child. He traveled incessantly around the county, though, making deliveries and picking up farmers' produce and specialty items for the Einhorns' store. Unlike Daniel or the rangers, he knew the going price of just about every commodity or product that might be purchased in the new times, both wholesale and retail, and his father had furnished him with a list of items and commodities to bring back if they were fortunate enough to find a proper boat.

In a little while, the two rangers and the two townsmen left Union Grove at a trot with a strong spring sun rising above Schoolhouse Hill to warm their backs and the temperature already climbing toward 60 degrees. They turned down the old state highway number 40, a two-laner that followed the ridge due south along the Hudson Valley. The pavements were fissured and broken from years of frost heaves and no maintenance and they walked their horses single file along the shoulder where the ground was softer and even. From the Route 40 ridge on the east side to Bemis Heights on the west side, the ancient Hudson Valley was four miles across, though the river itself was a mere ribbon of water one hundred to two hundred yards wide as it curled down the valley's center. With the foliage fledging out, it was rarely visible through the scrim of forest that had deepened and thickened over the years as the human population dwindled. At intervals they passed abandoned houses dating from the late twentieth century, once occupied by people who thought nothing of burning half a gallon of gasoline to fetch groceries or of driving forty miles back and forth to a job day in and day out. These people, who were neither town people nor farmers, had been left marooned in the collapse. In just a few years most had either left or died. Their homes were split levels and bunker-like ranches and the "colonials" beloved by the home builders of yore. Now the vinyl claddings were coming apart, the fake stone veneers were splitting off, and the particleboard underlayment beneath was disintegrating from rainwater leaking in. In many houses, the "picture" window was shattered, from weather or malice it was impossible to tell. Some had their front doors stoved in. The tawdry lack of permanence was a joke on the culture of waste that had produced these dwellings. Likewise, the businesses along the highway from the old times stood in uniform desolation: a swimming pool supply company in a tilt-up concrete box had mature box elders growing out its empty front windows. The Dairy Girl drive-in, once a happy scene of summer family frolics and teenage romances, was a grim skeleton of wood framing, all the plate glass gone and the equipment inside scavenged in the Great Collection of steel that had accompanied the war.

The warm air was gravid with the scent of lilac. The hardy bushes planted in the early settlers' dooryards still grew where no trace of the original dwelling remained, poignant reminders of fleeting human endeavor along the furrows of history. Farther down off the ridge, in the distance, where the Hudson bottomlands made for rich loamy soils with few rocks, farm laborers could be seen driving oxen and plow horses in fields that had the texture of fine dark brown fur. On three occasions along the way that morning they passed others going about their business. One was a scrawny boy of twelve driving a herd of flop-eared Nubian goats to better pasture up the road. He stopped and watched the four horsemen blankly, in tight-lipped terror that they would take one of his animals and roast it for lunch. Another was an old woman with a brace of six slaughtered partridges tied by their feet to either end of a pole that she carried across her shoulder. She could not have weighed a hundred pounds herself, had wild frizzy white hair, and wore an old-times coat of bright red plastic meant to look like patent leather, with an incongruous number of zippered pockets and one sewn-on belt too many. She marched past them with her chin thrust out, ignoring the men as though they were ghosts.

"You must be a deadeye shot, ma'am," the voluble Seth called after her, but the woman didn't even turn her head.

"I think she snared them," Elam said. "She ain't carrying a firearm."

The last was a grown man of forty-five who drove a cart filled with seed potatoes behind a spindly gray pony.

"No money, no money," he said extra loudly as he approached, assuming that the four were freeboot bandits.

"We're men of Jesus," Seth said.

"What . . . ?"

"Do you know the Lord, sir?"

"Is this the new style in robbery?"

"I tell you, we're foursquare and upright," Seth rejoined. "When we talk to God, he answers back. We're in his service, and he's at ours."

"He's a harsh employer, to my mind," the man said.

"He's love incarnate, my friend," Seth replied. "Lookit how your wagon box doth o'erflow in spuds. That's his doing."

"So you say. Almost killed myself diggin' them. Once upon a time I sat behind a desk in a comfortable chair you could adjust sixteen different ways, with a coffee machine right at hand, and a girl outside the door who took all my calls. Our office handled half the fire and casualty between Albany and Glens Falls. Now look what I'm reduced to."

"You could just as well say you been elevated."

"How's that?"

"That whole old-times way of life was false. You know that."

"I don't see it that way at all," the man rejoined rather vehemently. "If you are in communication with the alleged deity, please tell him we've had enough punishment."

"Okay, then. Go your way, sir, and God bless."

Shaking his head in puzzlement, the potato cart driver flicked his reins until the pony stepped lively.

TWENTY-SIX

Britney remained in the dead child's room all night with the door shut. Twice between midnight and sunrise, Robert knocked on the door asking to be allowed in, and both times Britney shrieked at him to go away. So early that same morning, as his son Daniel and three others rode south out of town along the Route 40 ridge, Robert slipped away to the parish house of the Congregational Church, where Loren lived with his wife, Jane Ann, and the four orphaned boys they had adopted the previous fall. Robert knew it was Loren's habit to rise early, before the boys, who were all under ten, turned the kitchen into a rowdy playroom. Indeed a little after daybreak Robert found his friend firing the big cookstove preparing to make tea and work in peace on his sermon for the coming Sunday. Robert took a seat at the big farmhouse table and sat wordlessly and hollow-eyed for a long time, and Loren did not press him, knowing that Robert would open up when he felt able.

"I'm afraid I'm going to lose her," Robert said eventually. Loren was startled for a moment, wondering if Robert meant the child, who he knew was already dead, and whether he was in his right mind. He placed a mug before Robert and slid the teapot closer along with the honey jar. The tea was a mixture of lemon balm and rose hips.

"Nothing's harder than losing a child," Loren said. Both of them had lost one before, of course: Robert a daughter, Loren a son.

"No. Nothing's harder," Robert agreed. He broke down and cried for a time. Loren did not try to intervene with psychobabble. He just abided with Robert and drank his own tea. The birds were really going at it out the window in the spring sunshine, their numbers greatly increasing in the new times as the load of chemical poisons in their world fell away to nothing. Eventually, Robert

subsided into sniffles and then, gazing out the window, began singing almost inaudibly a sad blues tune he learned years ago when he
played in a band with three fraternity brothers.

"What was that?" Loren asked.

"Skip James. 'Hard Time Killin' Floor Blues,'" Robert said and
poured himself some of the tea. "The thing is, we have to bury
Sarah now."

"I know. Let me take care of the arrangements."

"Okay," Robert said. His mouth was twitching again. "I don't
think I can bear losing Britney too."

"Well, you don't know—"

"The way she's acting."

"It's got to be the worst moment in her life."

"It's worse than when Shawn died, I'm sure," Robert said, referring to Britney's husband, gunned down the previous summer. "They
weren't getting along. Did you know that?"

"No. They never came to me for counsel."

"He was a pretty angry young guy," Robert said. "That whole
last year, she said, he was romancing one of the dairy girls at the
Schmidt farm. Britney can be a rough customer herself sometimes.
She's a tough girl. Hardheaded. But she's been wonderful to live
with. I've really loved her. And Sarah was a terrific kid. We were a
family." Robert began trembling again.

Voices and thumpings became audible from above. The children
were awake. They would be down soon with Jane Ann, creating
their breakfast circus.

"I'd better go," Robert said.

"I'll come over to your place a little later this morning," Loren
said, "and try to talk to her about making funeral arrangements."

TWENTY-SEVEN

Earlier, Britney heard Robert leave the house and, when she was sure he was gone, she carried Sarah's body downstairs, swaddled in a blanket, and placed it, with a long-handled shovel, in the chore cart Robert had built to convey his tools to the job site of any particular day. When she left the house on Linden Street, the eastern sky was streaked with pink and some lingering stars remained visible west of the zenith. She was well past the edge of town before the birds started singing in earnest.

A half hour up the North Road, pulling the wagon with a rope lead, she arrived at a house where she had lived between the ages of six and ten, before her father lost his job as a sales rep for the Holland and Vesey paper company in Glens Falls, two years after H & V was taken over by a so-called leveraged buyout firm, loaded up with superfluous debt, stripped of its remaining assets, and left for dead. Britney's father had worked there since before she was born and took his own life after another two years of fruitless search for employment led to his landing on the federal disability trash heap with a faked lumbar spondylolisthesis claim that humiliated him. In the process, the family lost their wonderful house.

It was a vernacular farmhouse with a fanlight in the gable end of the attic and a front porch big enough to use as an outdoor living room in the summertime. It was built in 1819 by a descendant of Revolutionary War patriot Ethan Allen, leader of the Green Mountain Boys. The original four-hundred-acre farm property had been subdivided, and the house was not in great shape when her family lived there, having last been renovated in the 1980s, but she remembered it with a searing, primal nostalgia. The rooms of the house were proportioned and arranged with superb fittedness to human psychology—they felt good to be in—and to the patterns of daily life. The parlor featured deep window seats where a nine-year-old girl could read or just daydream on a rainy afternoon. The big kitchen had its original fireplace with iron cranes for holding stew pots and a little bake oven on the side. The family ran two woodstoves in wintertime, consuming six full cords a season, and Britney remembered always being physically comfortable there, sometimes even too warm while blizzards howled outside. An old disused springhouse was her "fort," and there was a pond where she hunted tadpoles and turtles, and far behind the house lay pastures as broad as the Serengeti with other people's cows that Britney could pretend were giraffes and elephants, and behind these were upland woods full of mystery that seemed to go on forever. Her years there were the happiest of her life.

Now she pulled the cart onto the property and up the weed-choked driveway and stopped to regard the place. It was a ruin. Squatters, tramps, or pickers had managed to burn the place half down. An early-twentieth-century addition on the south side of the original building looked, strangely, like a roasted hunk of meat, a standing rib roast, say, with ugly brown-black char streaks feathering up from the windows to where the roof had collapsed in on itself. Part of the old main house was scorched, too, but something had stopped the damage there—two days of heavy autumn rain, in fact. The yard was crowded with sumacs and box elders that encroached on the windows and Virginia creeper grew up the broken remnants of the old rose trellis.

The dimensions inside were a little smaller than she remembered. The arrangement of rooms propelled her to a place that was not so much back in time as out of time. Unlike other junk-filled abandoned properties around the county, where families had been wiped out in one of the epidemics, or fled hastily in fear of being marooned with no gasoline, or harassed by pickers, her family's old place was utterly empty. Not any scraps of furniture remained, and everything made of metal had been scavenged, right down to the 1925 hot water radiators and the lighting fixtures. The emptiness comforted her, as though the place had been readied for her to reoccupy it. Part of the old plaster ceiling in the front parlor had come down in chunks on the hardwood floor. The window seats were still there, of course.

Britney carried Sarah's body inside and made a little cushion with the blanket in a window-seat nook for the two of them to abide for a while—Britney had no idea how long. Her thoughts were as far as could be from any temporal practicalities. All she knew was that she wanted to be with her daughter and that this was a good place where nobody was liable to interrupt their simply being.

TWENTY-EIGHT

That same morning, Brother Jobe dispatched his second in command, Joseph, to parley with Stephen Bullock about the impositions upon the local folk proposed by Mr. Buddy Goodfriend of the Berkshire People's Republic, and the possibility of mutual aid between Bullock's people and those in town in the face of it. Brother Jobe could have gone to see Bullock himself but there was so much ill feeling between them that he was afraid it would get in the way of any useful discussion. On the other hand, Bullock owed a debt of gratitude to Brother Joseph, who, the previous summer, had led the mission to rescue Bullock's trade boat crew when they were held hostage by the political boss of Albany, a notorious gangster named Dan Curry. All four boatmen were returned safely to Bullock's plantation, and Dan Curry was shot in the head for his exertions.

Joseph was glad to get away from the New Faith headquarters for a while. Such were his multiple and manifold duties day to day that he'd barely been out of Union Grove all year, apart from the journey to Albany. Often he didn't leave the New Faith compound for a week at a time. Along with Seth and Elam, he was a veteran of the military fiasco in the Holy Land but, unlike them, he'd been an officer there. Brother Jobe tended to defer tactical questions to Joseph, as he had during the difficult months of harassment in their previous (unsuccessful) settlement attempt outside Rising Sun, Pennsylvania. There they were beset by waves of refugees from Washington, DC, in the aftermath of the bombing that made the city uninhabitable, and from Baltimore and Philadelphia, too, when services and supply chains broke down there. Gangs had organized quickly in the face of these hardships and fanned out into the loamy Pennsylvania countryside to seize what means of survival they could. Joseph's son Aaron had died at the age of sixteen in the defense of the group's leased farm at Rising Sun and the New Faith had lost eleven others of their number before they decided to abandon the place and head north, far from the suffering cities.

Joseph rode a big roan gelding named Buck down into the Hudson Valley, where he turned onto the River Road and shortly came across the remains of the hapless picker Stephen Bullock had nailed to a black locust tree two weeks earlier. What remained of him now was considerably less than what Robert Earle and Terry Einhorn had first come across: just the upper portion of the thoracic cavity, half of one arm, and the head, of course, still secured in place by a landscape spike. The rest had been gnawed away by every sort of scavenger in the neighborhood from turkey vultures to coyotes to 'possums to blowflies. The sight of it brought Joseph back to the atrocities he'd seen in the Holy Land, and even with the temperature pushing above 60 degrees it sent a shiver through him. Also in the intervening days, Bullock had added a painted sign nailed to the tree above the corpse:

I was a thief like you
Pass by, stranger, and live

Brother Joseph could see the practical advantage of such a display, unappetizing as it might be. Over the past year he'd come to admire Bullock's operation, his vast holdings (more than four thousand acres), his exemplary projects (the sorghum mill, the cement works, the hydroelectric installation), the many workshops and barns, the excellence of his livestock, the village he'd assembled for his people on the property, the well-maintained mansion built by his ancestors. But he could not acquire a taste for the man himself, his imperious manner, despotic sway, and Yankee arrogance. It was men like Bullock, Joseph thought, who had brought about the ruination of his own land and people in Carolina generations earlier in the War Between the States.

He also could not fail to notice how poorly defended the plantation was as he walked Buck up the driveway. Anyone, like himself, could ride in. There was not so much as a gate. No guard was posted. When he got to the turnaround at the head of the drive, the stable boy Eddie Flake limped out of the barn and directed him to look for Bullock up the hill in a distant region of the property. Joseph rode on up.

There, at the edge of a three-acre field that he intended to plow for sorghum, Bullock and four other men puzzled over a utility tractor that had been refitted with a four-cylinder long-block Ford engine modified to 100 percent ethanol fuel. It was a pet project for Bullock, who maintained a deep romantic attachment to the power machinery of his youth. Apparently, the tractor had been able to cut two long passes in the field before it quit. Now, the engine would run only a minute at a time before sputtering out. Brother Joseph hailed Bullock from a distance of a hundred yards and rode up toward him. Bullock strode away from his men in the field and met Joseph on the road.

"Morning, sir," Joseph said, lifting his straw hat. "I bring you greetings from the New Faith and my boss, Brother Jobe."

Bullock, dressed in beautifully tailored buff riding trousers, shiny black boots, and a loose-fitted cotton blouse, looked to Brother Joseph like the second coming of George Washington. Bullock's mouth was even set firmly in a way similar to the familiar portraits of the founding father with his famously annoying dentures. Bullock held Buck's bridle while Joseph dismounted. Both were large men, but Joseph stood two inches taller than Bullock. He let go of the bridle with Joseph on the ground.

"If this is more business with the law," Bullock said, "tell your boss I resigned as magistrate and that's final."

"No sir, it's something else entirely. Is that the old Ford 5000 you got there?"

"Yes it is," Bullock said. "The 1980 model."

Joseph whistled, as in admiration of it.

"Wow. That's going back some," he said.

"I guess you noticed, they're not making them anymore."

Joseph let the snark pass. "What you running her on?" he asked.

"Grain spirits," Bullock said and glanced over at his crew. One of them worked the crank magneto that had been grafted to the engine in place of a suitable battery, which was unavailable now. The engine came to life briefly but then sputtered out with a feeble exhalation of white smoke from its upright exhaust pipe.

"You aim to plow with that?" Joseph asked.

"That's the general idea."

"We like mules."

"So your people keep telling me," Bullock said. "We've still got one foot in modern times over here."

"Well, the thing is, sir, how many acres of corn you got to sow to make the mash for your fuel, not to mention all the man-hours and additional trouble for fermentation and distillation, et cetera. You'd be altogether better off cropping animal feeds, don't you think?"

"I like machines for field work."

The men got the engine running again but it died just as quickly, with another smoky belch.

"Have you checked for vapor lock?" Joseph asked.

"We're still experimenting with the line feed. Alcohol's tricky."

"I'd go with the smaller diameter, it was my science project," Joseph said. "But I suppose it could be the coil. Not like you can send down to the auto parts store for a new one these days, though."

Bullock scowled. Meanwhile, one of his men cranked the magneto again and the engine started and stopped as before. A workman came over to where Bullock and Joseph talked.

"We're thinking maybe tow it back down to the shop and look inside," the man reported. "Shall I bring up the oxen, sir?"

"Fine," Bullock said, clearly annoyed and still glaring at Joseph. "Get the oxen." The man gestured to the others. They left the dingy blue and white tractor alone in the field and all four marched back down the road toward the distant barns.

"I'm sure the boss would lend you some mules for the planting season just to try out," Joseph said, "till you come around to see what fine beasts they are. Test drive them, so to say."

"I doubt you rode all the way over here to debate machine versus mule."

"No sir, I did not. We got what you might call a situation over in town and it goes something like this . . ." Joseph said, and proceeded to lay it out for Bullock. "I come to you with a request for solidarity, in case we have to resist these folks and their demands with force."

"You say they're like a band of Boy Scouts?"

"We suspect they have strength in reserve," Joseph said. "That what they have shown us so far is some kind of ruse. We don't think they'd come over all this way and try extorting money from folks otherwise."

"Try hanging a few of them," Bullock said. "See what comes out of the woodwork."

"They haven't done nothing yet except propose this here federation idea and that tax they call a subscription for signing on with them."

"I hope you told them to get lost."

"We're playing our cards a little closer to the chest right now, sir. You ever hear of a character name of Glen Ethan Greengrass?"

"Yes. He was head of the NPR radio station out of Pittsfield, Mass. Taught economics at Amherst College, I think. Ran endless fund drives just to hear himself talk. A blabbermouth of the first degree. That was years ago."

"They say he's their leader."

"What?"

"He wrote a book that's sort of their bible. Diversity and share the wealth and all like that."

"Yes, you see where that got us."

"Sounds like socialism."

"It's more like kindergarten. I'm surprised he's still alive."

"They say he's coming to Union Grove."

"Is that so? Don't let him near a microphone—just kidding. Seriously, though, why are you taking these jokers seriously?"

"The boss thinks we should be prepared for trouble."

"It's damned insolence, if you ask me. The world out there has gone insane. That's why I want less and less to do with it."

"If I might ask, how many able-bodied men do you have on hand?"

"I don't have any to spare," Bullock said. "I've dissociated my interests from the town of Union Grove. We're capable of defending this domain here, but I don't intend to risk losing any of my people over your way."

"That's disappointing, sir."

"That's the way it is."

"Can I give you a ride back down yonder?" Joseph asked. "Buck here is a sturdy boy."

"My men will be back directly with the animals," Bullock said.

"Good luck with that engine, sir. The Ford 5000, she was a good friend in her time. Just want you to know that whatever else happens you can depend on us, for we are men of Jesus."

Twenty-nine

When Robert returned to his house Britney was gone and so was Sarah's body. He doubted that Britney had taken it to the doctor's, where the village dead were usually kept awaiting burial in his springhouse turned morgue. But he went over there to inquire nonetheless because he didn't know where else to look. He found the doctor alone in his office at his desk, hungover, slumped in despair. Robert slid into an oak chair on the far side of the desk. A life-size plastic skeleton hung from a stand in the corner like a figure out of a medieval parable about the brevity of existence. The room smelled of alcohol.

"Was Britney here?" Robert eventually asked.

"No," the doctor said without looking up.

"Sarah died last night, you know."

"I know. Jason sent his boy over to tell me."

They sat silently for a while.

Eventually, the doctor said, "Maybe you're wondering, could I have done something to save her? For what it's worth, probably not. But forgive me for being too damn drunk to attend."

"I'm not blaming you, Jerry. I wasn't there for her either."

"Well, I'm blaming myself. I don't believe in God, so I can't blame him. We do what we can but it's not much. We're at the mercy of an indifferent universe. That's all. It wears me down. Sorry to burden you with my nonsense at a time like this."

"Well, she's taken the body somewhere," Robert said.

"Not here as far as I know," the doctor said. "You can go look if you like."

Robert did. It was ten degrees cooler inside the old springhouse with its clay floor, damp stone walls, and meager light. The table at center where the dead were laid was empty. Then he went home because he didn't know where else to look, and he was hoping that she might turn up there because, after all, it was her home too. But she was not there and Robert just sat quietly on the sofa in the parlor waiting for her to return, wondering how he might salvage their life together. After about an hour of painful rumination the door swung open and Loren entered.

Robert could not bear to hear himself say again that Britney and the child's body were not there and that he didn't know where to look. Just then, his eyes fastened on the German violin that he had found for Sarah the past fall. It was a lovely instrument with inlaid shell purfling along the edge of the top plate and an ebony crow inlaid on the back. It lay out on the table where she had left it upon realizing, days ago, that she felt too ill to practice, or even to put it back in its case. She had learned so well and so much in just a few months, it was an amazing testament to cognitive development in children. The recognition that the world was finished with Sarah and her development provoked such an upsurge of fury in Robert that he seized the instrument by its neck and brought it crashing down against the table with so much force that nothing remained in his hand but the peg box, the tailpiece, and the limp strings that connected them.

THIRTY

That afternoon, on a country crossroads 2.6 miles east of Union Grove, in the abandoned shell of a Sun Mart convenience store, with everything stripped out of it including the steel shelving and daylight visible through the disintegrating roof, Sylvester "Buddy" Goodfriend met with Duane Terrio, a one-sixteenth Pocumtuc Indian who, in the old times, had worked as assistant human resources manager of the SunEagle Casino and Resort outside Chicopee, Massachusetts, now defunct. A solid six-footer, forty-three years old, Terrio officially went by the name Wawanotewat, He Who Fools Others, in the Algonquin subdialect of his distant ancestors, but Goodfriend still called him Duane. In the performance of his duties, Terrio had adopted as well the costume of his ancestors. This mild spring day he wore a loincloth cut from an old blanket, leather leggings cinched above his knees, horsehide moccasins, and a red calico cotton blouse. Many coils of beads and bones hung from his neck and wrists, and his head was shaved except for a topknot gathered, bound, and slathered in a mixture of lanolin and blacking made from burnt wild grapevines, much as his people had done during their struggles with the English and the Mohawk back in the 1700s. His face was daubed with paint made of red iron oxide, with his eye sockets outlined in black. He carried a war club carved from a maple root and a short sword cinched into the belt that held up his loincloth.

"You look frightful enough," Buddy said. "Are your men comfortable?"

"They're anxious to get it on. We traveled light getting here. My boys are hungry."

"How many did you bring with you?"

"Eleven others. We'll have to take provisions soon."

"Take what you can where you can, but don't make a show of it. Not yet, anyway. We're going to start working these landowners today. The people in town, I dunno whether they're hardheaded or just dumb. There's opportunity here, though. I can smell it. I'll send a message when we need you to begin operations."

"Good luck, brother. Make it rain."

"Thanks, Duane."

THIRTY-ONE

Buddy Goodfriend left his pony, Che, hitched to his two-wheeled campaign cart in the shade of a white oak tree in Temple Merton's turnaround just after noon, expecting that the wealthy farmer would be present for lunch at the house, which, as it happened, was exactly correct. A servant girl answered the door and showed Goodfriend into the kitchen, where Merton and his girlfriend occupied a round table in a window bay that looked out on his fields, pastures, vineyard, orchards, and barns. Goodfriend introduced himself as the economic development director of the Berkshire People's Republic, on a diplomatic spring tour of neighboring states. He seemed clean, healthy, literate, and smartly attired in his old-times expeditionary casuals so, sharing a glance of mild incredulity, Temple and Lorraine invited him to the table.

"It's not often these days we get to meet new people from away," Lorraine said.

"I've never heard of this Berkshire Republic," Temple said. The servant girl brought a platter of fried smelts to the table. The delicate sardine-like minnows were running like crazy this time of year in the streams that fed the Hudson River and Adirondack lakes. In the Merton kitchen they were rolled in fine cornmeal, deep fried in lard, and eaten whole, bones, innards, and all, like french fries of yore. Lorraine had put up many jars of the smoky homemade ketchup that accompanied them to the table.

"Salt is scarce just now," she said.

"We've had some trouble with our supply chains," Temple elaborated. "We depended too heavily on certain Hudson River shipping arrangements that have been interrupted lately."

"People think commerce is boring," Goodfriend said, "but at the end of the day the people's well-being depends on it. We incorporated sixteen months ago. Communication is so poor these days, and that's one of the reasons for my journey. Obviously our part of the country and yours have many common interests and we're especially eager to improve trade and communication." He went on to explain the vacuum of governance in western Massachusetts and the social crisis it produced, and how the Berkshire People's Republic intended to rectify all that.

"Our office of sustainable technology is making great strides," he said.

"Strides toward what?" Temple asked.

"Reviving confidence, mainly," Goodfriend said. "The belief that progress is still possible."

"Ah, yes," Temple said. "Progress."

"We reject despair and resignation," Goodfriend said.

"Did you come here all alone?" Lorraine asked, as the servant girl brought three more plates to the table, each a perfectly composed salad of lettuces grown in Merton's greenhouse, with pickled beets, quartered hard-boiled eggs, and bits of smoked trout fillet.

"Others in the delegation are at the new hotel in town," Goodfriend said. "It must be exciting for you to see real estate development happen after these years of tribulation and decline."

"Yes, it's heartening to see new business here," Temple said. "We supply apple brandy to the tavern."

"We have high hopes for our part of the country," Goodfriend said, "with our heritage of civic engagement, our tolerance and progressivism, our wealth of water power." He went on at some length about the return of cottage manufacturing in western Massachusetts and the need to expand the market for their goods to neighboring states that had been cut off from each other in recent years. There was even serious discussion, he said, of rebuilding the railroad line from Greenfield, Massachusetts, over to Bennington, Vermont . . .

Goodfriend's palaver had turned rote because he found his attention focused more on the signal charms of Lorraine Moncalvo, and a portion of his brain was spinning scenarios in which he might possibly acquaint himself more intimately with her.

"You sound like a politician," Temple remarked good-naturedly, with a wink to Lorraine.

"Oh, but I am one," Goodfriend replied with an equal effort at good humor. "And so much of politics is salesmanship, isn't it? This outreach we're on, for instance. The need to sell an idea to people. The idea of commonwealth! Funny," his tone shifted perceptibly, "but I can't escape the odd feeling that I've met you somewhere before. There's even something about your voice."

"Mr. Merton was in the movies, back in the day," Lorraine said, because she knew Temple was averse to talking about that bygone phase of his life. "He was on TV too."

"Wait a minute," Goodfriend said and then snapped his fingers. "It's coming to me: *Boomtown*? On HBO?"

Lorraine nodded and beamed.

"Oh, that was such a great show! You played . . . whatsis-name . . . ? Oh, God . . . help me out."

"Lamont," Lorraine said. "Lamont Circe—"

"The guy who poisons . . . whasisname?"

"Ferdinand Belasco, the mayor."

"Right!"

"And about seventeen other characters before it was all over," Temple added, popping a quartered egg in his mouth.

"Well, isn't this something?" Goodfriend exclaimed.

"Did you see *The Big Lebowski*?" Lorraine asked.

"Oh, of course. One of my favorites."

"He was in that. He played Thug Number Two, you know, when those guys bust into the Dude's apartment and toss a ferret in his bathtub."

"Oh, yes! That was hilarious. That was you?"

"I was a much younger man," Temple said. "Plus the outfits and the hair—you'd never recognize me."

"He was in quite a few of the Coen Brothers movies. *O Brother, Burn After Reading, No Country for Old Men*."

"They were great artists," Temple said. "I hope their art doesn't disappear like the stage plays of the Roman Empire did."

"Oh, gosh, it's sickening to contemplate." Goodfriend shook his head.

"You know, we have no idea what the music of classical Rome sounded like," Temple said.

"Is that so? None?"

"There's no notation, no recordings, of course, nothing. Gone without a trace. And now we can see the stupidity in the old modern times of putting everything on digital media."

"I hate to think about it," Goodfriend said. "Believe me, I'll take this up with our people. We must do what we can to preserve the art of the cinema. But more to the point . . ." He then proceeded to lay out the actual business of his casual visit, just as the servant girl deposited a little dessert platter of honeyed nut cakes on the table and took the other lunch plates away. He told of the formation of the Berkshire People's Republic under their "foundational leader" Glen Ethan Greengrass, and their effort to build a greater New England federation under a central government, and of the need to raise subscriptions to support that effort. Temple grew visibly more uncomfortable the longer Goodfriend talked. Then Goodfriend took the paper money out of his coat and got to the heart of the matter.

Temple heard him out but replied as plainly as possible, "Are you out of your mind? I won't exchange silver coin for that stuff."

"Sir," Goodfriend replied. "You can't expect to operate a government with no revenue. We're determined to establish the federation and we are negotiating the terms of fiscal cooperation right now with your representatives in town. We're convinced that this subscription exchange is the fairest system anyone could come up with."

"You propose to run our affairs from over in Massachusetts?"

"No, just to coordinate regional cooperation and redevelopment—"

"Thank you for your company at lunch," Temple said, standing suddenly and dashing his cloth napkin on the table, "but I've got calves to attend to and fences to mend and a long list of routine chores to take care of. Thanks for stopping by and good luck with your scheme."

"It's not a scheme, sir. It's a task of nation building."

Temple Merton walked straight out through the pantry and the rear door.

"You see what Mr. Hamilton was up against in his day," Goodfriend said to Lorraine.

"Frankly, I didn't understand your pitch at all, apart from your love of old movies," she said cordially. "Come, I'll walk you to the door."

On the front porch, Buddy Goodfriend turned to her one last time and said, "We're going to make this happen. And we'll do whatever's necessary to raise the requisite funds."

"You know, there was so much about the crash that was tragic and terrible," she said. "But now that it's over we find ourselves enjoying a remarkable degree of freedom. And having tasted it, I don't think we'll allow ourselves to be pushed around again. That must be your pony over there."

"Yes."

"He's a sweetie. Enjoy your trip back in this beautiful weather."

Thirty-two

Ainsley Perlew, also known as Sonny Boy, crept up behind a hedgerow on the north-facing slope of Coot Hill Road nine miles northeast of Union Grove. Seven cows grazed in a pasture there about two hundred yards from his position. The sight of them lit up the parietal lobe of his brain like a pine knot flaring in a fire. Ainsley had avoided the roads out of town and ranged through the woods and edges of the fields in a transport of sensation and anticipation as he sought the opportunity to do what he was best at. In the service of that endeavor, he carried a backpack containing a disassembled bolt action rifle chambered for the Springfield .30-06 cartridge with a 24-inch matte stainless steel barrel and a superlight detachable carbon fiber stock. The weapon was fitted for a Leupold scope, a lightweight Hechman carbon fiber bipod, and a T-8 cell moderator sound suppressor, or silencer, that had cost more originally than the rifle when new. These had all been a gift, Buddy Goodfriend said when he presented them to Ainsley, from the great man himself, Glen Ethan Greengrass.

As a child in the old times, Ainsley had been diagnosed as an Asperger's syndrome case, closer to the more extreme end of the spectrum that bordered on autism. His father, the forest biology research specialist of the Toth Arboretum outside Worcester, Massachusetts, had been similarly equipped for life but navigated successfully through the doctorate program at MIT and then found a position that allowed him to work alone. Ainsley grew up on the three-hundred-acre grounds of that establishment, where from the age of seven he was free to ramble the trails and dells, to stalk small game, and develop his particular skills. He felt freer and happier in his solitary pursuits there than anyplace, school in particular, which had been a special hell for him with its horrifying social pressures.

He perceived people talking at him as a form of torture, while the world outside the arboretum, with its highway strips, cacophonous signage, bunker-like buildings, whirring color, and hostile movement, gave him migraines.

Now, with the automobiles all gone, and the economy reduced to a shadow of what it had been, and the human population winnowed steeply, the whole northeast region was turning into a kind of greater arboretum that Ainsley Perlew felt wonderfully at home in. His journey this day was a joyful symphony of sensation. The songs of birds and insects, the smell of growth and decay, the dappled sunlight in the tender new foliage transported him to a place of exultation where the perturbations of human society could not afflict him and he was free to be his essential self. The sensation of being in perfect unity with the world around him made his body seem to sing at the cellular level.

The temperature at two-thirty in the afternoon was a perfect sixty-nine degrees. From his perch along the old tumbledown stone wall, in the shade of the woods that followed the upland ridge of Coot Hill, he took a length of hard sausage from his coat pocket and gnawed on it as he surveyed the cows below. It amused him to the point of hilarity that cows had faces like people, like every other animal in the world, eyes, nose, a mouth. When the thought came to him that people's faces generally looked as dumb as cows, he almost choked on a chaw of sausage in the attempt to suppress his laughter.

When he finished his lunch, he took the various parts of his rifle out of the backpack, each piece lovingly wrapped in a little piece of blanket cloth and secured with a ribbon. He plugged the stock into the receiver body with the scope premounted, screwed in the barrel, attached the sound suppressor, fitted up the bipod, and locked in a ten-round magazine. He did it all in a leisurely manner, pausing to chuckle now and again over the cows' big round eyes, soft brown noses, and lolling tongues. Then, he found a nice flat rock along the tumbledown wall, positioned the rifle, flipped up the hinged lens caps, and had a look at the cows under magnification. The Leupold's lenses were so crisp he could count the flies orbiting the silly beasts.

Ainsley was intuitively very good at math. He made a series of calculations in his head in preparation for his shots: the distance, vertical drop between himself and his targets, wind direction and speed (negligible). He experienced math, especially calculus, as a matrix of flavors ranging from bitter to delicious the closer he got to putting the numbers in order properly. His first shot caught the nearest brown and white Guernsey directly in the left side of its head and dropped it in place like a big parcel on a doorstep. The others continued to graze. The silencer did not completely eliminate the report of the bullet, but toned it down considerably to about the level of, say, someone splitting stove billets with a kindling ax. It was only when the fourth cow dropped that the remaining three seemed to perceive some clue as to things not being right. They quit their grazing and began to stroll down the sloping pasture away from their fallen sisters, but did not make it very far before Ainsley managed to kill them all.

THIRTY-THREE

Karen Grolsch saw the crowd of some hundred people milling about and around the veranda of the Union Grove Hotel as she made her way up Hill Street. Word had been put out and artfully spread around town that the founding leader of the Berkshire People's Republic, Glen Ethan Greengrass, would be arriving this evening on an outreach campaign to open friendly relations with his New York neighbors and discuss coordinated improvements in public works, transportation, trade, and economic fairness. The "Berkies," as the townspeople soon came to call them, had also tacked up hand-lettered bills on street trees and old telephone poles that read:

> *Glen Ethan Greengrass*
> *Our Dear Leader*
> *Come Here [sic] Him Speak*
> *Union Grove Hotel*
> *7:30 p.m.*

Not a few denizens of Union Grove remembered Greengrass from his days as a public radio personality, always fighting the good fight for social justice, tolerance, diversity, inclusion, voting rights, women's reproductive rights, animal rights, marriage equality, income equality, while inveighing against corporate oligarchy, gun ownership, the surveillance state, fascism, racism, sexism, ageism, look-ism, militarism, capitalism, strict constructionism, and homophobia. He was such a permeating presence on the airwaves in the old times that his thin and nasal voice, like that of a perpetual nineteen-year-old, would often be heard, between programs, announcing simply: "Hi, this is Glen Ethan . . ." with no last name, as though he were head camp counselor to everyone living between the Connecticut River and Hudson River valleys, and that they would automatically know who he was and what he expected of them—that is, to contribute money in the everlasting quest for funds to run the radio station.

While not a few townspeople remembered him and his never-ending fund drives from the old times, they were intrigued by the notion that he had survived the great dislocations of the crash to emerge, apparently, as the political leader of a sovereign region, this so-called Berkshire People's Republic, and that he was leading a new movement to form a greater regional federation that would be a first step toward rebuilding the shattered sense of nationhood in the old cradle of the first American Revolution.

Rumors of big doings in town had spread that day, even among the laborers in the fields, the dairy, and the poultry barns at Carl Weibel's farm, and inspired Karen Grolsch to hurry home after work with her ducklings and prepare to report on the scene for Daniel Earle's newspaper. She was aware that Daniel had departed Union Grove for Albany that morning and she wanted to demonstrate her fitness for newspaper work upon his expected return in three days. Her late father had left behind several reams of printer paper and they had a drawer full of old ballpoint pens in the kitchen. Karen hastily stitched together a packet of paper sheets into a notebook of fifty pages, exchanged her farmwork clothes for a skirt and sweater, quickly scrambled two duck eggs and ate them with some of her mother's quince conserve, and set out across town to record the doings.

It was a lovely evening, warmest of the year so far, with the temperature lingering in the mid-sixties and the air rich with floral sweetness and the smell of horses. Karen could hear the buzz of conversation from a hundred yards away. The tavern was open and many of those on the hotel veranda held glasses of beer, cider, and spirits. The air of collective excitement and anticipation was more intense than any scene around town she could remember lately, even Christmas Eve before the musical festivities at the Congregational Church, or when the audience gathered in the music hall on the third floor of the old town hall for the debut of one of Andrew Pendergast's Broadway musicals, or even the recent grand opening of the hotel itself, where she had introduced herself to Daniel Earle.

The sun had just slipped below the shoulder of Schoolhouse Hill when a procession of mounted riders, carts, and box wagons made the turn across the bridge at Mill Street and up onto Main. In front of the vehicles marched the young Berkshire missionaries, including a few children who traveled with them. As they approached the hotel at the corner of Main and Van Buren the strains of that old-time popular song "This Land Is Your Land" rang out. Quite a few of the New Faith brethren in their black and white outfits peppered the waiting crowd and Karen pushed her way through the throng to Brother Jobe, who stood watching the proceedings braced against a sycamore tree in front of the New Faith barbershop with Brother Judah, who presided in that establishment. Like virtually everyone not a child in town, she understood the position Brother Jobe had come to occupy among them, but she was not intimidated by him.

"You don't know me, sir," Karen introduced herself boldly, "but I'm writing up events and doings for the *Union News Leader* newspaper, soon to be coming out, and I would like to talk with you."

"Is that so?" Brother Jobe said. "Well, I've heard of that endeavor and I congratulate you on trying your hand with it. Your boss is a fine young man. I hope you all make a go of it."

"Do you know what they're up to, these Berkshire folks, with all this hooplah?"

"Well, I can't speak to this here particular to-do tonight. I'm just spectating like ever'body else. But, having parleyed with some of these folks, I would say generally they are up to some sort of mischief where the interests of this town are concerned, and that is strictly on background, not for attribution."

"Excuse me?"

"By that I mean off the record."

"I'm sorry . . ."

"It means I'm giving you information you can use, but you can't attribute it by name to me telling you. That is an old-times rule of the news bidness. Is this not something you know about?"

"No, sir. The newspapers were all gone before I grew up."

"Well you mind the rules and we'll get along just fine. I'm your anonymous source on this here story. Me and your mayor, Mr. Robert Earle, are still negotiating with these birds, trying to feel out the situation, kinda playing for time to see what they're up to. Mebbe farther along I'll go on the record and you can quote me direct. You see how this works?"

"Yes, sir. I think so."

"All right then. Here's what's up so far. They've got wads of colored paper that they call money and they want to swap it with us for our silver."

"Why would we want to go along with that?" Karen asked, rapidly taking notes.

"We don't. I suspect it's no more than an old-fashioned protection racket."

"What's that?"

"That's where, say, a man comes to you with a proposition: if you pay him x amount of money, he won't set your house on fire or poison your livestock."

"People really do that?"

"You bet they do. It's one of the oldest games going, clear back to the savage barbarian times of antiquity—you pay tribute and they leave you alone."

"That's just bullying."

"More'n that, it's criminal extortion in the statutes, but the reach of the law is a little short and limp these days, and folks'll try whatever they can get away with, I guess. This bunch dresses it up in a lot of sweet talk about equality and so forth. But it's just pushing folks around to get money."

"Did you meet with this Greengrass fellow?"

"I ain't had the pleasure yet. But I aim to, soon as he lands and they fluff him up for company."

"Is the mayor here?"

"I don't know, ma'am. I expect he's about in the crowd some-wheres, though I ain't seen him yet. Say, it looks like something's up over there."

Indeed, a fancy box wagon with green and gold painted trim had pulled up before the hotel entrance and the Berkshire visitors were swarming around it.

"Thank you, sir. I'll mind those rules, don't worry," Karen said. She left Brother Jobe beside the tree, squeezed through the crowd in Van Buren Street, and edged around to see the commotion on the other side of the box wagon facing the hotel. Two of the big-gest and strongest young men among the Berkshire visitors were off-loading some bulky object from a side door of the wagon's cargo box. It turned out to be an old-times metal wheelchair. Sitting in it was a shrunken, frail figure swaddled in a blanket, with a knitted cap on and a scarf wrapped around his neck and lower face, concealing most of his features except his perfect ski-jump nose and, viewed by Karen from the side, his conspicuous bushy gray eyebrows. He was out on the sidewalk for only a few seconds before two big young men hoisted him and carried the chair up the front steps of the hotel, and then they disappeared inside. Buddy Goodfriend, who had been chatting on the porch, excused himself and followed the retinue upstairs. The crowd groaned and broke into a confused hub-bub, as if they'd been expecting more of a show. Meanwhile, Flame Aurora Greengrass strode up against the balustrade on the hotel veranda and called out to the crowd in the street in a powerful voice.

"Listen up everybody! Dr. Greengrass will address you folks from the window of his hotel room in just a few minutes, so be patient. Thank you all very much for coming out tonight. He'll be with you shortly."

Brother Jonah, the hotel clerk, came out to hang candle lan-terns from hooks along the eave of the veranda. A choir of twelve teenaged Berkies assembled there and broke into another old-times song: "We Shall Overcome." More Berkies carried luggage and some wooden crates into the hotel. Upstairs above the veranda, at the center of the building, in a second-floor window illuminated with candlelight, the seated figure of Glen Ethan Greengrass could be dimly discerned behind a scrim of filmy muslin curtain. Electronic crackling emanated from somewhere behind him, followed by the words "test, test, test." The townspeople gaped at each other. They hadn't heard an electric public address system for some time. The Berkies were running a 25-watt amplifier powered by a modified General Motors alternator with two teenaged boys taking turns at the crank. A feedback squeal preceded the once familiar reedy voice floating on a cloud of magic amplification out the window and over the corner of Main Street and Van Buren.

"Hi everybody, this is Glen Ethan. It's good to have your ear," he began. "Given the existence of a broken polity, as set forth in the founding deliberations of the People's Republic, with those who, for reasons unknown, promoted the continued relevance of oppositional thought, the will-to-progress is facing a crisis of confidence. The old Fourteenth Amendment talks about equal protection under the laws, but notice it leaves out unearned white skin privilege. And that was never something that should go up to a popular vote, whether blacks, Latinos, women, LGBTs, the differently abled, or other minorities should be equal first-class citizens. There wasn't a popular vote whether Jackie Robinson should join the National League. No, but plunged in the fires of racism he came out standing proud on his own two feet, up from all fours, a man for his time, but first and always a man! This is what we call Smart Power, using every possible tool, leaving no one behind, showing respect even for one's enemies, trying to understand and, insofar as is psychologically possible, empathize with their perspective and point of view, qua traditional political philosophy, helping to define the problems and to find solutions to the dissolution of the old Dumb Power elite that has left such a vacuum of policy and purpose. No minority should have their rights subject to the passions of the majority. This is a fundamental bedrock of what we used to stand for. And I get very concerned that we have created in these times—what we refuse to address, or call it like it is—that we've created a second-class citizenship."

He paused for a moment. The crowd buzzed and nodded at each other, seemingly pleased with the oration so far.

"Friends," he went on, "let's stop the ruse. Let's quit pretending. The facts are there, facts are facts, and considering what is much more to the point, we have among us two types of citizens right now: citizens like me, who, if I choose to marry somebody, I can marry somebody from a different area, a different state, and then they will breathe the same air, drink the same water as we all do. You have to breathe it too, in this part of the country: the same air. But my point is can you expect everybody's wagon to be pulled by a different horse, or even the same one? Watch what you assume. Look closely at the word and you'll see there's an ass before *u* and *me* in it. In wintertime, of course, the air is the same as the springtime. It's just colder, that's all. The air is the same. Look, people, I've got a right that if I die, and I'm married, my spouse is entitled to the horse I rode in on because I sure won't be taking it with me where I'm going. I talked to somebody last night who is looking to establish what many deny, though they always say, for reasons unknown, that time will tell. Do you even know what time it is? Can you tell time? The man I talked to had had enough of the perpetual shell game, the chicanery and shenanigans, sports of all sorts, bread and circuses. Statecraft is all about the ebb and flow of influence, friends! Who eats the losses, who pays, who gets sent out for lunch, who eats your lunch. You follow me? Equality under the law! Proportional representation! Go tell it on the mountain! Democracy now! Who can doubt it? I know at the end of the day I would not be here, my family would not be able to put food on the table for me, if it wasn't for the ideals of America. What's yours is yours and what's mine is yours and vice versa. This land is your land . . . this . . . my land . . ."

The public address system strained. It sputtered, crackled, squealed, and popped. The voice of Glen Ethan Greengrass came out in a few more broken spasms as the wire connection in the cord between the mic and the amplifier appeared to fail.

". . . economic parity . . . earth minorities . . . inclusion . . . abandoned . . . unfinished . . ." he said, and then the public address went completely dead. A murmur of uncertainty ran through the throng in the street. Up in the second-floor window, Glen Ethan Greengrass could be seen gliding backward as a shadowy figure moved his wheelchair. More commotion erupted on the hotel veranda as Flame Aurora Greengrass came downstairs again and strode through the hotel lobby back to the porch railing overlooking the crowd.

"Excuse the technical difficulties, ladies and gentlemen. It's old equipment. Glen Ethan has to rest now. It's been a long journey from over in Massachusetts. But he wanted me to tell you how glad he was to see you all and he looks forward to a great alliance between the people of the Berkshires and the Hudson Valley."

Karen had been scribbling furiously in her homemade notebook. She dotted a final *i* and turned to the man standing beside her, Charles Pettie, the cheese boss at Schroeder's creamery.

"What did you make of that, sir?"

"Quite a show. The sound wasn't so hot."

"How about what he said?"

"Well, the parts that I could make out, I didn't understand what the hell he was saying."

THIRTY-FOUR

The four horsemen of Union Grove, traveling south on the Route 40 ridge along the Hudson Valley, reached the town of Harts Falls across the Rensselaer County line at midday. The town's favorable location on a fourteen-foot drop of the Hoosick River made it the site of two water-powered mills, one for grains, the other for lumber, both constructed in recent years. The Hoosick River then continued below the falls two miles farther to the Hudson River where commodities could be loaded on barges and shipped to Albany or other points. The mills together employed forty men in season, but at this time of the year there was no Rensselaer County grain to grind. An establishment calling itself Guff's Lunch Room operated in an old foursquare house between the two mills. There, the four travelers were able to buy a meal of hard-boiled eggs, cheese, and sturgeon chowder. The great prehistoric fish had made a comeback in recent years, along with the teeming shad. The chowder was made of five simple ingredients: milk, butter, onions, potatoes, and fish. It lacked salt and, when asked, the serving boy said they had none lately. The cheese had an off flavor and a greenish tint, as if it had been made by amateurs. A crude sign above the pass-through to the kitchen told diners, "Sorry no bread today." The dozen or so workmen in the front room seemed to be making up for the shortcomings of the fare with beer. The men of Union Grove ate quickly and didn't linger at Guff's.

By late afternoon the temperature had climbed into the seventies, the warmest day so far that year. There wasn't a cloud in the sky and the horsemen decided to sleep out for the night, the empty houses along the way being full of mold, vile odors, or intimations of lives that ended badly. Fourteen miles north of Albany, they made a camp in a grove of black locust trees off the old Irish Road, close by a clear-running rill that afforded them drinking and wash water. They picketed the horses on a high line so they wouldn't step on their leads, with enough slack so they could touch their noses to the ground. The horses had stopped to graze in fields of clover more than once during the afternoon ride, and Brother Eben had supplied them with feedbags and enough oats for the journey down.

With their ground cloths spread and saddles for backrests, the men swapped around various food items all had brought along, expecting to spend a night or two out of doors in this way. The rangers had slabs of rich corn bread pudding, larded thickly with crumbled bacon and a mellow jack cheese made by the New Faith sisters. They also had a jar of pickled peppers, links of dry-cured sausage, and a sack of honey and oat cookies. Teddy Einhorn had an especially fine array of traveling treats: a plastic box of spicy smoked jerked-mutton strips (a staple on the counter back at the store), store-made potato chips, thick and oily with lard, a large sack of walnuts, another of dried apple rings, and a fondant log rolled in hazelnuts made by his mother, another store favorite. Daniel had brought some hard flat biscuits he made on his woodstove in the office with cornmeal, barley, mashed beans, and shards of desiccated ham. It was the best he could come up with on short notice. Elam remarked that they might be used as roofing shingles when they built the new mule barn.

At dusk they made a fire and boiled rose hips and water in their steel cups on a little travel grill that Seth had brought along, a wire shelf from an old refrigerator. They watched the stars come out. Between the four of them, they could identify the Big and Little Dippers, Polaris the north star, Orion with his three-star belt, the M-shaped Cassiopeia, and Draco, whose long tail wound between the two dippers. A shallow band of turquoise sky persisted above the horizon to the west when a box wagon wobbled up to the intersection of the Irish Road, came to halt, and then turned down the brushy field toward the campsite. A woman drove while a man with another woman walked alongside the wagon through the field of poplar and sumac scrub, with buttercup, garlic mustard, and clover between. The driver pulled the wagon up broadside to the fire and stopped.

"Good evening, gentlemen," the man said, flicking up the rim of his stiff-brimmed hat with a knuckle. He might have been fifty years old, handsome in an actorish way. His hair, whisking out beneath the crown of his hat, was a wavy gold-silver mix in the firelight, and his smile revealed teeth in good order. He stood a lean six feet, wore a gray-brown long coat, well made in a pattern cut, and a blue wool sweater vest with a loose-collared shirt. His trousers were buff canvas, also pattern cut and machine sewn, tucked into brown satiny leather boots. The female beside him was twenty-four, wearing tight-fitted old-times denim trousers that emphasized her extravagantly long legs, an open wool cape over a scoop-necked sweater, and a floppy wool beret with a pom-pom on top. Her straw-colored hair framed a big-eyed look of innocence accentuated by her half-opened mouth, as though perpetually in wonder at some small thing of the moment. She was as tall as the man. The wagon driver was a few years older than the first girl, long torsoed and well made, with an orange kerchief about her head. She wore a long skirt and a tight wool tunic with not all the buttons fastened and some mounded flesh showing pale in the firelight. Before saying anything, the man swept his left arm back to gesture grandly at the side of the wagon. Painted on the cabin wall, in jaunty lettering, it read:

Dr. Lowell Spinner, Mobile Care Unit
General Medicine, Holistic Healing, and Surgery

"I take it that would be you," Seth said.

"Yours truly," Dr. Spinner said. "And these are my clinical associates, Kelly and Annette, nurse and physician's assistant," the latter being up on the wagon seat. They both smiled and gave a little wave. "How's your health, gentlemen?"

"Pretty durn good, considering these times," Elam said, and gave a glance to his comrades to see if they agreed, and all did.

"You're a plucky fellow," Seth said.

"How's that?" Dr. Spinner asked.

"Why, for all you know, we're a pack of rascally bandits, and here you drive right in amongst us like you do."

"I don't take you for that."

"Ever'one else does," Seth said with a high-pitched giggle.

"I take you for Christians," Dr. Spinner said and that got Elam's eyebrows hoisted.

"Why, that's us exactly," Elam said. "What was the giveaway?"

"I'd like to say I had a nose for such things. But actually, it was just a wild guess."

"Well, I be dog," Elam said and proceeded to give the visitors a one-minute history of the New Faith, its journey north, et cetera.

"But it's true the highway's infested with pickers, riffraff, and scum nowadays," the doctor said, "and so we'd feel obliged to take our rest tonight in your company if that's all right. You know, security in numbers."

"The more the merrier," Seth said.

"There's a clear brook yonder for your horse," Elam said. "Ours are on a picket line there."

Annette attended to their horse and the other, Kelly, fetched bed rolls from inside the wagon.

"We're between towns of substance," the doctor said, "having made our circuit of the country people and farmers the past five days, and I wonder if you might have some extra food to share with us."

"Things must be sparse among your farm folks here in Rensselaer," Teddy Einhorn said.

"They don't have much to trade with this time of year," the doctor said. "It's the six weeks want, as they say. We're lucky to get the butt end of a sausage and some hominy porridge."

"Why do you bother making the rounds?" Daniel asked.

"These folks need help, especially this time of year after the long winter and all. Many of their ills are nutritional deficiencies and I can treat them for things such as lack of vitamin C and like that. Since the big change of times, the country people have gained in cunning but lost in knowledge, if you know what I mean. Sanitation is poor out there, and that accounts for a lot of unnecessary sickness—if only they would wash their hands after contact with their animals. Anyway, when we make the rounds again as the seasons wheel by, they have more to give and we're better rewarded."

"Why don't you set up in a town practice?" Elam said. "Let them come to you?"

"Because they won't," the doctor said. "They'll just hunker down on the farm and try to wait out their troubles, grin and bear it, pray, resort to witch doctoring, and like that. No, they need us to come out to them."

Teddy Einhorn had broken out his remaining edibles and the others did likewise, putting the items on an old nylon poncho beside the fire. Seth burrowed into his saddlebags and produced a quart bottle of spirits.

"Good Lord, what have we here?" the doctor said.

"This here is a nice peppy rye whiskey from up our way," Seth explained. "Half our farmers run a distillery for cash money."

"And a new tavern just opened in the village," Teddy added eagerly. "Union Grove is up and coming."

"Maybe we should have a look up there," the doctor said. "What do you say, ladies?"

By this time, the two women had taken their places on blankets to either side of the doctor. Annette shrugged and Kelly nodded indifferently.

"We've already got a doctor in town," Daniel said. "Friend of the family."

"Well, you're a fine bunch of gentlemen, nonetheless!" the doctor said, rubbing his hands, surveying the treats at hand. The visitors ate daintily but steadily and consumed all the items that were laid out for them, and all had more than one pull on the bottle. In the distance to the east in the Taconic highlands a chorus of wolf howls erupted with eerie musicality. The animals had more of a presence in the region every year as the human population went down by increments. Daniel tossed another stout branch on the fire.

"I hate to hear those monsters go at it," Teddy said.

"They have their place in the order of things," Annette put in. Her voice was husky and resonant.

"It's good to be here among friends, isn't it?" Dr. Spinner said. "And what brings you fellows out on the highway this time of year?"

"We're off to buy a boat at Albany so we can resume regular trade from our town with the outside world," Teddy Einhorn said, and proceeded to explain about the trouble with Mr. Bullock.

"What does a boat like that cost?" Dr. Spinner asked.

Teddy was going to toss out a figure but Daniel interrupted him, saying, "I guess we'll find out in a day or so when we get down to the boatyards." He and the two rangers all cut disapproving glances Teddy's way.

"Yes, I'm sure you will," Dr. Spinner said. "Say, any of you fellows interested in a relaxation treatment before you turn in? Both of my staff are capable of administering such, and there will be no charge, thanks to your generous hospitality."

"How does that work, then?" Seth asked.

"It's no work at all," the doctor said. "You just retire into the wagon with your choice of this one or this one, and she'll take charge."

"What kind of treatment is that, exactly?" Seth asked.

"It's a kundalini chakra cleansing," Kelly said. "An energy release technique combined with deep tissue massage that is purifying, relaxing, and pleasurable. You'll sleep well, even on this hard ground."

Seth looked at the others. Their faces were skeptical in the firelight.

"Will it do for sore muscles?"

"That and a good deal more," Kelly said.

"Well, I'm your man for that," Seth said. "What I have to do?"

"Leave it to me," Kelly said.

She got up, went around the fire to him, and extended her hand. Seth took it and she pulled him up. He looked back at the others, grinning, as she led him up into the wagon from a door at the rear. There was some muffled murmuring from in there but then the doctor commenced a disquisition on the many diseases and illnesses that they had encountered out in the country this season. A muffled moan could be heard now and again from within the wagon as he spoke, and the box shifted rhythmically on its creaky springs. The bottle went around again more than once. Young Teddy Einhorn could be heard snoring under his bedroll when the doctor went off on a tangent about the presentation of vitamin B deficiencies, Wernicke's encephalopathy, glossitis, pernicious anemia, beriberi, pellagra, dementia. He always saw a lot of it this time of year, he said, with the grain shortages and few green vegetables yet available.

Eventually, Seth and Kelly emerged from the wagon. He wore a sheepish smile and a scent of bergamot trailed behind him from the oily liniment that she had applied all over him.

"Feeling improved, my friend?" Dr. Spinner said.

"Yes, and all for the better," Seth said, reaching for the whiskey bottle, which was drawn down by a good two-thirds. "I suggest you give it a try, brother," he said to Elam with wink.

"I believe I had a treatment somewhat like it just last night," Elam said.

"Oh? Is that where you was at?"

"How about you, young fellows?" the doctor asked Daniel and Teddy, who had stirred blinking from his slumber.

Daniel made a little hand wave and just mouthed, "No thanks."

"Sure?" Dr. Spinner said. "Annette here is renowned for her healing skills. You look like you're a bit bottled up, wound kind of tight. She can uncork you, son."

Daniel declined again and cut a glance at Teddy, who seemed to weigh the matter and reluctantly shook his head. Daniel bunched up the sweater he intended to use for a pillow. Soon he was asleep. Elam put more tree limbs on the fire and watched Dr. Spinner and his girls drift off all bunched up together under a big maroon wool blanket. Seth fell out after them.

It was in the cold and darkness before dawn that Teddy Einhorn started awake to the feel of cold steel on the soft hollow between his chin and his throat. The fire had burned down to a few embers. But a light went on as Dr. Spinner struck a match to a torch of

rags soaked in a blend of beeswax and turpentine. He jammed the
pointed end into the soft ground. In the lurid torchlight, the girl
named Kelly held a straight razor under Teddy Einhorn's chin.
Daniel sat half up, blinking. Seth merely unfurled his eyelids, careful not to move one fiber of muscle unnecessarily. Dr. Spinner and
his assistant Annette both held firearms, she a .38-caliber police
revolver and he a pump shotgun.

"Is this another of your treatments?" Daniel said.

"I'll treat you fairly if you hand over the purse of money that
you must be carrying to the boatyard," the doctor said.

"What's the matter with him?" Annette said, pointing the muzzle of her pistol at Elam's bedroll. The blanket was bunched up to
his hat and his boots stuck out the end but he remained motionless.

The doctor crept forward and kicked the blanket. His foot
met no resistance. He snatched the end of the blanket and yanked
it down. Between the empty hat and the empty boots lay all the
party's saddlebags.

"You out there, friend?" the doctor called into the darkness.

"Yes I am," Elam called back from an indeterminate distance.

"All right, then."

"It's not all right."

"Yes, I can see how you'd get that impression," the doctor said.
"Are you armed?"

"Why don't you make a move and find out?"

The doctor appeared to reflect on the proposition a moment
before calling back, "What say we just call it a draw, go our own
ways."

"What, so you can rob other folks?"

"I assure you this is not our regular disposition."

"Some vitamin deficiency drive you to it?"

"We don't want any trouble."

"Too late," Elam said. "You found it."

"Are you going to kill us then?"

"I'm thinking about it."

"What kind of Christian men would do that?"

"We're the avenging angel sort."

Nurse Kelly backed away from Teddy Einhorn and huddled beside the doctor.

"Don't let him kill us," she whimpered.

"There must be some way we can settle this without bloodshed?"

"Yes there is," Elam said. "Place your weapons on my bedroll."

They hesitated, but then did as he said, including the razor. It was only then that Seth threw off his blanket revealing that he had a pistol in his hand, leveled all the while at the doctor. Elam strode in from the darkness holding a length of an ash limb about the size of an old-times baseball bat.

"Interesting, how you managed that," the doctor observed. "May I ask what aroused your suspicions?"

"Why, everything about you."

"What's next, then?"

"I'll ask the ladies to hitch up your nag and prepare to leave," Elam said.

"Hop to, girls," the doctor said. They hurried to the task.

Dawn was breaking. The doctor shivered. The torch was nearly spent. Daniel got the campfire going again.

"I just want to say, it was damn nice of you boys to share your provisions with us last night," Dr. Spinner muttered in a new and humbler way. "Despite what has happened, I want you to know that I really am a physician and that we really do serve the poor country people abroad in the county. But in these times, unfortunately, opportunity sometimes presents temptation."

"That's a pretty way of putting it," Elam said.

The rangers would not engage in further badinage with the doctor. They allowed him to just stand in place a few minutes and marinate in self-reproach while the girls prepared the wagon.

"We're ready to go, Doctor," Annette called eventually.

"I don't suppose you'll give us our firearms back," the doctor said. "We need protection out there on our rounds."

"Against rogues like yourself?" Seth said.

"There's worse out there than us, I assure you."

"Worse than cutthroats?" Seth said. "It don't need to get worse than that."

"All right. Point taken," the doctor said. "Will there be anything else?"

"Yes," Elam said. "I'm going to give you a hearty thrashing to remember this by, and mebbe you will stick to your true calling from now on, which could be doctor or whoremonger or both, I don't really know, but I recommend you leave off thieving."

And so did Brother Elam work over the doctor Lowell Spinner with a length of ash limb until he was limping, discolored, and bleeding in a few places. The women helped him up into the wagon, groaning, and then, as the sun broke over a distant Taconic hilltop, they were on their way.

Thirty-five

By ten in the morning the next day the four horsemen crossed the bridge at the former mill town of Cohoes, just north of Albany, where the Mohawk River met the Hudson in a maze of side channels and islands. A catastrophic fire had burned down the old downtown several winters ago. The jagged shells of three- and four-story brick buildings and piles of rubble in Remsen Street gave the scene the tragic look of an old World War Two photograph. A few sad-faced pickers scuttled among the ruins with their scavenging sacks but otherwise the place was uninhabited. The desolation continued along the sleeve of the Hudson shoreline south from there, past the ruins of the old Watervliet arsenal, where the U.S. military produced cannon carriages and ammunition beginning with the War of 1812 and then other ordnance all the way through Vietnam. The chain of industrial ruins ran from there to within a quarter mile of the new Albany waterfront at the base of the State Street hill, atop which stood the abandoned state capitol building. The legislature had not met in years, the vast state bureaucracy had shut down altogether, and the last governor, one Eric Champion, had disappeared in the chaos that attended the first visit of the Mexican flu.

The Albany of the new times was now concentrated along the river, where a score of boatyards lay in the shadow of the old elevated Interstate 787 highway, along with a new street called Commercial Row, lined by modest warehouses, wholesale mercantile establishments, shops, and two hotels. Since the demise of Dan Curry, a commission of business owners and boatbuilders had swept the rest of Curry's minions and hangers-on out of town, set up a new lawful administration, along with a court and paid constables, and a dockmaster's office, and installed a full-time town manager, a former Target executive named John Alonzo.

With its current population at 3,200, plus many transient boat-men, farmers, and men of trade on any given day, Albany was a much bigger town than Union Grove. Teddy Einhorn had never been in a place so bustling with commerce and activity. When he was a small child the national economy was still roaring but, paradoxi-cally, the towns and cities were dead. All the action took place in the ambiguous suburban periphery of chain store shopping and free parking. He dimly remembered the whir and flash of automobile traffic with a kind of thrilling nausea. As he recalled, there were no places in that old-times world where people walked down sidewalks and gathered around shop fronts. The people of Union Grove did gather in his family's general merchandise store—especially in win-ter with the woodstove burning. But on any given day most of the town's denizens were off at their jobs on the farms of the wealthy landowners, or at the sawmill, the creamery, the cider house, and so forth, so Main Street was generally sleepy. Albany's growing Com-mercial Row housed a score of businesses and emporia, with goods going in and coming out from daybreak to sunset, people likewise coming and going, and many of them lingering outdoors in the fine weather to talk business or socialize. With the great urban sink of New York in breakdown and disorder, the rising sea level aggravat-ing its problems, and international trade all but discontinued, the locus of remaining commerce had shifted inward away from the coast to the interior of the continent, and the Hudson River had once again become the watery main street of the region. Albany had become a center of exchange with its favorable position at the top of the Hudson estuary, where the tides were still felt and the water was yet slightly brackish, and with its connections both north to Canada and west to the vast inland empire of the old "flyover" states.

Much of the Albany business was wholesale trade, with produce and goods coming all the way from the Great Lakes down the Erie Canal and Mohawk River, and a lot of it went out as quickly, bound for markets as far away as Quebec or downriver to Kingston and Newburgh. The businesses on Commercial Row ranged from farm products to fishmongers, butchers, tools, farm implements, animal feeds, textiles and fabrics, pipes and fittings, crockery, cutlery, hardware, boots, pattern-cut clothing, sail lofts and chandlers for the outfitting of watercraft, even a new icehouse. Much of the merchandise for sale in these establishments was not new but salvaged old-times goods, and many stores had back workrooms where men and women labored to repair things and make them as much like new as possible. Customers most cared that these articles worked well and might last, not whether they were the latest thing or not.

As the men of Union Grove rode down the street, Teddy exclaimed to himself over and over, "This place is up and coming!" so enthralled was he by the noise, color, and motion. Seth and Elam remarked to each other how the scene had improved in just a year, looking much less like a frontier settlement than when the odious Dan Curry ruled. Daniel drew down the brim of his hat as he passed through Commercial Row, his thoughts harking back to Franklin, Tennessee, and his momentous deed there. His nerves entered a state of high alert as he glanced around and his eyes locked here and there with the casual gaze of shop clerks, tradesmen, and passersby. He had not been in a town of consequence since his weeks in Franklin, approaching two years ago, and even here among his own people, far from the Foxfire Republic, he fretted over the price on his head.

A new hotel, the Empire, had been erected the previous fall on Commercial Row, across from the dockmaster's headquarters. The hotel featured a fourth-story domed cupola at center and a sixty-foot-long, two-story veranda along the whole frontage. A big sign across the left side of the veranda said OYSTER BAR. Farther down the street, at the south end of Commercial Row, stood the poorly contrasting Slaven's Hotel, where the rangers had stayed the last time, now strictly the haunts of the lowest boatmen, while business people flocked to the Empire. The day market of pushcart vendors and farmers' stalls was also established in the vicinity of Slaven's, and pigs, some of them large, dangerous boars, roamed down there at night rooting in the gutters after the stalls closed.

A man named Grasso had established a day livery in the side street called Maiden Lane, a corral where the horses of day travelers could be rested, watered, and watched over while their owners went about business in town. The four men of Union Grove left their mounts there. The rangers, with their shopping list from Brother Jobe, went off at once to scout their purchases among Minnery's General Stocks, Hyde's Salvage and Made Goods, Van Voast's Import and General Trade Articles, and Aulk's Provisions, the food wholesaler. Daniel and Teddy Einhorn made for the boatyards. They all agreed to meet at the Oyster House of the Empire Hotel at four in the afternoon.

As the modern age waned, the practical design of inland waterway trade boats devolved to models long forgotten during the decades of motors and cheap oil. In the new times, the workhorse of the Mid-Hudson Reach was a flat-bottomed, shallow-draft, sprit-rigged sailing barge in the twenty-five- to forty-foot-long range, a homely but sturdy and capacious craft, easily maneuverable with leeboards to prevent side slipping, cheap to build, able to be managed by a crew of two, and with plenty of room on and belowdecks for cargo. They were denoted "Germantown tubs" because the prototype was first built in that village midway between Albany and Poughkeepsie.

Weems's Boat Works was one of several establishments that trafficked in previously owned watercraft along the Albany riverfront. Daniel and Teddy came to it after inspecting many boats in other yards, none of them suitable for one reason or another—spongy hulls, filthy bilges, bad rigging, sails not included, overpriced—and found one there that fit all their requirements. Ned Weems, the proprietor, had lost his twenty-year-old son the previous fall when a wooden loading crane up the street at Orvo's Marine Supply snapped and a stone counterweight flew out of its basket and cracked the young man's head open. Consequently Weems had a soft spot for young men, especially those seeking to improve themselves in difficult times, and gave the pair from Union Grove a very fair price for the tub called *Katterskill*, twenty-eight feet long, with striking red sails. They settled for ninety ounces of silver. They said they would sleep on her that night and sail away in the morning if that was all right. Weems said it was, and he would tidy up the cabin for them, and invited them for supper but they declined. Having business up the street, they thanked Weems and then the two went their own ways.

Teddy Einhorn had a long list of provisions to see about for his father's store and Daniel went in search of newsprint and things his father had asked for, in particular guitar and violin strings. They found mostly what they were looking for. Daniel bought five reams of 24 x 36-inch double-broadsheet paper at Van Voast's and was informed that weekly newspapers like his were starting up in Albany, Amsterdam, and Rhinebeck. He learned, too, that a weekly mail packet had just begun service between Albany and Peekskill and that he could arrange to distribute copies of his newspaper on it.

The four reassembled at the Oyster House bar at the appointed hour. The place glittered with luxurious furnishings. Its large room ran clear through the building from the veranda to a beer garden in the rear. Above the chair rail, mirrors lined the room, which amplified the available light. All the brass fixtures were brightly polished and crisply ironed white tablecloths lay on the tables. Even at four in the afternoon the bar was lively with patrons, many of them refined-looking, including not a few women of business, and the bar thrummed with conversation. A wire basket filled with lemons stood on the bar, a startling sight, and the burly bartender shook fancy drinks. A platter of smoked Lake Ontario whitefish and pickled onions greeted all comers gratis on a sideboard across from the bar.

Supper at the Oyster House was their reward, Elam said, for making the journey. Their boss had allocated extra coin for it, and they could order whatever they liked. The men found a table outside in the back and recounted their adventures of the day over a brew advertised as Cropseyville lager, reddish brown with a toasted malt flavor and no hops. A boy waiter, so young his voice had not changed, persuaded them to try the Cortland Blue Point oysters that had come to flourish on the reefs along the Tappan Zee, and when they were finished with six each of those he talked them into another order of Ossining Wiannos, both types served with horseradish cream. The menu consisted mostly of articles that came out of the river: shellfish, sturgeon, shad, bream, spring bluefish, smelt, eel, and white catfish, grilled, fried, smoked, or configured in chowders and stews. Potatoes, onions, carrots, parsnips, and turnips figured in. But even in Albany fresh vegetables were in short supply that time of year and there was no fresh fruit whatsoever besides the lemons, which came all the way from Maryland, the waiter said. Wheat bread was listed at a price that put it out of the question, but there was plenty of corn bread and ample fresh butter, now that cows could graze again. They ordered supper and, before their plates arrived, Elam announced that he and Seth would begin their return journey that evening and would have a good three hours of daylight if they left around five o'clock. They would take all four horses back, of course, as prearranged. They'd leave Daniel's and Teddy's bedrolls and personal gear at the livery. They expected to be home in Union Grove the following evening, unless they were detained by cutthroats, pickers, regulators, bushwhackers, bandits, or other riffraff, whom they were prepared to vanquish, Elam said with a grin.

Before they left, the rangers gave Daniel and Teddy a wad of receipts for the goods they'd bought, to be loaded on the new boat. The merchants' system was to convey bulk purchases to the docks by handcart, and would do so in the morning when presented with the papers. From dawn to dusk Commercial Row was full of carts pulled by cart boys who made up a special society of their own in the town. They lived in the orphans' "mansion" on James Street behind the crumbling elevated freeway. The late Dan Curry had set up the establishment, one of his few acts of civic generosity, because he had been an orphan himself, and had grown up sleeping in abandoned houses, and went for days without meals. At the mansion, the orphans ate as well as the merchants who employed them and slept in real beds.

Finally, Elam toasted the table, saying the journey down had been a fine one in good company—even including the antics of Dr. Lowell Spinner—and wished "the boys" a good trip home on their new boat. They were to look for a new landing on the river near Bullock's when they got home. Seth gave Daniel the .38-caliber revolver they had taken from Dr. Spinner's girl, saying he hoped there would be no reason to use it, but that having it would surely be a comfort. Elam kept Dr. Spinner's shotgun. Then the rangers drained their glasses and left the Oyster House.

"The boys" lingered out on the terrace. Later arrivals to the Oyster House seemed to prefer the glitter of the main barroom to the back garden, so there was no pressure to vacate their table. Daniel asked the waiter to bring any newspapers lying around and the boy came back with the latest edition of the *Kingston Pilot*. The news of doings in the rogue Foxfire Republic concerned one Trey Dansey, successor to the assassinated president Loving Morrow. Dansey was threatening to "capture and crucify" Milton Steptoe, president of New Africa. Armies of both breakaway nations had engaged in April in a series of battles between Corinth, Missis-sippi, and Florence, Alabama. The Foxfire government claimed the engagements amounted to a draw, but that raised the question: why was the fighting so close to the Tennessee border? The dispatch implied poor military leadership and low troop morale on the Foxfire side. There was no further news about the search for Loving Morrow's killer. Almost two years on, the incident seemed to have disappeared into the maw of history like a bawling animal of the wilderness sinking in quicksand out of earshot of God Almighty. In other news, the federal president Harvey Albright vowed to "rebuild the northern electric grid one county at time." A murrain thought to be viral rinderpest was killing cattle in the St. Lawrence River valley. A spring nor'easter had drowned Providence, Rhode Island, and it took two weeks for the waters to recede. The scant international news mentioned the ongoing breakdown of China into many autonomous states, despotic fiefdoms, and contested dominions. A devastating drought parched the breakaway nation of New South Wales, formerly of Australia. And there was a short item about the lynching of the Argentine dictator Ricardo Scarpa, plus five of his ministers, leaving the resource-rich country in a state of anarchy. Daniel read all the stories out loud to Teddy while they nursed their beers and enjoyed their leisure.

"The world is going to hell," Teddy observed.

"Everything changes, everything passes," Daniel said.

A gentle twilight descended over the back garden like a pleasant dream when Daniel spied a familiar face inside at the bar, about fifty feet away. It startled him and set his insides churning. This figure was the rough, brawny, moody boatman Daniel had journeyed west with on the Erie Canal almost three years ago on the barge *Glory*, Randall McCoy, the man who had tried to sell Daniel and his traveling companion, Evan Holder, into an indenture at the Lockport flight of locks, then under reconstruction by gangs of laborers. Daniel and Evan had barely escaped that fate, in the course of which Daniel discharged a pistol into the gut of one Bryan Farnum, superintendent of the works. They never learned the fate of Mr. Farnum, though they knew that a gang of mounted regulators was sent out after them. In the event, Daniel and Evan made it to Buffalo, and then slipped their pursuers on a boat out of Buffalo harbor. A week later that boat, a cargo scow not unlike the Germantown tub they'd just purchased, foundered in a storm on Lake Erie off the shoals of Sandusky, where Evan was lost.

"How about we go back to the boat, settle in for night?" Teddy said, quaffing the last of his beer. "It's been quite a day and I'd like to try her out for sleeping. Daniel . . . ?"

"Huh?"

Daniel's attention was riveted to the scene inside the barroom. It was McCoy, all right, no doubt, right down to the braids in his beard. He was in conversation with two other men at the bar and it did not seem an especially friendly confab. He looked physically slighter than Daniel remembered him, his hair a little thinner on top, and his once raffish clothing shabby. McCoy's face seemed ruddier, too, and Daniel watched him knock back two whiskeys in a span of a few minutes. One of the other two men placed a hand on McCoy's arm and McCoy brusquely batted it away.

"What do you say, Daniel? Get on back to the boat?" Teddy asked. "I found some honey nougats at Aulk's. We can share. Watch the moon rise."

"You go on," Daniel said, his gaze still fastened on McCoy.

"What's in there?" Teddy asked.

"Someone I thought I knew from when I was away," Daniel said.

"Are you going to have a glass with him?"

"No," Daniel said. He did not say that he was going to kill him, which was exactly the objective that had spun itself out in his mind as he sat and watched. "Do me a favor. Fetch my bedroll and things at the livery and bring them to the boat. I'll be back by-and-by."

"Well, all right," Teddy said a little diffidently and made to leave the table.

When Teddy was gone, Daniel rooted in his pockets and found an envelope of the machine-made guitar strings, one of several sets he'd purchased, and took out the third or G-string, sturdy brass-wound steel wire. He made loops at each end and formed rolling hitches around two metal spoons that remained on the table from the meal. He thrust the apparatus into a jacket pocket, keeping his eye on the scene within the barroom. The boy waiter returned and asked if he wanted a cigar, the Red Hook Monarch being the house specialty, he said. Daniel said maybe next time. Meanwhile, the two men palavering with Randall McCoy left him abruptly at the bar, apparently not on the friendliest terms. McCoy remained there slumped on his elbows and calling for two more whiskeys while Daniel watched. The sky above the outdoor dining terrace was filling with stars. McCoy demonstrably slapped some coin on the bar, as if he were angry, and walked toward the front entrance, unsteady on his feet. Daniel waited ten seconds and followed. Mentally, he was back on Channel Island, incandescent with the deadly training he'd received there.

At this hour, Commercial Row was quiet but not deserted. The merchants were just closing up, sweeping the plank sidewalks in front of their establishments. A few stragglers of the day's business lingered palavering in the feeble lantern light. Here and there a cart boy made his way with a late load, men rolled barrels inside a warehouse, a few wagons plied the carriageway, some loaded and some empty. Daniel caught sight of McCoy, listing from side to side, heading south on the sidewalk. He followed at a respectful distance. Soon the street life petered out altogether, the sidewalk ended, and a darkened zone began where the empty stalls of the farmers' day market stood between the heart of the waterfront and Slaven's Hotel at the other end, under a tangle of decrepitating freeway ramps. He and McCoy were the only pedestrians there. Up ahead, a candle lantern hung from Slaven's disorderly barroom, the type known among boatmen as a gully den. More lights burned within and the chords of a concertina playing a reel in a minor key carried up the street. A pig furtively crossed the street and disappeared in a lot filled with weeds, rubble, and trash. Daniel quickened his step and moved lightly until he was virtually on McCoy's heels, then spoke his name to the back of his head, which brought McCoy to a lurching stop. He wheeled around almost losing his balance.

"You following me?" McCoy said, peering intently into Daniel's face. His breath was sour and Daniel noticed that his lower front teeth were missing.

"I guess I am."

"Whaddaya want?" Then a little flare of recognition. "Say, I know you!"

"Yes you do."

"Help me out."

"Springtime, three years ago."

"Yeah, she comes around every year," McCoy said. "Look, here she is back again. Thank Gawd for that . . ."

McCoy cackled and wobbled in place, drunker even than Daniel had first supposed.

"The Lockport flight," Daniel said.

McCoy's features scrunched together at the center of his face. He canted his head sideways, one way and then the other, peering harder.

"Boil me for a shad," he muttered. "You! You rascal! Didn't you make a fine escape, though?"

"I did."

"That was some trick, you slippery sonofabitch. You know I lost my boat over that business?"

"Is that so?" Daniel said.

"Oh, it ruined me."

"You deserved it. You were going to sell us into slavery for twenty-five dollars."

"Wait just a minute," McCoy protested. "The indenture ain't slavery."

"It might as well be. How is it different?"

"Well, if you live through your term, you're free to go."

"In other words, you were going to let them try to work us to death."

"You two looked pretty sturdy," McCoy retorted and giggled. "Hey, it wasn't personal. Just business."

"I see," Daniel said. "And what business are you up to now?"

"I do a li'l this, a li'l that. I miss the canal. The lovely, easy life."

"It was a lovely," Daniel agreed. "Who were those men you were bickering with at the Oyster House?"

"Them? Oh, I work for them sometimes."

"Doing what?"

"You don't want to know," McCoy said darkly. "You had a friend along. Younger. What was he called?"

"Evan."

"Yes! Evan! A lively boy! Oh, we got on well, him and me. What happened to him?"

"Dead."

"Oh? How's that?"

"Lost in a storm on Lake Erie. Washed overboard."

"Sorry to hear that. She's bad when she's angry, Lake Erie is. Shallow, you know. That wind whips her right up, quick and fierce. Come on, le's have a drink—"

"What happened to Farnum?"

"Huh?"

"The super at Lockport."

"What happened!" McCoy echoed, with an edge of manic hilarity. "Well, you shot him, didn't you?"

"Yes I did. Did he live?"

"'Course not. He was dead before sundown. I forgot your name."

"Daniel."

McCoy's rheumy eyes opened wide. The concertina music emanating from Slaven's barroom segued into a merry, frenetic jig, "The Stool of Repentance."

"Daniel," he said. "Hold on now. You were in the paper a while ago. I saw the item. Why, there's a pretty price on you. Am I right?"

"That's correct," Daniel said, reaching into his pocket.

"And not just for shooting whatsisface. What else was it you done? I forget."

"It doesn't matter now."

"It was big as I recall. 'Course it matters."

"Not for our purposes."

"What purpose is that?" McCoy said.

"To answer one question."

"Being what?"

"How would you sum up your life."

"Sum up my life?"

"Yes. In a few sentences," Daniel said.

"Hmph. You really wanna know?"

"Yeah."

"All right, here goes." McCoy burped. "Grew up rough. Survived the troubles. Prospered on the Erie. Was beloved by my mules. Lost it all. Drank too much. And here we are. Why do you ask?"

"Because it's over now," Daniel said, and in a swift, deft motion he whipped the guitar string garrote over Randall McCoy's head and, pulling the spoon handles, tightened the apparatus around McCoy's throat, at the same time dragging McCoy on his boot heels by main force into a darkened empty market vendor's stall a few yards away.

"This is personal," Daniel whispered in his ear.

McCoy bucked and thrashed violently, but he was not as strong as he once was, and in a few minutes it was over. Daniel left him there under a plank table, knowing that the hogs would be back.

He left the scene at once, the frenetic jig from Slaven's gully den gaining in speed and violence as he departed. Walking casually toward the heart of Commercial Row, he felt the peculiar sensation of returning to himself after being not entirely present for an interval. The training still resided inside him like a sinister tenant dwelling in the attic of the house that was his psyche.

THIRTY-SIX

Beginning at sunrise, frantic with worry, Robert searched for Britney in the obvious places, though he was mystified as to how or why she would remove Sarah's body, or where she might take it, or what she might do with it wherever she took it. He had a look, first, in the family barn around the corner, where he discovered that Cinnamon the cow was in distress from not being milked for more than two days. He took care of her, dumping two whole pails of warm milk in the sand and leaving a third steaming in the chicken run. Anyway, Britney was not there, nor had anyone seen her at the New Faith compound, nor anyone along Main Street, including at Einhorn's store. He hiked a little way out of town to the rusted steel railroad bridge that crossed the Battenkill at the place along the river where Britney liked to gather wilds and there was no sign of her there. He peeked inside the ruins of the Kmart on his way back to town. Weeds were growing in there in places where sunshine came through the partially caved-in roof. He went to Daniel's print shop, knowing that his son was out of town, and knocked on the padlocked door there. Nothing. He tried the Congregational church. Nobody there, not even Loren. He trudged over to the Schmidt farm, then the Deaver farm on Pumpkin Hill, and then across town to the Weibel farm on the back side of Schoolhouse Hill. No one had seen Britney. It occurred to him that she might have just walked away from Union Grove altogether in a fog of despair, with no particular destination in mind, just walked away in torment and misery until she dropped, or got sick, or met roughnecks on the road, or encountered a dangerous animal, a catamount, a bear, a pack of wolves—of which, he was cognizant, there were plenty around these days. Or, he began to wonder, perhaps she had lit out with some destination in mind—Glens Falls? Bennington?—to deliberately start life over once again. But what about Sarah?

By midafternoon Robert himself had entered a fog of exhausted despair, partially induced by walking more than twelve miles all day without eating anything. He returned home to rest for a little while, found a pot of bean and potato soup in the meat safe, where the mice could not get at it, and devoured all of it cold. He couldn't help himself after that but fell asleep on the living room sofa amid the splinters of Sarah's shattered violin. And when he woke up it was with a vivid intuition, the residue of a dream, that he had missed looking in the most obvious place he should have gone to first: the childhood home up the North Road out of town where Britney had told him more than a few times she'd spent the happiest years of her life. So he pulled himself together and left the house again and hiked past the New Faith compound on the North Road out of town. Sure enough in a little while he came upon the handsome old white farmhouse all crowded around by sumacs, lilacs, box elders, and climbing vines, with its scorched addition and the yard filled with early spring wildflowers, the mustard cress, pink cranesbill, and subtle wild red columbine. The afternoon was windless, the temperature a perfect 70 degrees, and the landscape utterly silent except for the chatter of songbirds. As he stood in the empty road before the house, he noticed his chore wagon parked in the weeds and it was as if a great weight slid off his shoulders.

He stole in through the broken kitchen door, off all but one of its hinges, and entered. He paused to listen, hearing nothing, then crept stealthily toward the front rooms and it did not take him long to find Britney lying in the window seat wrapped in a blanket with her daughter's corpse. Britney was spooned up against the body with her long pale hair falling over the edge of the seat. She did not acknowledge Robert's presence. He was not altogether sure for a few moments that she was alive, but the room was filled with light and watching closely he soon observed the blanket rise and fall with her breathing.

"Brit," he said gently.

She did not reply. He stepped closer carefully. He wanted to lie down next to her and spoon against her in grief, but there was no room left in the window seat, so he squatted beside her and then slid his legs out so he could sit on the floor right next to her. He ventured to reach up and touch her and she allowed him to, and soon he was stroking the side of her neck by her ear, and rubbing the warm hollow between her neck and her shoulder, and after a little while Britney started to shudder soundlessly in tears, and Robert rose to his knees and buried his face in that familiar soft, warm, fragrant hollow between her neck and shoulder, saying, "Oh, Britney, I love you so much." He didn't repeat himself, but eventually her small hand swung out from under the blanket seeming to search and reach, and he took it and squeezed it and said, "I'm here. We're all here. Together."

Thirty-seven

Karen Grolsch got leave from Carl Weibel, a kind and understanding employer, to take a half day at the poultry barns for personal reasons. She had not taken a sick day all year and he considered her a good and valued worker. She had done such an excellent job as duck boss that Weibel was the chief supplier of cured duck sausage and preserved duck (bottled in its own fat) in Washington County. She walked back to town in lovely weather just after noon, changed into clean trousers and sturdy shoes, and set off on foot for Stephen Bullock's plantation, intent on talking to him about his quarrel with the town, the results to be published, she hoped, in the newspaper.

She had been to Bullock's place once before, at a levee a year ago to celebrate the rescue of his boatmen from Dan Curry's hostage racket in Albany. That had been a sultry summer evening of the purest festivity, unalloyed even by religious ceremony, and virtually everyone in town had been invited, though perhaps only a hundred or so actually came. Bullock himself was in fine form that night, such a striking figure with his splendid clothes, tall boots, long silver hair, and clean-shaven face, like a heroic figure in a fine painting from the nation's founding days. There was music and dancing and tables groaning with things to eat—old-times treats of meat and sausages in buns and little cornmeal crackers that the older people called taco chips and endless drafts of cider and beer—and swags of magical electric lights from tree to tree, and music amplified through loudspeakers, because Mr. Bullock was able to make his own electricity. Karen had gotten rather drunk herself and allowed a young man named Bruce (surname unknown to her), who worked on Bullock's orchard crew, to kiss her and fondle her breasts in the hayloft of the great barn while the band played the beautiful "Two Rivers Waltz" for the dancers down below. So her memory of Bullock's world was, on the whole, tinged with enchantment and she marveled that so much had changed in relations between Bullock and the town since then.

She had plenty of time on the way there to rehearse her introduction and review the questions she had for him. She had no appointment—a bygone formality in a world without phones or mail—but hoped for perhaps a quarter hour of his time. The journey was about four miles on foot, an hour and half at her moderate pace. Karen was aware that she had hardly ever in her life traveled any distance alone, apart from her daily trip to the farm. She had gone to other levees, holiday festivals, and dances out of town, to Battenville, Salem, and the great farm estates around the county, but never alone, always with friends, and usually in a cart or wagon. She was aware also that possible danger lurked along the lonely road outside the safety of the village. Mountain lions, or catamounts, were so brazen now that they sometimes ventured into village streets in broad daylight. And then there were those human predators reputed to roam the countryside looking for opportunity. She had never met a bandit, though she did not doubt they existed in more than rumor. So this spring day, in perfect weather, she marched along in confidence enjoying the feel of her own healthy, young body and her happy aspiration to be become more than just the duck boss at Weibel's farm.

She rambled past the intersection where the car dealers had battled for supremacy of annual sales, their vacant parking lots now miniature forests of poplar and sumac, the showrooms empty shells. The sight of these ruins and the monumental waste they represented made her momentarily angry. She knew that the people running things in the old times understood that their way of life was a dead end, and she could even imagine that they were so locked into their systems and habits that they were more or less trapped. What she couldn't grasp was their utter failure even to imagine another plan. So they took it as far as it would go and then just let it all crash. She remembered riding in cars, but they were all gone by the time she was seven years old, and then incrementally so were all the other things that had made life so comfortable. Yet she didn't especially miss it. She was used to the new ways and the new times, and ordinarily she didn't suffer from how it was now.

Along the River Road, Karen came to a slow water eddy along the Hudson where five New Faith brothers under the direction of Shiloh, the engineer, were building crib docks in preparation for the arrival of the new town boat. Brother Shiloh, a broad man of sharp angles, recognized her from town and she said she was out gathering the news for the soon-to-be-published newspaper, and so he gave her a little tour of the works. Shiloh's men were building log cribs—six-foot-square boxes like little cabins, joined together with half-inch iron pipe through auger holes, each box then filled with rocks, laid out in a line from shore, to be decked over with cedar planks coming down from Hokely's sawmill. The men had gotten two parallel sets of cribs in so far and hoped to have four altogether in place before the boat arrived, creating a slot protected from the current and the wind on two sides.

Karen scribbled notes as Shiloh showed her around and explained everything in his lilting Carolina accent. The new sights and sounds excited her tremendously: the smell of the skinned logs and the fishy overtone of the river, the afternoon sunshine, the bright little breeze off the water, the men working in the sun, in and out of the water, with their shirts off and muscles rippling. Mostly what excited her was the change of scene. It was so refreshing to be somewhere other than Mr. Weibel's poultry barns, or even at home. She told Shiloh that she was going to interview Mr. Bullock.

"Well, I'm not versed in the politics of it all," he said, "but as you get up the road you'll see that the squire has got a perfectly good boat docked there, not being used, along with a warehouse, and it's a dang shame that it's come to this. I had to pull these men off the hotel, which we are close to finishing. By-the-by, the boss is sending a wagon to fetch us back to town around five if you would like to hitch a ride."

"Thank you," Karen said. "I would appreciate that."

"Yeah, it's all uphill going back," Brother Shiloh said. "Mind if I ask: are you married?"

"No, I'm not."

"Got any feel for Jesus?"

"Probably not the way you mean."

"How is it you folks up here can't get that Jesus spirit?"

"We're not against him," she said. "I guess we don't think about it as much as you do."

"Well, you're a sturdy gal, anyways," he said admiringly with a smile. "My wife passed with that Mexican flu. You come back later and ride home with us, hear? And enjoy your session with the squire. I hear he's quite a character."

"Yes sir," she said, and she continued on her way.

Thirty-eight

The Reverend Loren Holder turned up at the New Faith compound after breakfast and found Brother Jobe in his headquarters, the old principal's office just inside the old high school's lobby. The whole building smelled of corn bread.

"Morning, Rev," Brother Jobe bellowed. "Glad you're here. I've sent a boy over to the mayor's house twice already, but he's not there, nor—"

"I have some bad news," Loren interrupted him. "Robert's girl—you know he lives with the young widow—"

"'Course I do. What about her?"

"She's lost her daughter."

"Lost?"

"Dead."

"What?"

"Tetanus, apparently."

"Oh, dear," Brother Jobe groaned. He backed up stiff-leggedly and sat on the edge of his desk. "Just like that?"

"I was there. She was in convulsions. Her muscles just kind of seized up. It was terrible."

"What'd the doc do?"

"He wasn't there."

"Why didn't someone fetch him there?"

"He'd been drinking at the tavern. Hard. Some of the men took him home in a wheelbarrow. He was too far gone to work any miracles. As it happened, Jason LaBountie was with the girl—"

"The ding-dang veterinarian? A little girl ain't a goat."

"Whatever you think of him, Jason's a science man."

"Well, he didn't save her, did he?" Brother Jobe snapped back.

"There was nothing anyone could do at that point. He told me to ask Jeanette, the doctor's wife, for some particular medicine that might have helped and she said they just didn't have any, so . . ."

"Lord."

The two men just remained silently in place, gazing into the linoleum, as though memorializing the dead. Eventually, Brother Jobe spoke: "You seeing about a funeral?"

"I don't know where any of them are. Robert, Britney. They're not at home, and the child's body is missing too."

Brother Jobe sighed.

"You don't suppose they went and done themselves in, do you?"

"No, I really don't see that."

"You know how people get in these times. Grief and all."

"Yes, I know."

"Well, then there ain't nothing to do but wait. Sooner or later they got to turn up."

"There's something else," Loren said.

"Huh?"

"There's seven dead cows in a pasture out on Coot Hill. All shot clean through their heads, one bullet each."

After a stunned interval, Brother Jobe said, "Ain't that elegant?" His thoughts then naturally turned to the curious personage called Sonny Boy, and he thought how he would like to wring his neck like a pullet's. "When it rains, it pours, don't it?"

"They belonged to a farmer named Temple Merton," Loren said.

"I've met Merton. Sold him a mule last September. Good man and a good farmer. He was on TV back in the day."

"Yeah, well, he sent one of his hands over to Einhorn's store and the message came up to me a little while ago. Apparently, he had a visit at his place the last day or so with one of these out-of-towners."

"You don't say? I wonder if it was the illustrious Mr. Greengrass himself, or his number two. Did you hear him address the multitudes from his hotel window last night?"

"I missed it," Loren said.

"Oh, it was a dilly. Near as I can make out, the man's a raving maniac. They're trying to put the squeeze on us, you know."

"I heard they asked for donations," Loren said. "For what, I didn't get."

"Subscriptions, they call it, for being part of their so-called federation, which ain't nothing that we would benefit from, far as I can see. In my opinion it's all a ding-dang smokescreen and a con. They think we're going to hand over good silver in exchange for their paper trash money. It's tribute, plain and simple. This Greengrass sumbitch is just a common grifter dressed up in socialist do-good glad rags. His troops don't amount to much. Buncha pimply-faced kumbaya-singing jackanapes. But I suppose he's got something up his sleeve, some kind of backup out there. What it's come to now with these dead cows is we really got to think about defending ourselves, and I mean start by running these birds out of the county ASAP. My next-in-charge man, Joseph, has been over to meet with the squire, to see if we can raise some strong-arm from his bunch. Well, Bullock flat-out refused to lend a hand. Now, if you can raise up mebbe twenty-five capable men from town, I can arm them. We've been laying in firearms and ammunition all year wherever we can scare it up—I hope this don't offend your sense of pastoral decorum."

"No, you're right, we have to defend ourselves," Loren said.

"I'm glad you see it that way," Brother Jobe said. "I expect my two rangers to return from Albany in twenty-four hours. They have tactical training and can lead the men we pull together. I've got perhaps thirty in this outfit can handle a fight. Greengrass and his inner circle are put up at my hotel. I aim to let them stay there long as they please, keep them close to hand, so to speak, and under a watchful eye. Of course, we should have expected something like this sooner or later in a land that's gone both lawless and godless. By the way, I know I ain't the only bystander who's noticed the doc has crawled into a bottle. Have you spoken to him about this, I wonder, in your pastoral capacity?"

"Yes, I have," Loren said. "Frankly, I think it's getting the better of him. I don't know what to do about it."

"Mebbe I'll parley with him," Brother Jobe said. "Put a different view of things on the table for him to chaw on. Oh, and let me know when you catch sight of our friend Mr. Robert Earle. It troubles me greatly that he and his girl have been touched by such tragedy."

THIRTY-NINE

Karen Grolsch proceeded north on the River Road, passing by the nameless wretch nailed to a tree by Bullock. There was even less of him remaining than since Brother Joseph's recent encounter: just a skull with a few leathery patches of flesh and some sparse strands of hair. Beyond the initial shock of recognition, she quickly regained her composure and began to make a sketch of it in her notebook. Then she plodded on, coming at last to Bullock's driveway. Before she arrived at the gracious turnaround at the top, between the handsome old manse and the great barn, she was met by a sturdy, dark-haired man of middle years with an air of authority and a rifle, which he proceeded to sling over his shoulder when he discerned that the visitor was a woman.

"Good afternoon," Karen said. "I've come from town to see Mr. Bullock."

"Do you have an appointment?" the man asked. This was Michael Delson, a car salesman in the old times and now a household attaché and security aide to Mr. Bullock.

"No, I don't," she answered.

When asked, and she stated what her business was—reporter for the *Union News Leader*, a newspaper starting up in town—Delson couldn't hide his amused interest.

"How can I get a copy?" he asked.

"You might have to wait a while," she replied. "The first one hasn't come out yet. But it will."

"We could use a newspaper around here," he remarked.

He took her to the kitchen door of the manse and left her in the care of the cook, Lilah Jaffrey, who put her at a table and gave her some tea, an herb blend of rose hips, Roman chamomile, and lemon verbena, and some buttery oat cookies. Lilah did all of the talking, while she adroitly evaded answering any question put to her by Karen. She talked about the old times and the children she had lost, and the husband who abandoned her when the old times lost traction and slipped into the new because there was no more office work for a municipal employee in the Glens Falls city purchasing department, and the unusual weather in recent years, and what a fine gentleman Mr. Bullock was, and how fortunate she was to occupy her place in the household, and eventually both women retreated into globes of silence while Lilah went about larding a leg of lamb for the Bullocks' evening meal. An hour went by, then another. Karen considered leaving but she felt that she had already made a certain investment of time and effort, and after exactly two hours and twenty minutes Michael Delson reappeared and said, "Come with me."

They passed through a center hall as wide and as well furnished as most people's parlors—or "living rooms," as they used to be called—and came finally to the library, where the (to Karen) near mythical Bullock himself slouched in a padded leather executive chair behind a large old desk carved with spiral pilasters at the corners and other neoclassical decorations. His moleskin vest was open and he had a two-month-old gray tabby kitten on his lap enjoying having its cheeks massaged. Karen stepped forward, introduced herself, and extended her hand across the desk. Bullock took it and gave it a squeeze rather than a shake. He gestured at the empty chair off a corner of the desk and she took it. He did not offer any explanation as to why he'd kept her waiting for more than two hours.

"That's a sweet little kitten," Karen said. "They're not so common in people's houses anymore."

"We like to keep some of the old customs alive here," he said. "Who doesn't love a kitten?"

"People have become superstitious about them," she said. "We have cats in the barn where I work. To keep the rats down."

"And where is that?"

"Mr. Weibel's farm. I'm the duck boss."

"Oh, his ducks are famous for miles around. You're a busy girl. I was informed that you also work for a newspaper out of Union Grove that is launching at some unspecified future date."

She told him about the forthcoming *Union News Leader*. And about the proprietor.

"I know his father very well. Years ago he built a Japanese teahouse for me. He brought his boy around then to help. A quiet, serious boy. Good worker."

"He's a grown man now, sir."

"Of course. I understand he left town a couple years ago and returned last Christmas. The minister's boy left with him. Didn't come back."

"Evan Holder," she said. "It's sad. He was a few years ahead of me at the big school, when it was still open. He was lively, full of fun."

The kitten stretched, jumped off Bullock's lap, and trotted out of the room. Bullock swiveled around in his chair to a counter behind him where a tray with a decanter and some glasses stood. He poured himself a drink.

"Want one?" he said. "You look like a grown woman to me."

"Thank you, I will. What is it?"

"My own whiskey. Made from my own barley. Distilled about three hundred feet from where we sit." He swiveled back around and handed a fine crystal pony glass to her across the table. "How do you like being in the center of the universe?"

"Is that what this is?" she said.

"It is to me," he said.

"Did you know there's a skull nailed to tree about a quarter mile south of here on the River Road?" she said.

Bullock recoiled slightly, then recomposed himself. "Yes," he said.

"Look, I made a drawing of it."

It was hardly what he expected. She opened her notebook and passed it across the desk. Examining it, Bullock took such a deep draught of his whiskey that he nearly drained the glass he'd just filled.

"That's quite good," he said, wincing, and passed it back to her. "Why'd you do it?"

"Well, I don't have a camera," she said.

"Point taken."

"Who was he?"

Bullock made a face. "Some riffraff caught stealing a horse. His name is recorded in a file somewhere around here. Offhand I forget."

"The people in town think that a feud exists between you and them," she said, pencil poised above a fresh page in the notebook.

"Is that so?"

"You stopped sending your trade boat to Albany."

"For now."

"They're running out of things in town. Foodstuffs, other goods."

"Oh?"

"Are you surprised, sir?"

Bullock's demeanor darkened. For a moment his mouth became a hard thin line.

"It became burdensome for me," he said after some reflection. "You know my boatmen were detained at Albany a year ago and held hostage for ransom. It was very inconvenient. And they could have been killed."

"They were brought safely home, though, by men of Union Grove."

"That's true. But I lost all the cargo that went down with them, including many barrels of good jack cider, worth a small fortune. I had to eat the loss."

"Eat it?"

"So to speak. Write it off. Kiss it good-bye. There's no such thing as insurance anymore, you know. In other words, the loss was all mine. So, you ask, why don't I want to keep at it? Well, because it's a very risky business. Those barrels of cider represented an entire apple crop."

"Don't you need some things from elsewhere too?"

"We're pretty self-sufficient here. When the need arises I'll weigh the situation and decide what to do."

"The town is having to get its own boat now."

"Good. They can enjoy the benefits and shoulder the risks. I'm aware that the Jesus people are building a landing downstream of mine."

"Isn't this all a duplication of effort, sir?"

"Redundancy is not necessarily a bad thing. It makes for resilience."

"How do you mean?"

"A healthy ecosystem has more than one way to keep itself alive."

Karen scribbled furiously in her notebook.

"You were elected magistrate last year," she said, taking a fresh tack.

"Didn't run, though," Bullock said. "Got elected despite my wishes. Served anyway. Was dragooned into it, really. Then was disrespected by the town during my term of service. So I handed in my resignation." He swiveled around and poured himself another three fingers of whiskey, then turned back. "You know what I want to talk about? Baseball."

"Huh? There is no more baseball."

"Of course there is. We play here."

"What does baseball have to do with anything?"

"Not so very long ago—last fall, I think—I had a conversation with your mayor, to whom we've already averred, Mr. Robert Earle, father of your newspaper editor, about getting a county baseball league together. Now I think that's an idea that deserves a bit of publicity in this so far alleged newspaper. What could be more entertaining on a summer evening! Get some friendly rivalries going! The equipment is easy enough to make. Why, the boys in my harness shop stitch up a damn good horsehide ball and fine fielder's gloves. Bats are easy to make and some of the old metal ones are still around. I don't know why we can't get started on this. It's May already! What else have you got going for yourselves over there?"

"I'll mention it if you want."

"You bet I want you to. Someone should tell Robert to get off his duff and start organizing over there!"

"Sir, you might not believe this but there are some people in and around town who just aren't getting enough to eat right now."

"Well, it's that time of year, the six weeks want."

"They're even running short of cornmeal."

Bullock rose out of his seat, came around the desk, and sat against the front edge of it, closer to Karen, looming. He seemed more than ever an imperial presence from a bygone age with his long white hair, tight riding pants going into fine boots, and broad shoulders thrust out of his moleskin vest. He gave off a tantalizing aroma of horse sweat mixed with whiskey.

"This is a new period of history, young lady," he said. "There are no more guarantees, no social safety nets. People have to learn to shift for themselves. I grant you, they haven't had much time to get used to it, but it's the new reality. Has anyone actually died of starvation over there yet?"

"Not as far as I know."

"Their diet may be more restricted for a while, and they may slim down a bit, but they'll be eating better soon. Surely this is the historic norm for the human race, not the extravaganza of pizza and granola of my halcyon years. That was the exception. Funny, in the old times they would have been delighted to lose a few extra pounds before summer. By the way, you're healthy looking. In fact, you have a fine figure, if you don't mind me saying. What's your secret?"

"Mr. Weibel provides generous food shares. He plans well. And I get all the duck eggs I want."

"I can do better than that. Want to work for me?"

"No, sir."

"Why not? It's nice here. I've got everything Weibel has going and then some. Does Carl have baseball over there?"

She had to smile. "No . . ."

"You'd be surprised what it adds to a small, isolated society. Have you got a boyfriend back in town?"

"Now you're embarrassing me, sir."

"Well, you put me on the spot. It's a simple question."

"No," she said.

"You're sweet on Robert's boy, though, aren't you?"

"I don't know him very well."

"I've got some very fine unmarried young men over here. Big, strapping, healthy specimens."

"I don't want to leave town, sir," she said. "Splendid as the life here may be—"

Just then, Bullock's wife, Sophie, came into the library. She was radiant as ever, having been out in her gardens all day, supervising three women who actually did all the digging, grubbing, planting, chopping, and pruning. She wore a simple armless, straw-colored linen sundress with a lace-up bodice that afforded some décolletage.

"Oh . . . !" she said, stopping short at the sight of Karen. "Am I interrupting?"

"We were just playing *Meet the Press*," Bullock said. "This young lady represents a newspaper starting up in town."

Bullock made introductions. Sophie swept to her husband's side at the desk. He hooked an arm around her waist. Karen rose from her chair. Sophie held out her hand and Karen took it.

"A newspaper," Sophie said. "How exciting. Did you reveal all our secrets, darling?"

"Ha! I'm an open book."

"Will you stay for supper?" Sophie asked.

"Thank you. I must go back to town. I have to get up early for work."

"Oh?" Sophie said. "You have another job?"

"She's Carl Weibel's duck boss," Bullock said, full of amusement.

"Ah," Sophie said. "Well, quack quack."

"How are you getting back?" Bullock asked.

"I'll walk."

"It's four miles!" Sophie said. "Mostly uphill. Oh, Stephen, have one of the men run her home in the gig."

"No, please," Karen said. "I'd prefer to walk. It's just an hour or so and there's plenty of daylight."

"Don't say we didn't offer."

The Bullocks, arm in arm, showed Karen to the door. As she walked back down the drive to the River Road, she was keenly aware of the bastion of solidarity the couple presented, and how skillfully she had been manipulated. Getting the news was not as simple and straightforward as she had imagined. People were subtle and more than the sum of their apparances, she mused.

It happened that Brother Shiloh was still waiting for her at the new landing when she got to it. The other men had already departed in a wagon. He had a big brown mule named Bunny with him and a simple stock saddle aboard. He wouldn't take no for an answer and they doubled up. She tried to avoid pressing her bosom against his back, but it was not really possible. He minded his manners, though, and rode her directly to the house she shared with her mother. All the way home she wondered about Bullock's world and its relation to hers, and how complicated it all actually was.

Forty

Seth and Elam had made twenty-five miles so far that day riding north up the old state highway 4 along the east side of the Hudson, with an excellent chance of making home before sunset, when they came upon a man in the ditch off the right shoulder of the road. There was no human settlement along this stretch of the road, midway between the depopulated villages of Stillwater and Starkville, just old farm fields going back to poplar scrub on the left side and third-growth forest running a quarter mile to the riverbank on the side where the man lay groaning in the weeds. The two rangers each had a riderless horse in train behind his own mount. The stranger lay in the tender spring wildflowers on his back looking up at a clear blue sky, the pink and yellow blossoms such a contrast to his grievous wounds. Only his lips moved but no sound came out. Seth dismounted right away and, panther-like, crept toward where the man lay.

"What happened, friend? Who done this to you?" he asked the man, who appeared to be no more than twenty-five years old, with neatly trimmed beard, brown hair made stringy with sweat, and well-made clothes that would have been elegant if not soaked with blood. His shoes or boots were missing and his pockets were turned out. By now, Elam had come over.

Seth took the man's hand. It was limp. He blinked his eyes strenuously as sweat poured into them. His breathing was shallow. Seth mopped his brow with his sleeve. Elam fetched a water bottle and tried to give the man a drink, but he appeared unable to swallow, or even comprehend that someone was trying to help him. The water just ran off his lips and down his neck.

"Let's have a look you," Seth said. He'd done some informal medic duty in the Holy Land after his unit was shot up at Nir Banim and their corpsman took one in the occipital lobe. He unbuttoned the wounded man's shirt, ran some water over his chest and stomach to wash the blood away, made an assessment, then rose up, took Elam by the arm, and led him ten paces up the road.

"There's at least three entry wounds up above, maybe more below," Seth said in a whisper, his words floating upwind, away from the wounded man's hearing, if he still had any. "Whoever done it shot him up more'n necessary and botched the job even at that."

"Is he a goner then?"

"I dunno. What do you want to do?"

"Can he be moved like this?"

"Pretty high percentage it would kill him," Seth said.

"I was thinking, maybe one-in-a-thousand shot, we could get him to the doctor."

"It's about ten mile and two, three hours or more to get back."

"We can't put him down like a dog," Elam said. "It wouldn't be Christian."

"'Course not," Seth said. "Okay, we got to sit with him and wait for it."

"He's a gentleman, from the looks of it," Elam said. "Someone gonna be missing him. Maybe a wife."

Seth used one of the man's socks as a sponge and dabbed cooling water on his forehead. Elam sat in the weeds behind him to shade his face from the bright afternoon sun and fanned him with his hat while he sang some hymns of the Appalachian gospel in a scratchy baritone: "Pass Me Not O Gentle Savior," "In the Garden," "Blessed Assurance," "Softly and Tenderly." Seth joined in on harmony for some. After an hour and a half, the man's condition had hardly changed.

"I never seen nothing like it," Seth said. "He flat-out refuses to die."

"Well, that settles it," Elam said. "We got to take him back, starting this minute."

"All right then, let's get him aboard."

They got him up over the empty saddle of Daniel's big black horse, Raven, in train behind Elam's mount, and trussed him to the tack so he wouldn't shift about.

"Kinda wish the sumbitches that robbed him might try the same with us," Seth said, "so I could blow them to Gehenna."

"That wouldn't be Christian, neither, old son."

"Yeah, well . . ."

Forty-one

Robert slept fitfully either sitting up beside the window seat where Britney lay with her dead child or curled on his side on the dusty floor just beneath them with his jacket up around his ears, falling in and out of febrile dreams of his shadow self battling with other shadows. The birds singing at first light woke him from his last ragged interval of slumber, in particular the sad, low, persistent coo of the mourning doves who nested in a dormer upstairs. The big parlor, shrouded in encroaching greenery, was still dim at this hour. As his head cleared, Robert detected a sour note of decay in the room, and knew at once where it came from, and felt impelled to finally take charge and do what was required.

He sat up, torqued his body around, and lay his hand on Britney, just above her hip, and squeezed it gently. She stirred.

"Can you hear me, Brit?" Robert said. The sound of his own voice reverberated painfully off the hard surfaces in the room.

She didn't respond vocally but he was pretty sure she heard him.

"We can't stay here like this forever, and now we're going to do what we have to do."

She continued to lie there in stoic silence. Robert hoisted himself to his feet. Without any further talk he went back out the rear of the house. He had seen the shovel lying in his chore wagon on the way in. He got it and searched for a suitable place to dig. About fifty yards from the back door he found a semiclear patch surrounded by the barest remnants of what had once been a garden fence. Here, the saplings were sparsest and he was able to cut through their young roots into friable soil. He dug for a good hour, at the end of which he had a hole that left him shoulder deep. It also left him frantically thirsty. He searched around the property and found an old hubcap with about a quart of rainwater in it. It did not look very clean, but he thought for a moment and took a chance. The water almost gagged him it was so sour, but it stayed down. He went back and tidied the corners of the hole. Then he jammed the blade of the shovel in the pile of excavated dirt and went inside.

Britney hadn't moved.

He knelt down beside her again and pressed his cheek against the side of her head. "It's time, now," he said, and kissed her behind her ear. She began shuddering again, but she allowed him to physically assist her getting up. It was difficult for her. She was stiff and terribly dehydrated. She wobbled on her feet but soon was able to stand on her own. She would not look at him but just stared into the floor, crying. He kissed her again on each cheek, and she allowed him to envelop her in his arms. At last, she responded instinctively by reaching around and squeezing herself into him. Then her crying turned vocal, a terrible keening wail, punctuated by hungry gulps of air and loud sobs. Robert didn't attempt to tell her to stop, or to say anything. He just allowed her to feel the full weight of her suffering. She continued until the sun crept over Moon Hill and sent beams of bright light streaming through the foliage into the room, and she let go of Robert and finally looked up into his face.

"I believe you came here because this is where you want to lay her to rest," Robert said.

Britney nodded and wiped the moisture from her face. Then she moved back to the window seat, bundled Sarah into the blanket so she was fully covered, and stepped aside. Robert took up the limp bundle in both arms. The rigor mortis had abated. He carried Sarah out the back door and the contrast between the beauty of the day, with all its birdsong, flower scent, and insect buzz, and the inert bundle in his arms struck him with a force like a blow. Britney followed him, blinking and weeping again as she stepped back out into the world. Robert carefully set the bundle into the bottom of the hole and then stood over it. Britney came to his side. They stood silently at the grave for a long time. Finally, Robert felt compelled to speak.

"We commit the body of Sarah Watling to . . . your care," Robert said, his mouth quavering. "Sarah was much loved and will be much mourned. We come into this world of struggle and we all depart for the same destination and we do the best we can in this beautiful mystery while we're here. We don't know why you took our Sarah —"

"And we'll try not to hold it against you, you twisted sonofabitch," Britney growled.

Robert waited to be sure she was finished.

"Rest in peace, dear Sarah. You'll live in our hearts."

Robert upbraided himself for speaking so unoriginally. They stood silently again for an interval. Then Britney went to the dirt pile, grabbed the shovel, and began heaving the earth back into the hole. Robert came around and she gave the shovel to him. She went to the rear of the house and sat on the steps there in a little patch of sunlight watching until Robert finished filling the hole. Then he took Britney home, pulling her the last half mile in the chore wagon because she was so weak with hunger and thirst.

FORTY-TWO

Having successfully received and loaded their cargoes early in the morning that day, tipped the cart boys, and acquainted themselves with the rigging, Daniel Earle and Teddy Einhorn trimmed their sails and heaved out of Weems's boatyard on a breeze blowing warmly from the southwest, perfect for tacking back and forth in a broad reach heading north up the Hudson River for home. Daniel took the tiller and Teddy, jumping gleefully about the deck in his bare feet, with his pants rolled up, worked the lines and the leeboards. They passed through the locks at Troy and again at Waterford, just above the junction with the Mohawk River, and finally at Mechanicville—each a silver dime toll to go through—and had good sailing thereafter the rest of the day, fighting a mild but steady current that kept their progress to about two miles an hour, about half the speed that a full-grown man might walk the same distance—the difference being that they carried a ton and a half of cargo.

After a long, bright, successful day of voyaging, watching the peaceful vistas of the countryside pass by, the sentinel forests and occasional bottomland fields, and the few little towns struggling to become a bit of something they once were before modernity dragged them down a cul-de-sac, Daniel and Teddy anchored while there was still some daylight in a little channel between narrow Splinter Island and the place where Mink Creek entered the river. There they ate a supper of delicacies, things purchased at Albany by Teddy for the store: pickled herring, smoked eel, salted ham, hard Duanesburg cheddar cheese, and a very dense sour loaf of dark groat bread made of rye, oats, and ground pumpkin seeds. Then, through a warm and spectacularly lingering twilight, they enjoyed the remaining nougats Teddy had bought the night before along with a sweet cider fortified with jack brandy, sold under the label Dickstein's Coxsackie Malmsey. It advertised itself on the label as a "reliable water purifier and vitality tonic." Teddy took out his pipe and tamped a thumb of burley tobacco into it. Daniel took out one of four cigars he had stashed in his inside coat pocket and lit up. Tobacco had lost its bad repute now that many farmers in the Hudson Valley grew it for cash and there was no more government to stifle production. They had managed to find machine-made matches in Albany and were bringing back a six-gross lot of matchboxes, sure to be a big hit at Einhorn's store. As the curtain of night fell they observed a fire burning on a hillside distantly to the west, not knowing whether it was a brush pile or somebody's house or a camp of pickers. Behind them to the east coyotes periodically yipped. The moon was not quite up yet, but its corona glowed above the treetops. Overhead the familiar constellations took their age-old positions again.

"It's grand being on the river, isn't it?" Teddy said, blowing a smoke ring in the still air.

"It's a fine life," Daniel agreed.

"You don't ever say much about what you saw when you were away," Teddy said. "I know you were on the Erie Canal. What did you see?"

"I saw most the length of it from Amsterdam to Lockport," Daniel said, dragging on his cigar, eyes squinting as he did. "It's lazy and sweet and slow and dreamy on the Erie Canal."

"Doesn't it go all the way to Buffalo?"

"It used to," Daniel said. "At the time, they were reconstructing the five-step flight of locks at Lockport, and that was as far as we went."

He didn't mention the trouble they met there: the threatened indenture, the shooting of superintendent Farnum, the desperate escape on Randall McCoy's mules.

"How does the Erie compare to sailing the Hudson River?"

"Oh, it's just as pretty but easier work. There's no rush to anything. You just walk your mules up the towpath, the sun shining, flowers blooming, and it's level all the way. The mules are gentle and obedient as if they know it's a great life for them too. It takes hardly any effort to tow a barge on quiet water where there's barely any current."

"What were the towns like?"

"Real nice," Daniel said. "A pretty girl in every one. Friendly people. Usually a tavern with good, cheap meals, nice beds."

"You got to Buffalo, though."

"Oh yes, we walked it from Lockport. The weather was ideal. Like now."

"Well, what happened there?"

"Nothing."

"You traveled on, though. They say you saw a great deal of America."

"Who says?"

"My pop," Teddy said. "The store is the center of town chatter, as you know."

"Of course." Daniel dragged on his cigar some more and took a long pull on Dickstein's Malmsey.

"So what happened then?" Teddy said.

"We, uh, bought a boat in Buffalo," Daniel said. "Something like this one. We thought we'd carry cargoes around the Great Lakes to make some money for a while, at least the summer, then figure out the next thing."

"What was it like sailing the lakes?"

"The lakeshore down along Pennsylvania and Ohio is one fine farm after another, practically shoulder to shoulder, a solid line of them, prosperous as can be. They were kind to us. The towns are nice. Hotels with restaurants. Here and there a newspaper. Good food. Pretty girls."

"Do they have the electric out there on the lakes?"

"No. It's like here that way."

"But it's prosperous."

"The land around the lakes is excellent."

"Okay," Teddy said, taking his turn on the bottle. "But then something happened to Evan."

"Well, yes. We were in a bad storm on Lake Erie, near Sandusky, where there are many islands and rocky shoals. Our boat sank in the storm. We got separated."

"You never saw him again."

"He was swept away."

"Did you search for him?"

"I was clinging to the capsized boat for dear life in a storm."

"Do you think he might have made it to land?"

"It's not out of the question. I never knew how far off the shore we actually were."

"But you were never able to find him."

"No. I never did see him anymore after that."

"I knew him slightly in school," Teddy said. "He was two years ahead of me. A great jokester. Everybody liked him."

"That he was," Daniel agreed.

"So then what happened to you."

"A ship came along, a schooner, a grand thing. I got rescued by it. It took me to Michigan. I stayed there all summer."

"Doing what?"

"This and that."

"Farm labor?"

"No."

"You don't want to say?"

"It was a big outfit. I did all kinds of things. Learned a lot."

"Okay. Then what?"

"I went south for a while."

Teddy waited for Daniel to tell him what he did down south, but Daniel just puffed his cigar. The moon came up behind them. They watched bats flit over the river eating the night caddis flies that were emerging from the muddy bottom.

"They say you were in that place calls itself the Foxfire Republic," Teddy ventured.

"Yes, I did get down there," Daniel agreed.

"What was it like?"

"Friendly people. Pretty girls."

"You say that about every place. What'd you do there."

"Nothing."

"You must have done something."

"I hung around for a bit. Then I had enough of it and came home."

"That's all, huh?"

"I met a girl there."

"What was she like?"

"She was complicated."

"But you left her there."

"It happened that she died," Daniel said.

"Oh, I'm sorry. What of?"

"She met with misfortune."

"What sort?"

"Let's just leave it at that."

"Oh . . . of course . . . pardon me."

"But there was no reason to stick around after that, so I left, and eventually I managed to get home. It wasn't so easy." He tossed the stub of his cigar over the side. It hissed when it hit the water.

"So many people dying before their time nowadays," Teddy said.

"Oh, it was her time," Daniel said. "I'm going below and turn in. Check the anchor lines before you come down, okay?"

FORTY-THREE

Brother Jobe stopped at the front desk of the hotel, where Brother Jonah sat reading a book.

"What you studying on?" he asked.

Jonah held up the spine to show: *Mayday!* by Clive Cussler. "It's about airplanes," he said.

"What do you know about airplanes?"

"They're a wonder. Maybe we can try to build one?"

"I was you, I'd study up on mules instead," Brother Jobe said. "You seen any sign of that Mr. Goodfriend or Mr. Glen Ethan Greengrass?"

"No. That Goodfriend, he comes and goes. The woman does too. Mr. Greengrass, I don't think he's left his room since they checked him in."

"That so? What number is it?"

Jonah told him. Brother Jobe went directly upstairs and knocked on the door. One of the teens opened it, a very large boy, well over six feet tall, but with a head that seemed as if it belonged to another body: small, undershot chin, a twenty-three-hair mustache, pimples on the forehead. Brother Jobe could see past him to where Glen Ethan Greengrass sat in his wheelchair facing the window, the back of his head to the door. Another large boy sat in a chair farther in near Greengrass. The overgrown boy who answered the door laid a finger across his lips and said, "Ssshhh. He's sleeping."

"Right in his chair like that?"

The guard shrugged.

"I'll come back," Brother Jobe whispered. "Tell him I'd like to parley."

The boy practically shut the door in Brother Jobe's face. He went back downstairs. At that evening hour on a weeknight the establishment was quiet. Two men from the Schmidt farm sat at the bar while Brother Micah puttered at his sinks. But Brother Jobe was more than a little interested to see Ainsley Perlew sitting at a table in the back, farthest from the door, eating supper. He crossed the room to him, his boot heels striking the new varnished plank floor sharply.

"Mind if I sit down?" he asked.

Perlew looked up from his soup bowl as though the sight of Brother Jobe mystified him. Brother Jobe took a seat anyway. He watched Perlew slurp his soup for a minute.

"That was you killed them cows out on Coot Hill, wasn't it?"

Perlew helped himself to another spoonful of the bean soup, watching Brother Jobe as he did.

"You don't talk much, do you?" Brother Jobe said. "But you hear what I'm saying."

Perlew swallowed and something like a smile, but not quite, drew his lips into a taut line.

"Did Mr. Greengrass or Mr. Goodfriend put you up to that?"

Perlew shook his head.

"Oh, it was your idear, then?"

Perlew stared back blankly and put his soup spoon down.

"Sonny Boy, I don't think you know who you dealing with," Brother Jobe said, and then he touched his right index finger to the outer corner of his right eye. Perlew's own eyes followed it. Brother Jobe captured his attention as surely as he might pin an odd specimen of moth to a cork. He easily entered the young man's mind. But what he found inside was a bewildering void like a hall of mirrors made of shimmering jelly. He was inside for only a moment when the mirrors seemed to shatter as if the place were booby-trapped, and then he found himself outside again seeing nothing but Perlew's pale, emotionless face, the boy's mouth slightly agape as if it were necessary for his breathing. Brother Jobe had never encountered a personality so strange and fractured. Perlew took up his spoon again and helped himself to more soup.

"You're an interesting piece of work," Brother Jobe said.

Perlew continued to eat his soup but did not grudge up a word of reply.

"You seem to be enjoying your supper," Brother Jobe continued. "When you're done, collect your things and get out of here. I don't care if the sun's down. You can sleep out in the fields. And when you wake, keep marching straight back to wherever you come from. If I hear that you're at large in the county after tonight I'll be sore vexed. If I hear about any more dead livestock, you'll find there is hell to pay."

Perlew's eyes lit up and he emitted a strange, brief high-pitched laugh.

"Are you the Devil?" he asked.

"People do wonder," Brother Jobe said.

FORTY-FOUR

Circumstances had gotten Duane Terrio, aka Wawanotewat, He Who Fools Others, and his eleven "Indian" warrior comrades into just the right mood for some mayhem. They had been sleeping rough for more than a fortnight since leaving Massachusetts, bathing in the cold, spring-fed brooks that flowed into the Battenkill, and eating irregularly. They had received their instructions and found their way easily to Temple Merton's farm near Summit Lake, and watched the house from the margin of the woods when twilight stole over the property, and saw someone light the candles in the kitchen and a room adjacent, and watched as figures moved around in there. Rough living had also necessarily sharpened their senses, and even at this distance they could almost smell the comfort, cleanliness, and nourishment emanating from the establishment. The aroma of corn bread baking was enough to excite their most savage instincts.

Six of the visitors stole down and brazenly entered the house through the open kitchen door while six waited in the woods. Once inside, they shoved the cook and the serving girl into the hallway. The women ran shrieking from the house out the front door. Three of the warriors remained in the kitchen, seizing everything that looked like food, stuffing their faces, and rifling the pantry, cabinets, drawers, bread boxes, pie safes, and meat safes for more. Terrio and two of his closest associates burst directly into the adjacent dining room, where Merton and his girlfriend Lorraine Moncalvo were about to address their supper of spring lamb and boiled potatoes arrayed on a platter for them.

"Hope we're not interrupting," Terrio said. He and the two others helped themselves to the tender pink meat and the parsleyed potatoes with their fingers. The platter was clean inside a minute. They washed it down with the bottle of Merton's own farmhouse cider, which they passed around, and wiped their hands on the table-cloth. "Go in there and bring me something else to eat," Terrio said to the Indian on his right, a former truck mechanic from Holyoke named Wally Eaton, now called Makkapitew, He Who Has Large Teeth. The one to his left was a former blackjack dealer from Aga-wam, Massachusetts, Eddie Wilczek, now known as Segenam, Lazy.

Oddly, Temple Merton's prior experience in the movie business, though years removed from the present moment, prompted him to admire the costuming and makeup of the noisy band that had just invaded his house. Terrio's blackened face with red eye sockets and a white spot on his forehead seemed particularly authentic and frightful, though his irises were blue. Both Merton and his girlfriend stared boldly at the invaders as if sheer contempt could disarm them. Meanwhile, Makkapitew returned with a large dish towel wrapped around various cheeses, links of hard sausage, a ragged piece of corn bread, and also a jar of preserved spiced pears. Terrio opened the quart-size pear jar at once, pried up the sealer lid, and drank up all the sugary juice before stabbing the nine-inch blade of his hunting knife into the fruit inside.

"What tribe are you boys?" Merton inquired.

"Me?" Terrio said. "I'm one-sixteenth Pocumtuc. The other guys, a mixed bag. Some are just honkies."

"Are you going to kill us, rape the women?"

Terrio laughed. "Naw, we're just going to burn your barns down and steal some stuff."

"Why stop there?" Merton asked.

"We have our instructions."

"Are you with that Berkshire outfit?"

"We're on contract for them. You have a lot of nice stuff here. I'm surprised nobody's taken it from you before."

"Just lucky, I guess. We're kind of off the beaten path."

"Then it's an honor and privilege to be first. Say," Terrio turned to Lorraine, "that meat was outstanding. There was some kind of rub on it. Something piney."

"Rosemary, salt, and a little honey," she replied.

"I'll remember that," Terrio said. "I like to cook myself when I'm not living off the land."

"What's the point?" Merton asked.

"Of cooking? You're kidding me. People have to eat. Why not do it right?"

"No, of pretending to be savages."

"That's not fair," Terrio said. "First of all, I'd call it going native, not savage, though I admit sometimes we have to play a little rough—"

He was interrupted by the sound of something crashing in another room.

"Like I was saying," he continued, jacking his thumb toward the hallway. "No, this is not like those historical reenactment clubs of old, you know, the Renaissance fair freaks and the Civil War dudes. Some of us think this—whaddayacallit?—this *collapse* has a ways to go yet and we're kind of seeing whether the Native American lifestyle might be an option for the long haul. I mean, you've got your situation here, right? What would you call this lifestyle of yours? White colonial settler?"

"I call it necessity," Merton said. "It's not a lifestyle or an act."

"Let's not have a semantic argument," Terrio said. "Don't get me wrong, I respect what you've got going here. I kind of wish I'd had the foresight to get something like this together. But I was leading a normal life—ha!—and got blindsided by what happened. I was one of those dumb bunnies still waiting for energy independence and economic recovery when the bomb went off in DC. Then, believe me, I got it, good, hard, and fast. And some of the guys at the casino—I worked over at the SunEagle in Chicopee—we put this going-native idea together. I've got to say, it's toughened us up a lot. Sometimes I'm out there on the land, looking up at the stars, and it's like old Christopher Columbus never landed. Well, we better get on with the job. I suppose this flatware is just stainless steel."

"That's right."

"Got any real silver?"

Merton didn't answer. He folded his arms.

"Okay, then. Where do you keep your coin?" Terrio persisted.

Merton remained silent, his chin jutting defiantly, so Terrio sprang from his seat and commenced smacking the older man about the head. Lorraine rose to defend him but Segenam rushed around the table to restrain her. In the process, he couldn't resist groping her abundant bosom. She screamed.

"You okay in there, sir?" a voice called through the open window from out in the back garden, one of Merton's hired men, nine in all, who had rushed from their quarters on the property when the two servant women raised the alarm.

"Not exactly," Merton yelled back, before Terrio whacked him again.

"What do you want us to do, sir?" the hired man yelled back.

"You don't have to turn this into a shit show," Terrio advised Merton.

"Just stand by," Merton hollered out the window.

Meanwhile, the other six of the Indian band came shrieking and whooping out of the woods with brands they had set aflame and ran down the pasture to Merton's great barn, and then his sheep barn, and then his carriage barn and carpentry shop, and began to set them alight. From his position at the table, Merton himself could see only the orange glow of the ensuing fire reflected on the landscape. Soon, animals could be heard shrieking. Merton's hired men could be heard shouting to each other to save them.

Two of the Indians who had gone upstairs entered the dining room. One of them, wearing an antique opera hat bedizened with turkey quills and a black, red, and gold U.S. Marine dress tunic above his loincloth and leggings, presented a sack that jangled as he opened it to show Terrio.

"Nice," their leader said as he peered inside. Then, to Merton, "Looks like we found what we were looking for. Guess we'll be on our way, then."

Hoofbeats could be heard as Merton's draft animals, released from the burning barns, stampeded past the house.

"Say, is it true you were an actor in a cable TV show back in the day?"

"Fuck you," Merton explained.

"If that's the way you want to be . . ." Terrio went around the table to where a large landscape painting hung on the wall. Dated 1911, it depicted a factory village on the Housatonic River in spring-time by the American impressionist J. Alden Weir. Merton had purchased it at a Christie's auction in Beverly Hills at the height of his earning years playing Lamont Circe in *Boomtown* on cable television. Terrio drew his knife from its porcupine quill–decorated sheath on his loincloth cord and slashed the canvas diagonally both ways. "Fuck you, too, then," he said, "and the boat of Western civ you sailed in on."

Forty-five

After Robert and Britney returned to the house on Linden Street, she went directly to the sickroom no longer occupied by Sarah, stripped off the sheets, put the room in order, swept up the splinters of the shattered violin in the parlor, and at last went up to the bedroom that she and Robert shared the past year to sleep away the rest of the afternoon. Robert did not trust her state of mind, and he was fearful of what she might decide to do, but he had no illusions about his ability to influence her. Their kitchen stores were low, but their four hens had been laying nicely as spring advanced. In the early evening he scrambled three eggs with some crumbled stale corn bread and chives from the garden mixed in, and some of Britney's own preserved hot pepper jelly on top, and brought this supper upstairs to her. She awoke and sat up in bed and accepted the plate and ate silently with the low evening sun pouring golden light into the room while Robert sat stoically beside her.

She cleaned the plate and, handing it back to him, said, "Thank you," before burrowing back under the blankets. Robert left her as the sun dipped below distant Schoolhouse Hill. He scrambled three more eggs and the rest of the broken-up corn bread for himself, weeded the flowering pea vines and puttered in the garden until the twilight faded, and then sat outside watching the stars, feeling like a shipwrecked castaway on the tides of time. He was conscious that his thoughts and feelings were the same utterly unoriginal torments of billions like him: the bewildering indifference of the universe, the pointlessness of suffering, the inescapable obligation to abide with it. Flickering vignettes of Sarah flashed across his memory leaving a contrail of melancholy that made his skin crawl and his eyes burn. He longed to play some airs in the minor keys on his fiddle but did not dare disturb Britney. Finally, he could only ask himself, what are the duties of the living? And the only answer that came to him was to keep living, and, in his case, to find his way back to the elusive gratitude for being that resided somewhere inside him.

It was chilly now. After a while the moon came up and he didn't need a candle to find his way around upstairs. He took off his clothes and stole into bed beside Britney feeling the heat of life radiate off her and inhaling the complicated scent of her hair and the soft skin where his face came to rest against the back of her neck. She stirred and reached back for his arm and dragged it over her side and held his hand between her breasts. Tenderness swelled within him, crowding out all the confounding existential conundrums as exhaustion overtook him. Before long, their breathing synchronized and Robert slipped effortlessly toward a place where anything was possible, even something as fugitive as happiness.

FORTY-SIX

When they returned to Union Grove just after sunset, Seth and Elam took the gunshot man directly to Dr. Copeland's house. The doctor had been teaching his son and medical assistant, Jasper, twelve, how to tie trout flies, specifically this evening a buff caddis fly imitation constructed solely of deer hair: wings, body, and tail. The deer hair was hollow and, when it was tied off on the hook, little air pockets were created that made the fly unsinkable. It was also nearly indestructible. You could use one fly all season long, he told the boy, and he had. The doctor knew that the delicate work required similar dexterity as surgery.

When the rangers came to the door and pointed to the figure hunched in the saddle, the doctor rushed outside with a candle lantern and asked his wife, Jeanette, to prepare the lab for surgery. He gave the lantern to his son to hold while the three men undid the lashings and carefully lowered the man off the big black horse. The doctor had obtained an articulated operating table from Glens Falls Hospital, his employer in the old times, before it closed permanently. They brought the man inside and put him on it. Jeanette set up a complex array of candles and mirrors on adjustable wooden stands and fired the alcohol burner of the autoclave. Then she cut the man's blood-stiffened clothes off with scissors while the doctor and his son changed into surgical gowns and scrubbed at the lab sink first with lye soap and then with full-strength ethyl alcohol. They cleaned off the patient with alcohol, put in a 110 millimeter plastic oral airway, inserted a rectal suppository of opium, the only anesthetic available, and proceeded to inventory his five wounds. The worst one had shattered his gallbladder, clipped part of his liver, and transited the pyloric canal of his stomach, finally exiting the right external oblique muscle. One lodged in the upper lobe of his right lung. One passed through his left upper trapezius muscle, missing the carotid artery and jugular vein by a few millimeters, and two had gone clear through the meaty part of his left thigh near the groin, apparently meant to unman him, but failing to.

"What a goddamned mess," the doctor said, as he retracted an approach to the lung wound through the first and second ribs. His wife and son assisted as he dissected and entered each region, found the lodged bullet, sutured tissues and muscles, sponged out fluids, put in drain tubes, and sterilized the thoracic and abdominal cavities with alcohol as best he could. He had Jasper stitch up the outer layers, while he moved on to the next site. They finished in just over four hours. The patient's blood pressure had gone as low as 72 over 40 but he was alive. They left him in place on the table, knowing that they would need more help to move him to a bed, if he lived through the night. The rangers had gone home, of course. Jeanette, too, had staggered back to the house in a pall of exhaustion.

"How do you like performing modern surgery in medieval conditions?" the doctor asked Jasper as they wearily took off their scrubs.

"You still have the knowledge," Jasper answered. "That's what matters."

The doctor cranked his head and could not help smiling at the boy, despite his fatigue.

"You'll be a better doctor than me when your time comes," he said. "Say a prayer for our patient before you tuck in. Go on now." He kissed the boy on top of his head and shoved him toward the door.

When Jasper left, the doctor went into the front room office of the old carriage house, poured himself three fingers of pear brandy in a pony glass, and stuffed some loose marijuana in a pipe he had carved himself. When he felt the mingled buzz come on, he returned to the lab, checked the patient's saline and glucose lines, and took his blood pressure again. It had climbed a bit to 78 over 46. He sat on a stool beside the operating table sipping his brandy, only two of the twenty candles still burning, and calculated that the man had roughly a 15 percent chance of surviving his ordeal. Arduous as it was, the surgery itself wasn't heroic. The doctor had seen much more complicated cases come through the Glens Falls Hospital emergency room in the old times: car and especially motorcycle crash victims, industrial accidents, shotgun wounds that just shredded people. The trouble, of course, was that he had no antibiotic medicines. The patient would be extremely fortunate to escape infection, or overcome it when it developed. Hard as people tried, and despite the persistence of knowledge about sanitary practice, the new times were septic times.

FORTY-SEVEN

Somebody was rapping on Robert's front door very early the next morning. Given the low angle of the rising sun and the time of year, Robert figured it was not yet six o'clock. Britney woke up, too, and rolled over to watch him pull his pants up.

"It's all right," Robert told her, though he suspected it was not.

Temple Merton was at the door. He'd left his farm when dawn was a barely visible gray glow above the treetops to the east. His bay gelding was hitched to the Japanese pear tree in Robert's dooryard.

"Sorry to bother you so early, Robert," Temple said. "Have you got a bucket of water?"

"Of course."

Temple brought it out to his horse. Meanwhile, Robert fired up the cookstove in the summer kitchen out back and put a kettle on. Temple came back and got right to the point: a gang of blue-eyed white men affecting to be Indians had burned his barns down and robbed his silver and gold. They were in the employ of the Berkshire People's Republic. He'd been visited two days earlier by one Buddy Goodfriend and had declined the offer of paying for a subscription toward their goal of forming a local political confederation. He assumed this was payback.

"Indians, for chrissake," Robert said.

"At least they weren't zombies," Temple said. He'd suffered through two decades of Hollywood's love affair with the various fabled undead. His cable TV series *Boomtown* was canceled in favor of the zombie-themed comedy *Death Comes Calling*, and two years later his sole directorial attempt, a sci-fi feature about time travel, was put into turnaround so the producers could pour their money into the would-be zombie blockbuster *BrainChild*, which went straight to video.

222 JAMES HOWARD KUNSTLER

"We had a parley with this Goodfriend," Robert said. "He gave us the song and dance about their federation and paying subscriptions. We were kind of waiting for their next move. But guys playing Indian . . . ?"

"They weren't playing," Temple said.

"How do you know they work for that Berkshire bunch?"

"Their head guy said so. In so many words."

"Frankly, it's the first I've heard of it."

"Also, the day before yesterday somebody killed seven of my cows in a pasture on Coot Hill."

"What? First I've heard of that too."

"They were shot in the head. One clean shot for each cow."

"These same guys?"

"I don't know. Could have been them."

"What about your neighbors? Have they been robbed or harassed?"

"I don't know yet. We were busy keeping the fire off the house until the wee hours of the morning. But when I rode out at dawn my place was the only one where you could see a column of smoke rising."

"Okay, I'll make the rounds and inquire," Robert said.

"They're going to hurt somebody pretty soon, you know," Temple said.

"I suppose you're right."

"We're going to have to play rough like them."

"We just haven't prepared for something like this."

"Well we can't just let them burn down barns and rob people."

"Of course not."

Robert stared into some intermediate zone beyond Temple's head as if dazed.

"What's the matter with you, Robert?" Temple said. "I'm not sure you're taking this seriously."

Robert recoiled, as though returning painfully to the present moment.

"We, uh, lost a child."

"Lost?"

"Dead. Tetanus."

"Oh, gosh . . . Just like that?"

"Yeah, night before last."

"What child was this?"

"I live with a young woman whose husband died a year ago. Her daughter. Eight years old. Named Sarah. A wonderful little girl. It was a horrible death."

"They couldn't do anything for her?"

"Nope."

"Forgive me. I had no idea."

"Of course."

"I'm sorry to lay all this on you."

"No, you were right to come here," Robert said. "We have able-bodied men in town. They're just not organized. No police force or militia. That New Faith bunch has some ex-soldiers, Holy Land vets, capable guys. We have to protect this community."

"I have nine men at my place," Temple said. "Of course they're farmhands not soldiers."

"Do you have any firearms?"

"Not enough to go around."

"I'll see what I can do," Robert said. "Did you lose any livestock in the fire?"

"Aside from those cows, my men got the rest of the animals out of the barns."

"As soon as this is over we'll help you rebuild your barns. That's a promise. And it's going be over. We'll put a stop to it."

"I guess I'll stand by, then."

"I'll see if I can get some more firearms over to you."

Temple offered his condolences again and departed. Robert made a pot of raspberry leaf tea with honey and brought a mug of it upstairs. Britney was actually sitting up in bed. She took the mug gratefully and held it close to her bosom.

"How are you feeling?" he asked.

"Still here in the world," she said without irony.

"You stay in it. Someday it'll seem like a better world than it does just now."

"I want another child," she said.

Robert did not know how to reply since he knew that she knew he had had a vasectomy when he was with Sandy, his wife, after they'd had the requisite two children.

"Of course," he eventually said.

"Who was that down there?" she asked.

"There's some trouble I have to see about it. Will you be okay if I leave for a while?"

"I'll be okay when I get another child," she said.

"We'll talk about it," Robert said.

"It'll take more than talk."

"Yes. But it won't hurt to talk."

FORTY-EIGHT

At eight o'clock Robert met in the office of the community laundry in the old repurposed Union-Wayland mill building with Brother Jobe and Loren Holder, his partners in the venture.

"I heard about your little girl," Brother Jobe said as he bustled in. "Terrible. Who can pretend to understand the mysterious workings of Providence. I suppose you and the rev here have made funeral arrangements."

Loren shook his head and mouthed the word *no*.

"We buried her ourselves, out in the country," Robert said.

"Huh?" Loren said.

"It's what Britney wanted," Robert said. "On a property where she spent part of her own childhood."

"Is she all right or what?" Loren asked.

Robert sighed. "I don't really know. She's fragile."

"Does she have other women she can talk to?" Loren asked. "She's not the only one who's lost a child in this town."

"She's kind of a loner," Robert said.

"Maybe Jane Ann can help."

Robert took it in and nodded his head, allowing an uncomfortable interval to pass, while Loren and Brother Jobe shared glances of concern.

"Thanks, sincerely," he said, "but I didn't call this meeting to talk about my personal problems." He told them about Temple Merton's visit and what had happened at his farm twelve hours earlier.

"White men dressed like Indians!" Brother Jobe said. "Ain't that just the last word in di-versity? We got to put an end to this monkey business. FYI, I caught up last night with that little freak Sonny Boy. He was enjoying a meal at the tavern like a grandee. I'm darn sure he's the one shot those seven cows belonging to farmer Merton.

Told him to get packing forthwith. I'm kind of sorry I didn't take him into custody. He's a psycho case if I ever met one—and I met a fair share in my law practice back in the day. He's probably out there now somewheres, laying for new targets. Shooting livestock is one thing. If he shoots any people I'll burn the sumbitch on a ding-dang brush pile."

"I've been around town talking to people," Loren said, drawing a folded piece of paper out of his shirt pocket. "I've got a list of twenty-three able-bodied men ready to take up arms."

He handed it to Brother Jobe, who scanned it.

"You send them over to my headquarters and tell them to hunt up Brother Amos, and he will provide weapons, including instruction on loading and care," Brother Jobe said. "And, by-the-by, my rangers are back from Albany."

Robert flinched, realizing how out of it he'd been the past several days.

"I forgot all about that," Robert said. "Is my boy back?"

"They say they purchased a fine boat and filled it with the requested cargo and your boy and Einhorn's are sailing it hither as I speak," Brother Jobe said. "Mission accomplished. We have a crib dock prepared for them just downstream of Mr. Bullock's wharf. We expect them sometime today. I'm sending four of the brothers over there this morning with wagons to wait and off-load their cargo."

"Make sure they can defend themselves," Loren said. "Especially as they'll be transporting valuable goods back to town."

"Roger that," Brother Jobe said. "Elam tells me they run into an interesting bandit on the way south. Styled himself as a country doctor working with two female assistants. Almost had to blow this fellow's head off. Then on the return trip they come across a gunshot man, robbery victim, apparently, lying in a ditch bleeding to death. Whoever it was shot him up, they even stole his boots, probably his horse too. That was ten miles downriver. And now we got Indians torching barns and pillaging up here. I tell you, there's mayhem and mischief breaking out all over the county. I don't like it."

"We've been lucky for years," Robert said. "And we got com-
placent about living in peace."

"People can be swept up by violence," Loren said. "And quickly.
It's a thin line."

"My people walk the straight and narrow, Reverend," Brother
Jobe said. "We're going to find out exactly where these birds are
roosting and flush 'em out, and I hope they will go back to where
they come from without any bloodshed. You tell your town men
after they fetch their firearms from Brother Amos to muster out
on our hayfield behind the school and I'll have my rangers ready
with a plan of action for them."

FORTY-NINE

At ten that morning, Terry Einhorn opened his general merchandise store on Main Street. His inventory of food commodities was low owing to the recent hiatus in trade and to it being the time of year when last season's stored-up fruits and grains ran near exhaustion. Shortly after he opened the store a box wagon pulled by two hard-used plug mares drove up outside the front window and seven boys ranging in age from thirteen to nineteen strode inside the store followed by a tall young woman in trousers and layered sweaters, who came up to the counter.

"Good morning," Terry said, a little awed by the swaggering figure before him. He remembered seeing her on the porch of the hotel the night that the Berkshire leader made his bewildering speech. The young men who came in with her made him nervous, fingering the merchandise and casting surly looks his way.

"Peace, brother," she said.

"What can I do for you?"

"I have a list," Flame said. She retrieved a folded sheet of paper from the fleshy cleft deep within her sweaters and handed it over theatrically. Terry was certain there was some kind of cologne on it, and he wondered if it was meant to somehow bamboozle him. It was a long list and the many items were designated in substantial quantities. As Terry read the list his eyes shifted from the paper to the woman and back again.

"Miz Greengrass is it?" Terry said.

"That's right."

"You're the people from out of town."

"Yes, we're from the Berkshire People's Republic," Flame said, "with our capital in Great Barrington."

"I've been there," Terry said. "Quite a while ago. I saw Vampire Weekend play at the Mahaiwe Theater."

"What was that?"

"They were a rock and roll band."

"Oh? Sexism, drugism, and music appropriated from people of color."

"It was more than that."

"They can't play it anymore with the electric off, can they?"

"Not like it was meant to be played."

"We're not enslaved by loud, violent music the way you old-timers were," she said. "Young people today put their energy into proactive politics. We're on our yearly outreach to bring justice, diversity, gender equality, and good government to the regions adjoining the BPR, and to unite with them against reactionary oppression, which is spreading like a plague across the broken land formerly known as the USA."

"Good luck," Terry said, cracking a smile that he could tell at once was not appreciated.

Flame's back stiffened.

"It's a bond of principle," she said. "A creed. A politics of fairness and decency. What have you people here got?"

"We're fair and decent," Terry said. "We've come through a bad patch of history and things have stabilized now, maybe even getting better, slowly but surely."

"Such as what in particular?"

"We have the new hotel and tavern."

Flame guffawed. "Do you have a government that cares? A government that shares?"

"We have almost no government," Terry said. "A village board of trustees. A mayor. We had a magistrate for a while but he resigned."

"Are you aware that your people are talking to our people about forming a federation?"

"I've heard rumors," Terry said. "I've also heard that our people are inclined to say thanks but no thanks."

"How can that be an option?"

Terry was not accustomed to political debate. Rather than answer Flame's question, he made a show of peering down the list she had handed him over his out-of-date eyeglasses and said, "I can't sell you all these things in the quantities you desire."

"Why not?"

"It wouldn't be fair to my regular customers, the people who live in and around Union Grove."

"You'll sell all these things sooner or later," Flame said. "What does it matter if you sell them sooner rather than later? They're just things."

Terry's amazement provoked him to smile again.

"Do I really need to explain?" he said.

"I think it would be only fair of you to try."

"Well, you see I've got a responsibility to ration out the goods I have on hand so our people can get through these lean weeks of the year when the crops are just going in and last year's stuff is running low."

Flame did not reply directly but rather just stared at Terry, as though to produce maximum discomfort in him.

"Yours is the only store anywhere around here," Flame said when she tired of staring. "You enjoy a monopoly. How is that? Who gave you permission to control the distribution of necessities?"

"Anybody else is free to open a store if they want," Terry said.

"The powers that be probably want the people to think so."

"There are no powers that be around here."

"No? You've got a handful of rich farmers who employ most of the workers in town. How is that not an oligarchy?"

"They're, most of them, decent people," Terry said. "They're not pushing us around. They're not telling me what to do. And the truth is, if they really mistreated everyone, the people would rise up against them. You don't see that happening, do you? Why's that? Because these farmers have provided some structure to people's daily life after it almost completely fell apart. You think the general run of folks could make a go at subsistence farming? They didn't have the skills. They needed the experienced farmers to organize a new system."

"That system is called feudalism," Flame inserted.

"I don't care what you call it," Terry said. "For now, it works, and nobody here is agitating to overthrow it. By-and-by it'll change. Things always do. As for me and my business, this town only needs one general merchandise store for the present time. We've got other businesses. There's a clothing store across the street, a barbershop, Russo's bakery, a livery where you can rent horses and carts, the new hotel. There's a fellow breeding mules and selling them all over the county. We've even got a new community laundry over on the river. This place is coming back and so are people's spirits. If you don't want to do business here with me, you can go up to Glens Falls, or back toward Bennington. If you want some of these things here," he hoisted the list, "then you'll take what I'm willing to sell and that's that. Do we understand each other?"

Flame shrugged her shoulders. "Whatever," she muttered.

"Okay then," Terry said. "I can give you fifty pounds of corn-meal, not a hundred . . ." And so Terry read down the list. Finally, he called for Buddy Haseltine, the young man with Down's syndrome he had adopted during the depths of the collapse, when the epidemics were raging regularly and Buddy, then a teenager, lost his parents. These days, wanting to be more independent, Buddy slept in the back of the store, serving as an all-around helper and night watchman. This morning, as Terry worked through the Berkshire outreachers' shopping list, Buddy lugged sacks of provisions, slabs of bacon, strings of hard sausage, flats of eggs, and a gallon tub of butter to the front from the storeroom out back, and Terry got all of the stuff assembled in the sitting area in front of the idle woodstove, warning the boys who came in with Flame not to start loading it out the door yet. And then the time came to settle the account. Terry prepared a handwritten bill of sale. It came to twelve and a half ounces of silver. He handed it to Flame and crossed his arms.

"You charged us for the plastic tubs," she said.

"That's right," Terry said. "If you bring them back, I'll refund the deposit. They don't make them anymore, you know."

Flame pulled a face, but then reached into her right trouser pocket and withdrew a fat wad of pinkish paper. She commenced to lay out twelve hundred Berkshire People's Republic dollars on the counter in various denominations.

"What's this?" Terry said.

"Money," Flame said.

"No it's not."

"It is. It's our money."

He picked up a note, examined it closely, and held it up to the daylight coming through the window.

"It's a shabby printing job," he said. "We don't take paper money here anymore, not even old U.S. Federal Reserve notes. You'll have to pay in silver."

"We don't go with silver in the BPR."

"You're not in your home territory. This is Washington County, New York, ma'am."

Flame bristled.

"Soon to be part of the Berkshire People's Federation," she said.

"Not if I have anything to say about it. Next time you venture over here, better bring more provisions with you."

"I'm sorry if you don't understand," Flame said. "This is what we're paying with. This is the people's money."

"It's worthless paper."

"Load the wagon, guys," Flame said over her shoulder, and several of the boys started picking up plastic tubs and sacks.

"Put that down," Terry barked. They made to hustle the goods out the door.

"Don't try to stop them," Flame said.

Terry came out from behind the counter and tried exactly that. He wrested a twenty-pound sack of cornmeal away from one boy, a brawny fourteen-year-old with some black mustache fuzz, and, as soon as he did, he was beset by several of the others. Another boy seized a broom from a hook near the front door and began

THE HARROWS OF SPRING   233

swinging at Terry's head with it. Three more boys ganged up on
Buddy Haseltine, smacking and punching him with their bare hands
until he curled into a ball near the window display of recycled plastic
tubs, cookware, and candle lanterns, where they continued to kick
him. Yet another grabbed an ax handle and landed several blows on
Terry's kidneys. He dropped the sack of cornmeal he had wrested
away from the young bandit and fell writhing on the floor. When he
was finally able to pick himself up the boys were gone, and Flame
with them, and all the provisions they had ordered up, too, together
with the wagon they came in on. Even the paper money had been
swept up off the counter and taken.

FIFTY

Brother Jobe strode wrathfully into the front room of his new hotel where Brother Jubal, the day man, was sweeping up.

"Is that Mr. Goodfriend about in his room?" Brother Jobe asked.

"I believe his key is yet behind the front desk," Jubal said, alluding to the house system whereby guests left their keys when out. It was not an easy matter to make a new key if one was lost.

"What number is the sumbitch in?" Brother Jobe said, storming behind the check-in desk himself. Jubal told him. Brother Jobe snatched the key off its hook and charged up the stairs, taking two at a time to the top floor. He didn't bother knocking, just unlocked the door and went in. Goodfriend's gear was scattered around the bed, the chest of drawers, and on the floor: shirts made of wondrous synthetic fibers, waterproof mountaineering pants, polarfleece outerwear, and a ripstop nylon duffel bag which, when he unzipped it, proved to be stuffed with bundles of red-tinted Berkshire People's Republic money.

Brother Jobe slammed the door in disgust and made for Glen Ethan Greengrass's room on the second floor. Lacking the key to it, he knocked. The same large, pear-shaped young man as before, six feet and three inches of him, came to the door again. He put his index fingers across his lips and said, "Sssshhhh."

"You tell Mr. Greengrass I got to see him."

"Please, keep your voice down," the young man said. "He's extremely ill."

"Is he conscious?"

"Barely."

"That's good enough for me. Let me in."

"No."

"Get out of my way, son."

Brother Jobe attempted to shove him aside, but he was too bulky and stolid to get past. In the commotion, two other large boys became visible farther back in the room.

"I can't allow you in," the young man at the door said.

"If your Mr. Greengrass is so sick, why don't you-all send for the doctor? We got one in town, you know."

"Doctors can't do anything for him."

"Is that your opinion or something you actually know about?"

"He doesn't believe in it," the boy said. "Who are you and what do you want?"

"I'm the owner of this ding-dang hotel."

"Come back later," the young man said. "He's better some times of day than others."

The door closed in Brother Jobe's face.

"Lookit here, son," Brother Jobe spoke into the door. "When I come back Mr. Greengrass better be ready to talk to me or I'm gonna throw his ass out of the hotel, and you-all with him. Hear me?"

If they did, they did not signify from behind the closed door.

FIFTY-ONE

The doctor was on his way up River Street toward the Congregational Church parish house when once again the enormous flock of black, brown, and white Canada geese down below stole his attention. They had marshaled on a wide bend of the Battenkill so thickly on the water that, the doctor mused, a mink could cross the river on their backs without getting its feet wet. The geese seemed to be going through some kind of population explosion. Their summer habitat in the Canadian far north had expanded with the retreat of the polar ice cap and now it was their time of the year to journey there. So absorbed was he that he did not notice the Reverend Loren Holder coming his way down the street until he was nearly upon him. The doctor turned, somewhat startled.

"Hey, I was just coming up to see you," he said.

"I was looking to talk to you too," Loren said. "Ever seen so many freakin' geese around?"

"No. It's got me worried."

"Last time I went fishing, there was so much goose shit in the water that weeds are starting to choke the Pothole," Loren said, referring to a pool famous among the trout fishers. "There were never weeds like that there before."

"I'm more concerned about when we're going to see another flu outbreak," the doctor said. "You must have noticed that the first two coincided with the spring migration."

"Only now that you mention it," Loren said.

"I think these geese are the vector."

"Is that why you were coming to see me?"

"No. I've got a patient in the surgery and I need help getting him into a bed. It's too much for Jeanette. Can you give me a hand moving him?"

"Sure. Anyone I know?"

"Young man. No name. Still unconscious. Those two army boys from the Jesus cult found him all shot up in a ditch down in Stillwater. Robbery, I guess. Even took his shoes. They brought him back here thinking he was going to die on the way but he made it. Now he's got to survive the surgery. So far, so good, but it's still early. What were you looking to talk to me about?"

"Your drinking," Loren said without any throat clearing.

"I don't know that I can stop."

On the way back to the doctor's house Loren said what he had to. The people in town needed the doctor. They couldn't lose faith in him. Everyone would soon know what condition he was in the night that little Sarah Watling died. It would get around.

"I couldn't have saved that girl," the doctor said.

"You certain about that, Jerry? Absolutely certain? I sure couldn't save her. I know that. Jason couldn't. He's just not an MD. But you? Anyway, we'll never know."

After a protracted silence, the doctor could only repeat himself: "I don't know how to stop."

"When you feel helpless before that bottle, you come and see me," Loren said. "I don't care what time of the day or night. You can get me out of bed if that's how it is. We'll go out walking. We'll walk in the daylight or the moonlight or by starlight. We'll talk. If it's raining, come into the house and we'll drink tea in my study. We'll talk some more. We'll go fishing in the goose shit and talk. You come and see me when you feel like you have to have a drink."

"All right," the doctor said.

"All right," Loren said.

By then they'd reached the doctor's place. He led Loren into the carriage house that was his office and his lab. Jeanette came in from the house a moment later. The gunshot man still lay on the operating table in the lab with a nasogastric feeding tube taped to his face and a massive bandage over his neck wound. The doctor explained carefully to Loren how they were going to transfer him to a gurney and take him into a bed in the recovery room behind the lab. Loren took the foot end. They managed the lateral transfer without incident. Loren provided the push to the gurney while the doctor helped steer through the door and Jeanette controlled the rolling glucose bottle stand. They did another lateral onto the bed, got the soiled sheet out from under the patient, and log-rolled him a half turn so he could be given another opium suppository. Jeanette pulled up the side rails on the bed. It was a bright, clean, spartan whitewashed room with nothing in it but the bed and a table. It was on the north side of the building and soft daylight came through the window, filtered by a lilac tree that perfumed a cool breeze stirring the gauzy curtains. The doctor checked the feed tube and the drip. Jeanette went off to fetch some clean dressings for the surgical wounds.

"You can go now, if you want," the doctor said to Loren.

But Loren hardly heard him. He was staring intently at the young man's bearded face from near the foot of the bed. Loren's jaw dropped. He came around the bed and peered closer. He reached over the bed and seized the doctor by his arm and squeezed so tightly the doctor said, "Ow."

"Dear Lord," Loren said. "That's my boy. That's Evan."

The doctor was so astounded to hear this that he swung around and knocked a candlestick off the bedside table.

Loren collapsed into the seat of the chair beside the bed. His hands began to rove over Evan's body as though he were trying to physically reassemble him in the form he remembered, a laughing boy of eighteen.

"Look," Loren said. "It's him. Oh, Lord."

"Better not to touch him."

"Huh . . . ?"

"Danger of infection."

Loren withdrew his hands and sat stiffly in the chair, nearly breathless with agitation, struggling to readjust the cognitive mechanism in his mind that had finally permitted him to accept his son's death and now had changed back the other way.

Even during the years before Evan left home to see the country with Daniel Earle, the doctor had barely attended the boy as a patient, for Evan was never sick. But he knew the family, of course, and Evan was always there in the background with the other children in town, so he knew him a little.

"I think you're right," the doctor said. "Oh, my goodness."

"He's a grown man," Loren said. "But it's him. It's my boy."

FIFTY-TWO

Following his aborted interview with Glen Ethan Greengrass, Brother Jobe was in turbulent spirits when he returned to the old high school. He consulted in the old basement boiler room with Brother Amos, and inspected the arsenal of firearms the New Faith brethren had managed to lay in over the past year, much of it in barter for their excellent mules. He instructed Amos to get fifty rifles and a thousand rounds of suitable ammunition up to the horse barn. The hayfield beside it, formerly the school's soccer field, had gotten its first scything and would be ready for the townsmen to receive their abbreviated weapons training. Next he summoned one Brother Gabriel, a former short order cook from Fancy Gap, Virginia, and told him to ready a horse cart to transport half a dozen rifles to farmer Merton's place on Coot Hill. After that, Brother Jobe confabbed with his two rangers and his second in command, Brother Joseph, informing them that, on top of these kumbaya rascals from Berkshire attempting to work a grift on the whole neighborhood, a pack of rogues got up like Indians were on the loose burning down barns. Plus which, he'd made the mistake of releasing a sharpshooting, cow-killing psychopath named Sonny Boy who was liable to be at large somewhere in the vicinity, armed and dangerous.

"What kind of Indians?" Seth asked.

"A farmer called Merton up toward Hebron told our Mr. Earle that they was blue-eyed white men in buckskins and like that. They torched his buildings with the livestock inside. His men barely managed to get the animals out alive—"

"What the hell?" Elam said.

"Since when you start cussing around here, son?"

"Sorry, Boss. Guess my old army mind tooken over."

"Might's well keep it switched on," Brother Jobe said. "You-all got to come up with some kind of plan to run these birds to ground before they hurt somebody. The town men are coming over to muster in the hayfield in a little while. They'll be joined by an equal number of our men. Amos is sorting out the small arms down below as I speak. Joseph, you got one afternoon to shape them into some kind of tactical force to deal with all this vexation. Seth and Elam, I want you to go out on a recon starting ASAP. I'm informed them kumbayas done moved their bivouac. Find out where they's holing up. Far as we know them Indian sumbitches is on the move too. And mind that lone wolf Sonny Boy is out there. Keep a low profile. Don't take no horse. You'll present too much of a target right out there on the road. Go out on foot and stay in the cover —"

Before he was quite finished, Sister Zeruiah burst into Brother Jobe's office and interrupted, saying he must hurry to Mary Beth Ivanhoe's chamber to witness "a strange and awesome transfiguration." Zeruiah was in an emotional state so tumultuous and agitated that Brother Jobe supposed that Mary Beth, the woman known variously as Precious Mother and the Queen Bee at the spiritual center of the New Faith sect, must be dying.

FIFTY-THREE

Loren steered clear of home, the parish house of the Congregational Church, and his wife Jane Ann. He could not tell her that the gunshot young man lying in the doctor's recovery room was their son, Evan. The doctor had warned him that the danger of infection and complication from surgery was hardly over, was really only beginning, and that, frankly, the chance that Evan would die was not a small one. In case he didn't make it, Loren would rather that Jane Ann never knew Evan had made it within ten miles of home, only to be gunned down by bandits. He'd been away from home for exactly three years now. The accepted story, Daniel's, was that Evan had been lost when their boat foundered in a storm on Lake Erie off the shoals of Sandusky, Ohio. Jane Ann would never get over the loss of a child—no parent ever does—but she had accepted it and moved on, as he had, Loren thought, and now she had the four orphaned small boys to look after, and at the level of practical, day-to-day existence, as he observed her, she was okay. She was able to laugh and find joy in the world and abide with the affections of her husband, and Loren didn't want to bring all that crashing down. The doctor promised Loren he would not tell Jeanette what they had discovered. If Evan didn't make it, the secret would remain between the two of them.

Loren sat with Evan for an hour afterward, talking to him, though Evan remained in a deep, heaving sleep all the while. Eventually, Loren left to attend to his own pressing duties. He rode a New Faith mare to Ben Deaver's farm, which was closest to town of all the big farms. Ben had six men available for the muster, and he sent a seventh man on a very fleet horse around to the other farms of Todd Zucker, Ned Larmon, Bill Schmidt, and Carl Weibel to inform the men they could spare to report to the old high school at midafternoon, and meanwhile Loren returned to town to round up the other available, able-bodied men who did not work as laborers out on the big farms.

FIFTY-FOUR

Robert Earle got a sturdy paint saddle horse named Mookie from the New Faith stables and set out for the rural townships with much on his mind besides the mischief of the Berkshire interlopers. As he left the village behind and ventured into the lush, mid-spring landscape, with pink and white phlox starting to bloom along the roadside and the trees fully fledged and the stupendous quiet of a landscape without motors, he was stunned as ever by the contrast between the world's beauty and its cruelty. And he marveled that it was possible for an ordinary man to function in that world made of those overpowering oppositions.

Britney was the main thing on his mind, like a musical refrain in a minor key stuck in his head. He knew her well enough to be sure that she absolutely required a child, just as she had said, and he knew for certain that he was unable to give her one. His vasectomy was his last encounter with modern medicine before the times finally turned. He'd gone with Sandy to the outpatient minor surgery facility in a strip mall outside Glens Falls. These were the first weeks when the electricity had just begun to falter. It would go out mysteriously for an hour or so every few days, enough to spook people without upsetting all of everyday life. It happened to go out that day fifteen minutes into Robert's procedure. He was under an IV sedative and a local anesthetic, and he was very much aware when the lights flickered and the emergency diesel generator kicked in. The doctor and other medical personnel carried on with a semblence of jaunty normality, as if it were England bedeviled by the Luftwaffe in 1942.

But the war in the Holy Land was far far away, and the situation was quite different. The nation was cracking under the weight of bloated modernity and all the patches pasted onto its excessive and malfunctioning hypercomplexity, and people were bewildered by the strange glitches, failures, and shortages. Going forward, nothing would really work anymore as it was designed to, yet the hope and expectation that it would all magically recover dominated the chatter in the rare moments when people could step back from their frantic lives and share a meal or a drink.

Now, this day years later, Robert carried a pistol as he rode the old county highways and back roads, alert for trouble in whatever form it might come in, but nothing untoward crossed his path. He stopped first at Holyrood's establishment, the county's leading cider works with several hundred acres of fruit, sixteen workmen resident on the premises, most with wives, all very busy in the orchards this week as the trees had blossomed and set fruit and needed a lot of tender love and care. Robert was relieved to see that Holyrood's barns, cider mill, and outbuildings were all unharmed, and Felix Holyrood himself had not heard of the arson at Temple Merton's place, which was seven miles away. He said he would set watchmen before sundown and that he had enough firearms and ammunition to put up a fight if someone came looking for trouble.

Robert proceeded from there, stopping at seven other farms in his planned nineteen-mile circuit. Of these farms, two had suffered arson and robbery by men dressed up like Indians following a visit by Buddy Goodfriend. One of the farmers, a goat dairyman named Brett Maun, had killed one Indian with a trenching shovel as the rascal was about to torch his birthing barn. He said it was the most startling thing in his life to be fending off an Indian attack, having been a small boy when that sort of thing happened only on TV. The dead man, suspiciously green-eyed, had lingered through the night after his cohorts slipped away into the dark woods. Maun and his wife gave him what attention they could, but his head was visibly cracked and he expired before dawn. He had been unable to speak while in their custody, so they learned nothing of his origins, purposes, or connections.

Robert completed his circuit of the rural townships late in the afternoon and set his course toward home, knowing that the combined town and New Faith defense force by now would have left the village seeking to evict the visitors from Massachusetts from their campground. He was a little sorry not to be there but confident with Brother Joseph in charge of the operation. Meanwhile, Robert knew Daniel was likely to have returned from his journey to Albany and, as he made his way home with the sun blaring in his eyes, an idea presented itself to him that seemed both inescapable and dreadful.

FIFTY-FIVE

Brother Jobe entered Mary Beth Ivanhoe's chamber gingerly, expecting a grim and ghastly vigil, only to find a stranger sitting up in the bed at the center of the room and daylight flooding in from the cupola above, from which drapes had been removed. The usual group of attendant sisters was nowhere to be seen. The woman in the bed appeared to be in her mid-thirties, sturdy and big-boned with the high cheekbones and sharp nose of her Appalachian ancestors, descended from Scottish border ruffians who came to America before the Revolution. Her light brown hair was short, rather pixieish, as if it was just growing in after a season of chemotherapy. She wore a plain cotton shift and was sitting outside the bed covers with her feet out and crossed at the ankles. She had been buffing her nails when Brother Jobe crept in, his face flushed and his heart up in his throat.

"Uh, where's, uh, Mary Beth?" he stammered.

The woman put down the smooth river stone wrapped in goatskin she'd been buffing her nails with and glared at him with slitty eyes and forehead all scrunched.

"What's the matter with you, Lyle?" she said. "It's me."

Brother Jobe took two steps back, as if recoiling from an object of incomprehensible bewilderment.

"That can't be you, Precious Mother," he said.

"Git used to it," she said, in a voice that retained some of its raw mountain screech. "And quit callin' me that."

"Where are all your . . . your helpers?"

"I told 'em to git lost. They's makin' me nervous, fussing and hoo-hahing all about. Where you been at, anyways?"

In fact, it had been days since the honcho of the New Faith had visited the previously bedridden seer and protector who had led the group north from the violent wilderness of Dixieland.

"I been busy," Brother Jobe said. "We got trouble in town. What all happened to you, Mary Beth?"

"First you tell me what kinda trouble."

"Don't you know? You can see things."

"Not anymore," she said. "I done quit that."

"That ain't something you resign from."

"Want to bet? I done it. Last time you come to see me, I was at death's door, remember?"

"'Course I do."

"Well, I went through that door a ways and up the elevator. Got some face time with the boss of bosses. He said, 'Mary Beth, we're not ready for you. I'm sending you back, and you gonna lead a normal life.'"

"Jesus said that?"

"He don't like to be called that up there. But it was him, all right."

"Mind if I set down?"

"Suit yourself."

Brother Jobe took a seat. He picked up a small metal tray from the bedside table and fanned himself with it.

"I'm movin' out of this hothouse," Mary Beth said. "Goin' down with the regular sisters. Maybe find a man amongst the brethren. Git back to regular living."

"So hold on a second—you don't have no more powers?" Brother Jobe said.

"What I said? You even listening? That was part of the deal. He said, 'You want to live normal, you got to act normal and be normal.'"

"What about your injuries? Your illnesses?"

"He done fixed all that."

"I be dog," Brother Jobe said. "Just like that?"

"You don't miss it when it's gone, believe me. Tell you the truth, I 'most forgot already what it was like to feel that way, all bloated up, achy and itchy, and them dang fits I used to git. Tell you something else I like. He said I could eat as much pie as I want now and won't never put on a extra pound again. I might work in the kitchen. The sisters tell me that's the place to be around here."

"Mind if I ask, what was it like up there where you had your meet-up with you-know-who?"

"It was nice."

"That all you got to say about it?"

"Kind of like I remember the penthouse suite of the Hilton Grand at Myrtle Beach. I was there one time before that sumbitch bashed me up with the car at the mall, 2006. A boy named Ramsey Burgwyn took me. He come in second in the NASCAR Coca-Cola Six Hundred sprint cup that year. It had a sitting room as big as the Ford showroom back home and a circular bed. He worked me over on it like an unfreshened heifer. The place smelt like a monkey house by the time we was done. Heaven's different that way. It smells like air freshener up there. Now, what kind of trouble you-all havin' in town?"

"Grifters and Indians," Brother Jobe said. "I'm afraid you wouldn't understand now."

"Well, I can't see through the veil of the humdrum no more, but it sure sounds like a bad combo," she said. "Think we gonna overcome?"

"I mean to see that we do. I guess we gonna have to wait to find out."

Mary Beth leveled her gaze at Brother Jobe. "Do you think I look pretty?" she asked.

"Yes, yes, I do," Brother Jobe said. "Why you're prettier than a blue bunting in a tulip tree. I confess, I had no idear what was underneath all that blubber and sickness. Turns out you could dance with the stars, if they was still at it."

Just then, another sister put her head inside the room and said, "We're ready for you down below, Mary Beth."

"Hot doggies," Mary Beth said.

Brother Jobe rose from his seat.

"You've had quite a life, girl," he said.

"And I ain't done yet," she said, climbing off the big bed and wobbling a little on her smallish feet. "Ain't that a novelty, though, standing up by my own self again. Sure feels dandy. Now make way for me, world. Mary Beth Ivanhoe is back in action amongst ye."

FIFTY-SIX

Brother Gabriel was provided a good map of the rural townships encompassing the village of Union Grove, and he made his way north along old County Route 62 toward Temple Merton's farm in a two-wheeled trap with its load of six rifles and a hundred fifty rounds of ammunition. He had reached the ruins of the old one-room schoolhouse at the intersection of Scotch Hill Road when he saw a figure hunkered by the roadside up ahead. He was alert without being especially alarmed at the sight of a lone stranger and kept his horse on pace on the level grade. As he drew closer, he began to apprehend that the figure was a woman, a young one at that. Her blond hair fell in frizzy ringlets on her shoulders. She wore mannish trousers but a loose button-front shirt and a sweater tied around her slender waist in the fair, warm weather. She rose off her haunches as he came near and he noticed that she was very comely indeed. She began to wave her hand, hailing him. He reined in his mare and the cart soon jostled to a halt nearly at her feet. From up on the driver's bench, he could see clear down the front of her shirt to a broad brown nipple at the end of a fleshy swell. His hormones reacted violently.

"Afternoon, mister," Flame Aurora Greengrass said attempting to approximate a friendly smile. "Catch a ride?"

"Why, sure," Brother Gabriel said, practically croaking like a frog. "How far you going?"

"Just up a ways."

"Climb aboard."

She scooched up onto the driver's bench. Brother Gabriel could feel her body radiate heat beside him while the vapors coming off her warm flesh and clothing made his head swim. He geed up his horse to a trot, stole a glance at her, then stole another. He could still see into her loose shirt at the creamy slot within. In an uproar of internal tension, he felt compelled to say something, and what came out was the default salutation of his people.

"Do you know Jesus, ma'am?"

He smiled strenuously but she only glared back in return. Next, she grasped the side rail on the driver's bench, turned toward Brother Gabriel, raised her long powerful left leg, and pushed him off the seat clear out of the trap onto the road, where he fell with a bright yelp. A little farther up the road a swarm of her comrades from the Berkshire People's Republic emerged from the woods on either side of the road and took control of the horse until they brought the rig to a halt again. Flame climbed down and uncovered the tarp behind the driver's bench, pleased to discover an assortment of rifles chambered for generic 5.56 x 45mm rounds and a wooden crate of the ammunition.

Back down the road, Brother Gabriel lay squalling in the dust unable to get up due to his shattered collarbone. The hijackers left him there despite his pleas and his prayers and took their prize to their bivouac in a hayfield down by the Battenkill.

FIFTY-SEVEN

Brothers Levi, Oren, and Titus were down at the new crib dock at the Hudson River awaiting arrival of Daniel Earle, Teddy Einhorn, and the new boat. Their two horses were released from their wagon harness and picketed in a sunny glade down by the riverbank where clover, phlox, and mustard cress grew. The men had a good enough lunch of hard cheese and corn bread. Their rifles were stacked in a tripod down by the dock. The day was warm and peaceful and a refreshing breeze came off the river. They occupied themselves all afternoon working on the small goods-storage building beside the road. The building was a simple twenty-by-fourteen barn with the sills posted up on stone footings. It would get a big sliding door for moving cargoes inside and narrow clerestory windows up under the soffit on one side to admit light while making surreptitious entry difficult. They were still in the early stages of construction, however, spending the afternoon hours nailing cedar shingles on the roof over the still-open framed walls. Oren remained on the ground splitting shingles from sixteen-inch cedar logs with a froe and a black locust mallet while the other two crawled about the roof, nailing the shingles into place.

Around five o'clock the boat still had not arrived. But a stranger drove by in a smart little pony cart. It was Buddy Goodfriend on his way to Stephen Bullock's plantation, about which he had heard told many wonders and marvels—especially of the treasures Bullock had laid up in the years since the events that brought on the hard new times. Goodfriend, feeling particularly buoyant this fine, sunny May afternoon, saluted the three New Faith brothers as his pony trotted up the River Road but he did not stop to palaver. He was anxious to get to his destination.

Not a half hour later the three brothers were still at work, still waiting on the boat, when an even more unusual sight than a man driving a pony cart presented itself: a band of eleven Indian warriors jogging up the River Road in loincloths, feather and claw necklaces, ear wheels, and deerskin moccasins, their heads shaved but for top-knots or spikey roaches stuck up in tallow. Their faces were painted in alarming motifs, red and black vertically and horizontally, ghostly white with blackened eyes and clown mouths, red bands, slashes, spots, handprints. They carried war clubs and hand axes, wore crude steel daggers in their loincloth waistbands, or carried bows and quivers over their bare shoulders. The three New Faith brothers stood stock-still in place as the Indians passed by in a kind of relaxed dogtrot. Only the Indian at the van of the party turned to look at them. His painted face evinced an utter absence of emotion, making him appear all the more sinister. The others of the party trotted by as if the dock and the barn and the brothers at work weren't even there. Nobody at either end of the transaction interrupted the bizarre moment, and then the Indians rounded a bend in the road and vanished.

The brothers remained frozen a good minute after the intruders were gone. Brother Titus, still up on the roof, murmured, "Now I seen everything."

"I'm wondering did I really even seen that?" Oren said.

"I'm pretty sure I seen it, too, brother," Levi said. "But I sure as heck don't know what to make of it."

Then they nervously resumed their work.

Twenty minutes later it was as if the Indians were but a dimly recalled hallucination when Teddy Einhorn cried, "Hey, hello, and ahoy," from the bow of the *Katterskill* a hundred yards out. The New Faith brothers dropped their tools, clambered down, and scrambled out to the end of the crib dock while Daniel brought the homely boat about in the breeze and Teddy reefed the mainsail, and they made a perfect landing between the two cribs. Daniel threw Oren a line and soon the craft was secure in its new landing.

"Isn't she a beauty?" Oren shouted.

The two boatmen jumped ashore.

"I wasn't sure this was the right place," Daniel said. "It's good to be home. Nice job on the dock, by the way."

Meanwhile, Levi and Titus got the horses and hitched them to their sturdy open hay wagon. Once the cargo was loaded on it, and tied down, Oren led the horses on foot with a lead line up the long hill and the other men followed the wagon, armed and alert for Indians or anything else untoward that might come their way.

FIFTY-EIGHT

Sylvester "Buddy" Goodfriend hoisted his blown brandy snifter to admire its floral etching against the amber evening light that poured through the windows of Bullock's gorgeous dining room. He'd visited quite a few of the local wealthy farmers in the district over the past week, but Bullock's establishment dazzled him by an order of magnitude. He was only sorry to hear that Bullock's hydroelectric generator was on the fritz, perhaps permanently, since the lord of the manor had exhausted his backup supply of Pelton wheels. It had been a long time since Goodfriend enjoyed the luxury of electric lighting and recorded music. But the evening and the company and the meal had been nonetheless extraordinary.

Everything in Bullock's dining room was museum-quality: first-rate landscape paintings by Gifford and Kensett, a fine portrait of a male ancestor, Moses Bullock (1742–1819), in his Revolutionary War artillery officer's bottle green uniform, the inlaid Hepplewhite sideboard (Goodfriend, an antiques dealer for a few years before the collapse, supposed he could have sold the piece for a tidy thirty thousand back when money was money), not to mention the impressive trove of silver flatware on the table, the Georgian candelabra, condiment dishes, salvers, and so forth. It made his brain ring like an old-times cash register.

Goodfriend had stopped by at about six o'clock in the evening supposing, as he usually and so reliably did, that supper might be on its way to the table and that in the custom of the new times a sojourning stranger of apparent good bearing would be invited to share the meal—which is exactly what happened after he introduced himself to Sophie Bullock, who swept into the front hallway in a sleeveless, cream-colored, scoop-necked toile dress that reminded Goodfriend of his grandmother, a former

Wilhelmina model (divorced from husband number three, convicted Wall Street fraudster Bucky Felsch), who used to take him to the Lenox, Massachusetts, country club for butterscotch sundaes.

Bullock himself followed, like an equestrian statue come to life. Costumed in his usual buff riding trousers, fine boots, and an old damask vest embroidered with violets, with his silvery hair down to his shoulders, Bullock looked like he could found a republic single-handedly before lunch. His outfit and bearing made Goodfriend self-conscious about his own showy old-times expeditionary raiment. But when Sophie explained that the visitor represented the Berkshire People's Republic, and its leader Glen Ethan Greengrass, Bullock's eyes truly blazed. He put an aperitif mint julep in Goodfriend's fist, clapped an arm around his shoulder, and ushered him into the dining room like a spider showing a fly to the web.

Goodfriend made his confederation pitch over the first course of fresh asparagus doused in morels, spring garlic, and a creamy sauce based on dandelion wine.

"And what would we have to do in exchange for all these awesome political blessings?" Bullock asked, filling Goodfriend's glass with a sparkling Riesling-type varietal produced on the premises. Goodfriend proceeded to sketch out the subscription procedure.

"How cunning," Sophie observed. "We'd pay for government the way we used to pay for cable TV."

"That's right," Goodfriend said. "A small monthly charge that you hardly notice."

"Can you pick and choose the services you get the way we used to?"

"Such as what, ma'am?"

"Oh, say, go with the free trade and dispense with the printed money?"

"Well, there's a certain core package—"

Just then, Lilah the cook brought in another course: pike quenelles in a puddle of arugula puree. Bullock refilled Goodfriend's glass.

"You shouldn't," Goodfriend said.

"Live large while you can," Bullock rejoined. "Tell me about this leader of yours, this Glen Ethan Greengrass."

Goodfriend was getting a bit high, a little sloppy, but he was always happy to lay out the colorful Greengrass story: child prodigy Northeast regional chess champion; batboy for the New York Mets (three seasons); PhD in statistical macroanalytics at age twenty from the City University of New York; leading Iraq War protester (member of the "Hadley Five," who organized the May Day riot at the Portsmouth Naval Base and was then prosecuted unsuccessfully for destruction of federal property); director of the First Action Prison Diversity Network; twice Green Party U.S. Senate candidate (lost twice); tenured economics professor at Amherst College, where the "Greengrass Inequality Index" was developed; editor of the radical left political journal *The Fisted Glove;* beloved progressive radio personality, CEO, and station license holder of WBGB-FM and its thirteen affiliates; confidant of the late, great folksinger Pete Seeger; and finally founder of the Berkshire People's Republic when the old nation finally crumbled under the weight of its own political mendacity and economic crime. By the time Goodfriend finished the saga, the crickets were chirping outside the dining room windows and Bullock had lighted the tapers in the Georgian candelabra. Also, Lilah had brought in the entrée: medallions of lamb with a fresh mint and shallot salsa and gratinéed hominy. Bullock had also switched to a bright red Grenache wine made by the monks of North Hoosick and Goodfriend had put away two glasses of it before he concluded the well-rehearsed biography of his mentor.

When Lilah brought in dessert, a maple crème caramel with cornmeal madeleines, Bullock brought out some of his own quince eau-de-vie, with the fruit in the bottle, a neat trick that Buddy Goodfriend asked to have explained to him as he quaffed a double dram of the fine spirit. (The end of the branch with its developing fruitlet was inserted in the bottle, which was suspended in situ from the tree until the fruit finished growing in October.) But he was so drunk that he kept on interrupting, saying, "Tha's marv'lous, jus' marv'lous," over and over, and finally ended the meal with his face planted squarely in what remained of the crème caramel before him.

Bullock rang for Lilah and told her to summon his subalterns Dick Lee and Michael Delson. Sophie excused herself from the table while Bullock waited and enjoyed his own dessert. The men appeared ten minutes later, coming, as they did, from their own cottages up the hill in Bullock's employee village. They were, at first, taken aback at the sight of Goodfriend, inert at his place.

"Evening, gentlemen," Bullock greeted his trusted aides jauntily, dabbing his mouth with a fine linen napkin. He had a bit of a buzz on too.

"Is he okay?" Dick Lee said, tilting his head at the disposition of the guest's face in the dish.

"Still breathing, but I've seen better table manners," Bullock said. "Take him to the blue room, will you, and freshen him up."

FIFTY-NINE

Seth and Elam stole over the landscape like a pair of panthers, keeping to the hedgerows and wooded ridges, searching for the new encampment of the Berkie bunch, as they called them. They had received the news of the brazen theft at Einhorn's store before leaving town. They were to reconnoiter a quadrant of the rural township where they thought the raiders were most likely to be, and meet up with Brother Joseph and his mixed band of fifty-three Union Grove and New Faith men at seven in the evening at the Center Falls bridge.

The late day was still and warm and the low sunlight cast every tree and rock in a stark chiaroscuro. They climbed the ancient folded ridge called Spook Hill only as high as necessary to survey the terrain to the west and north, an area that comprised about seven miles of the course of the Battenkill. They supposed that the Berkies would want to be near water if they intended to stick around for more than another day, for carrying water was the hardest chore of camping. From their position at elevation the rangers could discern columns of smoke here and there rising in the breezeless sky. Most of these were farms. But at one particular wooded place about two miles away in a straight line they counted thirteen thin columns of smoke and one greater one, which they took to be a likely bivouac of their quarry. Elam had just raised his binoculars to his eyes when the muffled thud of a pneumatically supressed rifle shot sounded, like a hand ax hitting a stove billet, and Seth watched Elam's head fairly explode in a cloud of red mist like one of the pomegranates they liked to use for target practice in the dull hours between battles back in the Holy Land. A moment later, the ranger's large and noble body crumpled in place like a puppet with its strings cut.

Seth knew instantly that his longtime comrade was dead before he hit the ground. He dodged to his left behind a tree as a second shot missed his own head. He wiped Elam's blood from his eyes, switching off his emotions as he had so many times in war when other friends dropped beside him. About a hundred yards farther up Spook Hill was an outcrop of pyritic slate where Seth saw a little cloud of gunsmoke hanging in the air, a result of the poorer quality propellant available in the new times for reloading cartridges.

Seth scrambled around to his right and crosswise, thinking that whoever fired on them facing downhill would instinctively move that way if he were right-handed. He climbed practically on all fours up and over the uneven terrain, careful not to disturb the brush and saplings, movement of which might betray his position to someone stalking him. Shortly, on a level shoulder of Spook Hill, he crossed a fresh trail of crushed bracken ferns, followed them awhile, and saw ahead a pileup of large glacial erratic boulders through a stand of hemlock. He stopped moving and could actually hear wheezing from there, as of someone with weak lungs attempting to catch a breath. He began to steal closer to the rocks a few footsteps at a time, until he was pressed against one as big as a cabin covered with pale green lichen. The heavy breathing had subsided but he could smell the odor of an unwashed human close by. He sat patiently for ten minutes, waiting for any other sounds that would betray the movement of his enemy. Seth remained as still and silent as if he had been deposited in place with the ancient glaciers.

By-and-by Ainsley Perlew left his hiding spot and ventured past the edge of the big rock where Seth waited. Ainsley held his rifle with both hands as if he expected momentarily to have to defend himself. But Seth easily seized him, spun him around, took away his weapon, and had him pinned on his back on the ground before the young man knew what was happening.

"Who are you?" Seth asked.

"What?"

"You with them Berkies?"

"What?"

Seth walked calmly three steps to his left and jerked a stout naked branch from a nearby fallen hemlock. In the meantime, Ainsley Perlew tried to scramble to his feet, but Seth caught him with a fierce blow to his left kidney. The young man shrieked and fell. Seth waited for him to stop squirming.

"What's your name?"

"Sonny Boy."

"How old are you?"

"What?"

Seth jabbed the pointy end of his branch in Ainsley's armpit.

"Ow! Nineteen!" he yelled.

"You still somebody's sonny boy at nineteen? Looks like you got a man's job."

Ainsley just glared back blankly, breathing through his mouth.

"Where are all them people parked?" Seth asked.

"What?"

Seth smacked him upside the head with the branch. "Them Berkshires."

"Down by the river."

They were only a few feet apart, but the distance between them might have been a million miles.

"What you think I oughta do with you?" Seth asked.

Ainsley shook his head.

"You just kilt as fine a man as they is. You know that?"

Ainsley began to cry rather stoically.

"Look at this weapon of yours," Seth continued, holding up the rifle. "That's a high-class sniper scope on this thing. What are you? An assassin? I think so."

Ainsley Perlew mutely blinked back at him through tears.

"'Course you ain't sayin'. Let me tell you something. They ain't no courts, no judges anymore. So I'm gon' have to judge this case myself. I can't turn the other cheek to what you done. Sorry. You kilt my best friend in cold blood. There ain't no shadow of a doubt about it in my mind. I would like to beat you to death with this here tree limb so you would die by degrees, mebbe regretting the wrong you done. But it would be less than Christian to do that. I will be merciful. I don't have no time to take you back to town where my people would judge you and hang you. Folks are waiting on me now and lives may depend on it. So I pronounce you guilty and sentence you to be gone from this world, and may the Lord have mercy on your soul."

Seth racked the bolt, then hesitated a moment. Their eyes met.

"I'm a good boy," Ainsley said.

"No, by God, you are not."

Without further ceremony, Seth tossed the branch aside, took aim, and lodged a bullet in Ainsley Perlew's heart. He flung the rifle at the slight figure now sprawled inertly on his back in the cedar duff with his unseeing eyes open to the dark treetops. Then he turned around, staggered to the cabin-size rock, and cried his own eyes out.

SIXTY

Dick Lee and Michael Delson had succeeded in freshening up Sylvester "Buddy" Goodfriend. His old-times expeditionary clothing had not prevented them from drenching him with bucket after bucket of water in "the blue room"—the bottling room of Bullock's distillery, in the basement of the building, with a tile floor and a drain in the middle of it. Once he was awake, they chained him by the wrists to a sturdy oak bench. Bullock came in from the manse after he had finished a cup of genuine coffee from his stash of culinary rarities. The blue room was dimly lit by a single candle lamp, hung from a hook in the center.

"Whatzis all about?" Goodfriend asked indignantly, clearly still drunk.

"It's about you," Bullock said.

"Well, I don' like it," Goodfriend said. "I'm not so inneresting. You're more inneresting than me, I'm sure."

"Perhaps. But my fate here tonight is not at issue and yours is. Later on, I'll be in bed with my wife, in an amorous frame of mind. We'll have a little roll in the hay and then, before lights out, I'll read some Anne Tyler to her. We're in the middle of *The Accidental Tourist* now. Are you an accidental tourist, Buddy?"

"Huh . . . ? No."

"Of course not. That was a rhetorical question. You came here for a reason. But now you know where I'll be later tonight and what I'll be doing. How about you, Buddy? Where will you be and what will you be doing, say, a couple of hours from now?"

"I hope I won't be here."

"The question is: will you be anywhere?"

"Aw, for chrissake . . ."

"You've strayed far from home in order to winkle money out of people like us, haven't you?"

"Not true!"

"Subscribe to a political union? I never heard such malarky."

"You can't run a federation for free."

"What am I going to do with you?"

"I think you're gonna hurt me."

"Yes, I could. Is there anything you could tell me that might prevent that?"

"Wha' could I tell you?"

"For instance? Do you have any backup out there?"

Buddy just sat on the wet bench, shivering and blinking. He remained silent.

"All right, then," Bullock said. "Have it your way."

He went and fetched a rubber apron that hung from a hook on the back of the door, took his time tying it on, then retrieved a twenty-four-inch bolt cutter from the bottling bench.

"Whazzat?" Goodfriend asked.

"I'll demonstrate."

Bullock and Dick Lee moved toward Goodfriend. Dick Lee put his boot up on the back of Goodfriend's chained-down hand, squashing it so that the fingers were splayed. Bullock positioned the jaws of the bolt cutter at the first joint of Goodfriend's right pinky finger.

Goodfriend began to wail: "Oh God, oh God, oh God, oh God . . ."

"You don't use that finger much, do you?" Bullock said. "But if we have to work through a few more of these, I'm afraid you won't be playing in the Berkshire Federation marching band anymore."

"Wait!" Goodfriend shrieked.

"Well?"

"There is something," Goodfriend said between wails and sobs. In another minute, stammering in desperate urgency, he betrayed Duane Terrio and his band of counterfeit Indians.

"You mean, they're here, out there on the property, as we speak?" Bullock asked.

Goodfriend nodded and broke down blubbering.

"Get the riot squad," Bullock told Michael Delson, who departed at once to alert the core of twenty dependable men among the denizens of the plantation who were trained to disarm bandits, pickers, and other interlopers. "Let's get this poor sot a drink," Bullock said to Dick Lee, his sturdy aide-de-camp, who didn't have to search far in the bottling room. He quickly located a jug of off-batch corn whiskey with a rather high fusel oil contaminent ratio, not good enough to sell and certainly not to consume on the premises.

Bullock pulled the cork and held the jug up to Goodfriend's lips, but they could not persuade him to drink any.

"What's the matter, Buddy," Bullock said. "Lost your taste for life's comfort?"

Goodfriend replied only with more blubbering.

"Very well, then," Bullock said. "We'll give you a little help."

He fetched a big red plastic funnel from the shelves and touched Goodfriend under the chin to prompt him to tip up his head. In a swift agile motion that took him back to his college EMT training days, Bullock jammed the neck of the funnel clean down Goodfriend's throat, past the base of the tongue and the hyoid bone into the esophagus. He grabbed a good fistful of hair so Goodfriend was immobilized while Dick Lee proceeded to empty the entire contents of the jug into the funnel. Goodfriend affected to gag, but the liquor was draining straight down into his stomach.

"Get another," Bullock said.

Dick Lee emptied a second jug of the 90-proof whiskey down Goodfriend's throat. They yanked out the funnel and held him upright by main force, still chained to the bench, for a good ten minutes, at which point Goodfriend went limp. Meanwhile, they heard a distant commotion and scattered gunfire somewhere outside the two-foot-thick stone walls of the distillery's foundation. The riot squad had engaged the enemy.

Sixty-one

Seth left both bodies on the shoulder of Spook Hill and hurried to his appointment at the Center Falls bridge. The evening sun had just ducked behind the treetops when he saw the fifty-three armed men waiting where the road crossed the river, some squatting in the broken pavement, some leaning over the old iron railing watching trout fin the Battenkill below, and Joseph standing somewhat ahead and apart from the others, as though he knew that his comrades would show up exactly as they were supposed to. Then Seth appeared alone, hurrying down the road.

"Where's Elam?" Joseph asked.

"Shot and killed, sir," Seth said plainly, his own tears having dried in transit.

"Oh, my good Lord," Joseph said as though rocked by an ocean wave. "By who?"

"Young bushwhacker from the outfit we's after," Seth said. "I done put an end to his career. His remains is up there too." Seth watched Joseph struggle to get a hold of his emotions. "We'll sort it out later, sir," he went on. "Our objective is about two klicks yonder in a hayfield on the river." He pointed up the road he'd just come from, opposite the setting sun.

Joseph mustered his men to attention and explained what they were about to do next: march up the road a mile or so, duck into the woods, and take up positions around a hayfield, pinning the Berkshire raiders with their backs to the river, then round them up and march them in custody back to town, where the village trustees would determine what to do with them.

"It's going to be twilight time we get there," Joseph told them. "Not the best visual conditions. I believe we can git this done without violence. They are many amongst this bunch no more than children, so don't you be trigger happy. All right, let's move out and set a double-time pace. We can make our objective in fifteen minutes, maybe still be able to see what the heck we're doing."

A half mile up the road they came upon Brother Gabriel groaning in a ditch. That was the first they'd heard that the Berkies had hijacked his trap cart and its cargo of six rifles and ammunition. Joseph left two men with him in expectation that they would return soon with wagons and transport him back to the doctor in town.

The rest were shortly upon the Berkshire bivouac. The hayfield had gotten a first cutting. The grass was laid in rough rows to dry before stacking. A half dozen horses were picketed near the river and the various wagons parked in a line between the field and the road. Many individual campfires were lit before the ragtag of tents, and also one larger communal one at the center of the grounds. The men of Union Grove deployed stealthily in the darkening woods on two sides of the hayfield, with several more riflemen stealing behind the idle wagons to defend that egress. The Berkshires had been cooking a communal meal at the big fire, turning out crude cornmeal and water hoecakes baked on a shovel over the coals and attempting to boil up beans in several pots on a piece of chain-link fence that was their grill. The men in the woods overheard a mixed thrum of chatter, palaver, complaint, plus the shouts and cries of children playing indefatigably and a cacophony of various stringed instruments being plucked. Somewhere in the hayfield, a child shouted, "I can't eat this," and an older voice shouted back, "You'll eat it if you know what's good for you!" Orange and green twilight lingered in treetops. When he was satisfied that all his men were in position, Joseph strode out of his cover in the woods into the open and discharged a shot from his rifle into the sky. The chatter and shouts ceased. Some of the young ones dropped closer to the ground. Heads turned toward Joseph as if viewing a fearsome apparition.

"All of you in there, listen up!" Joseph bellowed to them. "Drop whatever you are doing and assemble over on the road."

None of them moved or spoke.

"Do not tarry," Joseph said.

"Who are you and what do you want?" a husky female voice replied from near the big fire. It was a voice familiar, at least, to Seth.

"We are the authorities from Union Grove," Joseph said, "and I am placing you under arrest."

"We don't recognize your authority."

"You don't have a choice in the matter," Joseph said. "You are surrounded on all sides. Assemble up on the road and do not waste another minute."

"He's bluffing," one of the older boys shouted across the campground. "It's a trick."

"This is no bluff and no trick," Joseph said. "Get up to the road or we will come and drag you up there."

"Stay where you are!" the same boy retorted.

There was no further reply. Joseph waited thirty seconds and gave the signal to press inward, which was transmitted all round the hayfield. The men of Union Grove began to emerge from the woods in the dim light and press in. As they did, they were met by the muzzle flashes of rifle fire from the center. They dropped to the ground and commenced to return fire in withering volleys, their own rifles well outnumbering their adversaries'. The fierce exchange lasted barely ten seconds. When it was over, groans, shrieks, and weeping could be heard all around. Joseph and ten men on the south side of the hayfield swept into the campground. The men on the other sides followed, snagging many of the youngsters as they attempted to escape into the woods or past the line of wagons. In the chaotic hour that followed, with daylight extinguished and only the big campfire at center providing any illumination, all the young adults and children of the Berkshire spring outreach were rounded up under armed guard and accounted for, including Flame Aurora Greengrass, their weapons taken from them. Nine of their number lay dead, all ages from a girl six years old to a boy of seventeen, lined up like windrows in the hay stubble. Seven additional wounded were placed in the wagons. One man of Union Grove lay dead: Bob Bouchard, a woodcutter on Robbie Furnival's crew, shot in the eye.

One Ralph Horsley, a laborer on the Ben Deaver farm, broke his ankle tripping over a log. Joseph left Seth with five men behind to wait for daylight, when they could inspect the premises for anyone and anything of value left behind and retrieve the two bodies off Spook Hill. Everyone else, the living, the groaning wounded, the dead, returned to town in procession as the moon rose over the old county highway.

At the head of the procession Joseph drove the trap cart that the Berkies had taken from Brother Gabriel earlier that day. A sickness of spirit gripped Joseph all the way back to town as he realized that the action of this evening would resound in infamy far, wide, and long: the massacre of the children. History would not care about the actual circumstances, that he and his men were fired upon and responded instinctively as men under fire will. Nobody will see or care about any part of this story except the children gunned down by grown men, Joseph thought, a slaughter of innocents, whether it was true or not.

SIXTY-TWO

Robert went to Daniel's newspaper office and living quarters directly, before he even brought Mookie back to the New Faith stable. A light burned deep within through the front window. He tied the horse to a lilac bush beside the building, tried the doorknob, and entered without knocking. Daniel was seated at the end of the long table near the woodstove, eating a supper of the remaining things he and Teddy had brought back from Albany: some smoked sturgeon, hard cheese, and what was left of the groat bread. He was also working on a bottle of Kinderhook rye whiskey.

Daniel stood up abruptly as Robert entered. Father and son regarded each other for a long moment across a yawning gap of age, experience, and expectation.

"We only returned a little while ago," Daniel said. "We were on the river all day long. Then we had to off-load the cargo. I was going to come over to the house later."

"I guess you found a suitable boat."

"A fine one. Got hold of some good broadsheet newsprint paper too."

"Great," Robert said. "Can I sit with you awhile?" He seemed agitated and abstracted to Daniel.

"Sure," Daniel said. He fetched another glass from the nearby hoosier cabinet and poured Robert a double dram of whiskey. "You smell like a horse."

"The whole world smells of horse," Robert said. "I've been riding all over the county." He helped himself to some of the smoked fish with his fingers.

"You must be hungry," Daniel said. He fetched another fork and plate for his father, sliced off some cheese, and carved up the heel of the groat bread to share.

"Whoever smoked this fish knew what they were doing," Robert said.

"It's from a provisioner in Albany. Aulk's."

Robert told Daniel about the barn burnings, the men gotten up like Indians terrorizing the farmers, the shakedowns and robberies, the phantom presence of Glen Ethan Greengrass holed up in the new hotel.

"I heard about some incident at Einhorn's store today," Daniel said.

"What incident? I was gone all day."

"Late morning, a bunch of those Berkshire kids looted the place. They roughed up Teddy's father and the retarded boy."

"How bad?"

"They'll be all right. They beat them with a broom handle."

They ate silently for a while. The whiskey got into Robert's bloodstream quickly. He looked up at Daniel. His eyes were moist and he appeared to have difficulty forming words.

"What is it, Dad?"

"Something terrible has happened to us," Robert said. A sound came out of him that was something between a groan and a bark. He covered his face and sobbed. Daniel had not seen his father in such a state since his mother, Sandy, died. He nervously got up from the table and stood back in the dimness beyond the corona of the candlelight, as if he had to physically put distance between himself and his father's torment.

"Our little girl died," Robert said, his voice full of phlegm and grief.

"Huh?"

"Sarah."

"What? Just like that? While I was gone?"

Robert nodded.

"Oh no . . ." Daniel moaned and doubled over as if someone had kicked him in the gut. He struggled to control his own breathing. He had come to know Britney's little girl as though she were his own sister.

Robert struggled to compose himself again. He managed to tell Daniel the story in a string of succinct sentences: tetanus, the death scene, the burial at the old house. When Robert was finished, Daniel rolled his eyes in a gesture of cynical contempt for the malign and capricious entity some called God.

"I'm so sorry," he said. "She was a dear, sweet child."

Robert nodded but choked up on a tangle of words unspoken and fell to weeping again with his face buried on his arms on the table. Daniel came around the table and squeezed his father's shoulder. He was sure that anything else he might say would be fatuous. Eventually, his father pulled himself together again and Daniel returned to his seat, thinking he could just abide with father and his grief for a while. He poured himself another whiskey and refreshed Robert's glass.

Robert knocked it back in one gulp.

They sat together silently awhile longer, Robert slumped in his seat, eyes unfocused, looking inward, really.

"Britney wants another child."

"Do you love her?"

"I do," Robert said. "And I don't want to lose her."

"Then give her another child."

"I can't."

Daniel puzzled over that a moment.

"When I was recovering at the house," he said, "I was pretty sure you two were . . . doing it."

"Yeah," Robert said. "We do it."

"So keep doing it. You know, on the right day when she's—"

"I had a vasectomy back . . . after your sister was born."

"A what?"

"You don't know what a vasectomy is?"

"I never heard of it."

Robert just stared at Daniel for a moment, putting it together. Of course Daniel had never heard of a vasectomy. It was no longer part of adult life in the new times of America, hadn't been since Daniel was a small child. There may have been a number of things

Robert took for granted that Daniel had never heard of because they no longer existed: radiation therapy, Prozac, dialysis, liposuction, stents, CAT scans, gastric bypass.

"It's an operation where they snip the little tubes that carry your sperm into the stream of semen," he explained.

"Like castration?"

"No, no. Your testicles still produce male hormones. But you're effectively sterilized. You can't get a woman pregnant."

"You had that?"

"Yeah. It just was after we'd moved here. The economy was just starting to fall apart. We had no idea it would get to this, but we were afraid to bring any more children into the world. Anyway, it's done. They can't undo it. I can't give Britney a child."

They sat at the table in the candlelight silently for a long time after that, working on the Kinderhook rye.

"So I've been thinking," Robert said eventually.

"Yes. What about?"

"Maybe you could . . . you know . . ." Robert had been staring into the refracted light of the candle flame in his whiskey glass. He looked up at Daniel and they locked into each other's gaze.

Daniel did not say anything. He just nodded his head to signify that he'd comprehended.

"Just . . . an idea," Robert said. "Maybe you could think about it."

Daniel nodded again. Robert drank down the whiskey remaining in his glass and pushed back from the table.

"I guess I'll be going," he said.

SIXTY-THREE

Joseph left the injured and dead children at the doctor's with four New Faith brothers and several townsmen to assist the doctor in moving them in and out of his surgery and the springhouse that served as his morgue. Then he hurried to the old high school and dispatched some of the sisters who had experience nursing the invalid Mary Beth Ivanhoe when she was ill down to the doctor's place as well. The fifty-nine Berkshire children and teens arrested but not injured were taken to the sanctuary, formerly the school assembly hall, where blankets were found for them, and guards posted to watch over them sleeping on the proscenium stage until it could be decided what further to do. Joseph took Flame Aurora Greengrass to a special solitary cell, a small chapel that had been a teachers' lounge in the old times, and placed her under guard there. Finally, he faced the awful task of informing Brother Jobe what had happened.

The pastor and honcho of the New Faith Covenant Brotherhood Church of Jesus was in his quarters, the old principal's suite on the first floor, where he'd been waiting anxiously all evening for the return of the defense force. He sat behind his desk, where he'd been trying without much success to compose a sermon for the coming Sunday service titled: "Getting in the Glory Land Way for Dummies." Joseph entered without knocking. Brother Jobe shot out of his seat.

"You're still up, then," Joseph said.

"'Course I'm up," Brother Jobe retorted. "Did you find them birds?"

"Yessir," Joseph said, fingering his hat.

"You round 'em up and bring 'em back?"

"Yessir, we did."

Brother Jobe waited for more.

"Well, don't just stand there like a seegar store injun."

"It didn't go down so smooth, sir."

"Let's have the details, then."

When he learned that the stalwart Elam was dead Brother Jobe's legs wobbled. He lunged for the back of his desk chair and lowered himself gingerly into the seat as if he might fall down on the floor and shatter like a porcelain statuette. Then, when Joseph went on to say that they had killed and wounded over a dozen children in the skirmish, Brother Jobe cradled his forehead in his hands, leaned forward on his elbows, and struggled to keep from hyperventilating. Joseph gave him the rest of it briefly and gently: Seth remained at the site of the fray and would bring back the bodies of Elam and his murderer at daylight. The wounded were at the doctor's. The rest of the children were in custody on the premises and the woman known as Flame was sequestered from the rest under guard in the little chapel.

Brother Jobe remained humped over at his desk.

"Git Boaz, Zuriel, Shiloh, and Eben down here," he muttered, without raising his head, referring to four of the most mature and reliable brothers. "Fit 'em out with sidearms. We got to see about something right away."

"What's that, sir?"

"That'd be Mr. Glen Ethan Greengrass, the author of all this mischief and tragedy."

SIXTY-FOUR

Daniel was cleaning up the dishes, half dead on his feet, half drunk, when he heard somebody else at the door, rapping timidly. He considered pretending he was not there but nobody in these new times would leave a home or a workplace without extinguishing any live flames and a candle still burned on the table. So, with his heart in his gut, he went to see who was at his door. It was Karen Grolsch. A smile ignited on her face at seeing him.

"I heard you were back," she said.

Daniel was shocked to realize he'd all but forgotten about her in the rush of events and was startled to see how radiant she was.

"Are you okay?" she asked.

"Uh, yes, I'm okay," he said.

"Can I come in for a moment."

"Uh, yes, please come in."

He threw the door all the way open. She smelled of soap and lilac as she stepped past him. She was tall, only a few inches shorter than him, but lithe, sprightly in a light blue summer frock and a thin cardigan sweater, her movements like music in their liquidity. He watched her eyes take in the big room with all its printing equipment and the contrasting domestic areas, the sitting area, the kitchen, the bed—two worlds in one place.

"I've been drinking some," he said. "Forgive me."

"That's okay," she said.

"We were on the river for two days. Out in the sun. Long days."

"Yes, I heard. You got that boat."

"We did," he said. "We brought back a nice boat."

"I've been busy while you were away," she said. She carried a canvas tote and pulled out bundled sheafs of papers covered with handwriting. She began laying them out on his kitchen table. "This is my interview with Mr. Bullock—"

"How did you manage to do that?"

"I just went over there and asked to see him."

"You're brave."

"He was gracious. He talked to me for an hour in his study and gave me whiskey. This other report is about the speech that the visiting Mr. Greengrass, founder of the Berkshire Republic, made from the window of his hotel room while you were gone. I transcribed it the best I could, but it didn't make much sense. I got a lot of comments from the villagers. They didn't get it, either, so it wasn't just me. This other one is a report on the robbery that took place today at Einhorn's store."

"I heard about it."

"Yes. It's all here."

"You have been busy," he said. "Are you still the duck boss at Weibel's?"

"Quack quack," she said. "That means yes."

"I'm impressed," he said.

"I told you I would take this seriously. Maybe now we can put out a newspaper."

He looked down at the packets of papers neatly arrayed on the table before him, then back at Karen, and said, "Yes, yes, I believe we can."

She saw something darken his features. He rocked on his heels. He put his hand to his mouth as if his insides were rebelling.

"What is it?" she asked. "Are you sick?"

He tried to look away.

"Tell me," she said.

Gasping for air, he told her.

SIXTY-FIVE

Loren had been sitting beside his son Evan in the room behind the doctor's surgery when the men from the village defense team brought in the wounded and the dead. The place had been exceptionally quiet up to that point, just a sweet spring evening with the sounds of new life bourgeoning outside the window: night birds, insects. Loren had been reading *Huckleberry Finn* to Evan by candlelight. The young man remained unconscious but did not show any gross signs of infection or fever. His brow was dry. From time to time he sighed or shifted slightly in bed. Then the others came from the battlefield about an hour or so after nightfall and the old carriage house turned clinic erupted in a commotion of cries, weeping, prayer, groans, and shouted orders, as the dead were laid out, the wounded were sorted, and the laboratory prepared once again for surgery. Loren left Evan and offered his assistance. Three New Faith women arrived claiming to have nursing experience and set to tasks at once. The doctor and his wife and son donned their scrubs, arrayed their instruments, and fired the autoclave. The candle stands and mirrors were deployed along with fresh linens, grain alcohol antiseptic, opium suppositories, cloth dressings, and bottles of intravenous fluids. And then the surgeries commenced.

They would be at it until sunrise. In the event, the doctor was able to save three of the seven wounded, including a seven-year-old girl who survived the amputation below the knee of her shattered leg. A teen with a head wound died as soon they brought him to the table. Others did not survive their blood loss, trauma, and shock during arduous ordeals under the knife. Loren, who was physically large and strong, was given the task of holding down the patients on the table, as the opium anesthetic did not render the patients completely unconscious, lest the dose kill them outright. Their agonies could be heard over much of the east side of the village, and people began to venture from their homes and collect on the street before the doctor's establishment to see what was going on. Among those who had ventured down from the Congregational Church's parish house was Jane Ann Holder, who was enlisted at once in helping to care for the surviving children in a new postoperative ward set up in the infirmary on the second floor above the surgery, unaware that her own son lay in the ground-floor back room recuperating from his own ordeal.

SIXTY-SIX

Brother Jobe and four of his men marched across town from the New Faith headquarters directly to the new hotel in the center of Main Street. Even downtown they could hear the commotion up at the doctor's, a sound cloud of anguish. Inside, Brother Jonah sat behind the desk, as usual. The bar was closed this night, because Brother Micah, the tavern manager, had turned out for the village defense force. Jonah had been trying to read another Clive Cussler adventure novel, *Valhalla Rising*, but was unable to concentrate owing to the distant screams and howls abroad on the night air, even after he'd closed the windows in the front room.

"What all's going on out there, sir?" he asked when Brother Jobe and the men marched in. "Sounds like banshees and goblins on the loose."

"It's just some people got hurt in a skirmish," Brother Jobe said. "Is that Mr. Greengrass yet up in his room?"

"His boys come down now and then," Jonah said, "but I ain't seen the man himself since he come in. I think he might be ill, sir."

"Yeah, so they say. We gonna personally examine the sumbitch. Come on, let's go."

The New Faith men lit a candle and followed Brother Jobe upstairs to the door of the Greengrass room. Their polite knock on the door was answered by a surly retort, "What do you want?"

"We want to speak to Mr. Greengrass."

"He's very sick."

"That's what you said before."

"Nothing's changed."

"No, things *have* changed. Open the door or we gonna bust it down."

Brother Jobe and his men waited. Eben and Zuriel hoisted their pistols from their waistbands. Brother Jobe nodded to Shiloh and Boaz, who threw themselves against the door and shattered the jamb. The door flew open. Inside, two hulking young men saw the brandished pistols in the mix of candlelight and the moonlight streaming through the window. Every surface of the room was occupied by empty plates and glasses from the meals they'd ordered up. A hand of playing cards lay on a tea table arrayed in the gin rummy way, with the wheelchair as one of the seats there.

"Git over in that corner by that chiffonier," Brother Jobe told them. They shuffled past the card table to the designated spot. "This place stinks like a hog pen."

"What's all that screaming out there?" one of the young men asked timidly. In the old times, he might have been a linebacker on the high school team but he had the soft, unformed face of a child and the voice of a choirboy.

"That's the sound of you-all's youngsters all shot up," Brother Jobe said.

"Who shot them?" the other young man asked.

"Just shut up," Brother Jobe said, then called across the room: "Mr. Greengrass, can you hear me?"

"He's sick—"

"You keep saying. And didn't I tell you to shut up?"

"Leave him alone!"

Shiloh smacked the boy upside the head with the flat of his hand.

Brother Jobe approached the bed warily. Glen Ethan Greengrass lay inert on the bed. He was not tucked within the bedsheets but rather lay on top of the undisturbed blankets with a thin white-tufted bedspread pulled up to his shoulders. He appeared to be wearing clothing under the bedspread. Brother Jobe leaned closer with his candle. Greengrass's face was sunken and shriveled. In the meager light the concavities beneath his cheekbones were so deep they looked like excavations. The skin was like old parchment. His hair was unnaturally dark and full and carefully combed. The lips were shrunken back to such an extreme that the face appeared to be deviously grinning.

"Don't touch him!"

Shiloh smacked the boy again.

"Didn't he tell you shut up?"

"What are you?" Brother Jobe muttered, reaching out to draw down the bedspread, which he then flung aside, revealing the full shrunken figure in a tattered old business suit several sizes too large, the tips of bony fingers like claws on a bird of prey, and shiny black shoes on its feet that looked several sizes too large. An odor as of rot overlaid with disinfectant spirits rose off the figure. Brother Jobe turned to look back at its two young guardians. "What is this? Some kind of puppet?"

One of them gaped with his mouth open. The other tried to look away as if frightened or ashamed. Neither replied.

Brother Jobe slid his left hand under Glen Ethan Greengrass's head. As he attempted to lift it, the full, dark hair fell away all of a piece, revealing an incision that circumscribed the skull. Brother Jobe slid his left hand farther down under the figure's shoulders and his right hand under its hips and lifted it up in both hands. The figure was as stiff as a four-foot length of two-by-six lumber and didn't weigh as much as that. Brother Jobe looked down on the thing in his hands with disgust and amazement. He turned so that his men could behold it. As he did, its head drooped backward and, with a slight tearing sound, came loose and fell off the body and onto the floor, where it bounced once. Grains of sawdust and wood chips fell from the aperature that had been his neck.

"I be dog," Brother Jobe said, "if Glen Ethan Greengrass ain't a ding-dang mummy!"

His two young guardians let out howls that drowned the screams of the dying children emanating from four blocks to the east. One fell to his knees and began to throw up.

Brother Jobe turned to gaze down at the shrunken remnant of a former person in his hands and said, "My thoughts exactly."

THE HARROWS OF SPRING 283

Then he heaved the body clean out the open window in a forceful arc that made it appear, for a moment, as if it might take flight. But gravity intervened and it landed in the street with a faint thud. Finally, Brother Jobe picked the head and the wig up off the floor and stuffed them in a pillowcase.

"Take these two gomers back and put 'em in with the others," he told Shiloh and the men.

Sixty-seven

As he made his way home on horseback across the village from Daniel's quarters, Robert heard the commotion at the doctor's place and then saw the people on the street and stopped to ask what it was about. Charles Pettie of the church music circle was one of the several dozen neighbors on the east end of the village who had gathered there. They carried candle lanterns as in a vigil.

"What happened?" Robert asked him.

"Weren't you in on this?" Charles said. "They got up a militia, you know."

"No, I had to go out in the county and see about the mischief there."

"I would have gone with them but for my bad knees," Charles said. "The Berkies fired on our people. Some children got hurt. More than a few. Dear God . . ."

Robert asked him to hold on to Mookie while he went inside. The doctor's waiting room had been turned into a triage unit where the New Faith nurses were trying to comfort and console those awaiting surgery. Among the men acting as orderlies, moving the patients in and out, was Tom Allison, the former college dean who ran the livery now. Robert went over to him.

"It's going to get around that we killed a bunch of kids," Tom said. "I hope you're prepared."

"I don't even know what happened," Robert said.

Tom laid out what had gone down in the hayfield.

"They fired on us," Tom said. "After that, well . . ."

Robert attempted to comprehend the scene.

"We're good people," Tom insisted. "We are."

"I know," Robert said.

"I've got to go," Tom said. "They need me now."

Robert realized that in the close quarters of the chaotic scene he would only be in the way, so he went back down the driveway and spoke briefly as mayor to the gathered townspeople to convey what he'd learned of the situation. He saw no point to remaining out there among them and he rode the horse back to the New Faith stables. None of the brothers was on duty there when he came in. Enough moonlight entered through the cupola so he could see what he was doing. He took off Mookie's tack, put him in a stall, found some oats in the grain room for him and a fat flake of hay, and brought him a bucket of water. Then he walked the rest of the way home to the house on Linden Street. It was upwind of the doctor's place and the cries of the wounded and dying were so faint as to be barely audible. When he stepped inside he discovered Britney sitting on the sofa in the front parlor.

"You're sitting in the dark," he said, realizing it was a self-evident and stupid observation.

"The moon's full tonight," she said.

"Well, that's true."

"I was alone all day."

"I'm sorry I couldn't be here. We've had a sort of emergency."

"What sort?"

Robert realized she had virtually no idea what else had been going on for days. He didn't want to spell out the terrible result: children dead and dying.

"Trouble outside of town. I had to ride around the county all day."

"Are we being invaded?"

Robert hesitated. "Just some bandits," he said.

"I thought I heard screaming far away. Is someone having a baby across town?"

"No. The doctor's working on some people who are hurt."

"Anyone we know?"

"No. Just the bandits."

Britney nodded.

"Can I sit with you?" Robert asked.

"Yes."

He slid in beside her. He could feel her warmth through the flannel bathrobe and the sweater on top of it.

"How are you doing?" he asked.

"I'll never get over this," she said.

"I know."

"What do you know about it?"

"Well, I lost a wife and a daughter," he said.

"Of course," she said. "Forgive me. I'm ashamed of myself."

"It's okay," he said. "It was a long time ago."

"Did you ever get over it?" she asked.

"No," Robert said. "But I found you."

She turned to him.

"Let's make a child," she said. "You and me."

"We've been together a year, you know, and you haven't gotten pregnant."

"I know when I'm ovulating. I can feel it. I've been extremely careful all these months. I didn't want to tell you."

He reached over and touched her cheek, pulled some of her long hair away from her face, and tucked it behind her ear.

"Do you know what a vasectomy is?" Robert said.

Britney nodded. Then, suddenly, her tears ran as if a faucet had just been turned.

"Oh shit oh shit oh shit oh shit," she said and twisted herself way from him pressing against the back of the sofa.

Robert let her cry herself out. He tried to rub her neck and shoulders but she batted him away. Finally, she turned back around, looking forward. Not saying anything, just struggling with her sadness.

"I have an idea," Robert said.

She was sniffling and it took her a while to heave a big sigh and say, "What's your idea?"

"You could get pregnant by ... other means."

Her eyes widened as if he'd said something crazy.

"Haven't you heard?" she said. "There are no more fertility clinics."

"I mean somebody else could do it."

"You want another man to get me pregnant?"

"I know you want another child."

"But it wouldn't be your child."

"What if the other man was Daniel?"

This time her face expressed a collapse of all hope.

"That would never work," she said.

"It would be partially mine," he said.

"It would never work," she repeated. "Never. Never ever."

He saw no benefit in arguing about it. His face also sagged in futility.

"It was just a thought," he eventually said, sunk in embarrassment and resignation.

She reached for his hand and squeezed it damply, though as she did she turned her head to front again and did not look at him.

SIXTY-EIGHT

Brother Enos sat in the hallway outside the little chapel room where Flame Aurora Greengrass was confined. That wing of the old high school, which otherwise contained classrooms turned to workshops, was quiet as a mausoleum at this hour. Brother Jobe trudged down the hall carrying the sack that he'd brought from the hotel. A candle burned on a stand next to Enos's chair and he just stared ahead into space.

"Whyn't you read a ding-dang book or something while you sittin' here," Brother Jobe said. "Improve your mind a little."

"Yessir, I'll do that next time."

"You can read, can't you?"

"Yessir."

"There's a whole doggone library down yonder hallway."

"You want me to go get a book right now, sir?"

"No. Next time will do. Open the ding-dang door. And lock it back up whilst I'm inside."

Enos took the key that hung on a cord around his neck and unlocked the door. It opened with a creak. Brother Jobe carried his own tin candle lantern into the room. The twelve chairs set up for Christian meditation were shoved to one side of the room and a cot had been set up in one corner. Flame Aurora Greengrass had been lying on it. He could see where she had attempted to stack up two chairs in hope of getting to the clerestory windows near the top of the wall. But the window openings were only nine inches and someone her size could never have wiggled out, even if she'd been able to get up to them, which she hadn't. Flame propped herself up on an elbow squinting in the meager light as Brother Jobe pulled up two chairs close to the bed and sat down on one of them.

"Sit up, young lady."

"Think you can label me whatever way you like?"

Brother Jobe ignored the remark.

"Do you know who I am?" he said.

"You're some little fat man in funny clothes."

"I'm your fate, sittin' here right next to you, taking a special interest in what you done and what you going to do."

"What does that mean?"

"For starters it means you'd best be polite. Go on sit up now, right here acrost from me."

Flame stared back impudently a moment, then hauled herself upright on the cot facing Brother Jobe.

"Are you some officer of the law?" she asked.

"I'm the chief executive and pastor of the New Faith Covenant Brotherhood Church of Jesus, and that's as much authority as you got for the time being."

"I have a right to an attorney?"

"As it happens, I'm an attorney myself."

"You're kidding."

"You want me to go git the Duke University sheepskin? Don't bother answering. Maybe some other time."

"I have a right to remain silent."

"I wish you would because then I could get on with the bidness at hand."

Brother Jobe picked up the sack he'd brought in with him, reached in, carefully removed the mummified head of Glen Ethan Greengrass, and set it upright against the backrest on the other chair beside him. Flame recoiled at the sight of it and placed a hand over her mouth.

"Yeah, I know it ain't a pretty sight," he said. "Maybe this here'll help."

He took the wig out of the sack and put it on the mummified head without quite being able to determine how it was supposed to fit.

Tears began to squirt out of Flame's eyes and she drew her knees up into her chest.

"That your daddy?"

Flame nodded her head.

"Looks like he ain't been among the living for a while."

"He . . . lives . . . in our hearts," she said.

"As the departed should. But you been traveling all about the countryside with him for some time trying to scare folks, and rob them, and now you gone too far. You brung a lot of misery down on your own fellow travelers. There's thirteen of yours dead and three more shot up but alive, one of them a seven-year-old girl that had to have her leg cut off. Plus one town man you shot in the head and one of my rangers killed today," Brother Jobe said, his voice both rising in pitch and breaking, "one of the finest human beings I ever known, bushwhacked by that sharpshootin' runt of yours, who's dead now too, by the way." He struggled to regain his composure. "There's at least half a dozen common laws of conduct that I could hang you under."

"We don't believe in capital punishment."

Brother Jobe smacked the seat of the adjoining chair so hard that the head of Glen Ethan Greengrass fell on the floor and rolled under the cot. He did not bother to retrieve it. Flame shrieked and began to hyperventilate.

"It don't matter what you believe," Brother Jobe hollered back at her. "Not anymore. What matters from now on is what I require of you. Where's that sumbitch Buddy?"

Flame shook her head wildly.

"You don't know or you ain't sayin'? I'm fixin' to hang his ass too."

Brother Jobe watched Flame blubber awhile.

"Let me ask you something," he said eventually. "Do you know why Achilles chased Hector around the city of Troy three times?"

She continued to shake her head while her eyes blazed and her nose ran.

"Because he was just that pissed off," Brother Jobe yelled at her again and rose halfway out of his seat doing so. The tendons in his neck stood out like they were piano wires. "And you got me feeling much the same way. Where's that Buddy at?"

She would not reply but only glared back in opposition.

Brother Jobe brought his right index finger out vertically in front of Flame's face. He captured her attention and it was all he needed.

"Lookit here now and follow," he said.

He swerved his index finger up to the outside corner of his right eye. At the same moment, the glare went out of Flame's eyes. She let go of her knees and came to sit primly on the edge of the cot, psychologically his captive.

"I'm amongst your mind now," he told her. "Can you feel it?"

"Yes."

"Where's Buddy at?"

"Bullock's," she said.

"Was he aimin' to rob Mr. Bullock?"

"Yes," Flame said.

"From what all I know of Mr. Bullock, Buddy done picked the wrong fellow to try and snooker. I'd calculate that Mr. Bullock done disposed of him by now. You think I'm quick to anger? Why, Mr. Bullock, he's a human magnum load with a hair trigger. Those men playin' Indian go with Buddy?"

"Yes."

"He's probably got them strung up like Christmas lights down along the River Road. Mr. Bullock don't have no patience for bandits. Nor mercy. He's a harsh man. I don't like to think that I'm like that. But you and your bunch have really tried my Christian patience. Can you give me a reason why I shouldn't hang you?"

"I'm pregnant," she said, without a particle of emotion.

It was Brother Jobe's turn to be startled. He left his position at the threshold of her mind and ventured deeper into the dark realm of her memory and experience. What he discovered there stunned him.

"You're carrying Elam's child," he said.

"Yes," she said.

Brother Jobe sat quietly for quite a while, his own emotions in turmoil, weighing the situation and all its ramifications as he explored more deeply the mind of the young woman before him. The damage of her upbringing and her passage into the difficult new times was as plain to him as the injuries suffered by Mary Beth Ivanhoe after she was crushed by an SUV automobile.

"You prepared to bear this child?" he asked at length.

"Yes," she said.

"You understand you will have to dwell with us?"

"Yes."

"I'm gonna make a special provision for you. You'll live in a special place. You will be cared for and looked after and watched over. It ain't gonna be like the life you led before. Understand?"

"Yes.

"Henceforth, you'll be known among us as . . . Sister Venus. Flame is gone. She done sputtered out. A new you has took her place. Understand?"

"Yes."

"I'm gonna count backwards from ten and you gonna fall asleep. When you wake up, you won't remember none of this, but you got a new place and a new role in this world. Understand?"

"Yes."

"Ten . . . nine . . ."

When he arrived at one, Brother Jobe reached out and helped ease her down onto the cot, where she reposed in stillness with her head on a pillow and her hands clasped beside her face as if in prayer. He left his chair, retrieved the mummified head of Glen Ethan Greengrass from under the cot and the wig that had come off again, and stuffed them back in the pillowcase he brought them in with. Then he went to the door and told Enos to unlock it. Enos peered inside.

"She asleep?"

"She gonna be for a good while," Brother Jobe said.

"Mercy," Enos said.

"She's out of the woods now, I judge. I'm gonna send some of the sisters down to set with her. By-and-by they gonna bring her upstairs. She won't cause nobody no trouble no more."

When he got back to his own personal quarters at half past four in the morning, Brother Jobe found his all-around man Friday and confidential assistant Brother Boaz waiting in the office.

"What'd you do with the better half of Mr. Glen Ethan Green-grass's mortal remains?" Brother Jobe asked.

"I got him in the janitor's closet yonder, in a box."

"Well, take this here," Brother Jobe said proffering the sack with the head and the wig in it, "and go bury him out in the corn somewheres. It'll be light in little while."

"Yessir."

Boaz made to leave.

"Wait!"

Boaz halted in midstep.

"On second thought, make a nice fire out there and cremate the sumbitch. Then scatter what's left to the four winds."

SIXTY-NINE

Karen Grolsch did not leave Daniel's place that night but retired with him to the big bed between the Hoosier cabinet in the kitchen area and the printing office that occupied the rear two-thirds of the building. There they did what young people hungry for affection, affirmation, and amity will do, and they did it repeatedly through the long hours of night, and remained awake even after that, so thrilled were they in the unfolding discovery of each other's bodies and beings. Moonlight poured into the room through the transoms of the fine old windows. They were far enough across town that the cries of the surgeries did not carry there.

"They say you've been out west," Karen murmured, folded halfway over Daniel with her long, elegant fingers tracing the valley between his pectoral muscles.

"I was in Michigan for a while."

"How did you get there?"

"On a beautiful ship. A big schooner. On the Great Lakes."

"What did you do in Michigan?"

"I fell in with the government," he said. "With what was left of it. What people now call the Federals. They moved their headquarters there, a town they named New Columbia. I stayed offshore at a place called Channel Island, out in Lake Huron, where most of the officials lived. I was enlisted into an agency called the Service and went through their training there."

"What were you trained to do?"

"I was trained to kill people," Daniel said.

Karen hoisted the top half of her body above Daniel to take in his face. Her breasts dangled before him. He cupped one and kissed it.

"Did you kill anyone?" she asked.

"Yes."

She lowered herself back down and tucked her head beside his shoulder.

"Were they bad people?"

"They were bad enough in a particular way," he said. "I'm not sure that anyone is evil through and through."

"Did you decide who you killed?"

"One I had instructions to kill. The others I had to decide on my own due to the circumstances. One I had reason to kill, and he pretty much asked for it, but I let him go. I'm telling you this because I believe I can trust you. But you need to know who I am and what I've been."

"You can trust me," Karen said. "I think I know what you are."

"What do you think that is?"

"It might shock you."

"Go ahead."

"You're a warrior."

Daniel struggled to digest it.

"I never thought of myself that way," he said. "I agonized over my mission."

"Then you're the best kind of warrior."

He was so disconcerted he searched for a way to reply.

"Does it scare you to be with someone who could do such things?" he asked.

"I feel safe with you. I feel you would protect me."

"I would," he said. "I'm grateful that you aren't judging me."

"I'm not afraid of you. We must take the world for what it is and who we become."

"Maybe you have some warrior in you too."

"Right now I'm just the duck boss. Quack quack."

"Translation?"

"I think I love you," she said, and her lips went searching for his again.

SEVENTY

The table in the conservatory was laid for a morning meal as Duane Terrio, aka Wawanotewat of the Pocumtuc people, was led in hobbled and shackled by Dick Lee, Stephen Bullock's estimable majordomo and Michael Delson, his second aide-de-camp. The latter two were armed and took wicker seats in opposing corners of the lovely room with its orchids, bromeliads, and other interesting specimens. Bullock was not there yet. The early morning sun traced a lacy pattern through the tangled vines that grew along the walls from brick-lined beds. Lilah the cook brought in a tray with two juice glasses on it. They were filled with a purplish liquid. She set them down and smiled at the prisoner. She had never been in a room with an Indian in native costume before.

"Morning," she said, taking in his topknot and his exotic accessories.

"Morning to you, too, ma'am," Terrio said. "You don't happen to have a key to these handcuffs, do you?"

She shook her head, smiled again, and withdrew.

"Isn't this pleasant?" Terrio observed.

After a suitable interval, during which Terrio grew increasingly nervous and the other men remained silent, Bullock swept in through the door in his riding togs, having been out since dawn inspecting his domain on a fresh Hanoverian gelding named Plutus.

"Why you're looking bright-eyed and bushy-tailed, my fine-feathered friend," he said. "Forgive the mixed metaphor. How'd you sleep, by the way?"

"Oh, just great. All chained up on a wet tile floor in a basement."

Bullock sighed, then said to no one in particular, "Why do people think that sarcasm enhances communication, I wonder. Saying the opposite of what you mean for effect." Then he turned his attention back to his guest at table. "Anyway, I'd think you'd be used to sleeping rough, living as you do."

"We don't sleep wet, generally."

"I take your point. But then, admit it, you've been a rather naughty fellow. Trying to burn down my horse barn and scaring the servants. Of course I treated you harshly. But not as severely as your compadres, who sleep in bliss like never before because they are all dead now. Every last one of them. I've got them stacked like cordwood over in the apple storage barn. And Mr. Goodfriend, your patron? Why, he's as stiff as a board this morning having, unfortunately, drunk himself to death."

Terrio flinched and then squirmed in his comfortable wicker chair.

"Take off the cuffs, Michael," Bullock said. Delson handed Bullock his rifle and freed Terrio's hands. Terrio shook them to get the blood circulating. Delson returned to his seat with his weapon. "So perhaps now you're thinking why have they kept me alive?" Bullock continued. "Are you thinking that?"

"Maybe."

"Come on, be a little more definite?"

"Okay, I'm thinking that."

"Good, now we have some basis for conversation. Cheers!" Bullock hoisted his juice glass and drank down the contents.

"What is that stuff?" Terrio asked.

"Sumac tonic," Bullock said. "Loaded with vitamin C. Try it. It's great for you."

"You want me to be healthy, huh?"

"Well, you seem a little wan. It's not so easy living off the bounty of field and forest, I suppose."

"We've gotten better at it," Terrio said.

"But mostly you steal stuff, right? Come on, be frank."

"Okay, we had to supplement our diet."

"But I give you credit. You must be a pretty clever fellow to even attempt this aboriginal thing. Ah! Here come the blessings of Western culture!"

Lilah reentered with another tray and slid plates before Bullock and his guest, along with a basket of freshly baked corn bread and little ramekins of butter and blackberry jam.

"Dig in."

"I'm not hungry."

"Oh please! Of course you are. Running around the countryside like a goddamn savage, looting and burning. Doesn't that work up an appetite?"

"Mister. You scold me for being sarcastic, but you talk in circles," Terrio said. "Why don't you just get to the point. How come you're keeping me alive?"

"Well, all right, then. First, I wonder if you might clarify this Berkshire People's Republic baloney. What was that all about?"

"It doesn't exist," Terrio said.

"I suspected as much."

"Just a line of bullshit to get hard money out of suckers. We're from over there, but it's no better off than this part of the country, maybe worse. It was all Buddy's idea. He picked up kids with no family, no parents, along the way to front him. Then he brought us into the picture and things got a little rougher. Now, here we are."

"Yes, here we are," Bullock said. "How do you like it here?"

"What? This place?"

"Yes. Does it seem comfortable? Civilized?"

"Civilized," Terrio echoed him. "I've been struggling with that."

"Evidently."

"Look, the old me would say it's a hell of an operation," Terrio said. "I was sorry to try and burn it down."

"Why, thank you," Bullock said. "And so now I'm thinking, perhaps this man—you—may prove useful in an enterprise like this, a person with the skills you have, and elastic scruples. You're like a good piece of equipment, a weapon of war, say, that might come in handy. So why throw it away? Do you see what I'm getting at?"

"I think so."

"Of course I had to sacrifice your traveling companions. I couldn't keep such a crew around, wondering if you'd try to cut our throats some night. Please taste the omelet. It's our own cheese and the ham comes from pigs that are finished off on acorns before we slaughter them."

Lilah returned with a pot of coffee and filled each man's delicate pink luster cup, then set down the cream pitcher and honeypot.

"Is that real coffee?" Terrio said.

"Puerto Rican arabica, a sassy Mondo Nuevo."

"Damn. Where do you get it?"

"If you make a little effort you can get stuff," Bullock said. "We get stuff."

"Okay, what can I do for you?" Terrio said, and hoisted his fork to address the contents of his plate.

"Do you know what a Pelton wheel is?"

"I got no idea."

"It's the key part of a hydroelectric generator system. I have such a system here. The Pelton wheel is what the running water hits to spin the turbine. As it happens, mine broke. I thought I was being clever to lay in several backup replacements, but they broke too. Serves me right. They were manufactured in China. If the goddamn thing was working, we'd be listening to some Erik Satie right now—just the thing for a beautiful spring morning. Did you know that Satie and Claude Monet were born in the same town in France about twenty-five years apart?"

"No," Terrio said.

"I think of them as absolutely complementary, the music, the paintings—like *fromage* and *jambon*."

"Huh?"

"You wonder what was in the air of Honfleur in those days."

Terrio just shook his head and tucked into his omelet. They ate silently for a minute.

"Why didn't you go solar?" Terrio eventually said.

"Intermittancy," Bullock said. "Sometimes the sun shines, sometimes it doesn't. The Battenkill always flows."

"Even in the depths of winter?"

"Oh yeah. The penstock is well below the ice formation."

"What's the penstock?"

"It's a pipe that concentrates the flowing water into the turbine."

"Oh—"

"But this is getting didactic."

"Huh?"

"Too much information," Bullock said. "The thing is, I know a gentleman over in the Camden Valley, just over the Vermont line, who purchased the exact same system as I did. Name of Blake Harmon. He's doing pretty well over there, considering these times. He laid in some extra parts too."

Bullock hoisted his coffee cup.

"You want me to go over there and get 'em?" Terrio asked.

"I was thinking of something along those lines," Bullock said.

"I could do that. I could get 'em for you."

"Then maybe I could find some other ways you can be useful here. You'd have to live on the property, of course."

"I could live on the property."

"And not in some silly-ass wigwam, either."

"I can return to your ways."

"Oh, come on. They were your ways, too, most of your life. Plus, you have to wear regular clothing. Grow your hair back like a normal person. Halloween's over."

"Whatever."

Bullock dashed his damask napkin into his empty plate and downed the last of his coffee.

"I think we've reached a framework for understanding," he said.

Terrio lifted his coffee cup, a wary smile for the first time lightening his not unhandsome features.

"Cheers to that, sir, and second the motion," he said.

"That's the spirit. All right fellows, take him back."

"Huh? You're putting me in that hole again?"

"Well, I have to think about this," Bullock said. "Weigh the pros and cons."

"But you said we had an understanding."

"Yes, a nice framework for an agreement. I won't shilly-shally over it. Don't worry. But this is a large establishment with a lot of complex parts and relationships. And it's my responsibility to consider the big picture." Bullock turned to his aide. "Oh, Dick, better put the cuffs back on."

"What!"

"Just a formality. To preclude any transitory temptation."

"Oh, fuck you, mister . . ." Terrio said.

"See what I mean? How am I supposed to keep you around if you fly off the handle so easily?"

"Okay, okay, I'm sorry," Terrio said. "I apologize. Really. Go ahead, put the cuffs back on. Look, I'm cooperating."

"Noted," Bullock said, then he left the table. Dick Lee and Michael Delson led Duane Terrio back to the basement of the carriage barn.

Ten minutes later, Bullock emerged back into the courtyard, where Dick Lee held the reins of a fresh mount for him. His lumber crew was cutting some old-growth cedar on Lily Pond Hill two miles over at the west end of his property and he wanted to make sure they didn't overdo it.

"I've been thinking it over, Dick," Bullock said as he put one leg on the mounting block.

"Yes?" Dick Lee said.

"That fellow's just not going to work out."

Dick Lee nodded.

"It was worth a try," Bullock added.

"I'll take care of it, sir."

Bullock climbed on board his fresh horse and rode off to supervise the morning's work.

Seventy-one

Britney told Robert that she was going out gathering wilds. The morning was warm, dry, and so clear that, to Britney, the air itself seemed to magnify every detail of the waking world, every leaf, every cloud, every living, flying, buzzing thing. Robert had gotten up before her to make their breakfast, but when she came downstairs she said that her stomach was too upset to eat. She said good-bye through the door while he was in the bathroom and left the house without a sack or basket to carry her wild gatherings home.

She took Main Street east out of town, past the ruined Kmart, and hiked up the empty highway through a landscape raucus with birdsong until she got to the old railroad right-of-way that led just a short distance to the decrepit steel truss bridge across the Battenkill. She walked carefully down the old rotting wooden ties that lay across the rusty girders, cognizant of the irony in watching her step. She stopped about two-thirds of the way across. Forty feet below, the large glacial erratic boulder called the Priest by fly fishers of the old times waited in a current reduced in force from its early spring flow. The Battenkill made a lush green tunnel an eighth of a mile down to a bend in the river where yellow iris blazed in a sunbeam above a quiet shoal. Cedar waxwings dipped back and forth across the stream eating caddis flies as they shed their larval armor and took flight as adults. The insects that dallied in the surface tension skin of the water, drying their wings too long, were slurped down from below by hungry trout, who made little dimples in a pool downstream of the Priest as they fed.

Britney could not reconcile the stupendous beauty of the world with its sadness. The birds, the fish, and the insects that performed in the spectacle before her all owed some duty to violence and death, Britney thought, and so did she. There was no escape from it. In the old times, which she remembered very well, there was a multitude of distractions to allow you to forget these primal obligations to existence. Some people never even encountered them until their final moments, when it turned out to be the biggest surprise of their lives. The last thing she would be, Britney thought, on this warm, bright spring morning, was surprised.

A waist-high strut ran the length of the bridge on the edge of the carriageway deck. Britney leaned against it breathing deeply. Her pulse raced and her head pounded as she contemplated what she willed herself to do. A sour bile rose into her throat as if a reminder of creation's bitter ruthlessness and her vision blurred as her eyes filled with tears. She made a short speech in her head thanking Robert for his kindness and care, apologizing for the way she'd said good-bye, and wishing his forgiveness, and then she stepped on a diagonal brace to climb to the top of the strut.

Jane Ann Holder saw the figure on the bridge from about fifty yards down the tracks on the far side of the river. She had been earnestly gathering wilds herself—nettles and burdock in a sack and morel mushrooms in a basket—as a way to get outside and clear her head after the ordeal of the night surgery. She had been relieved in the recovery room at seven in the morning by Bobbie DeLand, who had been a geriatric nurse. The horror of the dying and mutilated children still left Jane Ann wobbly and a night without sleep amplified the raw emotion roiling inside her. When she halted in her footsteps up the tracks from the bridge, and realized that the woman in the thin white frock was Britney, she put down her sack and basket and called out to her. As Britney turned her head to see who was hailing her, Jane Ann hurried the rest of the way onto the bridge. Britney clambered onto the strut, looked down at the Priest and at Jane Ann rushing toward her, and let go of her grip on the vertical girder post. For a moment she hung suspended between the world and the not-world. But Jane Ann was six inches taller than Britney, and strong, and she gripped Britney around the hips and wrenched her down off the strut. In the process, both women fell in a heap on the railroad ties that formed the flimsy, rotting deck, Britney shrieking and flailing at Jane Ann with her fists. Jane Ann held tight to Britney until her shrieks became sobs and she stopped struggling.

"Let me go," Britney sobbed.

"Only if you promise to be still," Jane Ann said.

She hesitated to agree and Jane Ann held on. Finally Britney said, "Okay, okay, okay, okay . . ."

Jane Ann relaxed her grip. She could see daylight and rushing water through the railroad ties and girders beneath. She torqued her body and hauled herself upright. Then she reached down and took hold of Britney's slender but muscular upper arms, hoisted her up, and allowed Britney to fall into her embrace.

"Come, let's sit together awhile," Jane Ann said.

Britney nodded.

Jane Ann led the smaller woman the rest of the way across the bridge to a mossy embankment cut through the land a century and a half earlier by the railroad builders. The gentle slope there was as soft as a carpet.

"Come sit."

They lowered themselves onto the moss. Sunlight shimmered in the silver beeches across the tracks as a mild breeze stirred the glittery coinlike leaves. Britney cried again for a long time and Jane Ann simply held her hand until she ran out of tears.

"Please don't tell anyone," Britney said.

"I won't."

"What am I going to do in this world?" Britney asked.

Jane Ann hesitated, struggling to contain her own emotions.

"I heard what happened to you," she said. "I know what it's like to lose a child. Evan has been gone for three years. Every day

I have to battle with the empty hope that he'll turn up. I don't win the battle. But even so, something inside me remains grateful to be in this world. I don't want to leave it, even if he's gone. If anything, I feel a stronger duty to remain here."

"This world is vile," Britney said.

"No, it's a strange and mysterious gift. But it's up to us to care about each other and somehow, after a while, that leads to caring about being here."

"I don't know if I can bother trying anymore."

"There's a child who needs you," Jane Ann said.

"What child?"

"One of the kids wounded yesterday."

Britney looked bewildered.

"You don't know what's happened?"

Britney shook her head. "Something about bandits, Robert said."

"These were not bandits," Jane Ann said. She described the incident in the hayfield. The casualties. The night surgery. The survivors.

"How terrible," Britney said.

"There's a little girl, six, maybe seven, we're not sure. No name yet. Her lower leg was shattered and the doctor had to take it off. She'll need a home. She's not going back to where she came from. None of them are. Would you consider taking this little girl in and caring for her?"

Britney appeared overwhelmed.

"I don't know," she said.

"Would you come see her with me?"

Britney brought the heels of her palms up to her eyes, struggling to find the will to reply.

"You're a good mother," Jane Ann said.

Britney dropped her hands, nodded her head, and resumed weeping.

"Okay," she said between sobs. "Okay."

Jane Ann put an arm around Britney's shoulder and drew her close. They sat in a little patch of sunlight until Britney came back to herself.

"Come," Jane Ann said. "Let's go see her."

She helped Britney to her feet. Jane Ann retrieved her sack and her basket. Together they crossed the old railroad bridge and made their way back to town.

SEVENTY-TWO

Bullock returned from the timber cutting at midday for lunch with his wife. Sophie brought a basket up to the Japanese teahouse that Robert Earle had built some years ago beside the half-acre pond stocked with trout. They sat on cushions at a low wooden table in the open pavilion with blue clematis climbing up the trellis on each side. The table was weather-burnished the same vivid silver color as Sophie's hair. She took the various items out of the basket and arranged them on the table: a small teapot and two porcelain cups, a glass box containing negimaki—grilled rolls of thin-sliced beef around spring onions—and another of mushroom dumplings, a tiny ceramic jug with a wooden stopper containing soy sauce made on the premises, and a shaker containing ground red pepper. They ate off the blue Karakusa plates that Bullock had shipped home from Japan during his post-collegiate sojourn there. The whole operation thus far had been conducted in a kind of formal silence they often observed for these teahouse lunches, a retreat from the morning's busyness into ceremonial Zen-like calm. Today, however, Sophie's concerns could not be palliated by simple stillness.

"Dear," she said, lifting her teacup.

"Um . . . yes?"

"A favor, please."

"Yes, sweetheart?"

"Those trespassers you captured last night?"

"Yes. Very bad men."

"Of course. Did you . . . you know . . . ?"

"Yes, it's done."

"Where are they?"

"Laid out in the apple storage cooler."

"I hope you won't make a morbid display of them on the River Road?"

"You never go down there," Bullock said.

"Yes. But they frighten other people."

"Gosh, hon. That's the idea," he said, spreading his hands out as though a banner hung in the air between them. "Message: thieves and riffraff will be dealt with severely."

"A painted sign might do as well, don't you think? Perhaps with a picture of a hanged figure."

"Frankly, I disagree. There's something more persuasive about a ripe corpse hanging from a tree picked over by buzzards."

"Stephen! We're eating," she said, placing a delicate hand demurely over her midriff to denote gastric distress.

"Sorry," he said, brandishing a chunk of negimaki between two chopsticks, "but you know those savages came this close to burning the place down last night."

"I understand, darling."

"Who knows who or what might blow this way next. Cannibals, thrill killers, Visigoth wannabes."

"The thing is, dear, after a few days they begin to stink."

"It can't be helped." Bullock made a helpless face, a moue, as if his samurai demeanor had suddenly and mysteriously turned French.

"A south wind comes up on a hot day and it's so bad I go all cross-eyed," she said. "It even gets into the draperies and the linens."

"Actually, I think the smell is a most effective element in the total presentation—"

"I insist, darling. You must find some other way to dispose of them. Or I may be forced to, I dunno, withhold my affections."

"Oh, don't say that."

"I feel rather strongly about it."

Bullock popped the beef morsel in his mouth and chewed contemplatively for a minute.

"Oh, all right," he said. "I don't want to make you unhappy."

SEVENTY-THREE

Later in the afternoon, the Reverend Loren Holder sat beside the bed of his wounded son in the doctor's back room. The young man had not shown any signs of fever or infection but he remained asleep on tapering doses of opium. People had come and gone all day outside the door and upstairs where several children lay recovering from their surgeries, along with Edward Tenant, who had come through his ordeal with the sawmill splinter.

Loren stayed at his boy's bedside downstairs. He slept a few hours on the floor beside the bed but remained depleted from the travail of the night surgery. He did not think about food. He drank water from a pitcher on the table beside the bed and he peed out the window into the bushes when necessary. Now he was reading *Lolita* by Nabokov, marveling at the lost world of the mid-twentieth century, and the sly mastery of the author's manner, when he looked away from the page and saw his son looking right up at him with his eyes half open.

"I think you're my father," Evan said in slow, slurred, weak voice.

Loren dropped the book.

"I am your father," he said, and fell to his knees beside the bed so that he and Evan were face-to-face. "It's me, son."

"How'd I get here?"

"Some of our men found you on the road and brought you back."

"Hey, I'm really stoned. This is like some kind of dream."

"The doc's got you on opium."

"I think I prefer whiskey," Evan said. He laughed slightly and then coughed. "Really, where are we? Heaven?"

"No. You're home."

Loren brought his hand up and tenderly brushed the hair off Evan's forehead.

"Home? Oh, that's where I was going. I made it then."

"Yes you did. I'm so glad."

"What happened?"

"I thought you might tell me," Loren said.

Evan sighed. "I don't know. I was on a horse. What happened to my horse?"

"I think the people who shot you stole it."

"They shot me?"

"Yes. Several places. Dr. Copeland worked on you. You're in the room behind his lab."

"Oh, gosh ..."

Evan tried to move his body.

"Careful," Loren said.

"These sheets are too tight. Untuck them a little."

"I think the idea is to keep you from moving."

"Aw, Dad, my butt is sore. Give me a little room in here."

Loren did as he asked. Evan shifted slightly.

"Ouch. Whoa. I got a lot of sore places. What are these tubes?"

"Glucose and water. Are you hungry, thirsty, do you want anything?"

"How do I pee?"

"He's got a catheter in there."

"Oh, jeez ... Where's Mom?"

"She doesn't know you're here."

"Huh? You didn't tell her?"

"You had a lot of surgery. If you didn't make it, I didn't want her to know you came all the way back home and ... you know ..."

"You were gonna not tell her?"

"Yeah, that was the plan."

"Jeez ... Hey, maybe I won't die after all."

"I'm thinking maybe you're going to be okay."

"Well, maybe you should go tell her I'm here."

Loren burst into tears and touched his cheek to Evan's, kissed him several times, and in a voice choked with emotion said, "Yeah, I think I'll go get your mother now."

SEVENTY-FOUR

Daniel came by the doctor's place well after sundown, when word reached him that Evan Holder was there. Loren and Jane Ann had been sitting with Evan for hours as he alternately slept and woke, and he was alert when Daniel got there. Evan's parents gave the small room to the two young men who had not seen each other for more than two years, since their misadventure on the way west ended in the foundering of their boat on Lake Erie.

Daniel took the chair that Loren had been sitting in. Such was their amazement at finding each other again that they couldn't stop beaming, or find the way to begin.

"Well," Daniel said.

"Well," Evan said. "Bet you thought you'd never see me again."

"That's a wicked fine beard you've got going," Daniel said. "Last time we were together you hardly had to shave."

"Yeah? Think I should keep it?"

"There's a barbershop in town now."

"You don't say."

"Things are a little different here now."

Their smiles faded and neither spoke for a while. A candle burned brightly on a table at each side of the bed.

"I'm told you got shot on your way home," Daniel said.

"I've been shot at before. But this was the first time they actually hit me."

Daniel was able to laugh before he gagged on his surging emotion.

"You can't imagine how many times I've thought about that storm on the lake, and watching you slip away, and not being able to save you." Daniel reached for Evan's hand and took it and squeezed it. "I'm amazed to see you and so glad you're home. So glad."

"Maybe when I'm around for a while you'll change your mind," Evan said.

Evan closed his eyes and subsided into sleep. Daniel watched Evan's chest rise and fall. A minute later his eyes reopened.

"Was I asleep?"

"Yeah. Only a minute or so."

"My father says I'm on opium. It's a weird feeling."

"They say you're doing fine. Can you tell me what happened to you when our boat broke up?"

Evan coughed, tried to order his thoughts.

"Well, you wouldn't believe how close to land we were," he said. "I saw a light in the distance and just swam for it. I dunno, a half mile maybe. I was half frozen to death when I crawled out of the water. A place called Kelleys Island, not far off Sandusky Harbor. I washed up on the rocks and yelled at the light. It was the cottage of a fisherman named Peter Sale. He lugged me inside, wrapped me in blankets, and poured hot water and whiskey into me. I survived. I had no idea how to go looking for you. So I didn't."

"Same for me," Danel said. "Go on."

"I worked with him on his boat until August, netting whitefish and smoking them there on the island. He was a fine, fair fellow, and I felt that I owed him, but I couldn't stay at it. It was a lonely life there, just me and him. Once every two weeks we'd go to the mainland with the smokers. So that one time late in the summer I didn't go back to the island with him."

"What happened to your silver and gold?"

"I had to drop my pants in the lake. They were dragging me down."

"It was in your pockets?"

"Yeah, lost it all. Had to. I got work in the market in town, loading freights. As soon as I had a little silver I went back to cards. I got some decent clothes and made my way around that part of the country playing cards. It was what I was good at, turns out. I ranged as far as Wisconsin. I had a fine career. Oh, the lakes are grand. I was on my way home with thirty-two ounces of gold sewn into the lining of my coat when this happened. I don't even remember getting shot."

"Where's the coat?"

"Oh, I suppose the robbers have it now."

"That's a damn shame."

"Tell you the truth, I've won and lost a few fortunes since we were traveling companions on the E-ri-o. Now tell me. What happened to you?"

Daniel did, mostly, in the rest of the hour that they were alone together, though he was not ready to tell his old friend what exactly he had done in the Foxfire Republic.

SEVENTY-FIVE

In the week that followed, Stephen Bullock disposed of the bodies of the interlopers he'd had executed. To spare his workmen the chore of digging twelve graves, he put them to the less arduous task of building a wooden raft fourteen feet square, and on it he stacked the bodies amidst a great pyre of firewood. He towed the floating crematory several miles downstream with his schooner and had his men ignite it. A northwest wind blew the smoke in the direction of Massachusetts, the ancestral home of the Pocumtuc Algonquins. Sophie Bullock was satisfied with the arrangement and did not withhold her affections from her husband.

Jane Ann Holder met Robert Earle and Britney Blieveldt at the doctor's infirmary to visit the seven-year-old girl who had lost the lower part of her left leg. Her name was Elizabeth or Liza Kellner, a scrappy, bright-eyed child eager for life on the new terms it offered to her, and grateful for the prospect of being taken into a household with something like a real mother and father after her time in the custody of Sylvester "Buddy" Goodfriend and his minions.

All but seven of the surviving Berkshire youngsters were taken into the New Faith compound and other households among those townspeople who felt comfortable enough with their care and upbringing. Those other seven, all boys sixteen and older, were escorted in wagons to the boundary where Washington County, New York, met Vermont and released with the warning never to venture across it again.

A funeral for Brother Elam (old-times name, Hugh Parmelee) was held in the Union Grove graveyard, where he was buried beside Brother Minor, son of Brother Jobe, who had been shot the previous year by the villain Wayne Karp. Many of the regular villagers who had come to know and admire Elam turned out for the ceremony.

The euology was delivered by Seth, his devoted friend and comrade, recounting their many adventures in the Holy Land and then in the not so united states of America in the years since.

Fifty volunteers combined from the village and the New Faith, under the supervision of Brother Shiloh, the engineer and builder, journeyed to Temple Merton's farm and camped there for three days restoring his barns and outbuildings, and then moved on to the other farmers who had suffered vandalism and rebuilt their barns too.

Daniel Earle published the first edition of the new *Union News Leader* with its editor and publisher denoted as one "Orlando Heathcoate." The top story in the upper left-hand column of the crowded broadsheet was a frank report under the byline of Karen Grolsch about the tragedy at Ramsdell's Hayfield, as the property was subsequently called, because it belonged to farmer Frank Ramsdell of Battenville, including the strange events and depredations leading up to it and the horrific aftermath. Another column reported the executions of one Sylvester Goodfriend and eleven bandits captured in an arson and looting attack at Bullock's plantation. Copies of the newspaper were sent far and wide when the Germantown tub *Katterskill* made its maiden voyage down the Hudson River to Albany with a crew composed of Teddy Einhorn, the new pilot, and Corey Widgeon, his sole crew, an old schoolmate of Daniel Earle's. The *Kingston Pilot* and other papers replied over the following weeks with censorious editorials about "bloody Washington County." Stephen Bullock, for one, considered these the best advertising conceivable to ward off future incursions of pickers, bandits, rogues, and riffraff who gave passing thought to visiting the locality.

In the middle of June, Robert Earle received a written message from Stephen Bullock, hand-delivered by Dick Lee. It was a proposal to put to rest all the ill will of the bygone year and an invitation to a baseball game to be played that Saturday night between the men of Bullock's plantation and the men of Union Grove, including any members of the New Faith brethren who felt competent to take the field. Bullock's hopes were pinned on his center fielder, Cecil

316 JAMES HOWARD KUNSTLER

Fullmer, a onetime minor league prospect for the New York Mets' Class AA Binghamton club (now in charge of Bullock's ox barn). The game would be played, Bullock proposed, in the old VFW field on the south side of Union Grove, tucked behind an abandoned Chevrolet dealership and the village road-sanding storage facility and garage, no longer in use.

Brother Jobe was interested in the proposal, for the sake of improving relations, and supplied four brothers to the Union Grove nine who had played at various times in their youth in the Babe Ruth League, the Army Ranger League, or the Carolina Collegiate Coastal Plain League, including his pitcher, Brother Seth. Bullock offered to supply fielder's gloves and several serviceable balls sewn in his harness shop. The bats were indestructible aluminum ones found in the old high school basement, likely to survive the next several ice ages. Brother Jobe offered to rebuild and groom the VFW field, bringing in five wagonloads of fine red clay from the deposits around the western base of Schoolhouse Hill. His men meticulously set down foul lines and the batter's box with powdered lime and scythed the field a few hours before the game.

It rained a little that Saturday morning but the skies cleared, the temperature rose, and at six o'clock in the evening the weather was perfect. Terry Einhorn had assembled an operation for grilling sausages, Brother Micah of the New Faith Tavern arranged for a setup of beer and cider kegs off the third base line. The two managers of the ball clubs, Bullock and Robert Earle, confabbed with the umpire at home plate. That crucial role was decided by a drawing of straws between the village trustees and the winner happened to be Brother Jobe. An announcement of the game was broadcast in the second edition of the *Union News Leader*, and word spread quickly, with families driving to the game in carts and wagons from as far away as Hoosick Falls, Argyle, and Cossayuna. The pitcher for Bullock's nine completed his warm-ups on the mound, and the lead-off hitter for Union Grove, Eric Laudermilk, stood in the on-deck circle with his arms hooked under a thirty-four-inch Miguel Cabrera model bat manufactured years ago under the Sam brand name. A stillness fell over the several hundred spectators gathered off the foul lines on benches or on chairs they had carried to the field themselves or just standing. Then, a clarion tenor voice rose from among them, belonging to Andrew Pendergast, director of the Congregational Church music circle and choir, posing the musical question:

Oh, say can you see, by the dawn's early light,
What so proudly we hailed at the twilight's last gleaming?

The people both on and off the field glanced around to one side and another and by the middle of the stanza, before the anthem's soaring bridge, all joined in the strains of a song they had not sung, or even heard, for a very long time.

And that is all there is to tell about the events of the year that concerns us in this history of the future where the people came to live in a world made by hand.